MOON 月詠 (つくよみ) PHASE 2

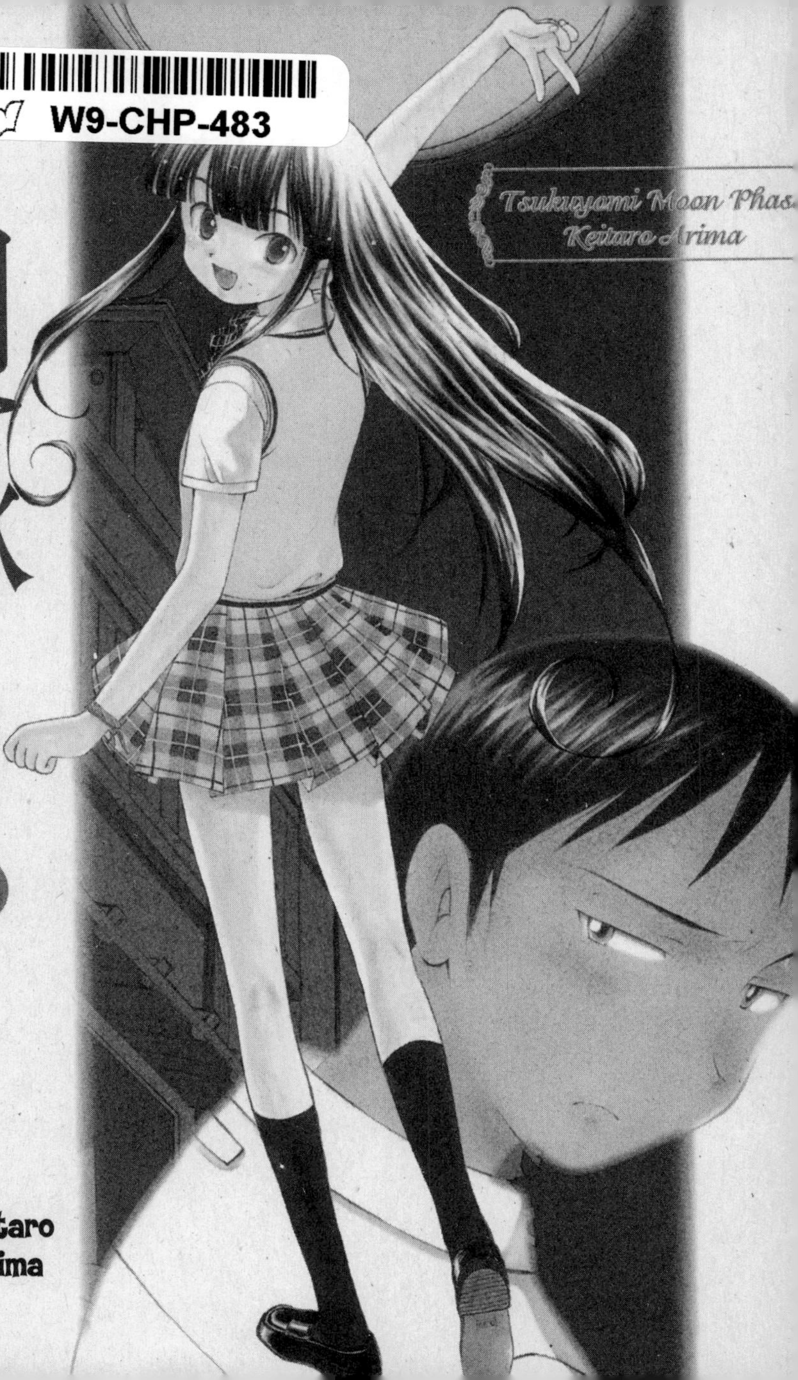
Tsukuyomi Moon Phase
Keitaro Arima

Keitaro Arima

Cameraman Kouhei Midou is researching Schwarz Quelle Castle. When he steps inside the castle's great walls, he discovers a mysterious little girl, Hazuki, who's been trapped there for years. Utilizing her controlling charm, Hazuki tries to get Kouhei to set her free. But this sweet little girl isn't everything she appears to be...

TSUKUYOMI

Moon Phase 月詠

CREATED BY: KEITARO ARIMA

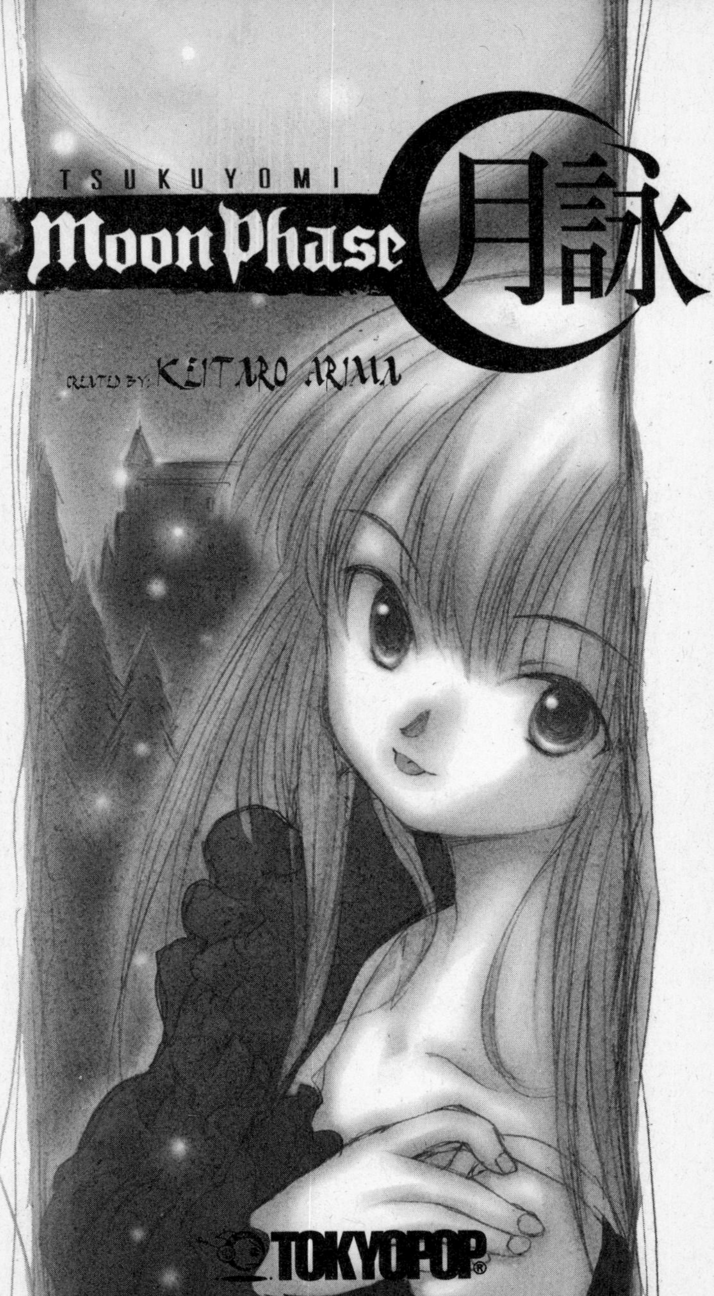

TOKYOPOP®

HAMBURG // LONDON // LOS ANGELES // TOKYO

Tsukuyomi - Moon Phase Vol. 2
created by Keitaro Arima

Translation - Yoohae Yang
English Adaptation - Jeffrey Reeves
Copy Editor - Hope Donovan
Retouch and Lettering - Vincente Rivera Jr. and Alyson Stetz
Production Artist - James Dashiell
Cover Design - Seth Cable

Editor - Julie Taylor
Digital Imaging Manager - Chris Buford
Production Managers - Jennifer Miller and Mutsumi Miyazaki
Managing Editor - Lindsey Johnston
VP of Production - Ron Klamert
Publisher and E.I.C. - Mike Kiley
President and C.O.O. - John Parker
C.E.O. and Chief Creative Officer - Stuart Levy

A  Manga

TOKYOPOP Inc.
5900 Wilshire Blvd. Suite 2000
Los Angeles, CA 90036

E-mail: info@TOKYOPOP.com
Come visit us online at www.TOKYOPOP.com

ISBN:1-59532-949-8

First TOKYOPOP printing: March 2006
10 9 8 7 6 5 4 3 2
Printed in Canada

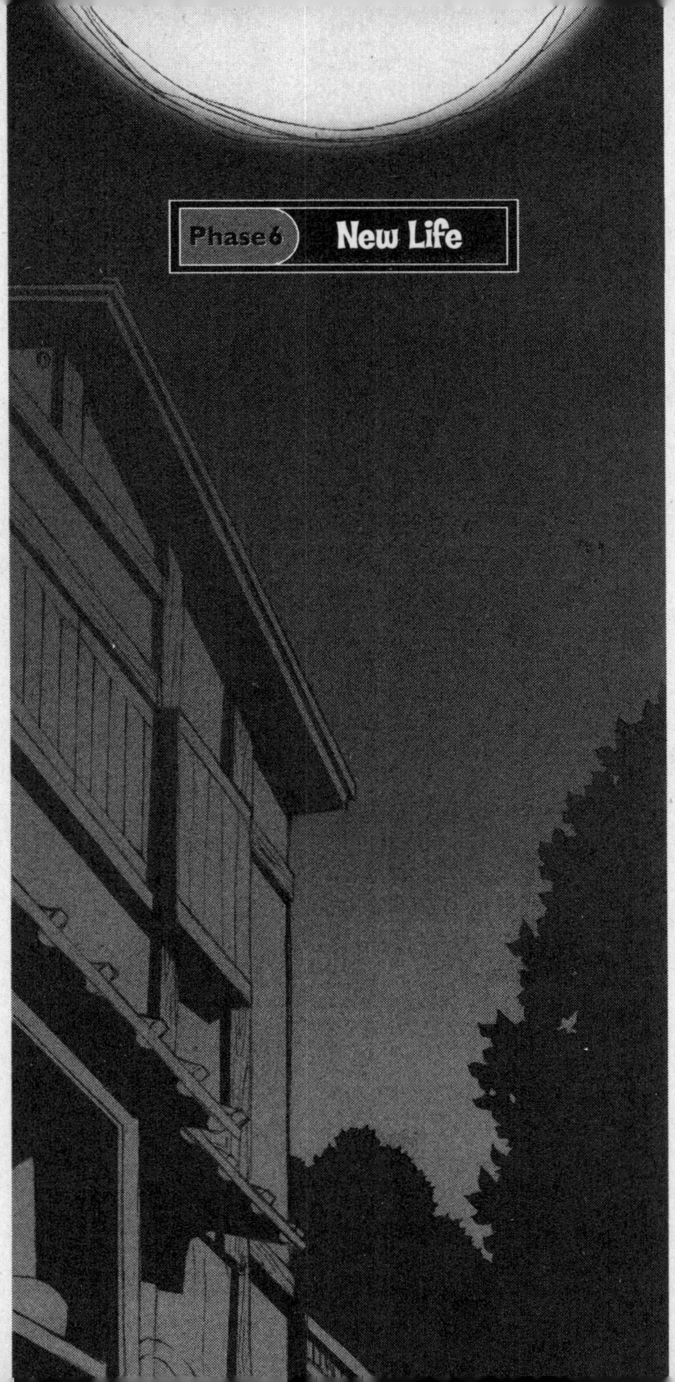
Phase 6
New Life

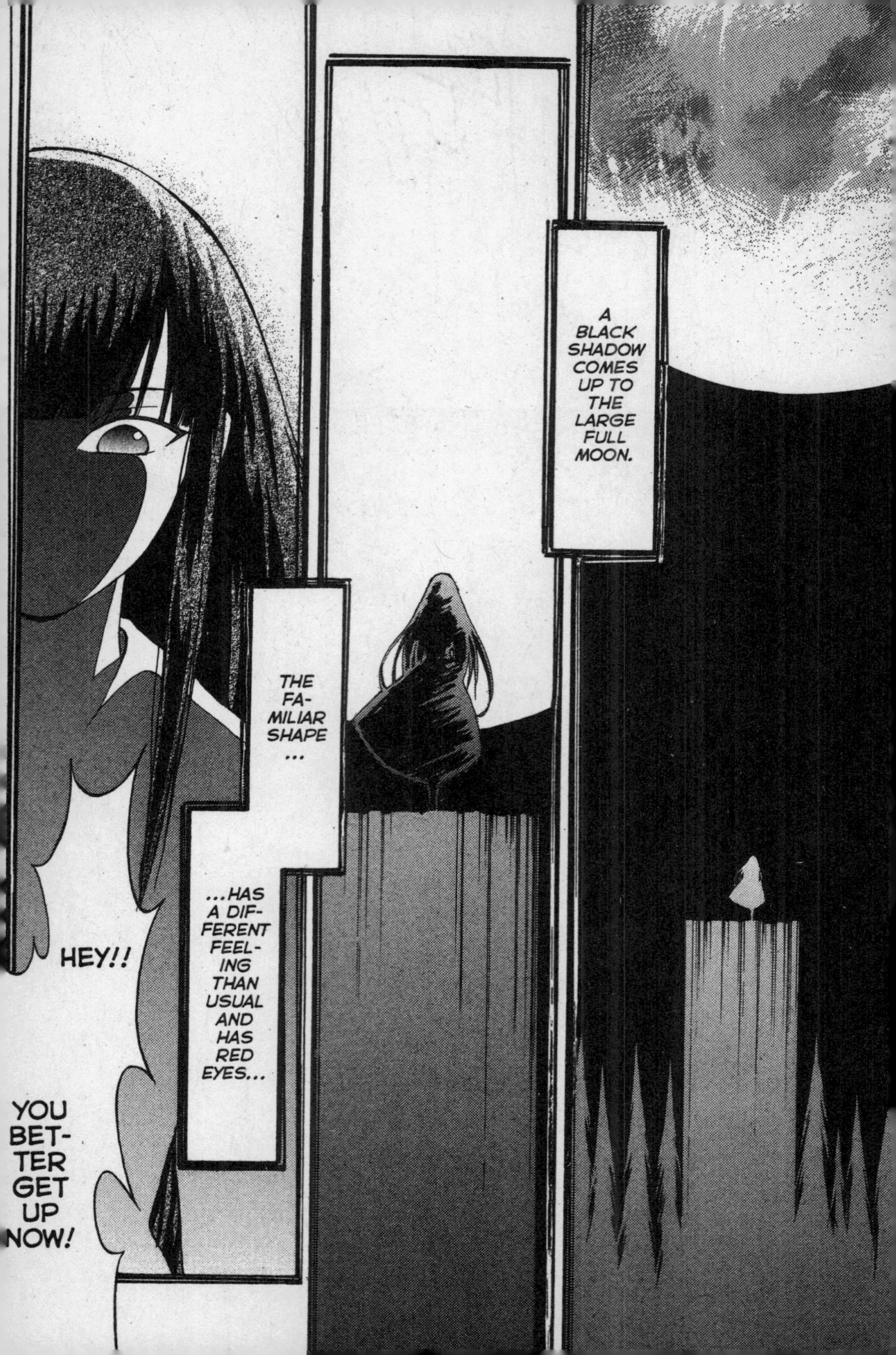
A BLACK SHADOW COMES UP TO THE LARGE FULL MOON.
THE FAMILIAR SHAPE...
...HAS A DIFFERENT FEELING THAN USUAL AND HAS RED EYES...
HEY!!
YOU BETTER GET UP NOW!

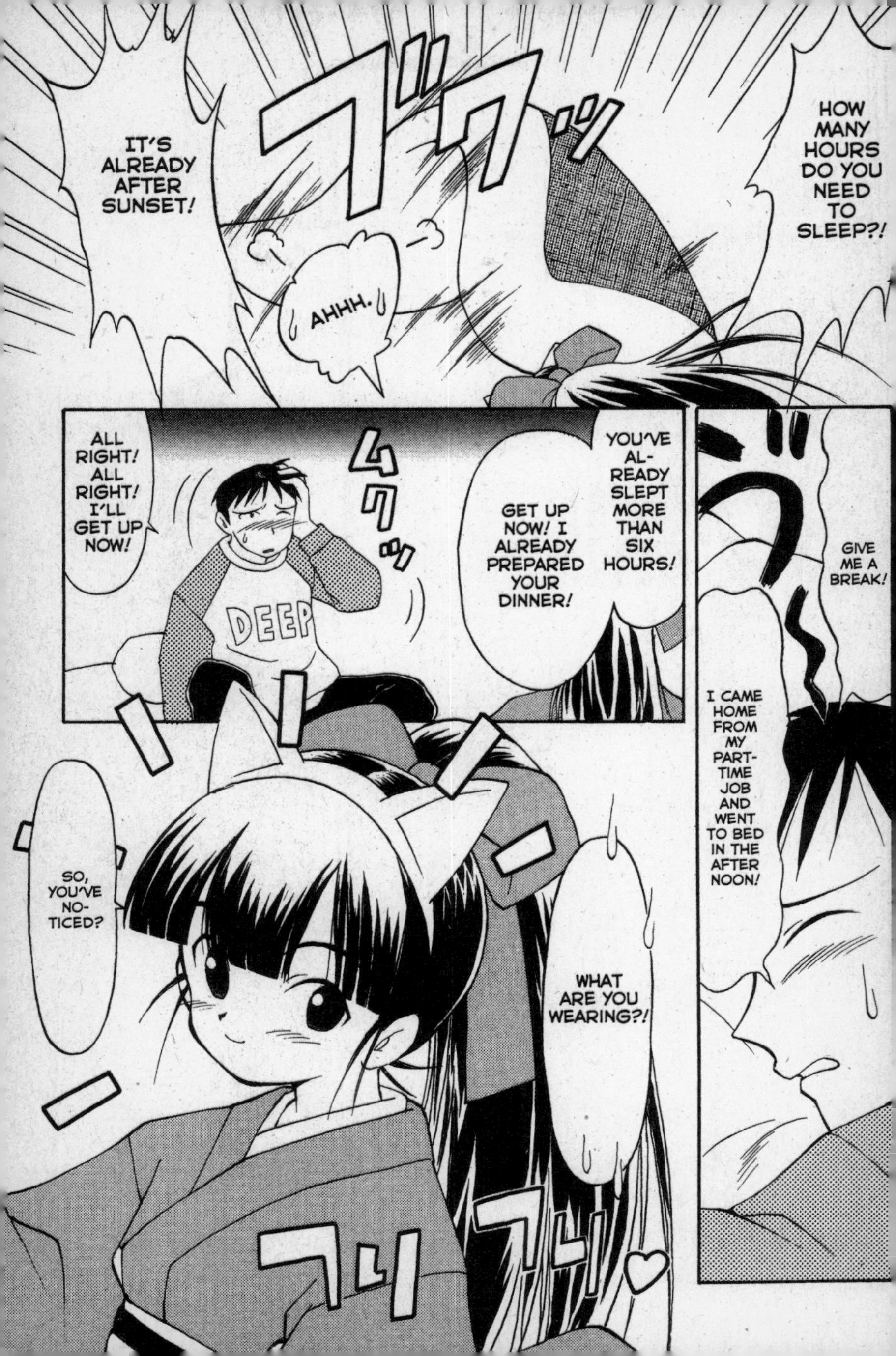
HOW MANY HOURS DO YOU NEED TO SLEEP?!
IT'S ALREADY AFTER SUNSET!
AHHH.
GIVE ME A BREAK!
I CAME HOME FROM MY PART-TIME JOB AND WENT TO BED IN THE AFTER NOON!
YOU'VE AL- READY SLEPT MORE THAN SIX HOURS!
GET UP NOW! I ALREADY PREPARED YOUR DINNER!
ALL RIGHT! ALL RIGHT! I'LL GET UP NOW!
DEEP
WHAT ARE YOU WEARING?!
SO, YOU'VE NO- TICED?

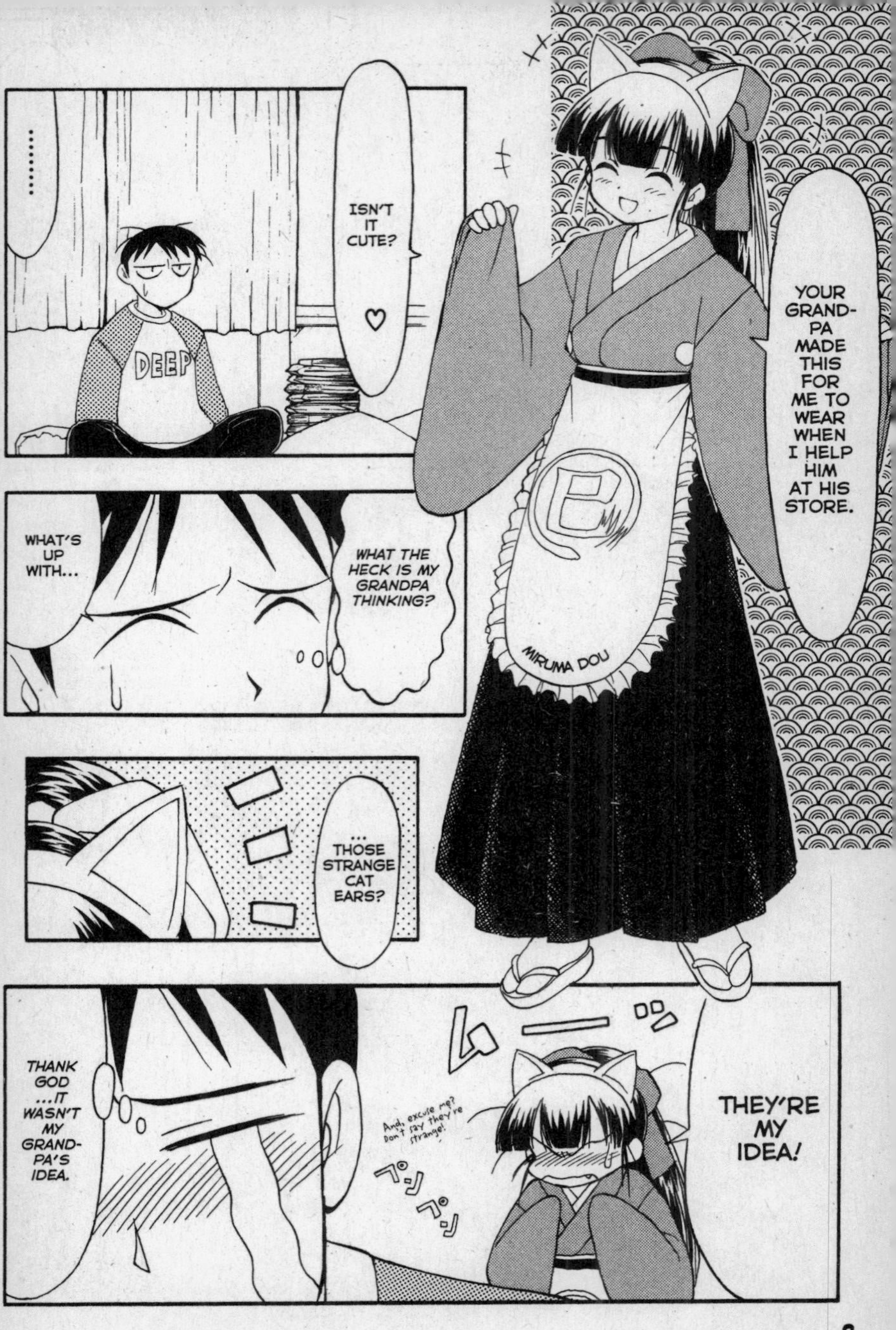
YOUR GRAND-PA MADE THIS FOR ME TO WEAR WHEN I HELP HIM AT HIS STORE.
ISN'T IT CUTE? ♡
MIRUMA DOU
......
WHAT THE HECK IS MY GRANDPA THINKING?
WHAT'S UP WITH...
... THOSE STRANGE CAT EARS?
THEY'RE MY IDEA!
And, excuse me? Don't say they're strange!
THANK GOD ...IT WASN'T MY GRAND-PA'S IDEA.

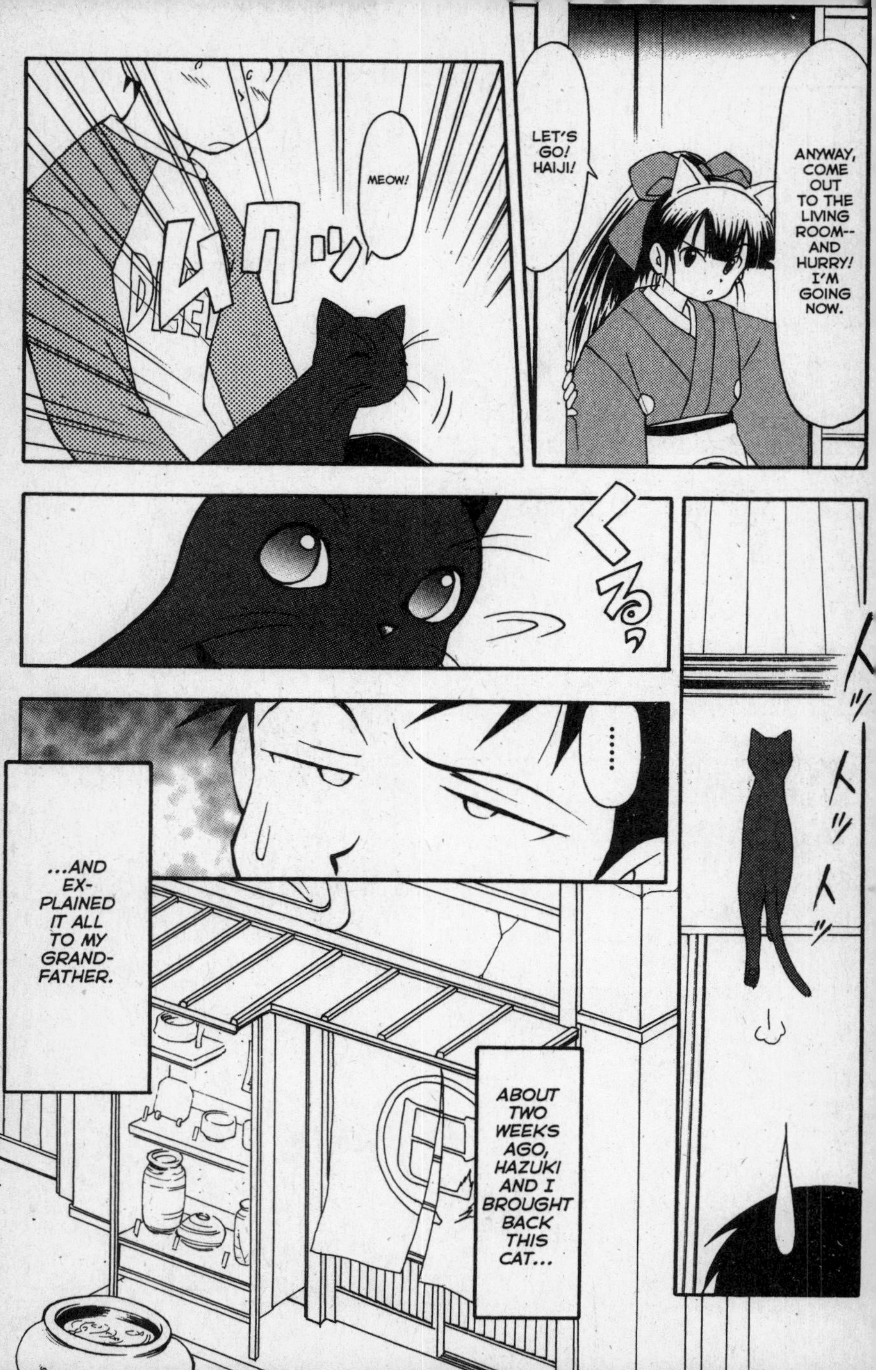
ANYWAY, COME OUT TO THE LIVING ROOM-- AND HURRY! I'M GOING NOW.
LET'S GO! HAIJI!
MEOW!
......
ABOUT TWO WEEKS AGO, HAZUKI AND I BROUGHT BACK THIS CAT...
...AND EX-PLAINED IT ALL TO MY GRAND-FATHER.

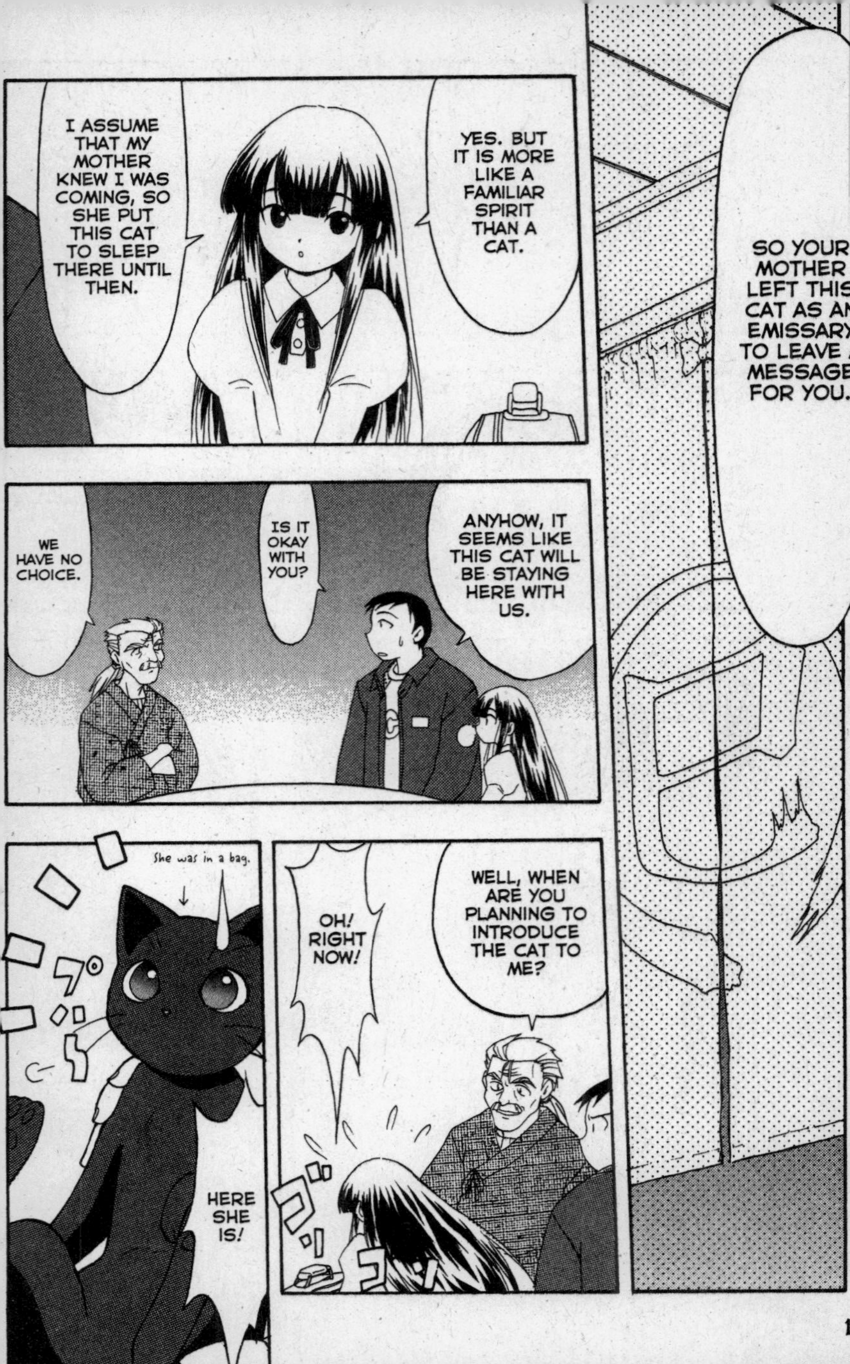
SO YOUR MOTHER LEFT THIS CAT AS AN EMISSARY TO LEAVE A MESSAGE FOR YOU.
YES. BUT IT IS MORE LIKE A FAMILIAR SPIRIT THAN A CAT.
I ASSUME THAT MY MOTHER KNEW I WAS COMING, SO SHE PUT THIS CAT TO SLEEP THERE UNTIL THEN.
ANYHOW, IT SEEMS LIKE THIS CAT WILL BE STAYING HERE WITH US.
IS IT OKAY WITH YOU?
WE HAVE NO CHOICE.
WELL, WHEN ARE YOU PLANNING TO INTRODUCE THE CAT TO ME?
OH! RIGHT NOW!
She was in a bag.
HERE SHE IS!

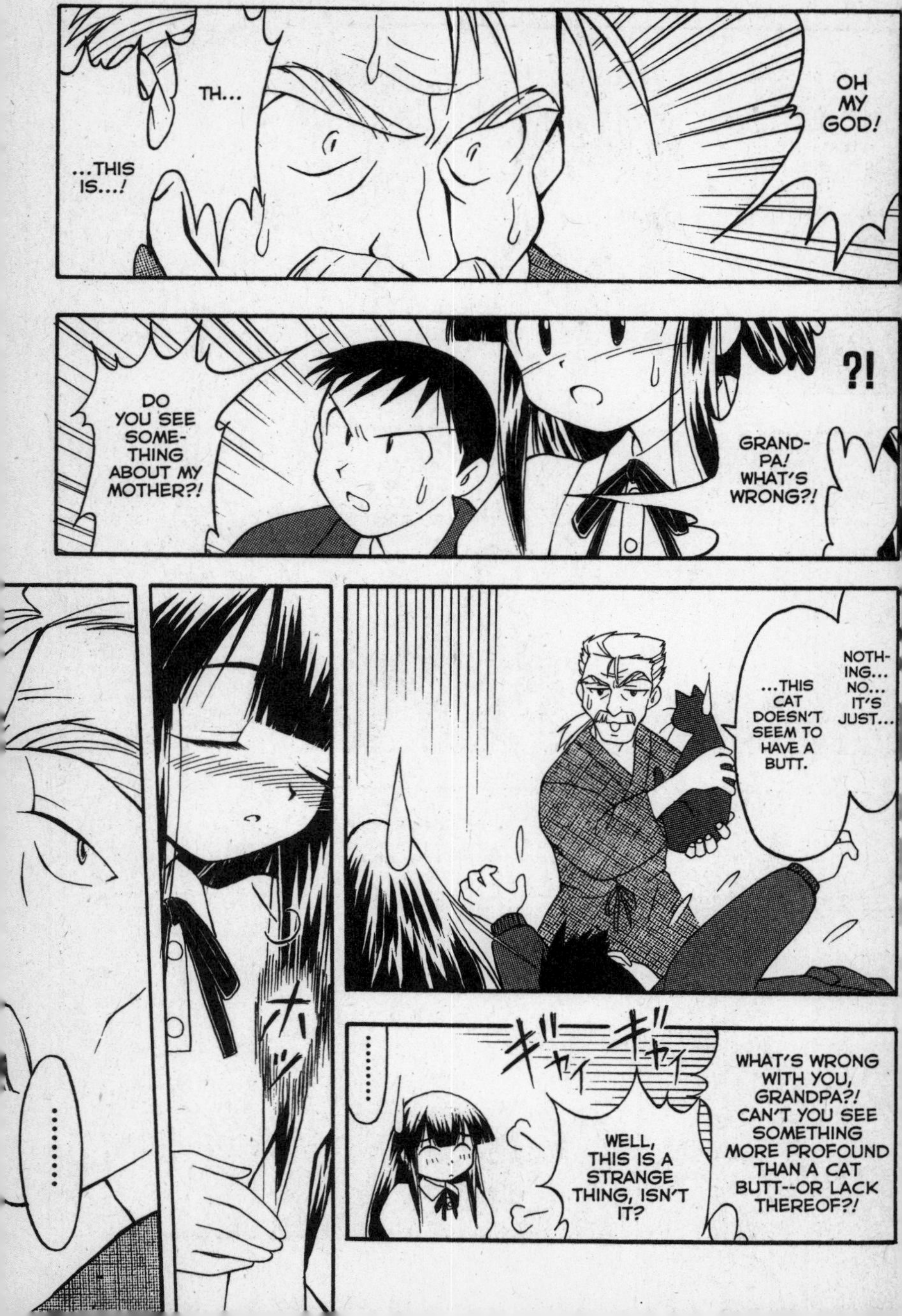
OH MY GOD!
TH...
...THIS IS...!
?!
GRANDPA! WHAT'S WRONG?!
DO YOU SEE SOMETHING ABOUT MY MOTHER?!
NOTHING... NO... IT'S JUST...
...THIS CAT DOESN'T SEEM TO HAVE A BUTT.
WHAT'S WRONG WITH YOU, GRANDPA?! CAN'T YOU SEE SOMETHING MORE PROFOUND THAN A CAT BUTT--OR LACK THEREOF?!
WELL, THIS IS A STRANGE THING, ISN'T IT?
......
......

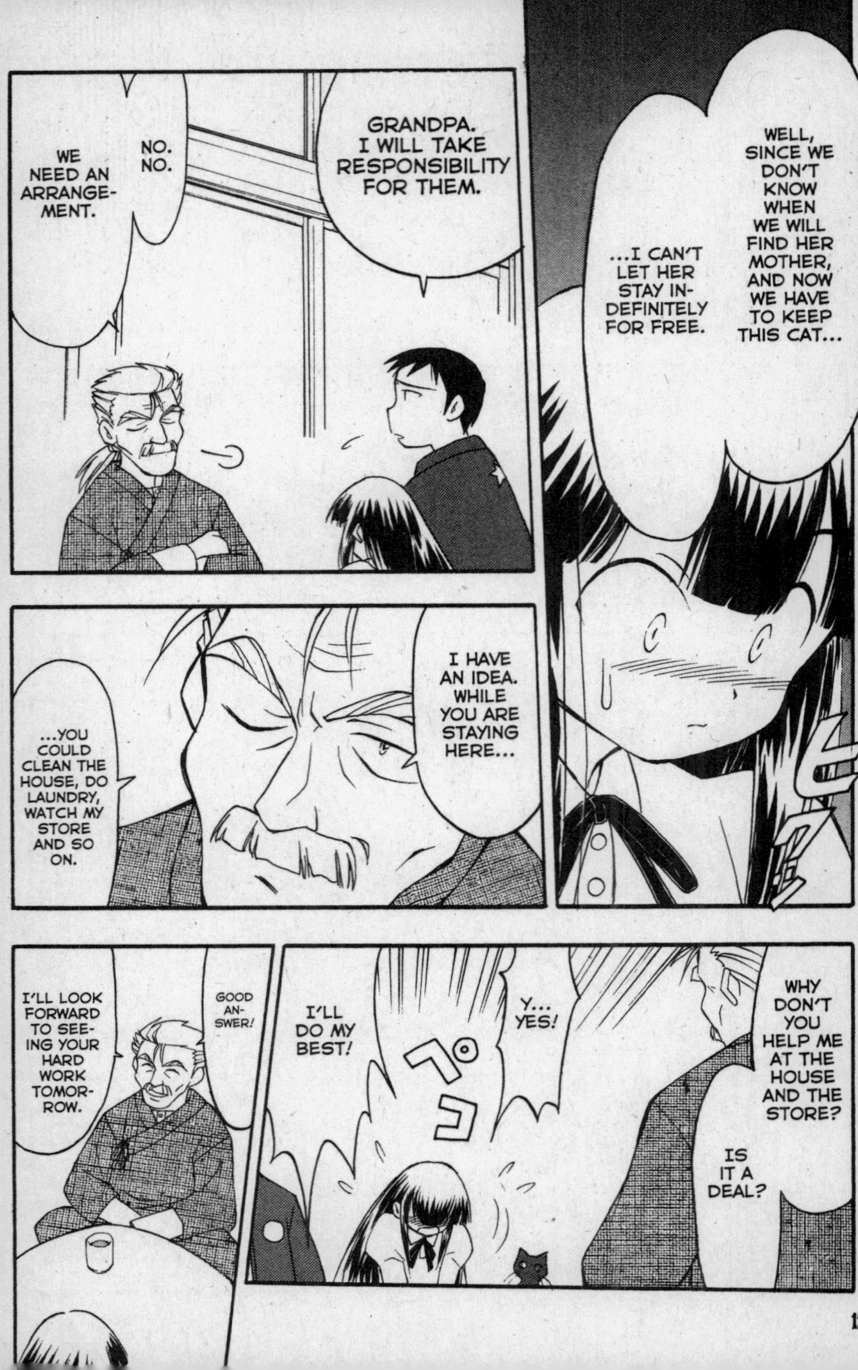

WELL, SINCE WE DON'T KNOW WHEN WE WILL FIND HER MOTHER, AND NOW WE HAVE TO KEEP THIS CAT...
...I CAN'T LET HER STAY INDEFINITELY FOR FREE.
GRANDPA. I WILL TAKE RESPONSIBILITY FOR THEM.
NO. NO.
WE NEED AN ARRANGEMENT.
I HAVE AN IDEA. WHILE YOU ARE STAYING HERE...
...YOU COULD CLEAN THE HOUSE, DO LAUNDRY, WATCH MY STORE AND SO ON.
WHY DON'T YOU HELP ME AT THE HOUSE AND THE STORE?
IS IT A DEAL?
Y... YES!
ペコ
I'LL DO MY BEST!
GOOD ANSWER!
I'LL LOOK FORWARD TO SEEING YOUR HARD WORK TOMORROW.

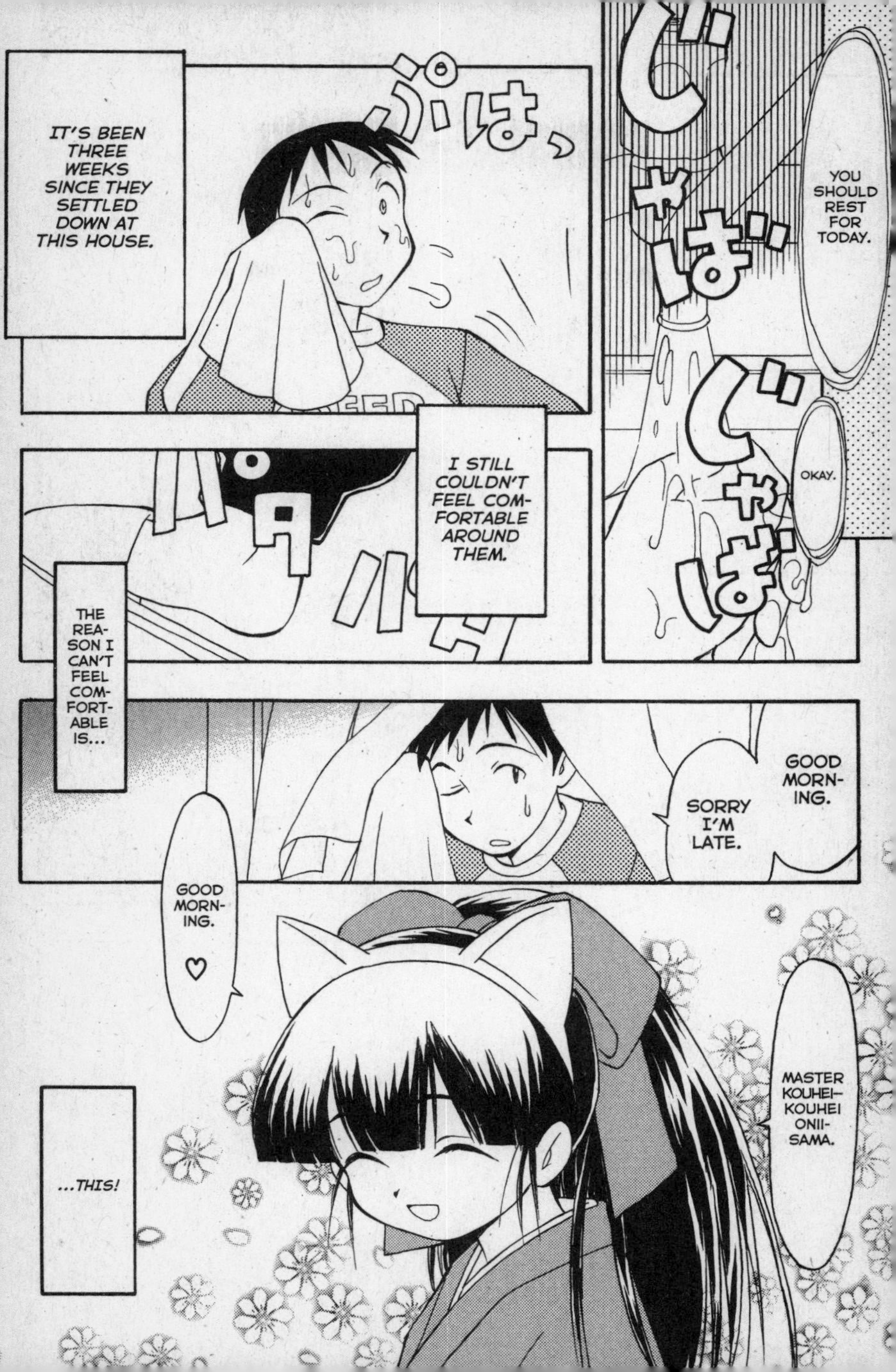
じゃばじゃば
YOU SHOULD REST FOR TODAY.
OKAY.
IT'S BEEN THREE WEEKS SINCE THEY SETTLED DOWN AT THIS HOUSE.
ぷはっ
I STILL COULDN'T FEEL COMFORTABLE AROUND THEM.
GOOD MORNING.
SORRY I'M LATE.
THE REASON I CAN'T FEEL COMFORTABLE IS...
MASTER KOUHEI-KOUHEI ONII-SAMA.
GOOD MORNING. ♥
...THIS!

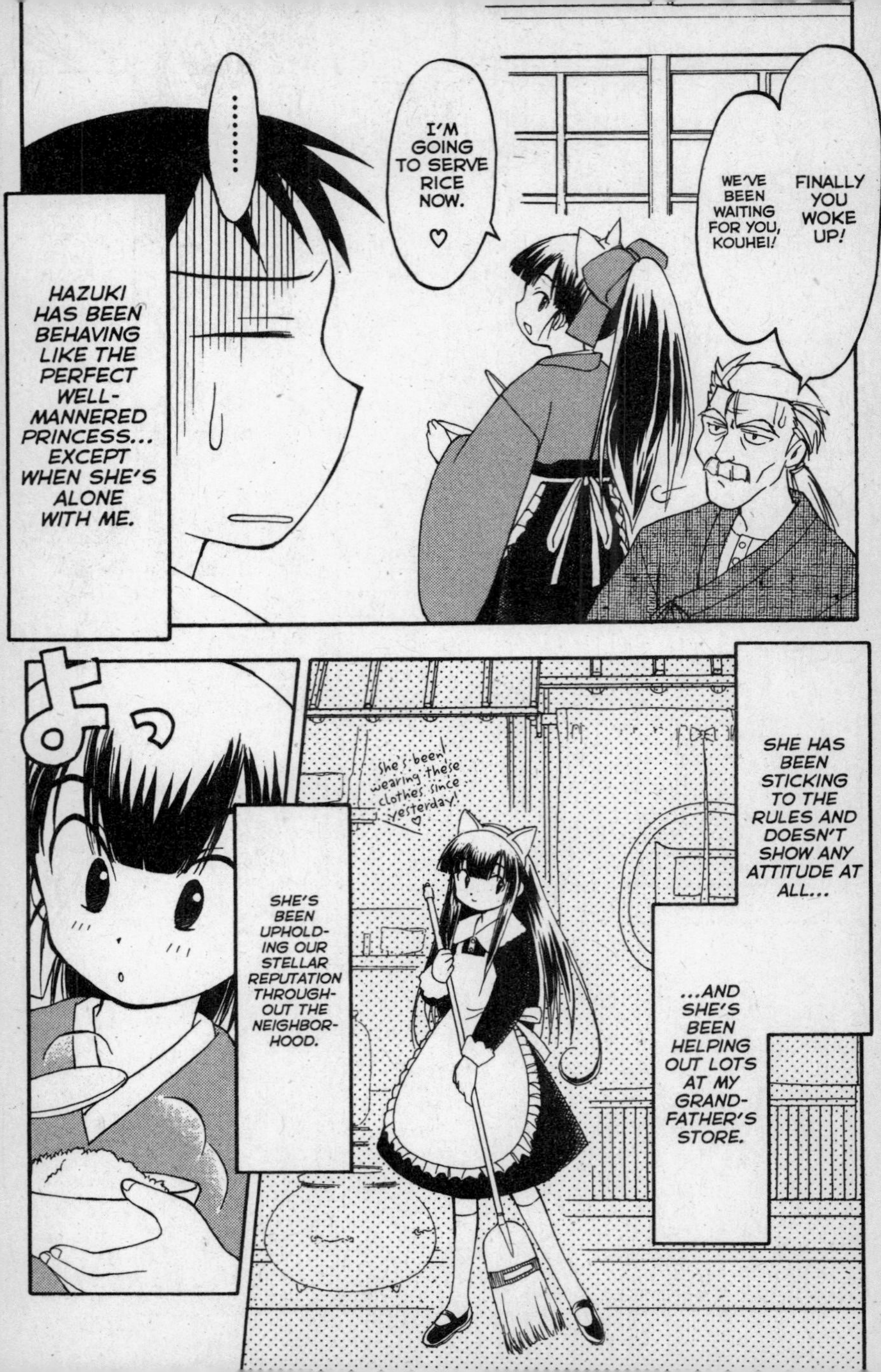
FINALLY YOU WOKE UP!
WE'VE BEEN WAITING FOR YOU, KOUHEI!
I'M GOING TO SERVE RICE NOW. ♡
......
HAZUKI HAS BEEN BEHAVING LIKE THE PERFECT WELL-MANNERED PRINCESS... EXCEPT WHEN SHE'S ALONE WITH ME.
SHE HAS BEEN STICKING TO THE RULES AND DOESN'T SHOW ANY ATTITUDE AT ALL...
...AND SHE'S BEEN HELPING OUT LOTS AT MY GRAND-FATHER'S STORE.
She's been wearing these clothes since yesterday! ♡
SHE'S BEEN UPHOLD-ING OUR STELLAR REPUTATION THROUGH-OUT THE NEIGHBOR-HOOD.
よっ

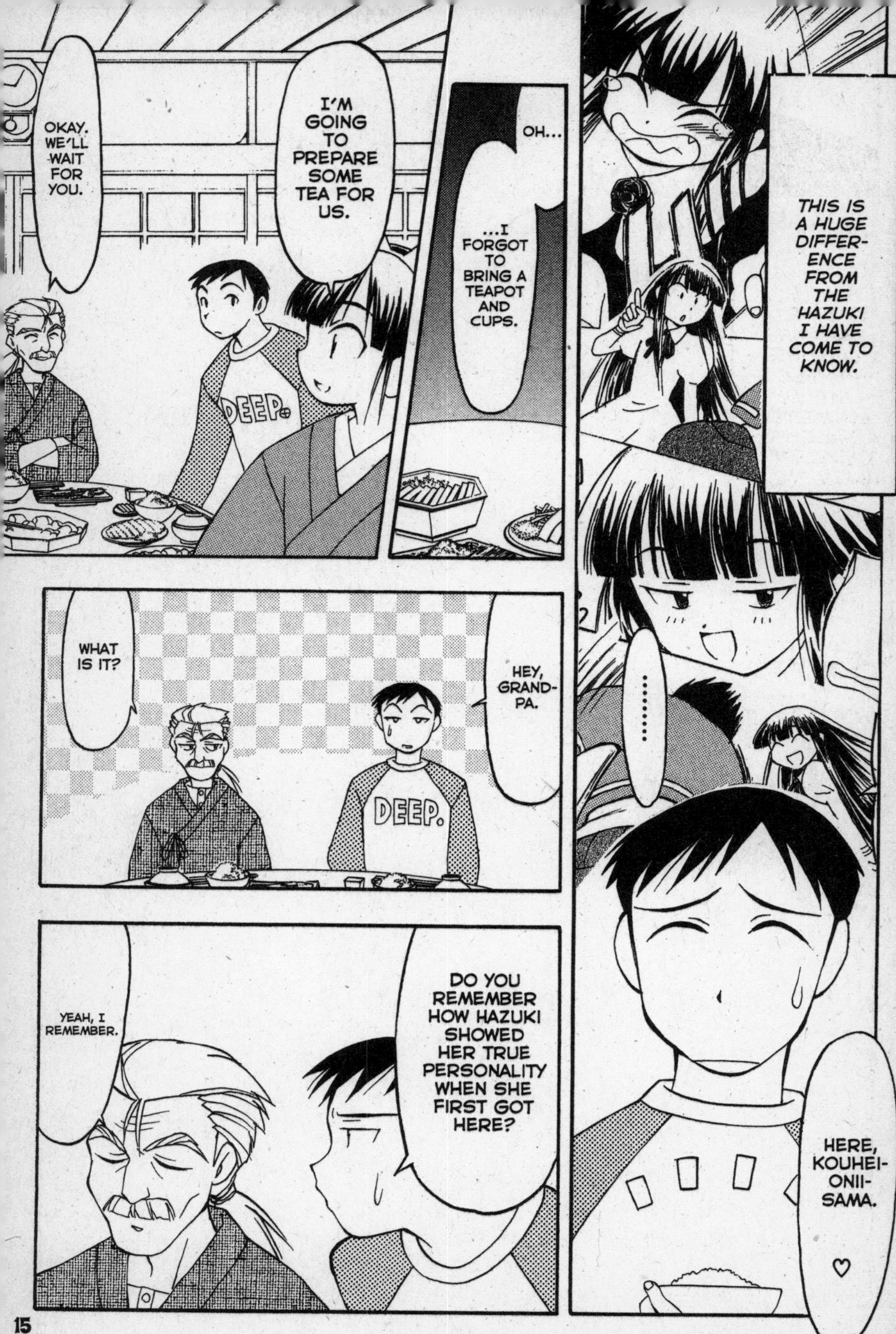

I'M GOING TO PREPARE SOME TEA FOR US.
OKAY. WE'LL WAIT FOR YOU.
OH...
...I FORGOT TO BRING A TEAPOT AND CUPS.
HEY, GRANDPA.
WHAT IS IT?
DO YOU REMEMBER HOW HAZUKI SHOWED HER TRUE PERSONALITY WHEN SHE FIRST GOT HERE?
YEAH, I REMEMBER.
THIS IS A HUGE DIFFERENCE FROM THE HAZUKI I HAVE COME TO KNOW.
......
HERE, KOUHEI-ONII-SAMA. ♥

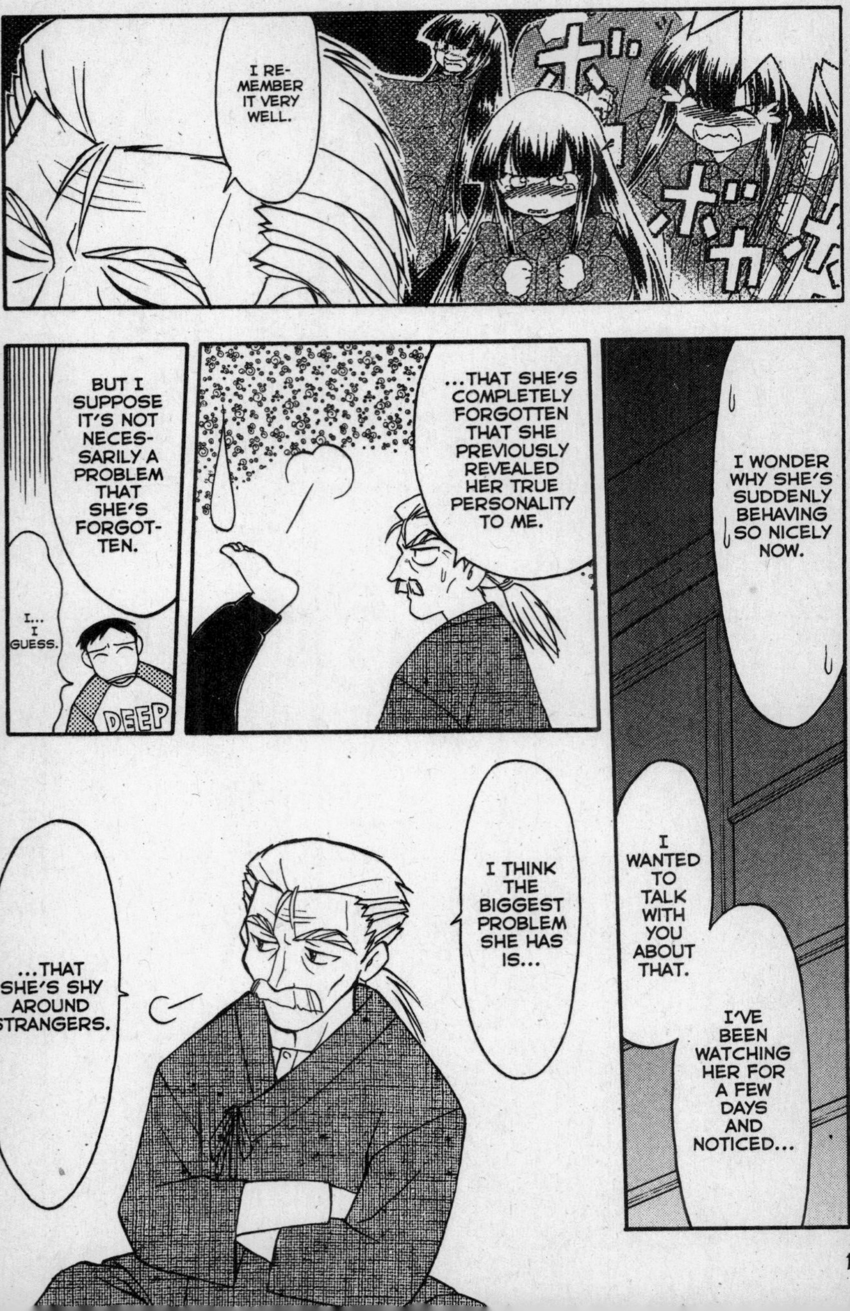
I REMEMBER IT VERY WELL.
I WONDER WHY SHE'S SUDDENLY BEHAVING SO NICELY NOW.
I WANTED TO TALK WITH YOU ABOUT THAT.
I'VE BEEN WATCHING HER FOR A FEW DAYS AND NOTICED...
...THAT SHE'S COMPLETELY FORGOTTEN THAT SHE PREVIOUSLY REVEALED HER TRUE PERSONALITY TO ME.
BUT I SUPPOSE IT'S NOT NECESSARILY A PROBLEM THAT SHE'S FORGOTTEN.
I... I GUESS.
DEEP
I THINK THE BIGGEST PROBLEM SHE HAS IS...
...THAT SHE'S SHY AROUND STRANGERS.

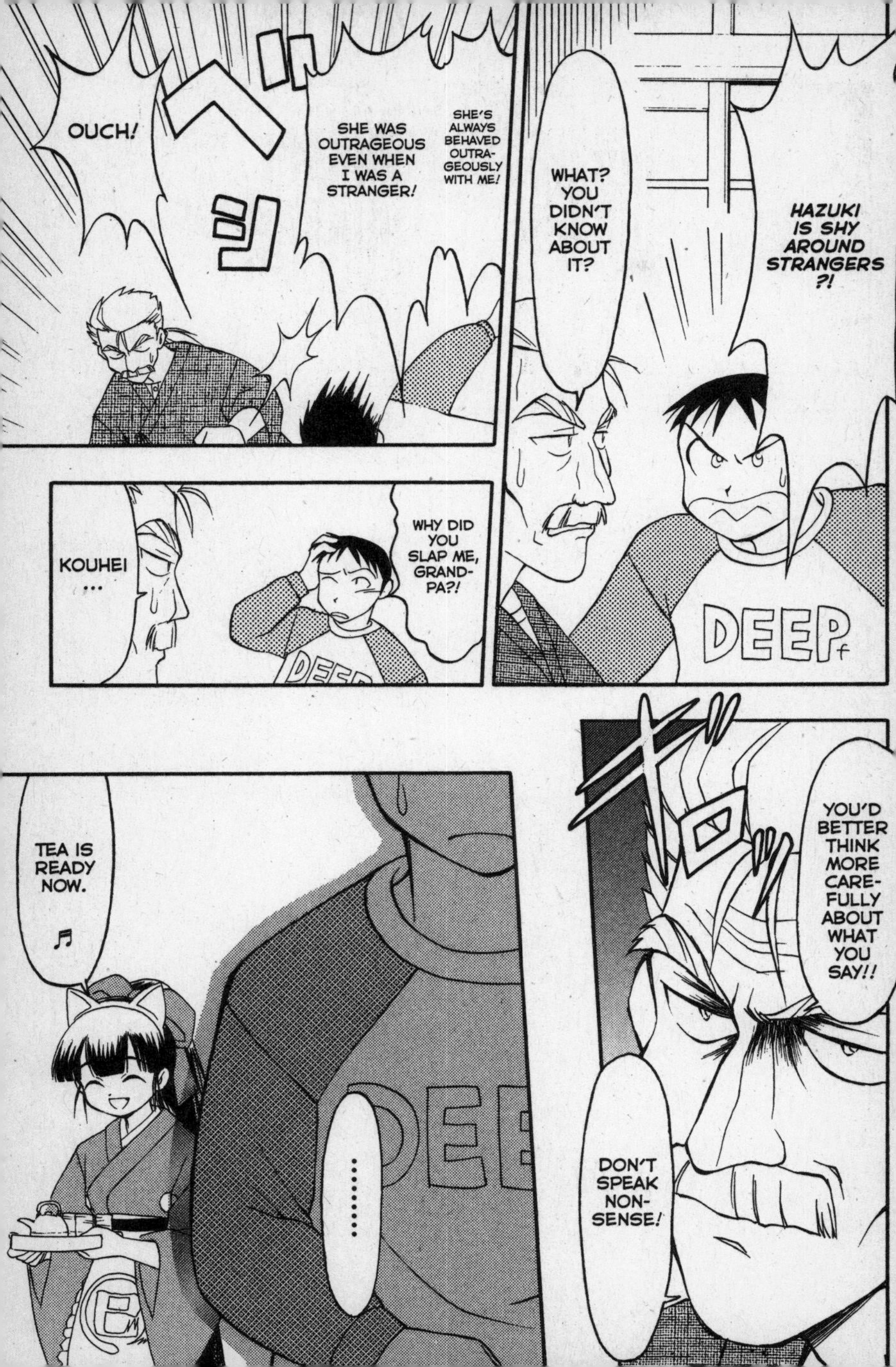
HAZUKI IS SHY AROUND STRANGERS ?!
WHAT? YOU DIDN'T KNOW ABOUT IT?
SHE'S ALWAYS BEHAVED OUTRA-GEOUSLY WITH ME!
SHE WAS OUTRAGEOUS EVEN WHEN I WAS A STRANGER!
OUCH!
WHY DID YOU SLAP ME, GRAND-PA?!
KOUHEI ...
YOU'D BETTER THINK MORE CARE-FULLY ABOUT WHAT YOU SAY!!
DON'T SPEAK NON-SENSE!
....
TEA IS READY NOW. ♪

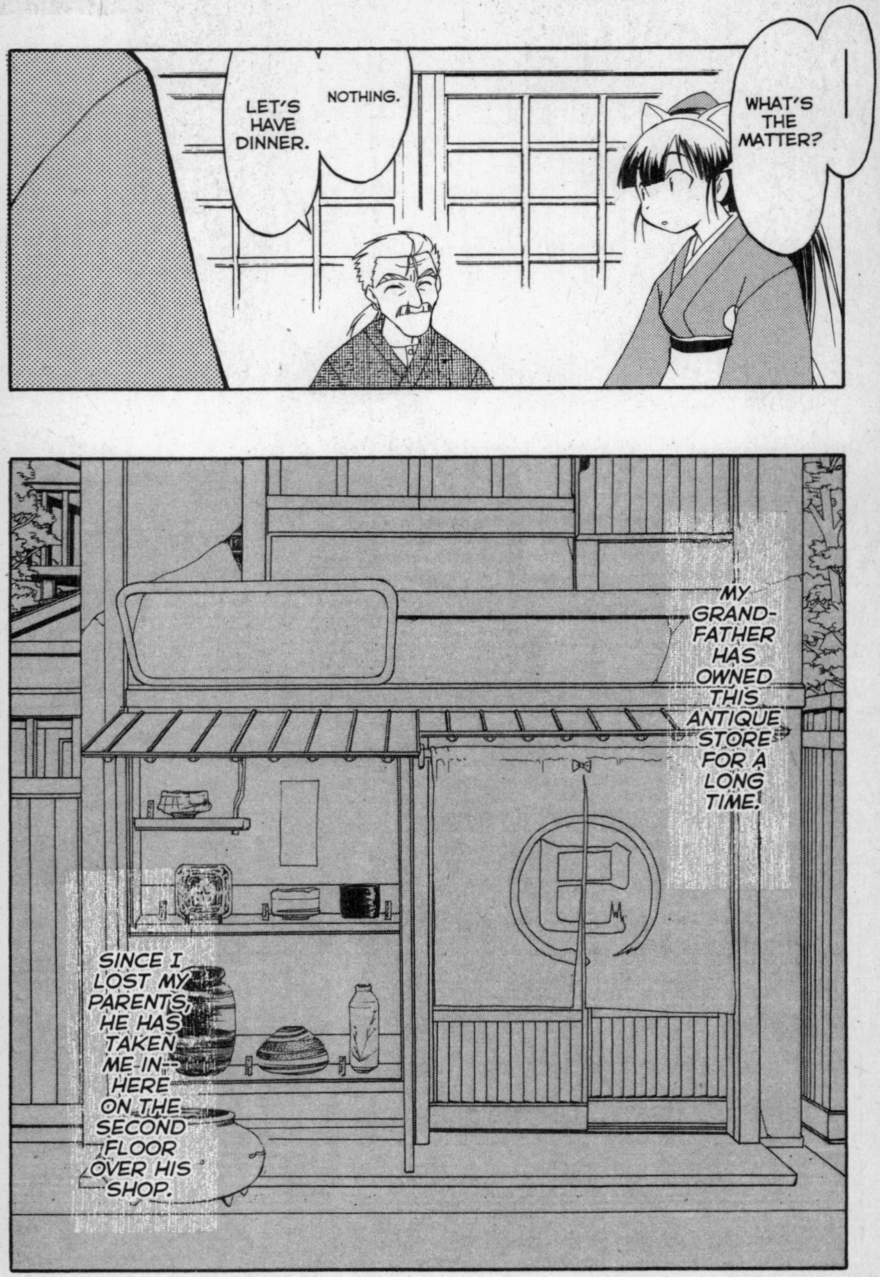
WHAT'S THE MATTER?
NOTHING.
LET'S HAVE DINNER.
MY GRAND-FATHER HAS OWNED THIS ANTIQUE STORE FOR A LONG TIME!
SINCE I LOST MY PARENTS, HE HAS TAKEN ME IN HERE ON THE SECOND FLOOR OVER HIS SHOP.

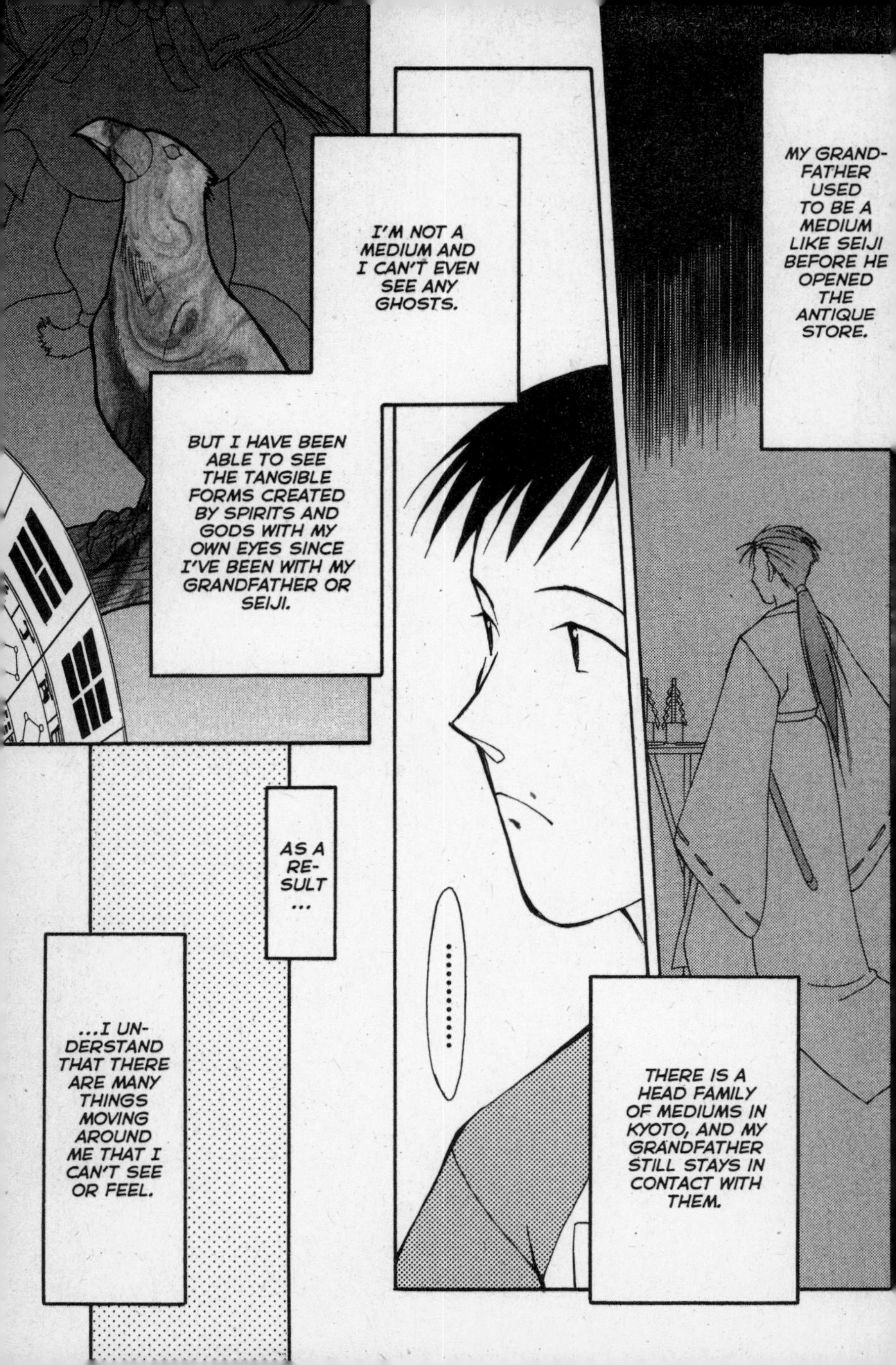
MY GRAND-FATHER USED TO BE A MEDIUM LIKE SEIJI BEFORE HE OPENED THE ANTIQUE STORE.
THERE IS A HEAD FAMILY OF MEDIUMS IN KYOTO, AND MY GRANDFATHER STILL STAYS IN CONTACT WITH THEM.
I'M NOT A MEDIUM AND I CAN'T EVEN SEE ANY GHOSTS.
BUT I HAVE BEEN ABLE TO SEE THE TANGIBLE FORMS CREATED BY SPIRITS AND GODS WITH MY OWN EYES SINCE I'VE BEEN WITH MY GRANDFATHER OR SEIJI.
....
AS A RE-SULT...
...I UN-DERSTAND THAT THERE ARE MANY THINGS MOVING AROUND ME THAT I CAN'T SEE OR FEEL.

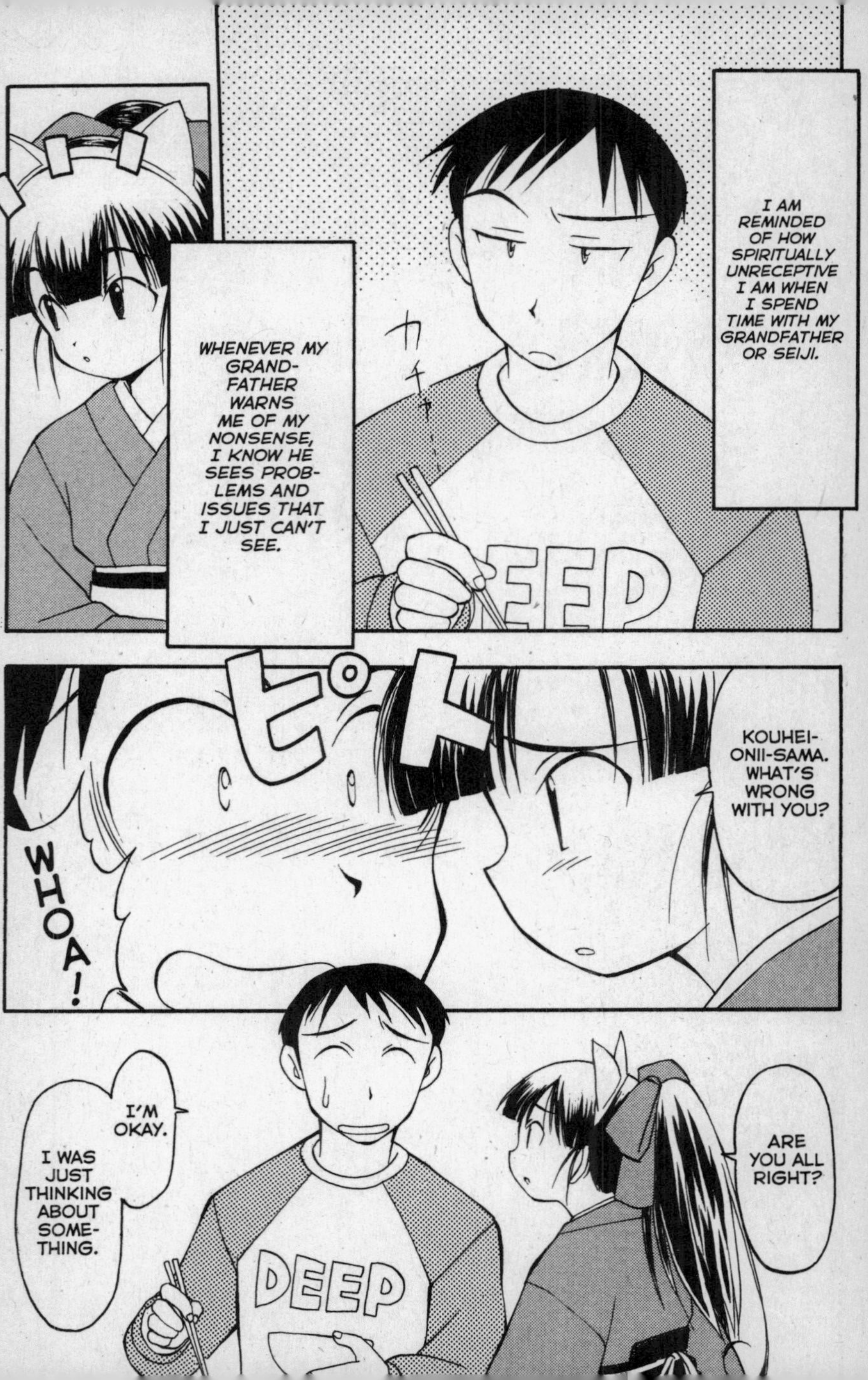
I AM REMINDED OF HOW SPIRITUALLY UNRECEPTIVE I AM WHEN I SPEND TIME WITH MY GRANDFATHER OR SEIJI.
カチャ
DEEP
WHENEVER MY GRAND-FATHER WARNS ME OF MY NONSENSE, I KNOW HE SEES PROB-LEMS AND ISSUES THAT I JUST CAN'T SEE.
KOUHEI-ONII-SAMA. WHAT'S WRONG WITH YOU?
ピト
WHOA!
ARE YOU ALL RIGHT?
I'M OKAY.
I WAS JUST THINKING ABOUT SOME-THING.
DEEP

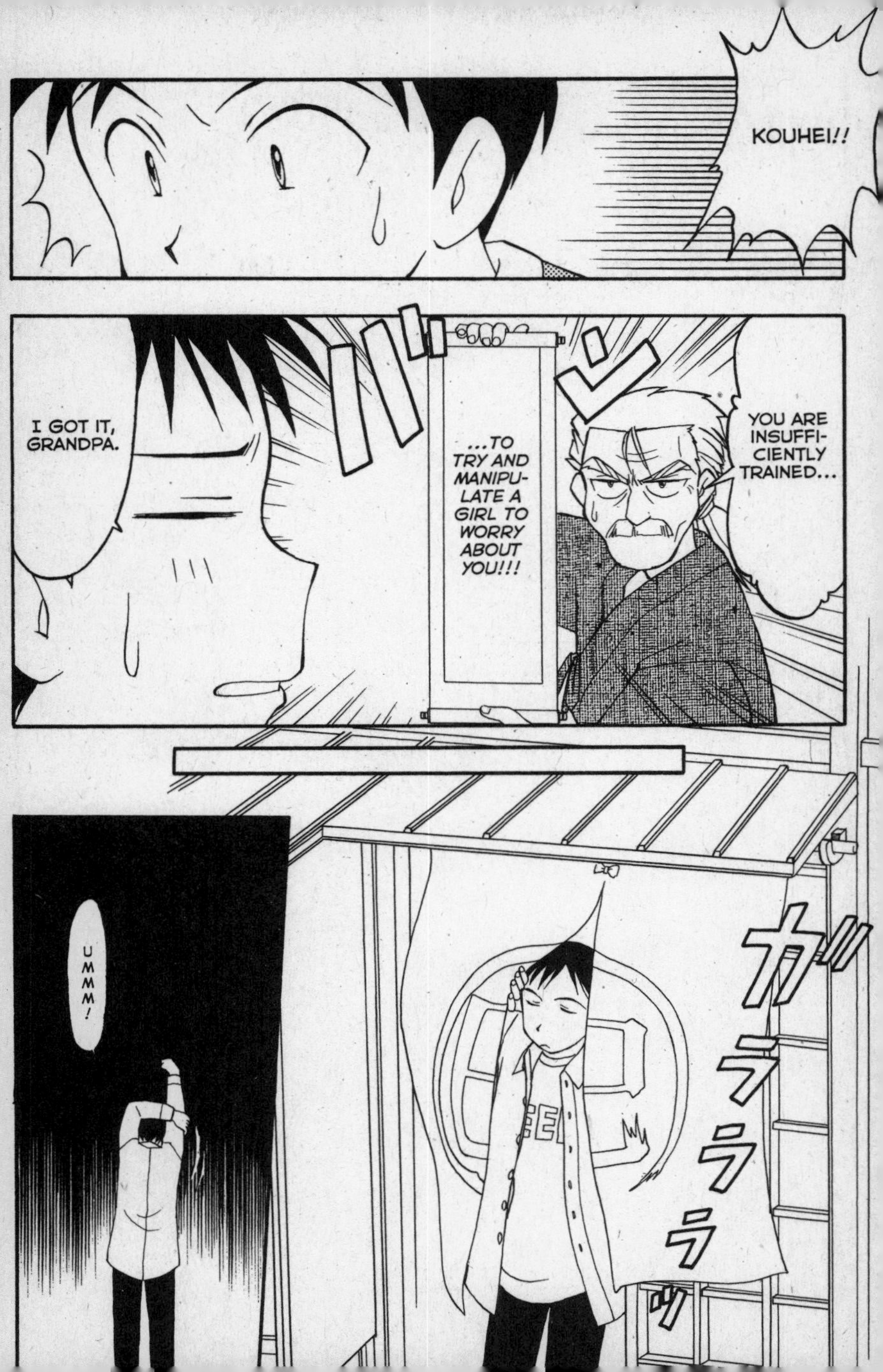
KOUHEI!!
YOU ARE INSUFFICIENTLY TRAINED...
...TO TRY AND MANIPULATE A GIRL TO WORRY ABOUT YOU!!!
I GOT IT, GRANDPA.
UMMM!

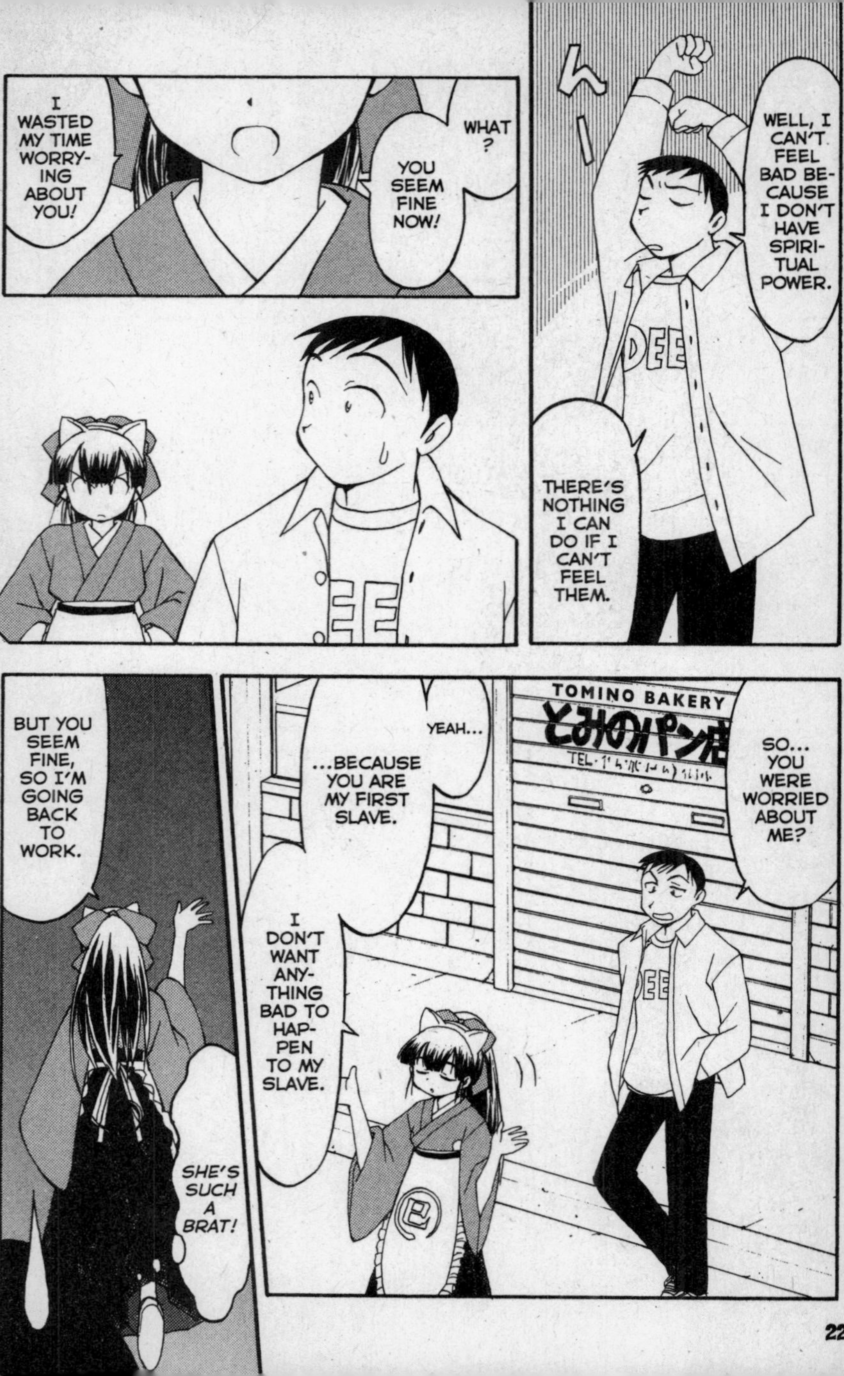

WELL, I CAN'T FEEL BAD BECAUSE I DON'T HAVE SPIRITUAL POWER.
んー
THERE'S NOTHING I CAN DO IF I CAN'T FEEL THEM.
WHAT? YOU SEEM FINE NOW!
I WASTED MY TIME WORRYING ABOUT YOU!
TOMINO BAKERY
とみのパン店
SO... YOU WERE WORRIED ABOUT ME?
YEAH...
...BECAUSE YOU ARE MY FIRST SLAVE.
I DON'T WANT ANYTHING BAD TO HAPPEN TO MY SLAVE.
BUT YOU SEEM FINE, SO I'M GOING BACK TO WORK.
SHE'S SUCH A BRAT!

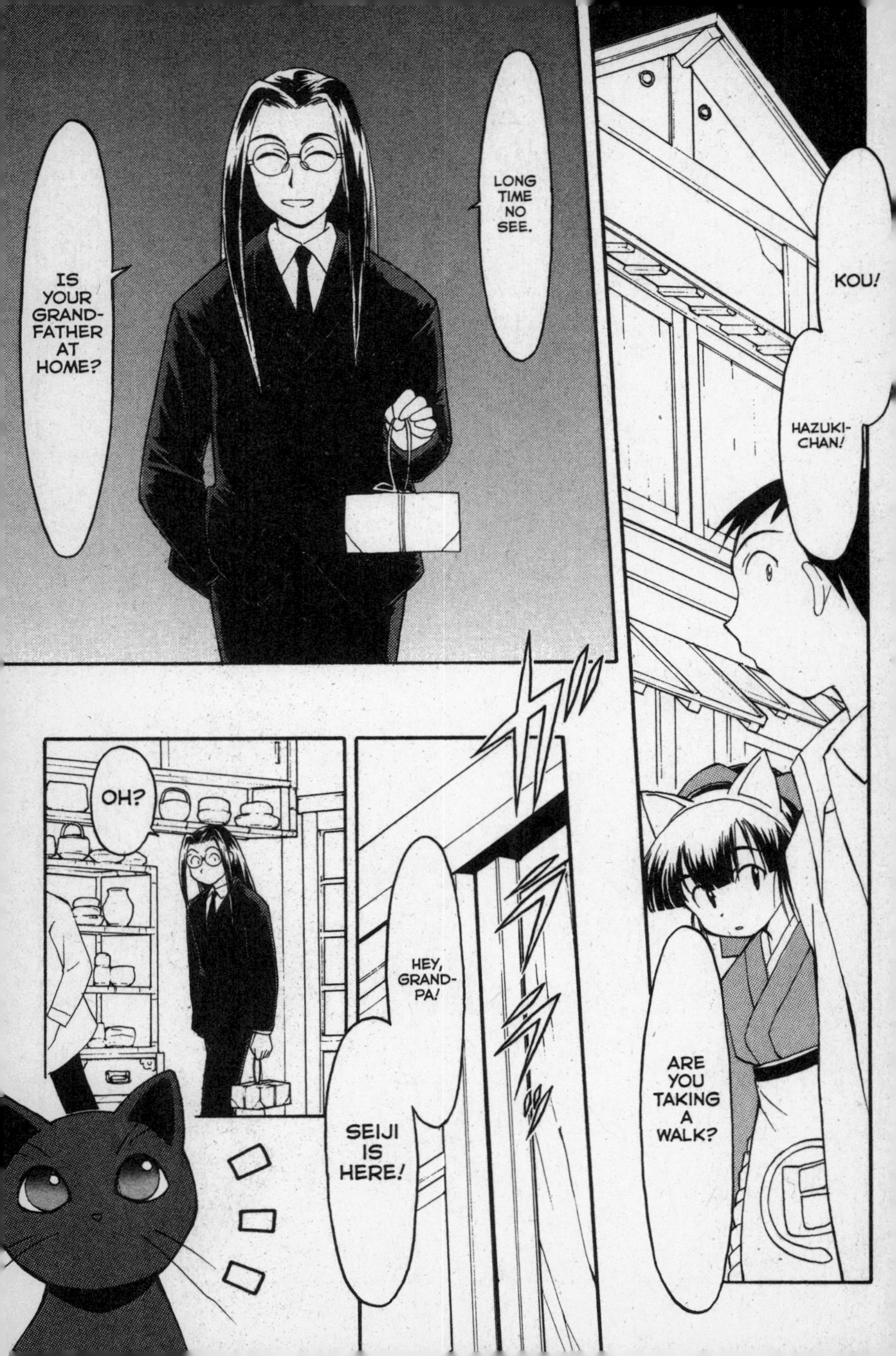
KOU!
HAZUKI-CHAN!
ARE YOU TAKING A WALK?
LONG TIME NO SEE.
IS YOUR GRAND-FATHER AT HOME?
HEY, GRAND-PA!
SEIJI IS HERE!
OH?

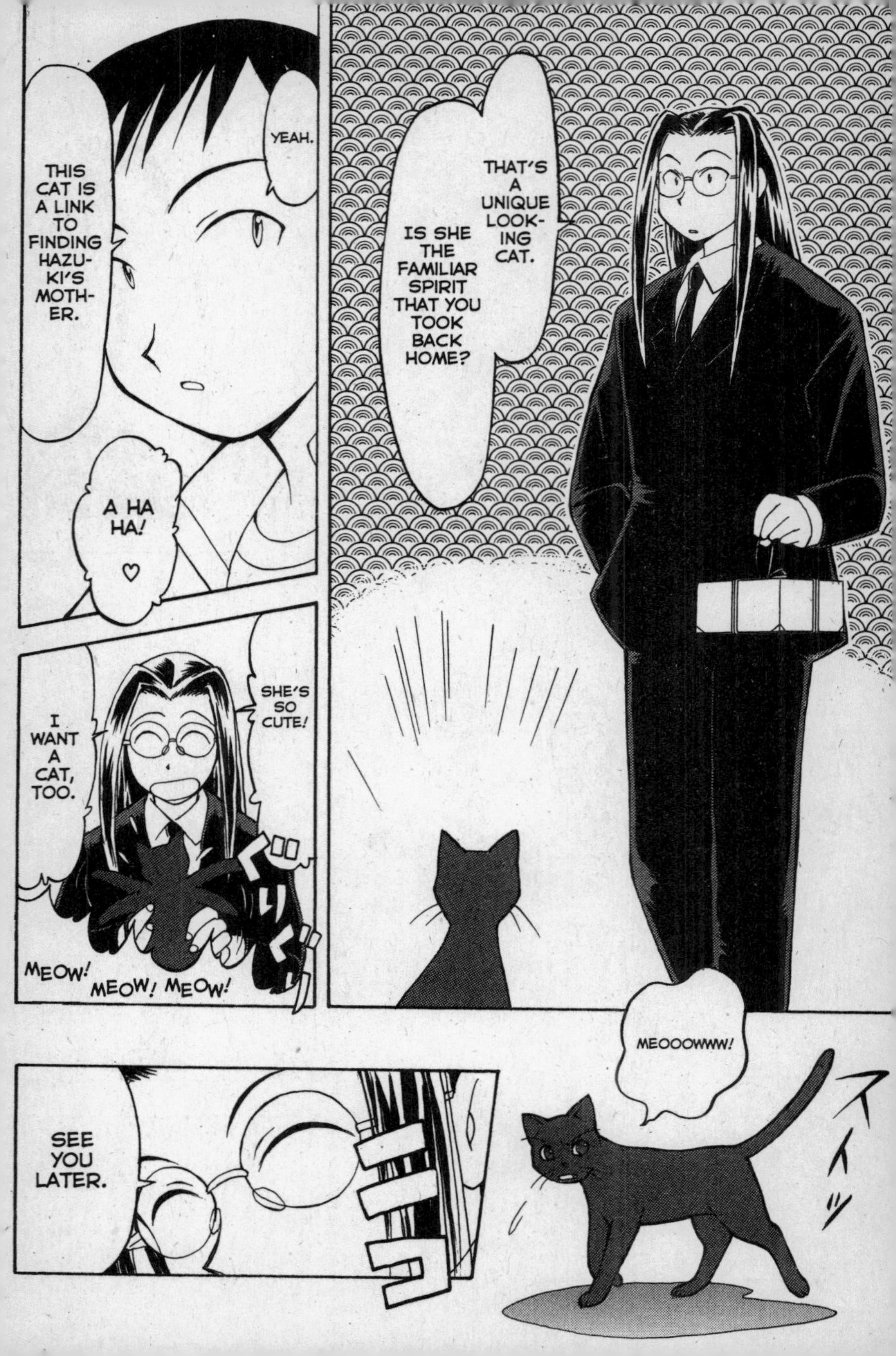
THAT'S A UNIQUE LOOKING CAT.
IS SHE THE FAMILIAR SPIRIT THAT YOU TOOK BACK HOME?
YEAH.
THIS CAT IS A LINK TO FINDING HAZUKI'S MOTHER.
A HA HA! ♡
SHE'S SO CUTE!
I WANT A CAT, TOO.
MEOW! MEOW! MEOW!
MEOOOWWW!
スイッ
SEE YOU LATER.

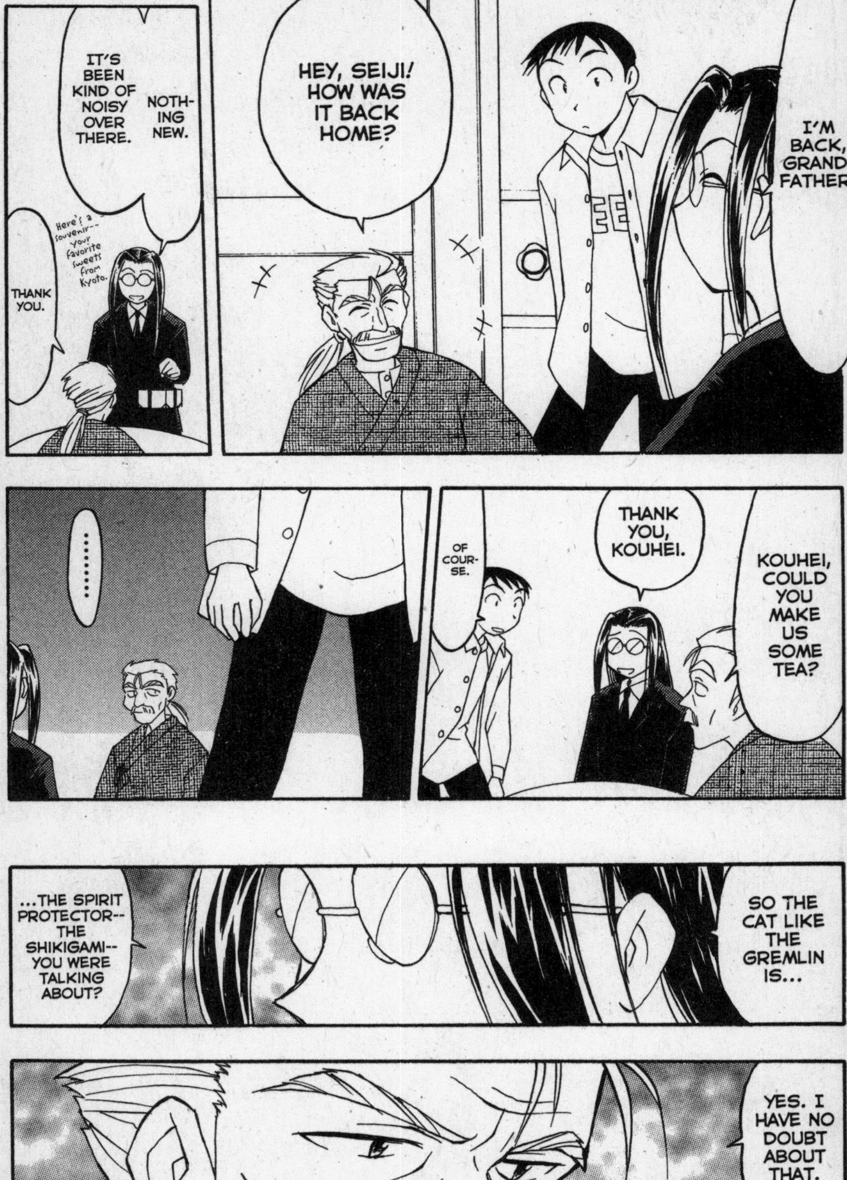
I'M BACK, GRANDFATHER.
HEY, SEIJI! HOW WAS IT BACK HOME?
NOTHING NEW.
IT'S BEEN KIND OF NOISY OVER THERE.
Here's a souvenir-- Your favorite sweets from Kyoto.
THANK YOU.
KOUHEI, COULD YOU MAKE US SOME TEA?
THANK YOU, KOUHEI.
OF COURSE.
......
SO THE CAT LIKE THE GREMLIN IS...
...THE SPIRIT PROTECTOR--THE SHIKIGAMI--YOU WERE TALKING ABOUT?
YES. I HAVE NO DOUBT ABOUT THAT.

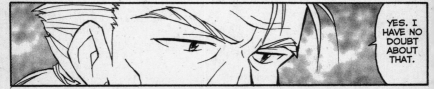

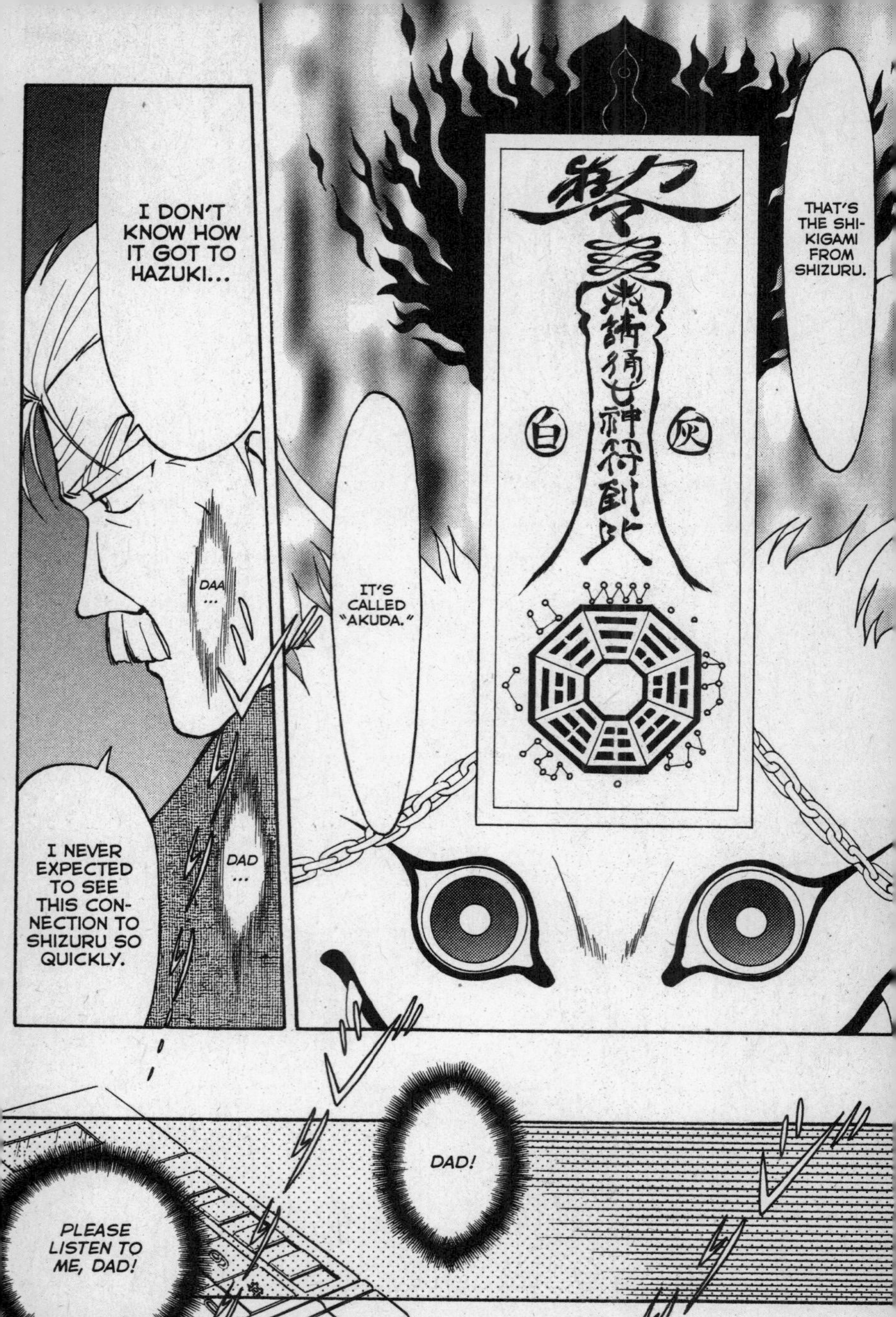
THAT'S THE SHI-KIGAMI FROM SHIZURU.
IT'S CALLED "AKUDA."
I DON'T KNOW HOW IT GOT TO HAZUKI...
DAA...
DAD...
I NEVER EXPECTED TO SEE THIS CON-NECTION TO SHIZURU SO QUICKLY.
DAD!
PLEASE LISTEN TO ME, DAD!

VAMPIRES REALLY EXIST!

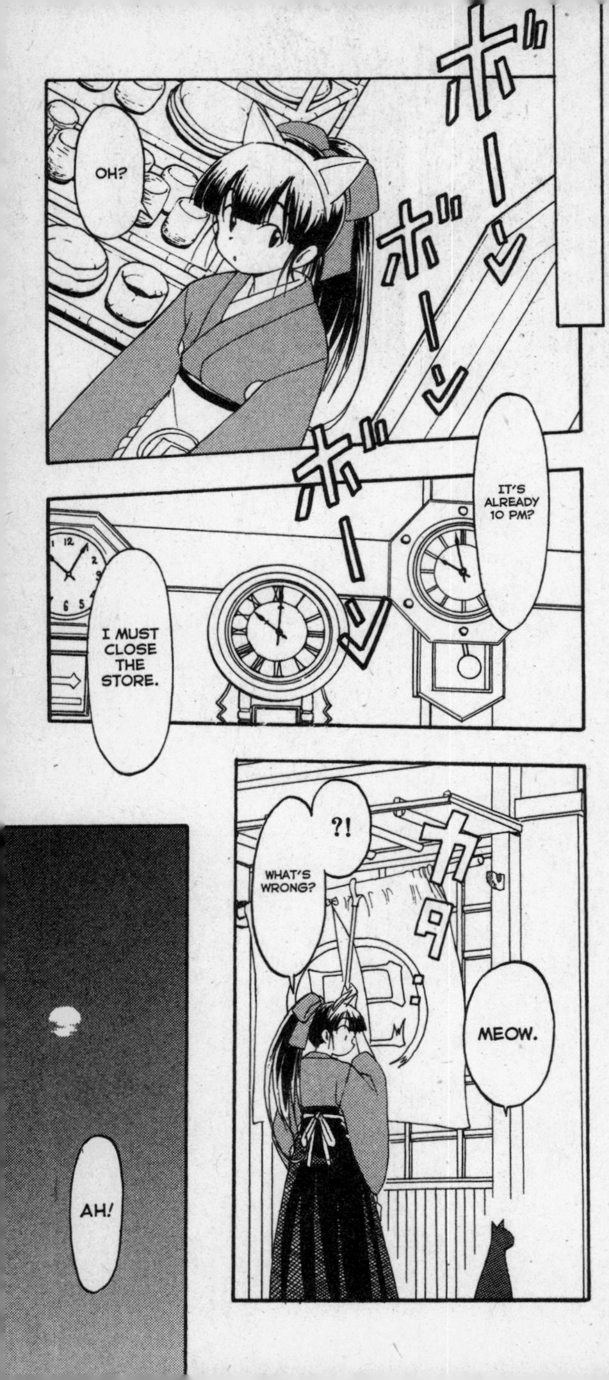
ボーン
ボーン
ボーン
OH?
IT'S ALREADY 10 PM?
I MUST CLOSE THE STORE.
カタ
?!
WHAT'S WRONG?
MEOW.
AH!

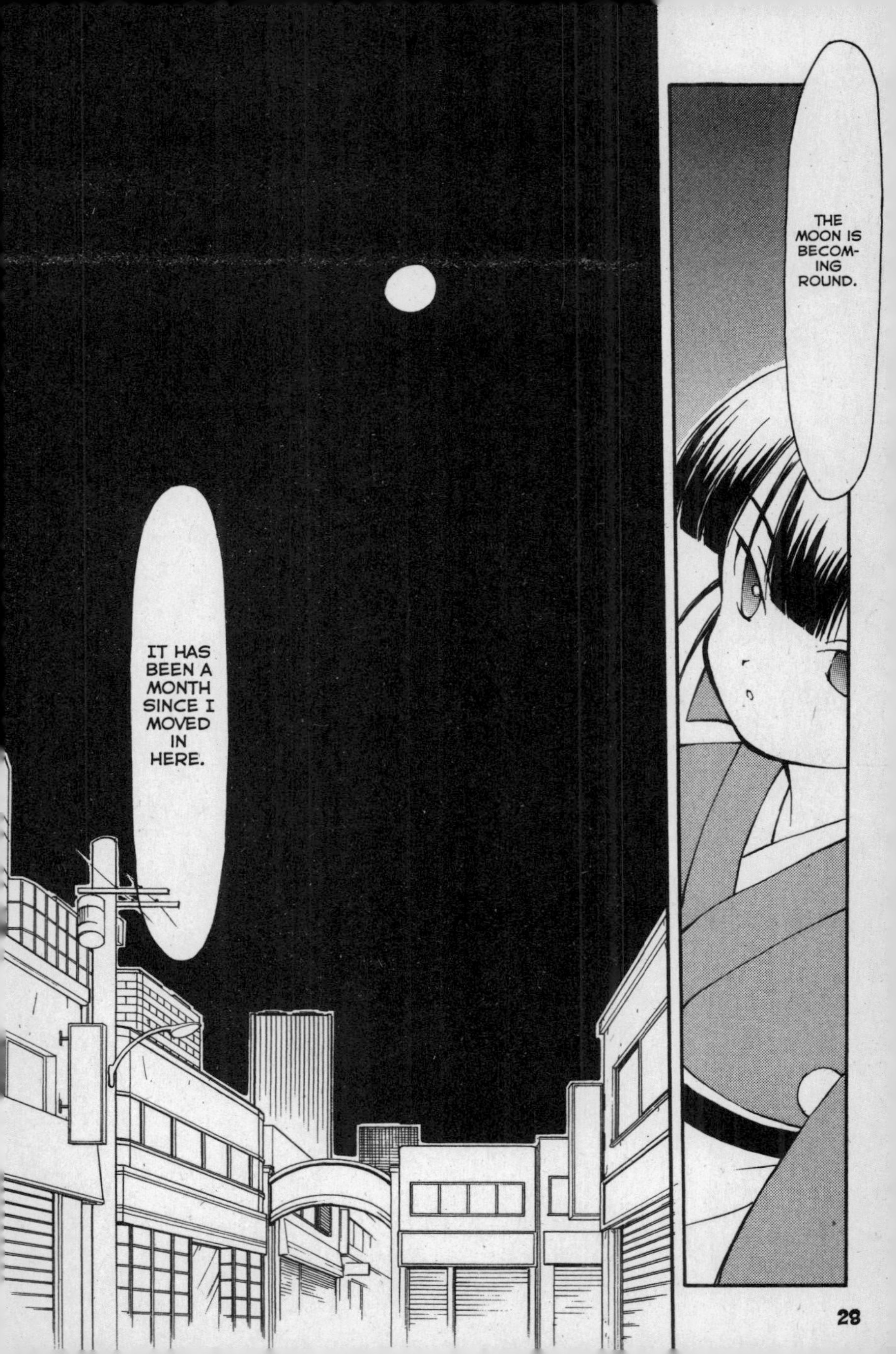
THE MOON IS BECOMING ROUND.
IT HAS BEEN A MONTH SINCE I MOVED IN HERE.

Grandfather's Words of Wisdom

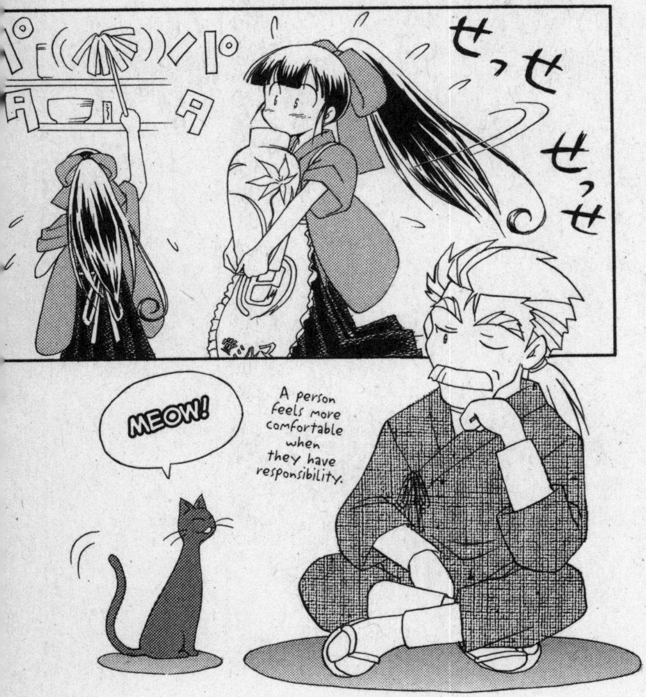
せっせ
せっせ
パタ
パタ
A person feels more comfortable when they have responsibility.
MEOW!

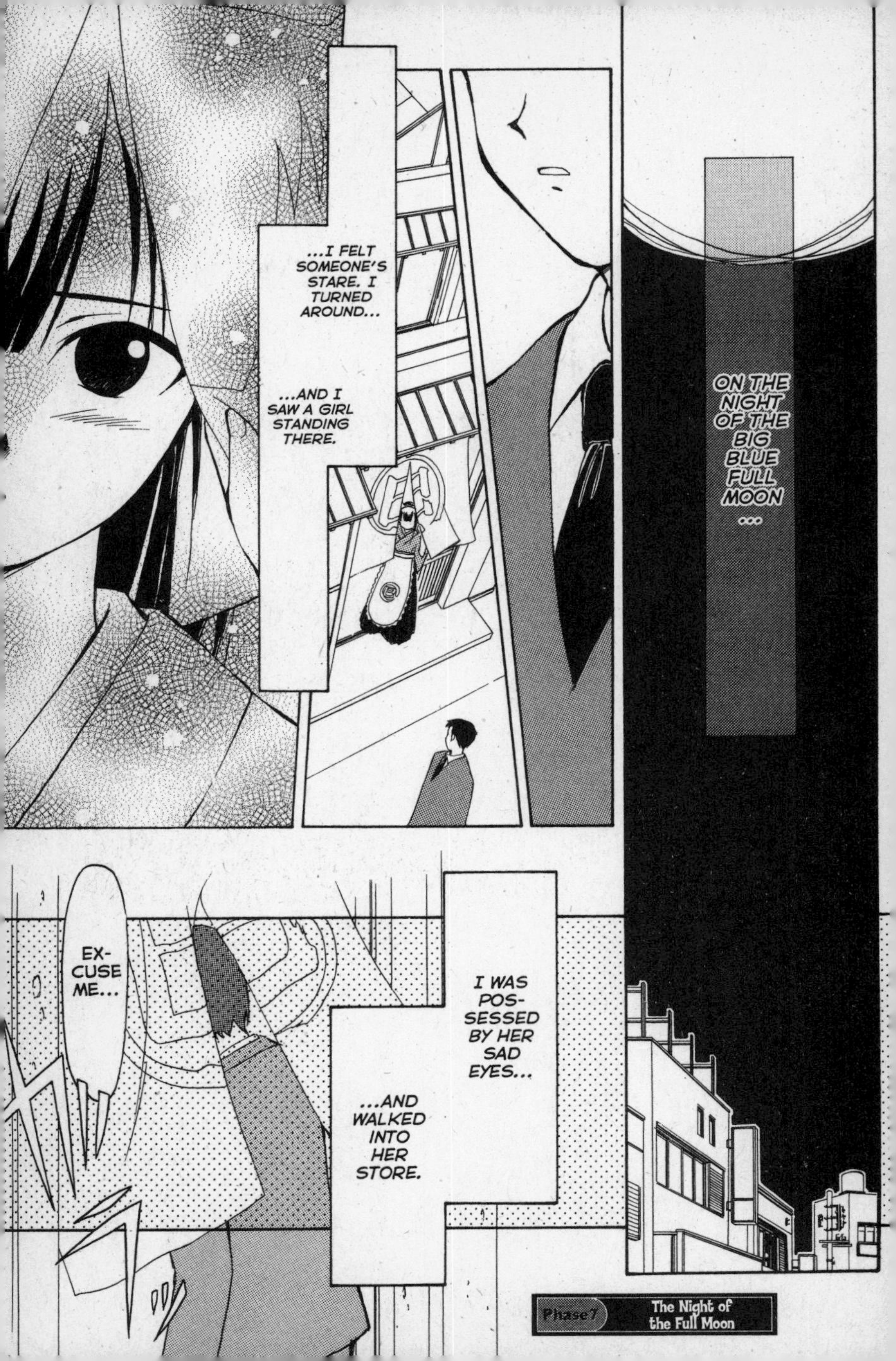
ON THE NIGHT OF THE BIG BLUE FULL MOON...
...I FELT SOMEONE'S STARE. I TURNED AROUND...
...AND I SAW A GIRL STANDING THERE.
I WAS POSSESSED BY HER SAD EYES...
...AND WALKED INTO HER STORE.
EX-CUSE ME...
Phase 7
The Night of the Full Moon

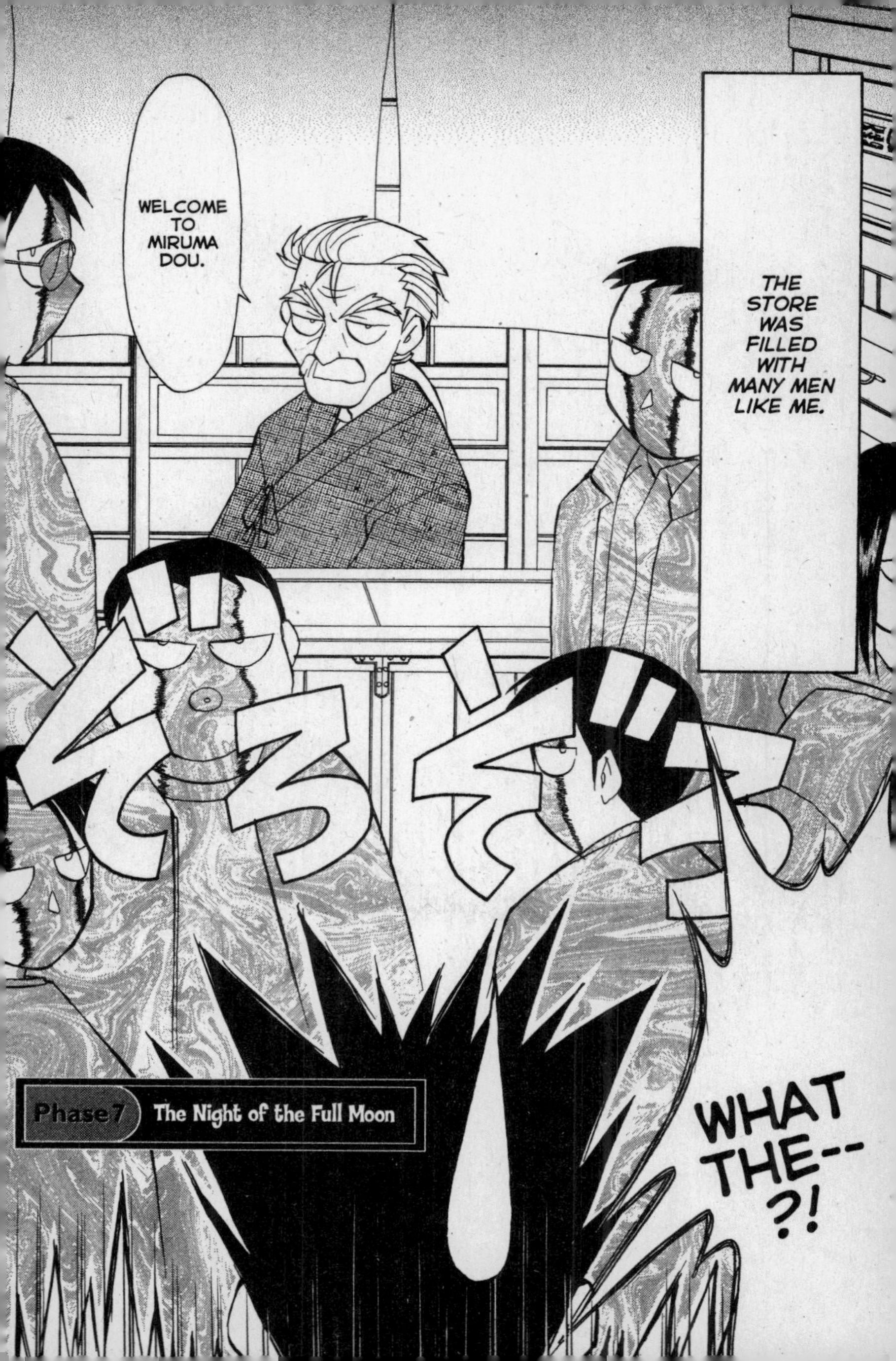
THE STORE WAS FILLED WITH MANY MEN LIKE ME.
WELCOME TO MIRUMA DOU.
Phase 7 The Night of the Full Moon
WHAT THE--?!

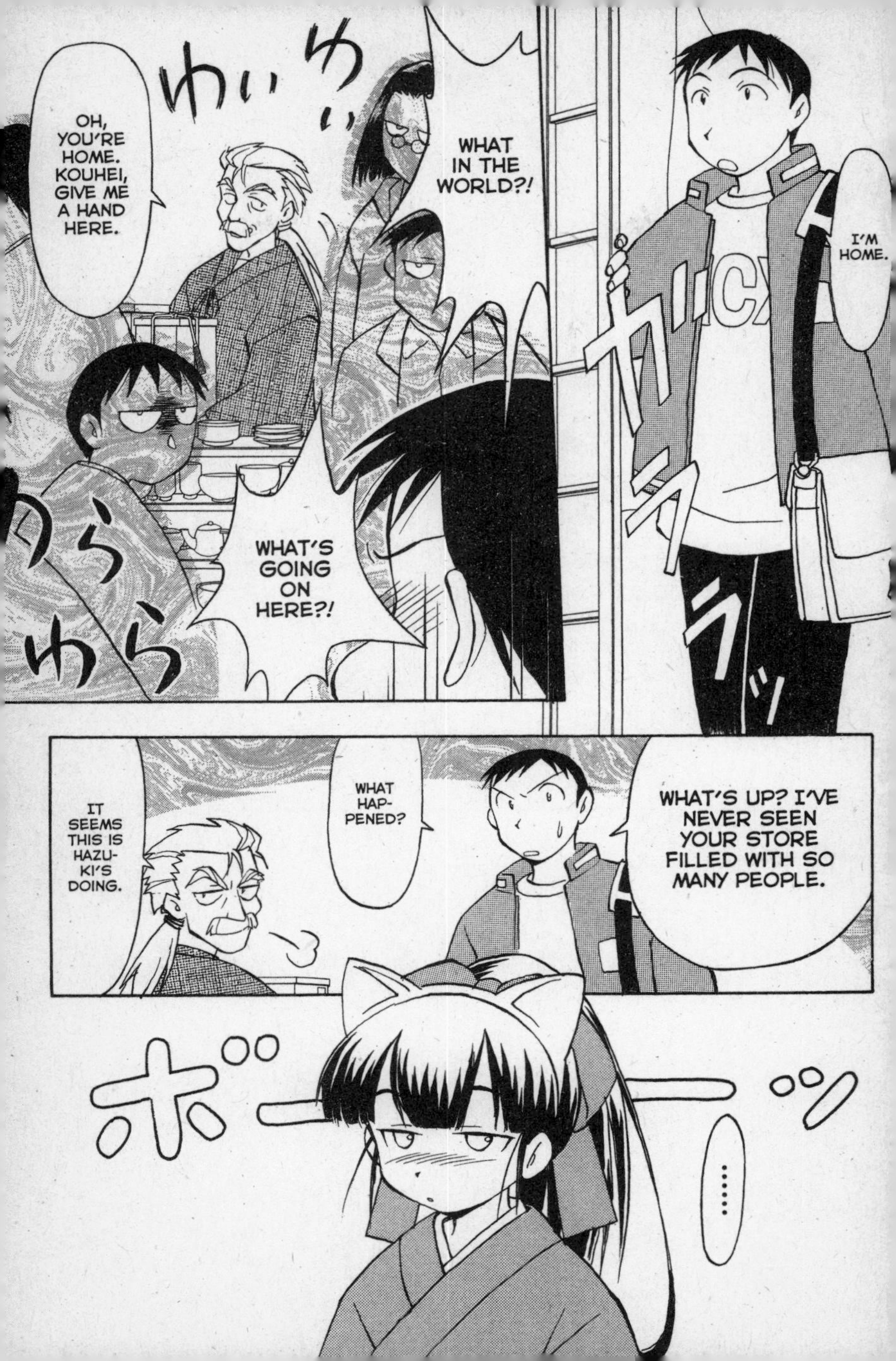

I'M HOME.
ガラッ
WHAT IN THE WORLD?!
OH, YOU'RE HOME. KOUHEI, GIVE ME A HAND HERE.
WHAT'S GOING ON HERE?!
ゆら ゆら
WHAT'S UP? I'VE NEVER SEEN YOUR STORE FILLED WITH SO MANY PEOPLE.
WHAT HAP-PENED?
IT SEEMS THIS IS HAZU-KI'S DOING.
ポーッ
......

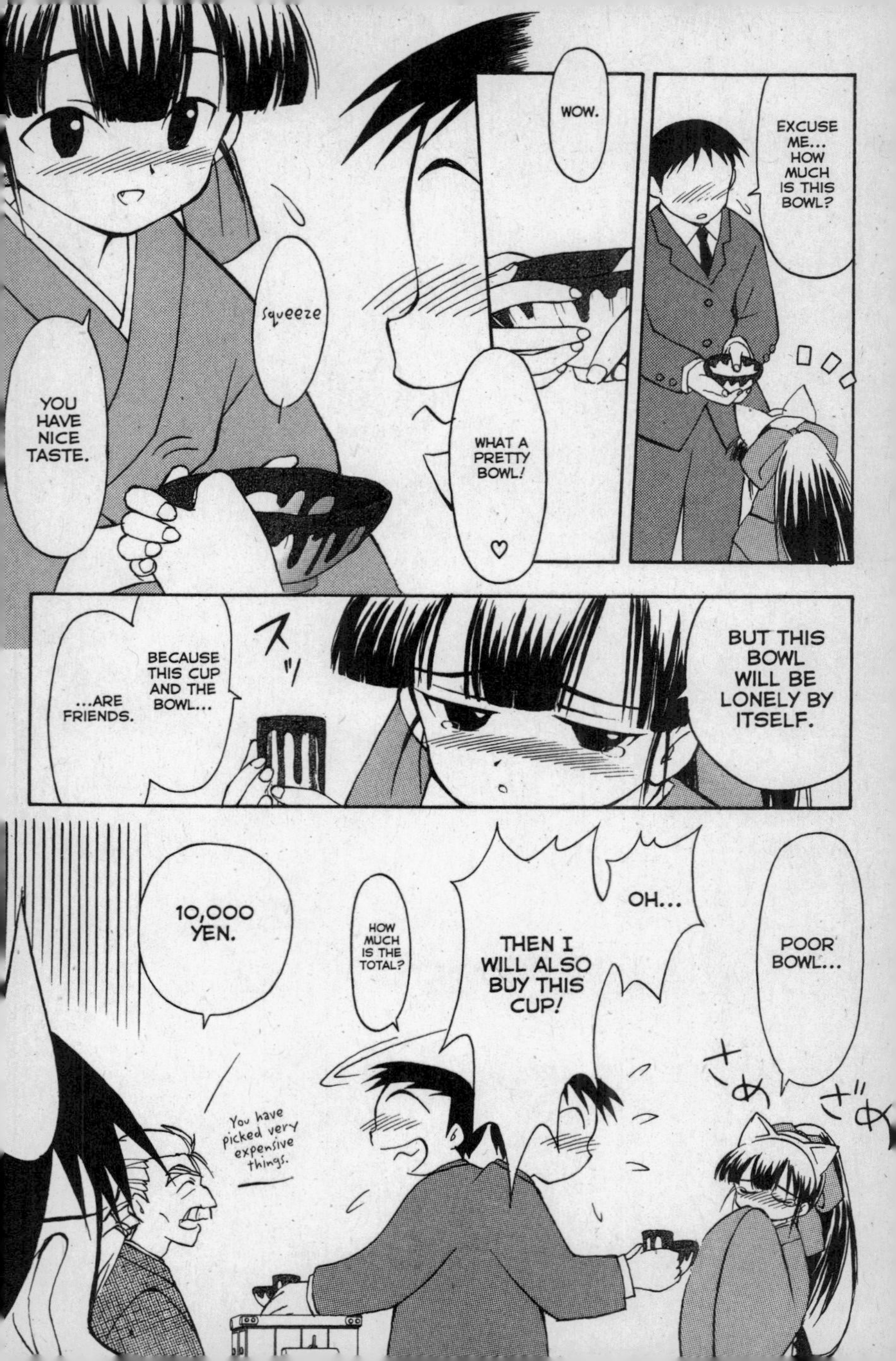
EXCUSE ME... HOW MUCH IS THIS BOWL?
WOW.
WHAT A PRETTY BOWL! ♡
squeeze
YOU HAVE NICE TASTE.
BUT THIS BOWL WILL BE LONELY BY ITSELF.
スッ
BECAUSE THIS CUP AND THE BOWL...
...ARE FRIENDS.
POOR BOWL...
さめ ざめ
OH...
THEN I WILL ALSO BUY THIS CUP!
HOW MUCH IS THE TOTAL?
10,000 YEN.
You have picked very expensive things.

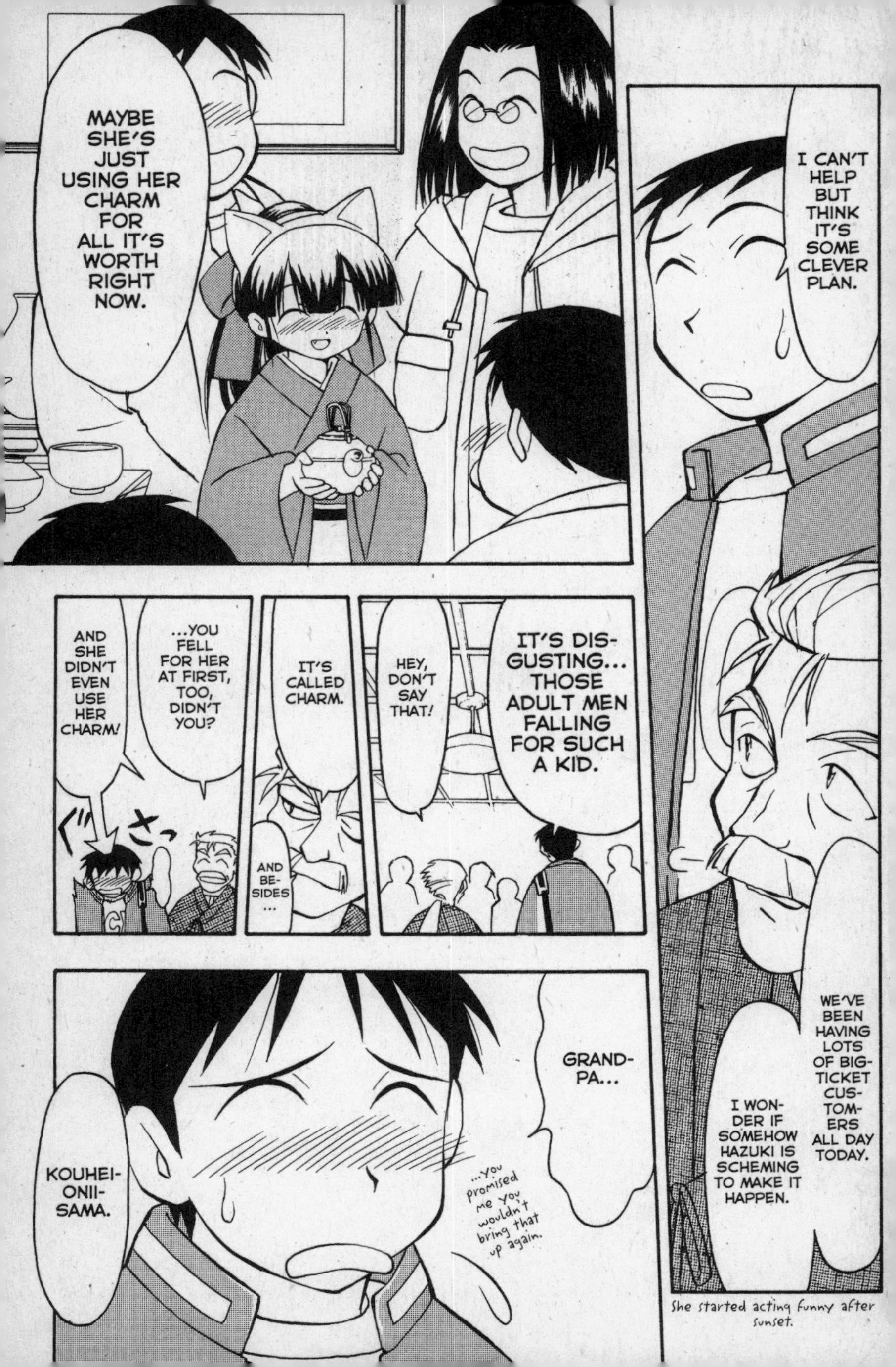

I CAN'T HELP BUT THINK IT'S SOME CLEVER PLAN.
MAYBE SHE'S JUST USING HER CHARM FOR ALL IT'S WORTH RIGHT NOW.
WE'VE BEEN HAVING LOTS OF BIG-TICKET CUS-TOM-ERS ALL DAY TODAY.
I WON-DER IF SOMEHOW HAZUKI IS SCHEMING TO MAKE IT HAPPEN.
She started acting funny after sunset.
IT'S DIS-GUSTING... THOSE ADULT MEN FALLING FOR SUCH A KID.
HEY, DON'T SAY THAT!
IT'S CALLED CHARM.
AND BE-SIDES ...
...YOU FELL FOR HER AT FIRST, TOO, DIDN'T YOU?
AND SHE DIDN'T EVEN USE HER CHARM!
ぐ
さっ
GRAND-PA...
...you promised me you wouldn't bring that up again.
KOUHEI-ONII-SAMA.

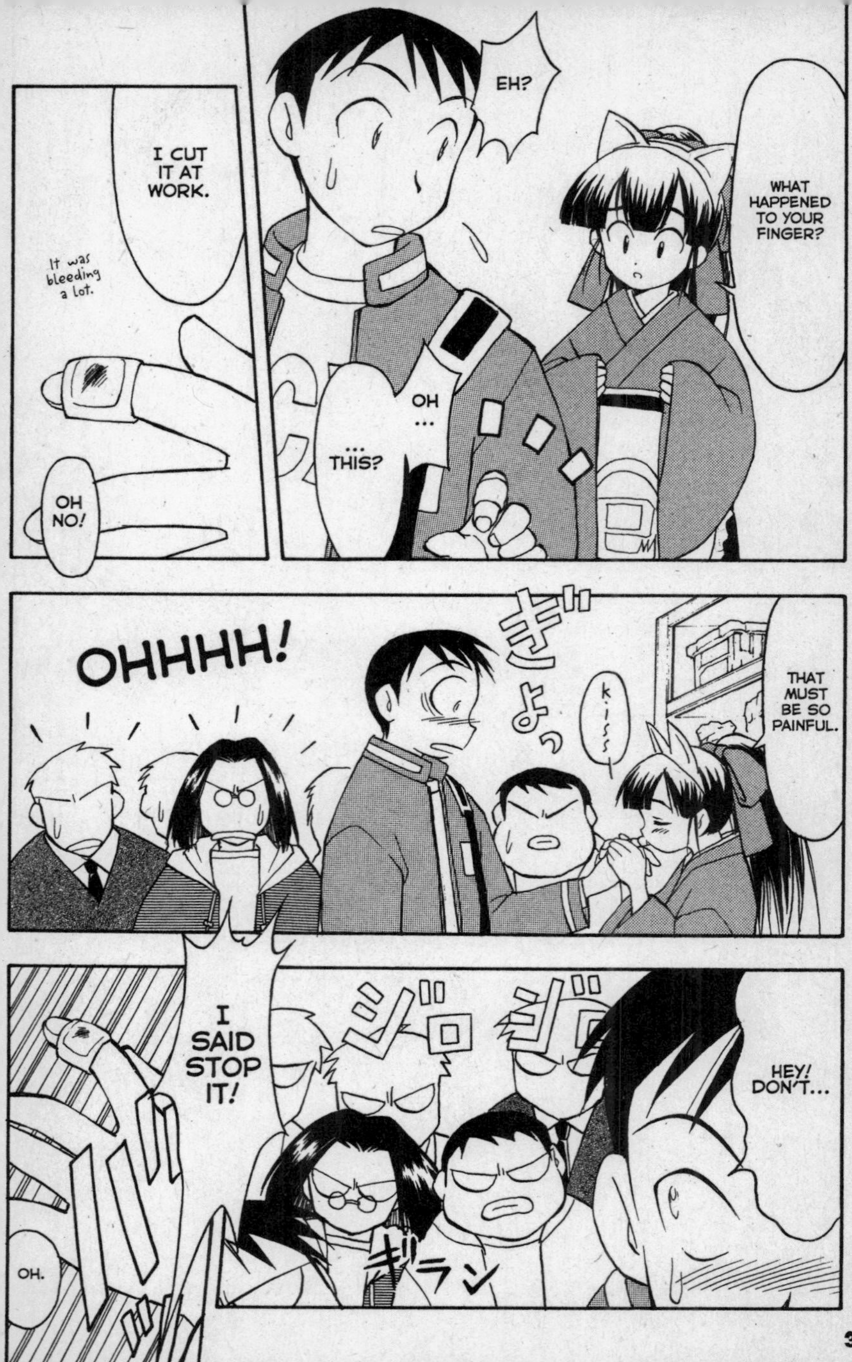
WHAT HAPPENED TO YOUR FINGER?
EH?
OH ...
... THIS?
I CUT IT AT WORK.
It was bleeding a lot.
OH NO!
THAT MUST BE SO PAINFUL.
kiss
ぎょっ
OHHHH!
HEY! DON'T...
ジロ
ジロ
ギラン
I SAID STOP IT!
OH.

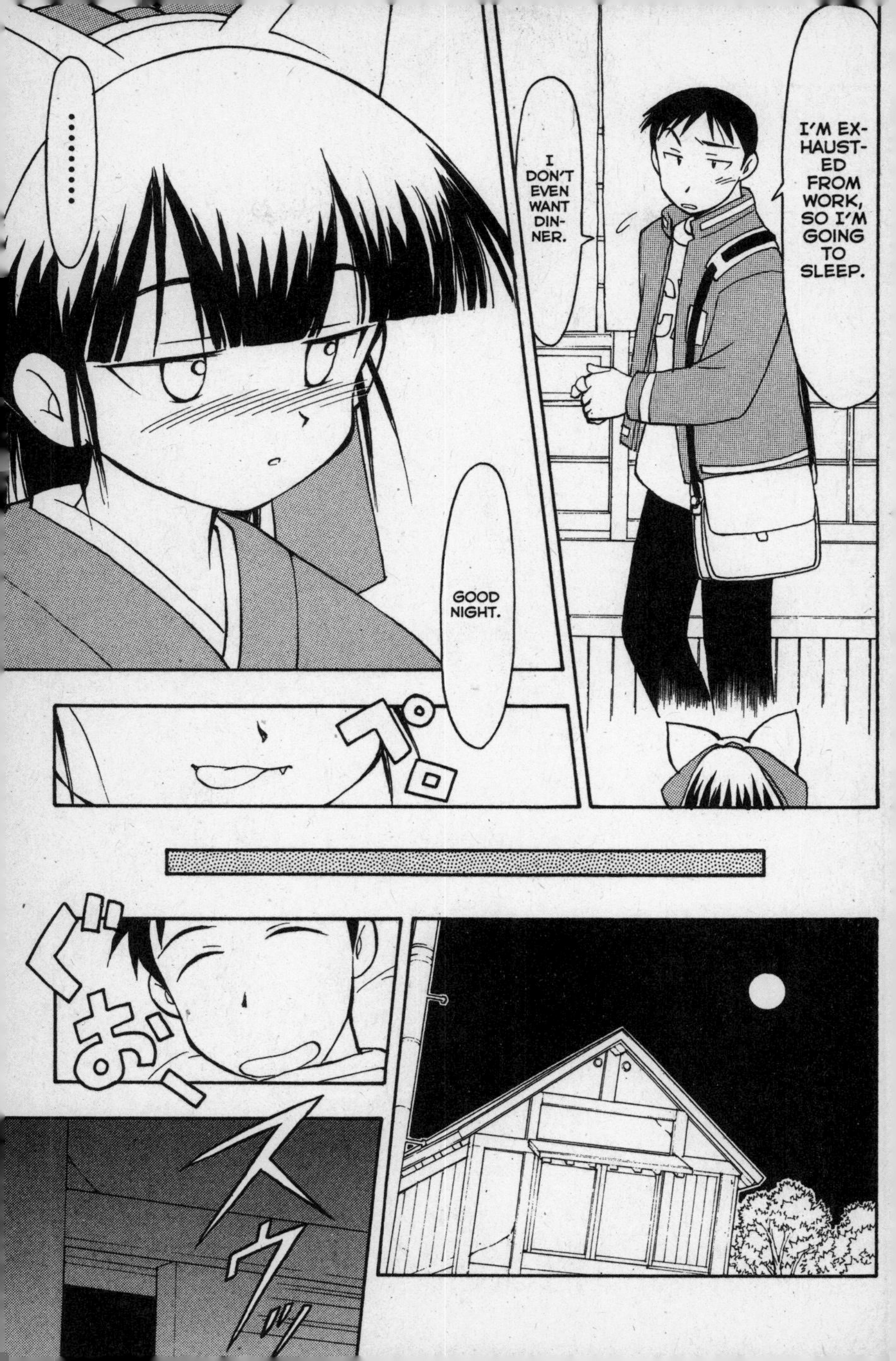

I'M EX-HAUST-ED FROM WORK, SO I'M GOING TO SLEEP.
I DON'T EVEN WANT DIN-NER.
GOOD NIGHT.
......
ペロ
ぐぉ〜
スゥ

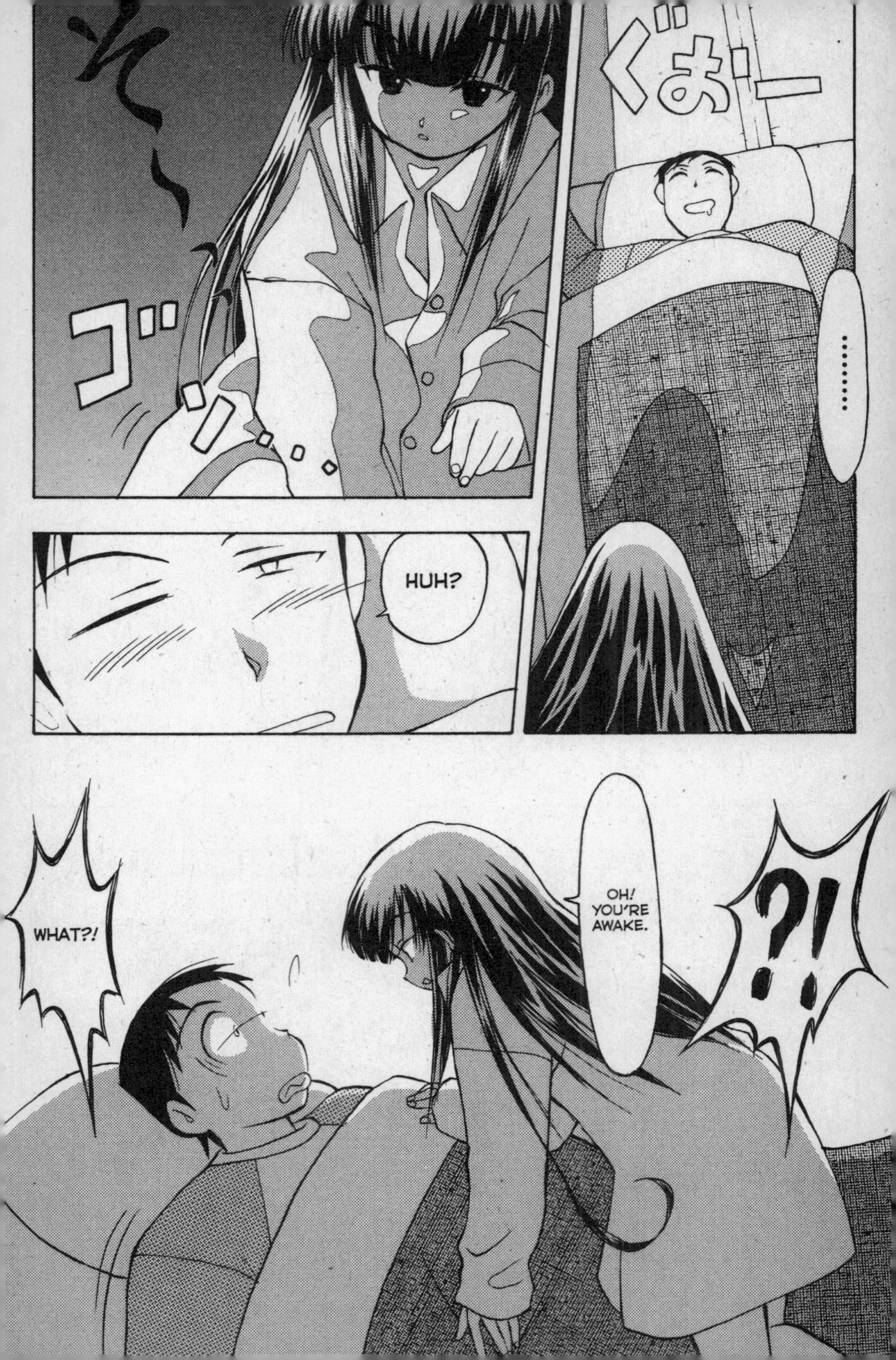
ぐぉーー
......
ゾくぅ
ゴゴゴ
HUH?
OH! YOU'RE AWAKE.
?!
WHAT?!

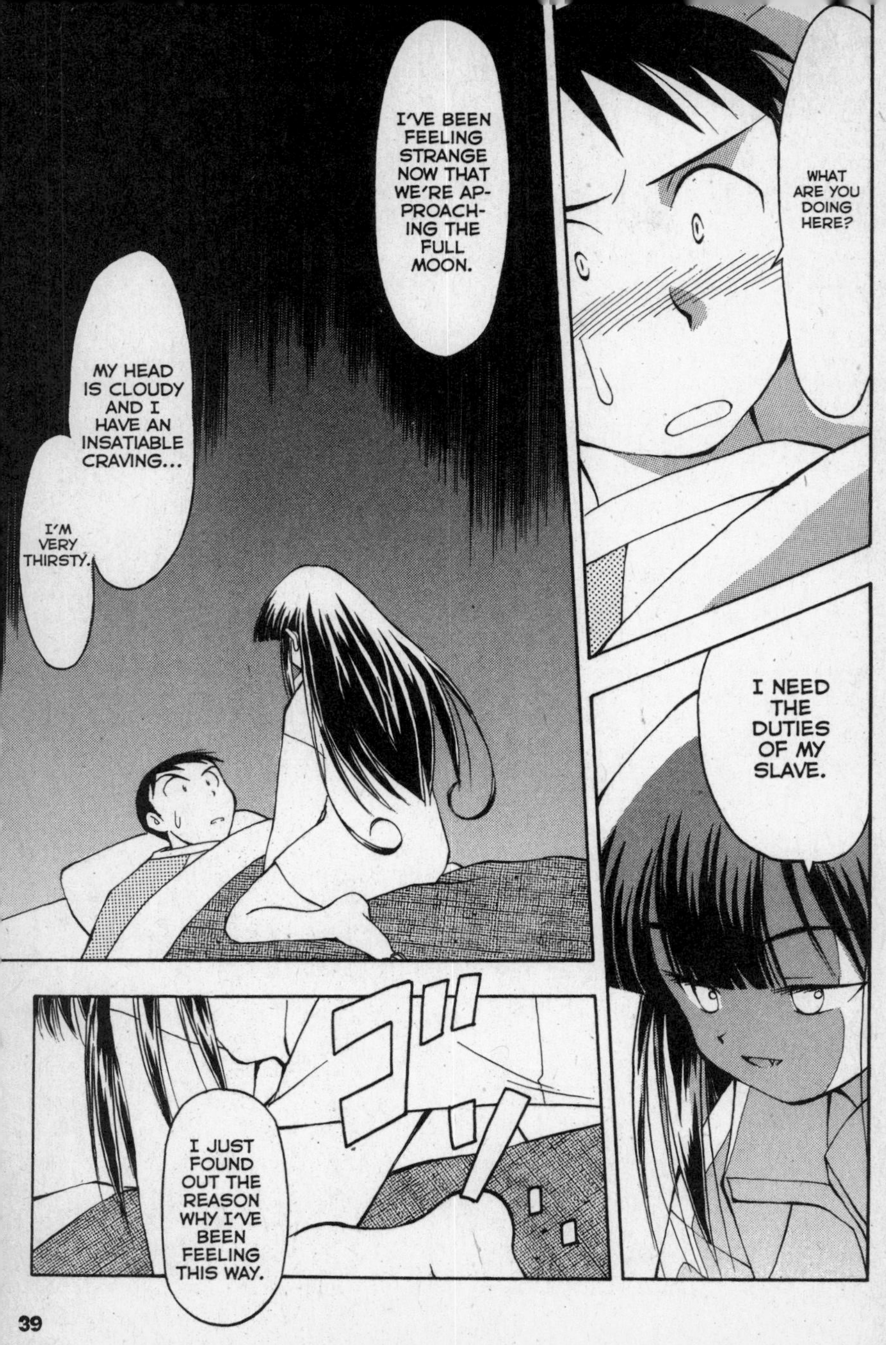
WHAT ARE YOU DOING HERE?
I'VE BEEN FEELING STRANGE NOW THAT WE'RE AP-PROACH-ING THE FULL MOON.
MY HEAD IS CLOUDY AND I HAVE AN INSATIABLE CRAVING...
I'M VERY THIRSTY.
I NEED THE DUTIES OF MY SLAVE.
ゴゴ
I JUST FOUND OUT THE REASON WHY I'VE BEEN FEELING THIS WAY.

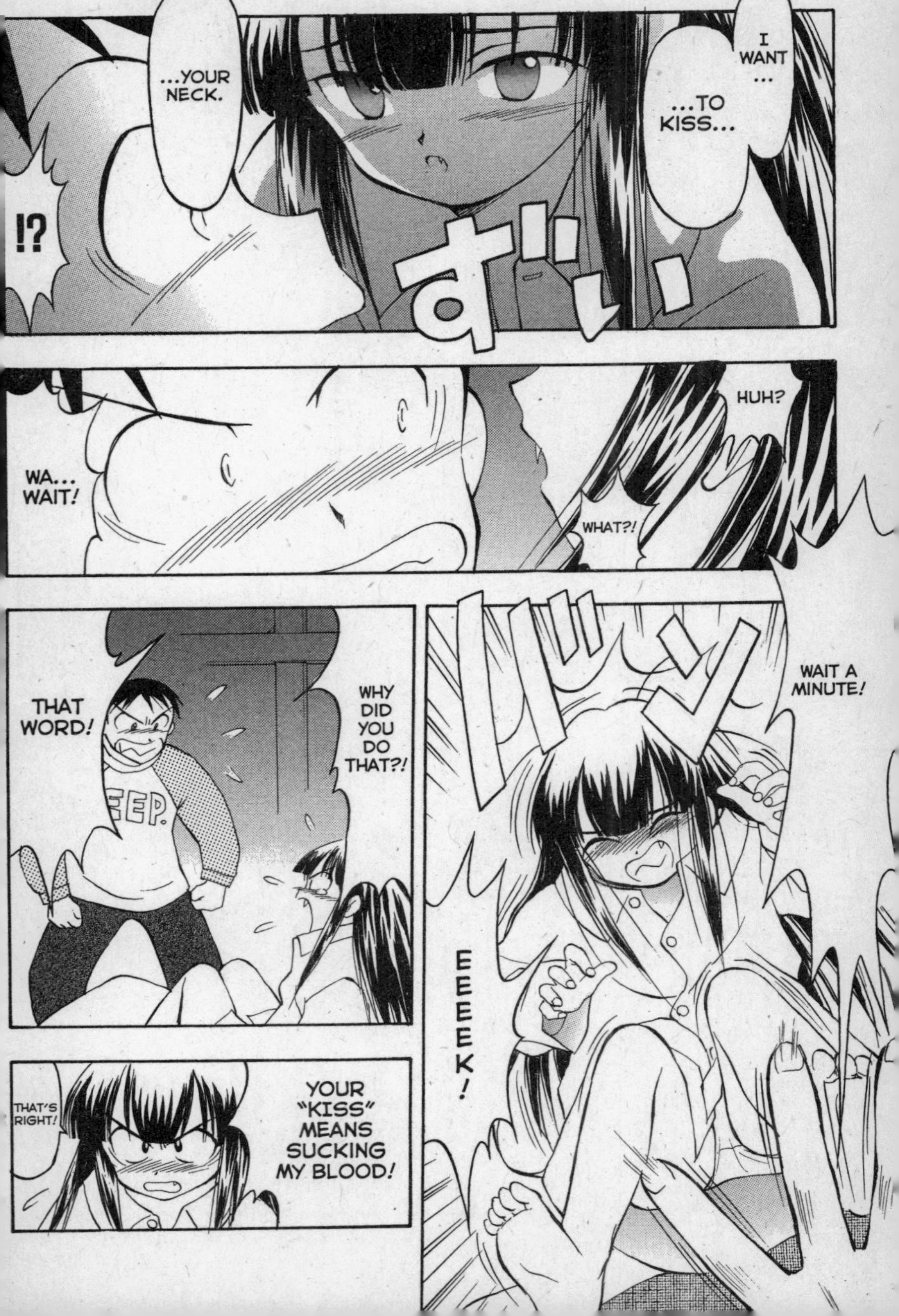
I WANT...
...TO KISS...
...YOUR NECK.
!?
HUH?
WHAT?!
WA... WAIT!
WAIT A MINUTE!
EEEEEK!
WHY DID YOU DO THAT?!
THAT WORD!
YOUR "KISS" MEANS SUCKING MY BLOOD!
THAT'S RIGHT!

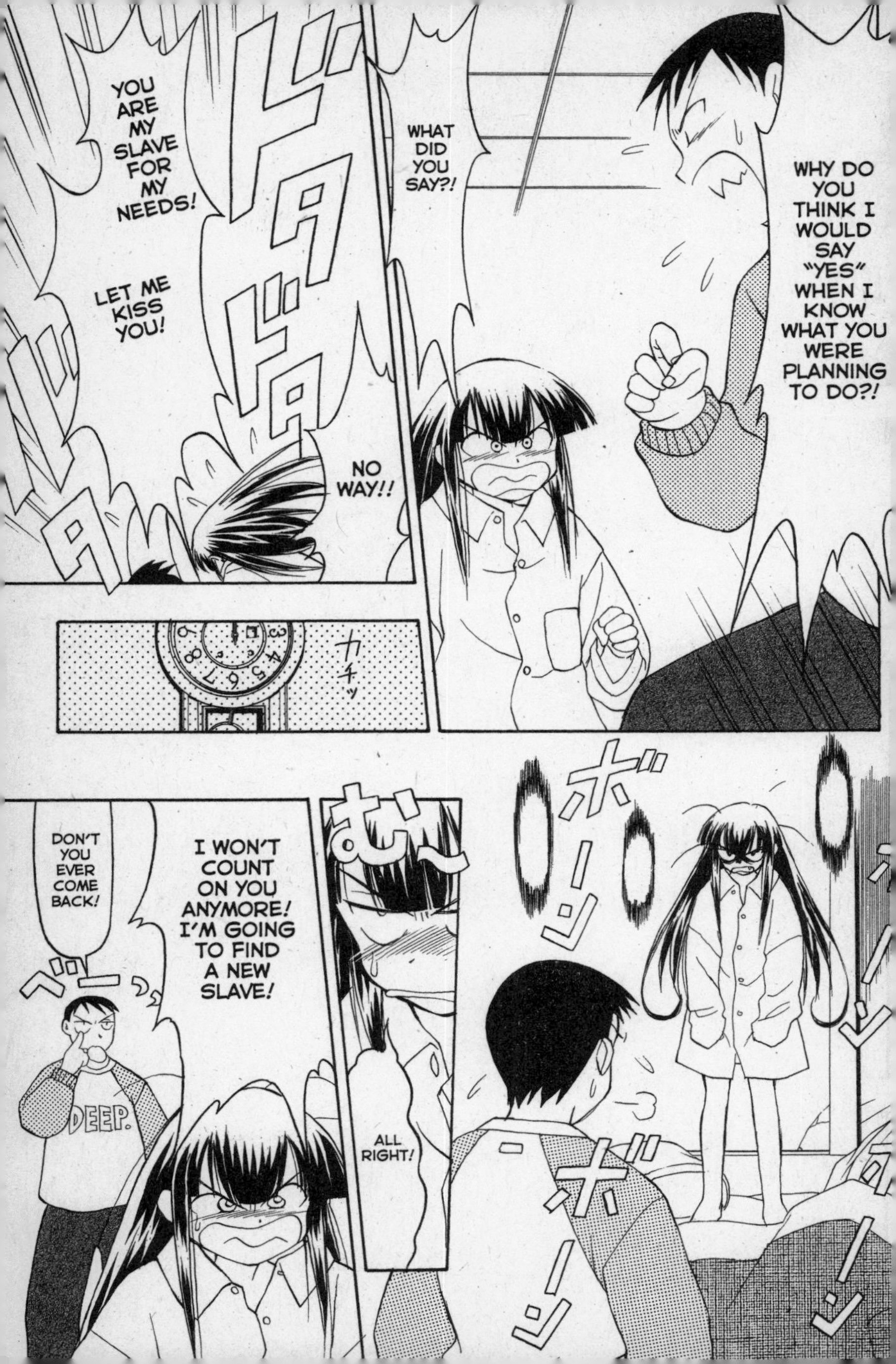
WHY DO YOU THINK I WOULD SAY "YES" WHEN I KNOW WHAT YOU WERE PLANNING TO DO?!
WHAT DID YOU SAY?!
NO WAY!!
ドタドタ
YOU ARE MY SLAVE FOR MY NEEDS!
LET ME KISS YOU!
カチッ
ボーン
ボーン
ALL RIGHT!
むー
I WON'T COUNT ON YOU ANYMORE! I'M GOING TO FIND A NEW SLAVE!
DON'T YOU EVER COME BACK!
べーっ
DEEP.

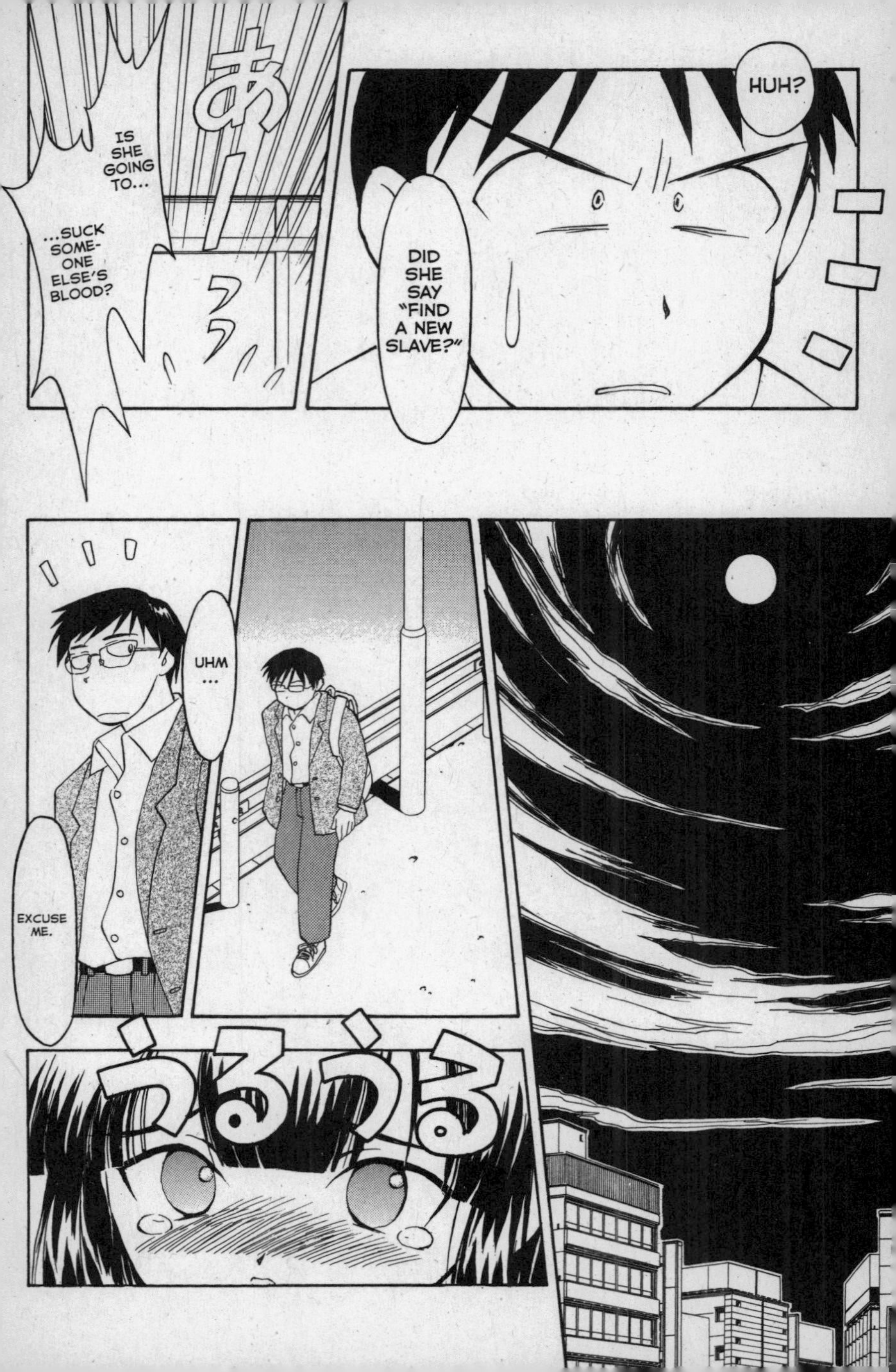
HUH?
DID SHE SAY "FIND A NEW SLAVE?"
あ
IS SHE GOING TO...
...SUCK SOME-ONE ELSE'S BLOOD?
UHM...
EXCUSE ME.
うるうる

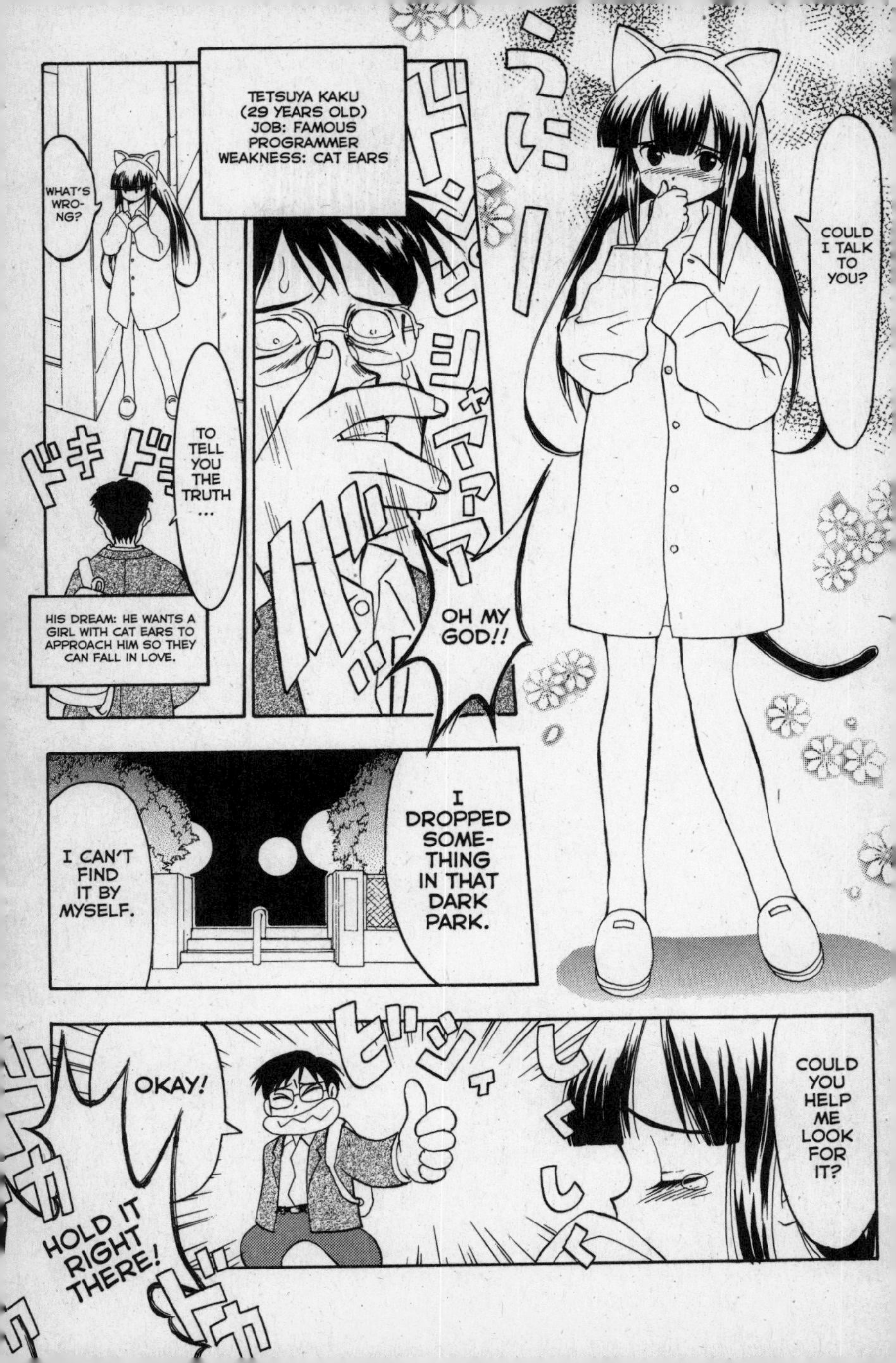
COULD I TALK TO YOU?
TETSUYA KAKU (29 YEARS OLD) JOB: FAMOUS PROGRAMMER WEAKNESS: CAT EARS
OH MY GOD!!
WHAT'S WRO-NG?
TO TELL YOU THE TRUTH ...
HIS DREAM: HE WANTS A GIRL WITH CAT EARS TO APPROACH HIM SO THEY CAN FALL IN LOVE.
I DROPPED SOME-THING IN THAT DARK PARK.
I CAN'T FIND IT BY MYSELF.
COULD YOU HELP ME LOOK FOR IT?
OKAY!
HOLD IT RIGHT THERE!

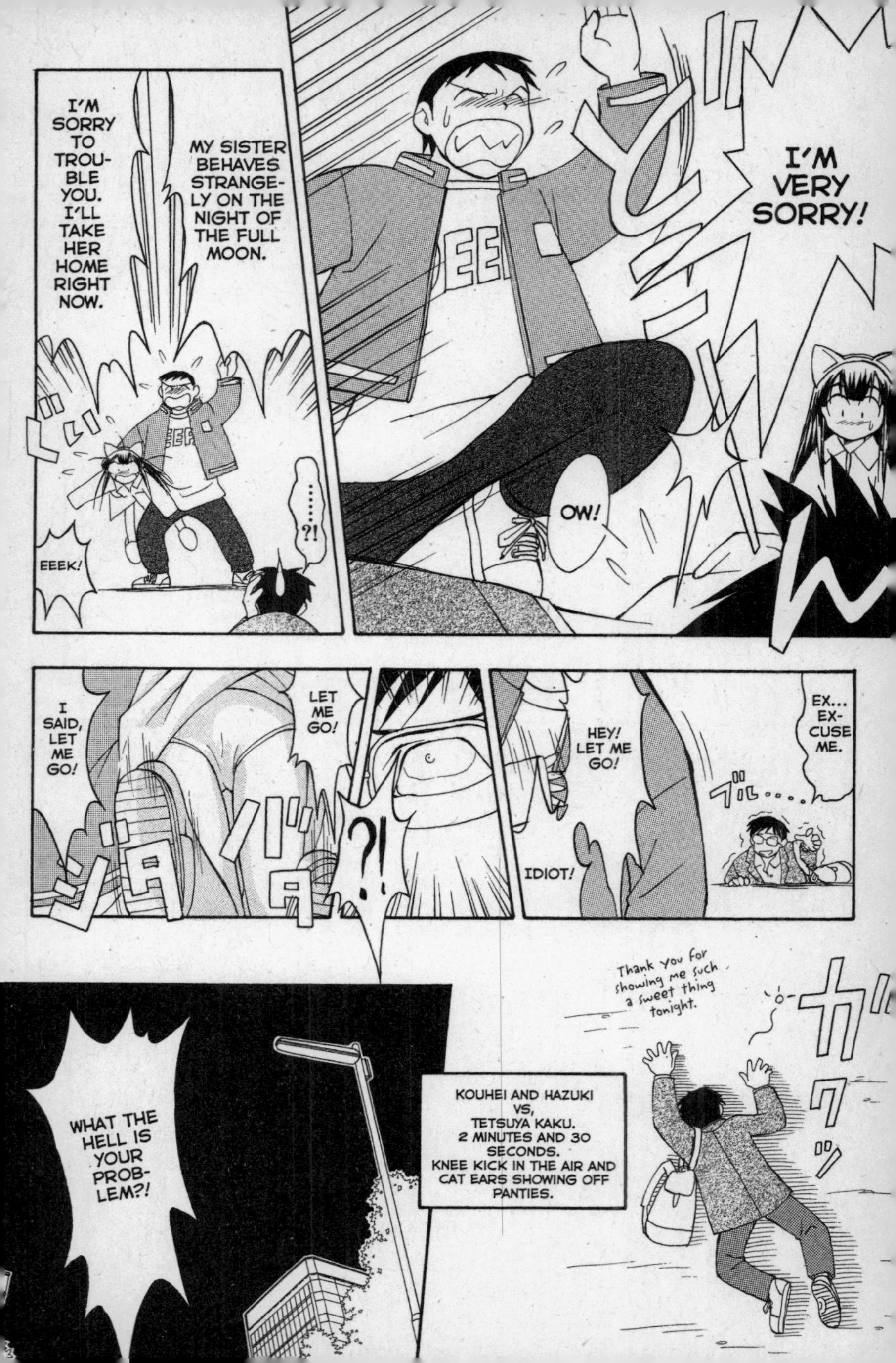
I'M VERY SORRY!
OW!
MY SISTER BEHAVES STRANGELY ON THE NIGHT OF THE FULL MOON.
I'M SORRY TO TROUBLE YOU. I'LL TAKE HER HOME RIGHT NOW.
......?!
EEEK!
EX... EXCUSE ME.
HEY! LET ME GO!
IDIOT!
LET ME GO!
?!
I SAID, LET ME GO!
Thank you for showing me such a sweet thing tonight.
KOUHEI AND HAZUKI VS, TETSUYA KAKU. 2 MINUTES AND 30 SECONDS. KNEE KICK IN THE AIR AND CAT EARS SHOWING OFF PANTIES.
WHAT THE HELL IS YOUR PROBLEM?!

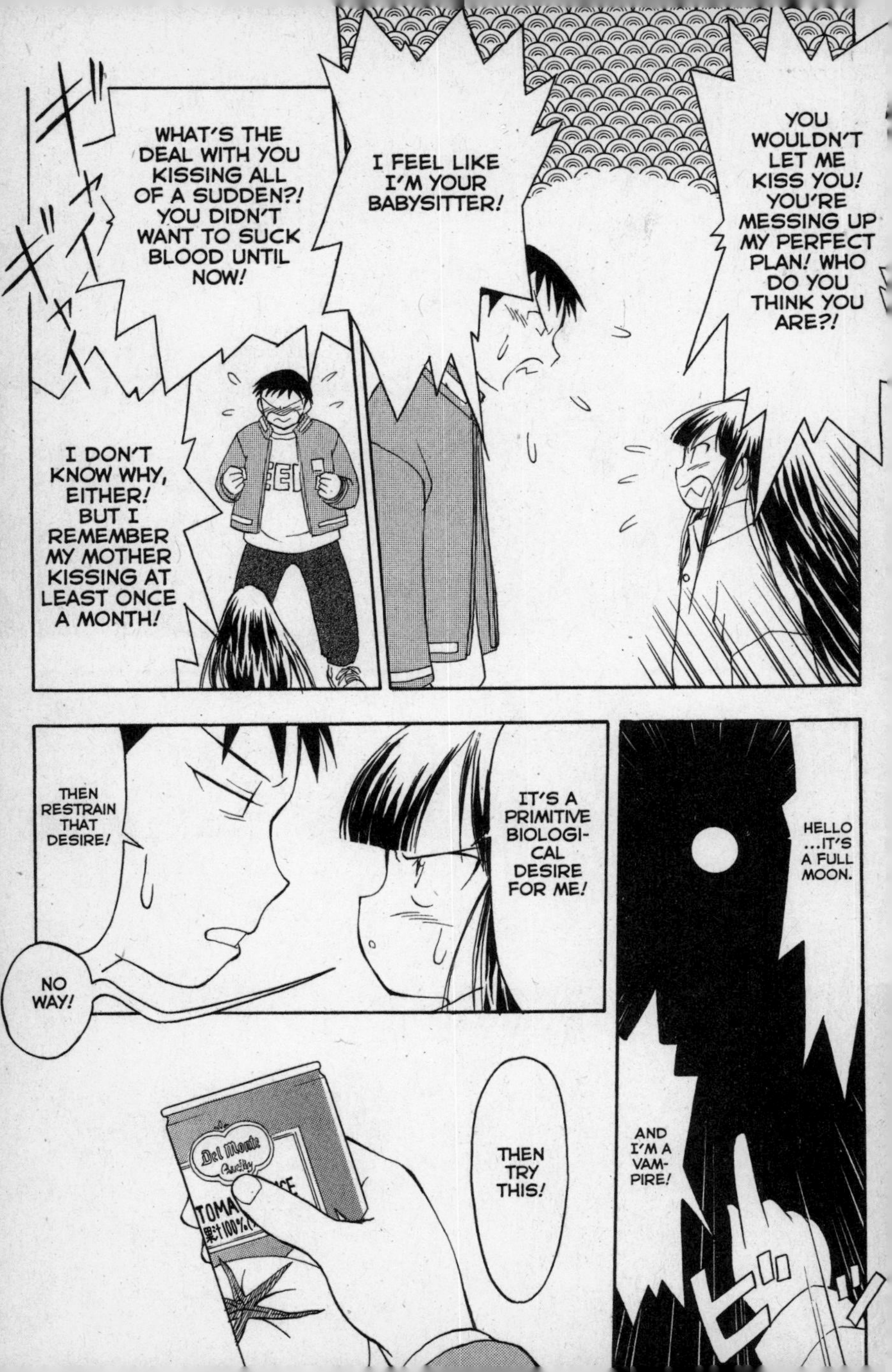
YOU WOULDN'T LET ME KISS YOU! YOU'RE MESSING UP MY PERFECT PLAN! WHO DO YOU THINK YOU ARE?!
I FEEL LIKE I'M YOUR BABYSITTER!
ギャイギャイ
ギャイギャイ
WHAT'S THE DEAL WITH YOU KISSING ALL OF A SUDDEN?! YOU DIDN'T WANT TO SUCK BLOOD UNTIL NOW!
I DON'T KNOW WHY, EITHER! BUT I REMEMBER MY MOTHER KISSING AT LEAST ONCE A MONTH!
HELLO ...IT'S A FULL MOON.
AND I'M A VAMPIRE!
IT'S A PRIMITIVE BIOLOGICAL DESIRE FOR ME!
THEN RESTRAIN THAT DESIRE!
NO WAY!
THEN TRY THIS!
Del Monte

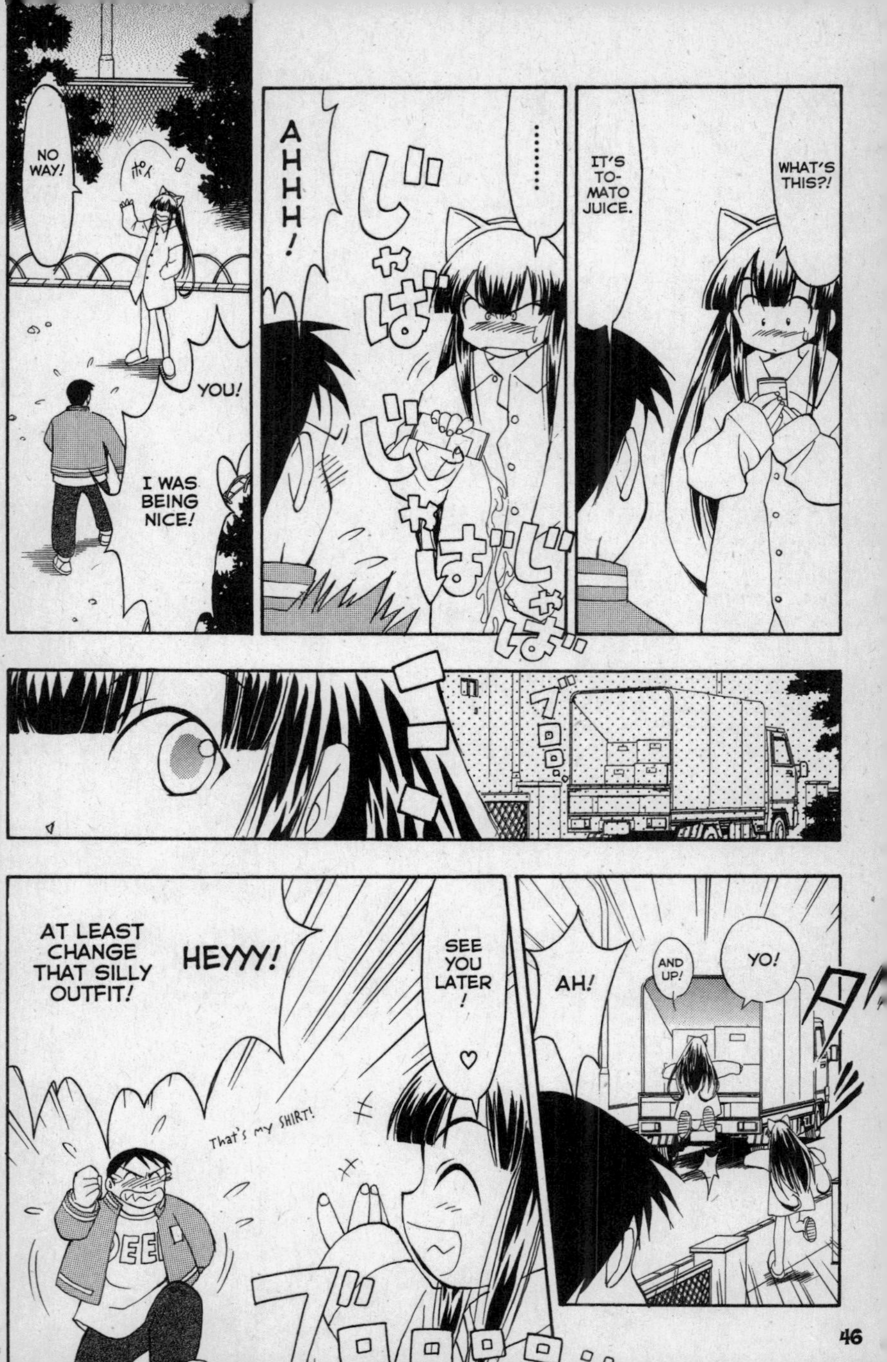
WHAT'S THIS?!
IT'S TO-MATO JUICE.
......
AHHH!
じゃばじゃば
NO WAY!
YOU!
I WAS BEING NICE!
YO!
AND UP!
AH!
SEE YOU LATER! ♥
HEYYY!
AT LEAST CHANGE THAT SILLY OUTFIT!
That's my SHIRT!

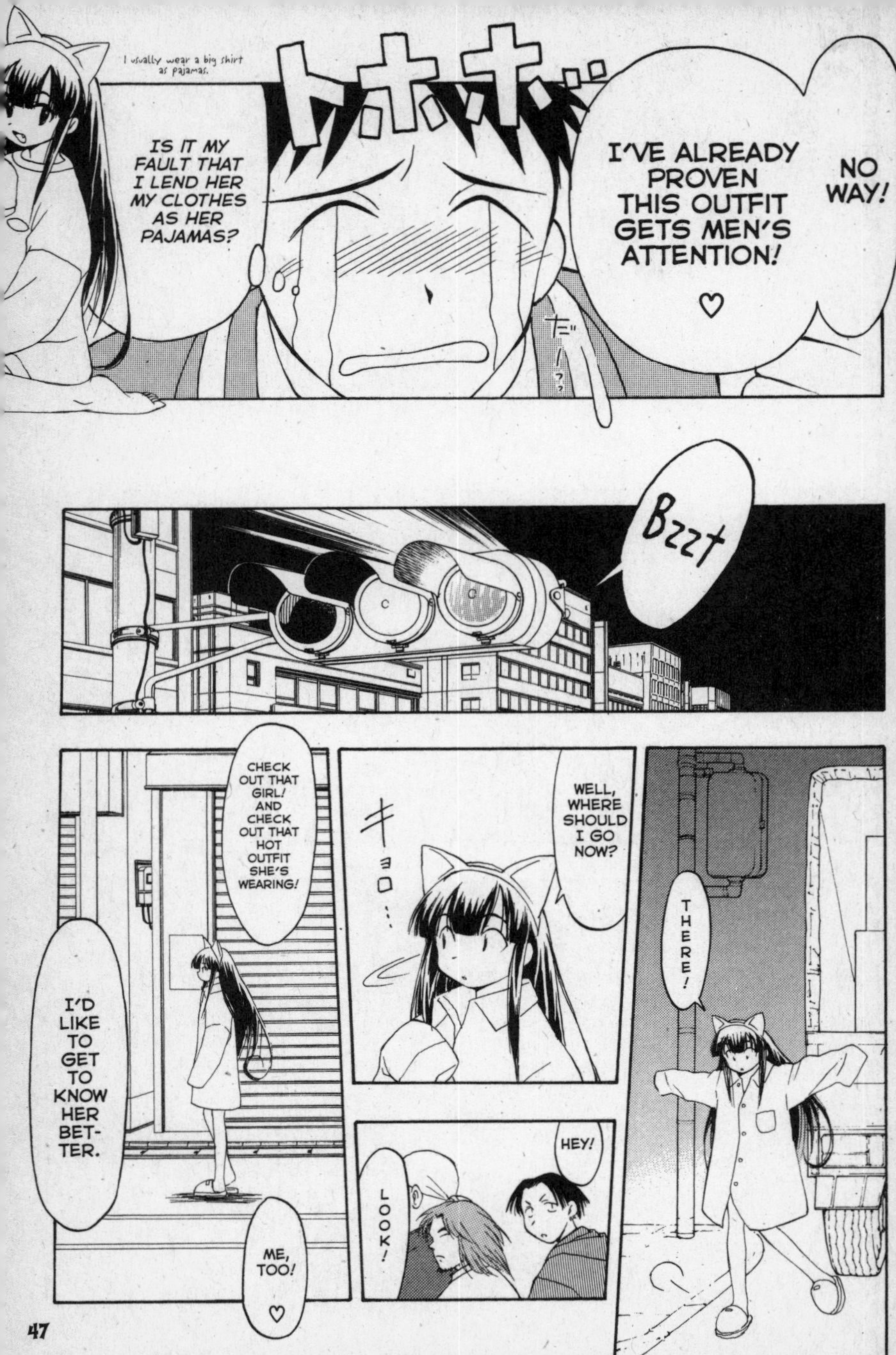
NO WAY!
I'VE ALREADY PROVEN THIS OUTFIT GETS MEN'S ATTENTION! ♡
IS IT MY FAULT THAT I LEND HER MY CLOTHES AS HER PAJAMAS?
I usually wear a big shirt as pajamas.
Bzzt
THERE!
WELL, WHERE SHOULD I GO NOW?
キョロ...
HEY!
LOOK!
ME, TOO! ♡
CHECK OUT THAT GIRL! AND CHECK OUT THAT HOT OUTFIT SHE'S WEARING!
I'D LIKE TO GET TO KNOW HER BET-TER.

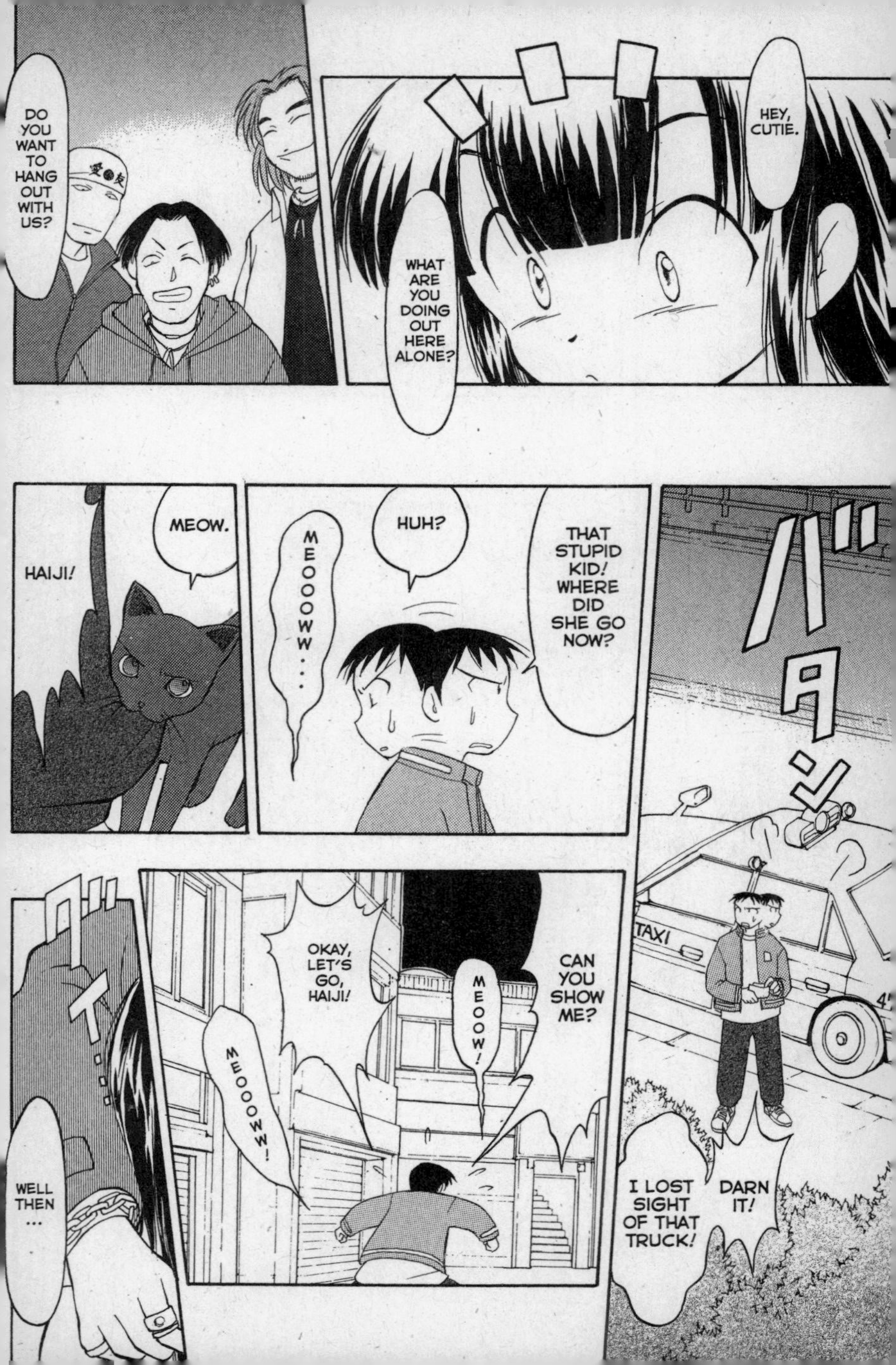
HEY, CUTIE.
WHAT ARE YOU DOING OUT HERE ALONE?
DO YOU WANT TO HANG OUT WITH US?
バタン
TAXI
DARN IT!
I LOST SIGHT OF THAT TRUCK!
THAT STUPID KID! WHERE DID SHE GO NOW?
HUH?
MEOOOWW...
MEOW.
HAIJI!
CAN YOU SHOW ME?
MEOOW!
OKAY, LET'S GO, HAIJI!
MEOOOWW!
グイ...
WELL THEN...

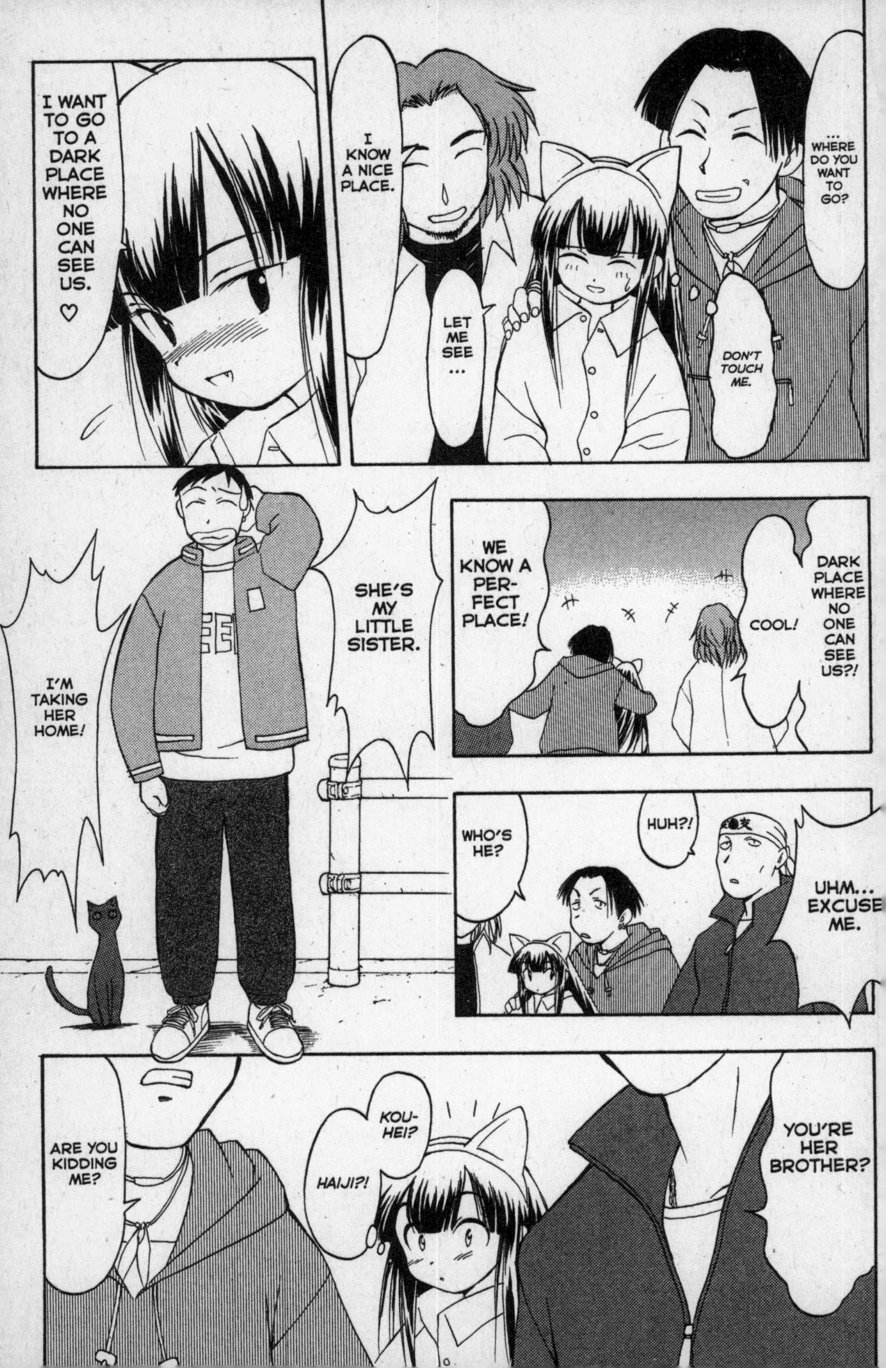

... WHERE DO YOU WANT TO GO?
DON'T TOUCH ME.
I KNOW A NICE PLACE.
LET ME SEE ...
I WANT TO GO TO A DARK PLACE WHERE NO ONE CAN SEE US. ♡
DARK PLACE WHERE NO ONE CAN SEE US?!
COOL!
WE KNOW A PER-FECT PLACE!
UHM... EXCUSE ME.
HUH?!
WHO'S HE?
SHE'S MY LITTLE SISTER.
I'M TAKING HER HOME!
YOU'RE HER BROTHER?
KOU-HEI?
HAIJI?!
ARE YOU KIDDING ME?

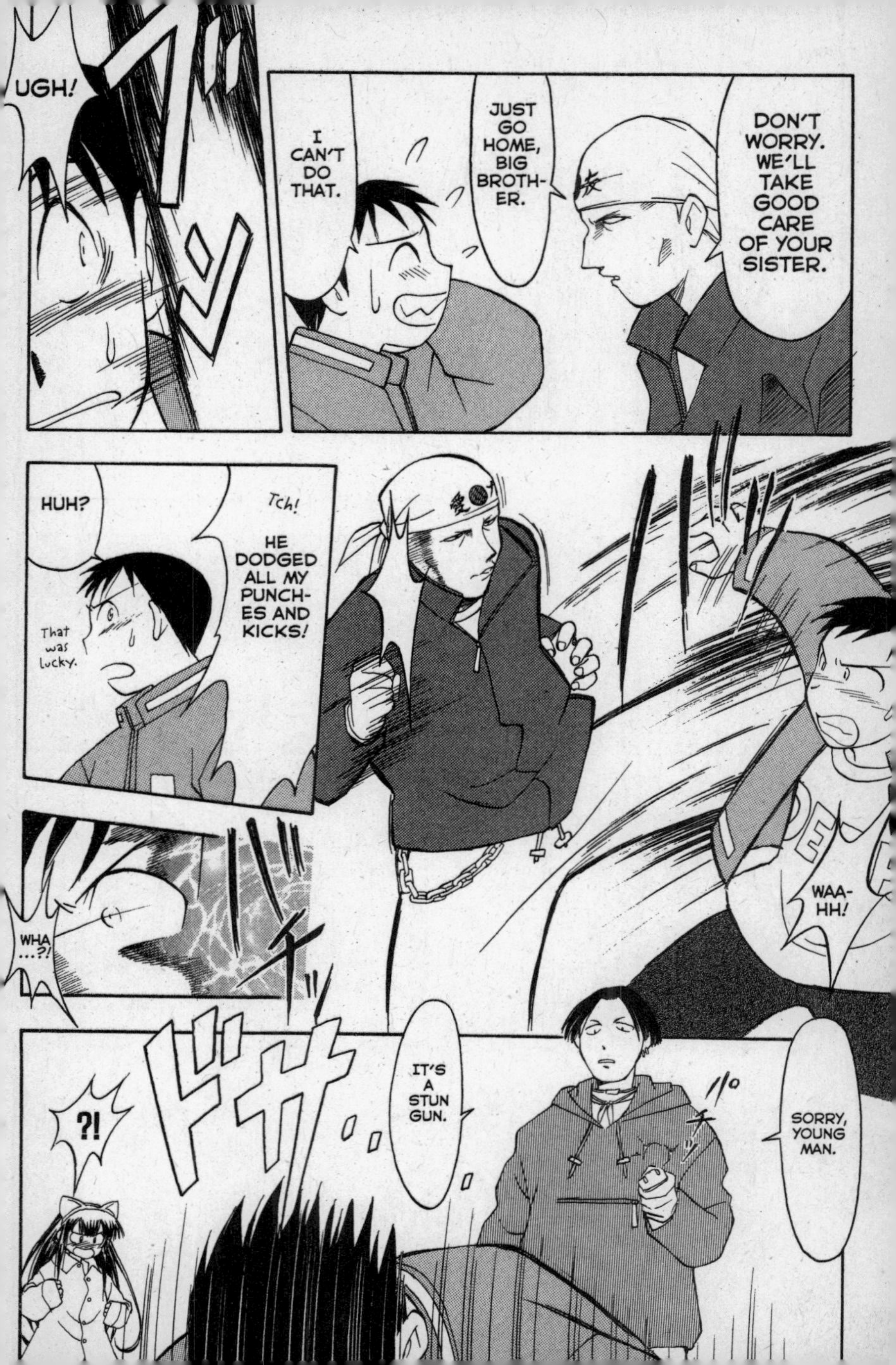
DON'T WORRY. WE'LL TAKE GOOD CARE OF YOUR SISTER.
JUST GO HOME, BIG BROTHER.
I CAN'T DO THAT.
UGH!
WAA-HH!
Tch!
HE DODGED ALL MY PUNCH-ES AND KICKS!
HUH?
That was lucky.
WHA ...?!
SORRY, YOUNG MAN.
IT'S A STUN GUN.
?!

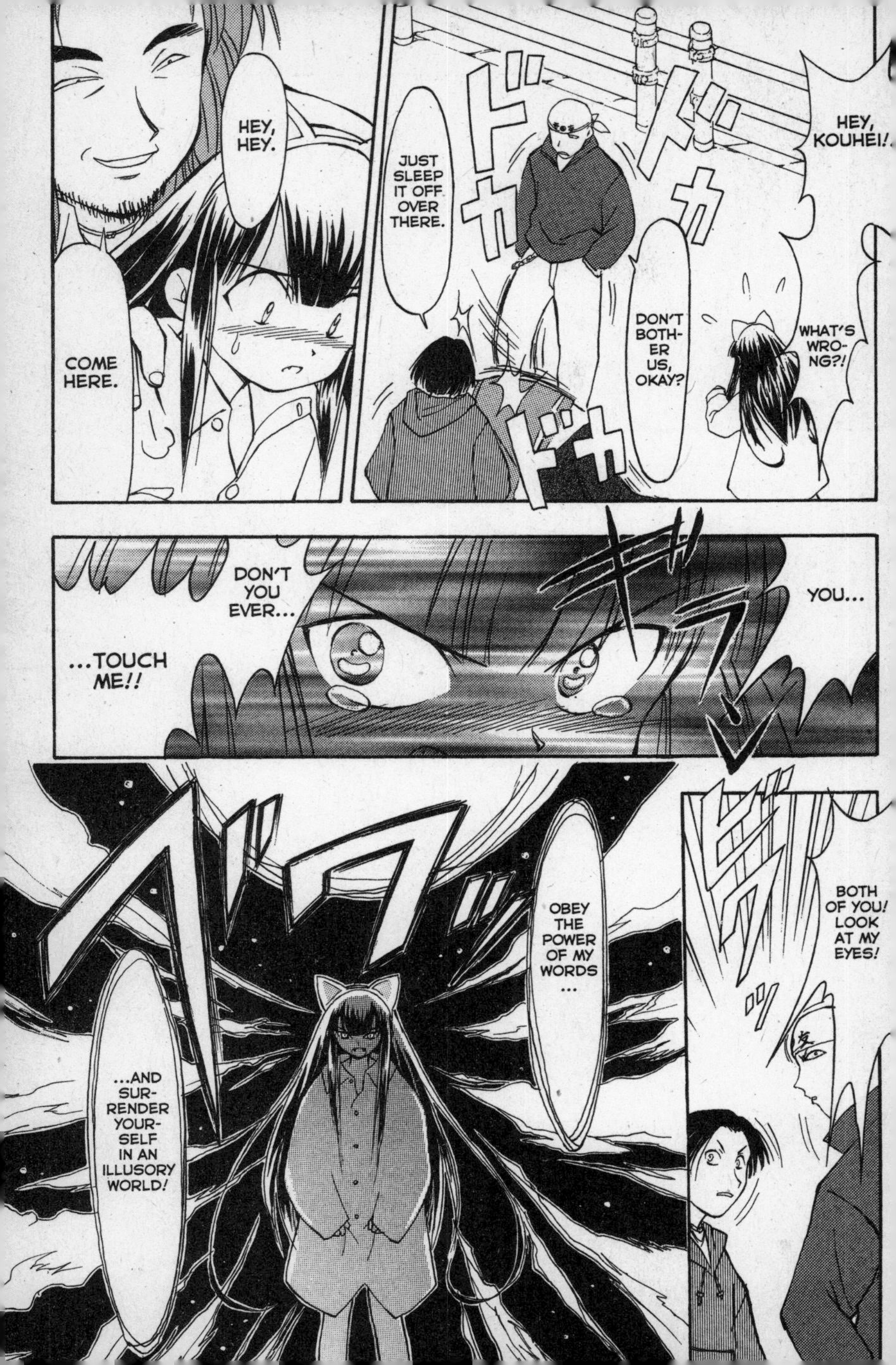
HEY, KOUHEI!.
WHAT'S WRONG?!
DON'T BOTHER US, OKAY?
JUST SLEEP IT OFF OVER THERE.
HEY, HEY.
COME HERE.
YOU...
DON'T YOU EVER...
...TOUCH ME!!
BOTH OF YOU! LOOK AT MY EYES!
OBEY THE POWER OF MY WORDS...
...AND SURRENDER YOURSELF IN AN ILLUSORY WORLD!

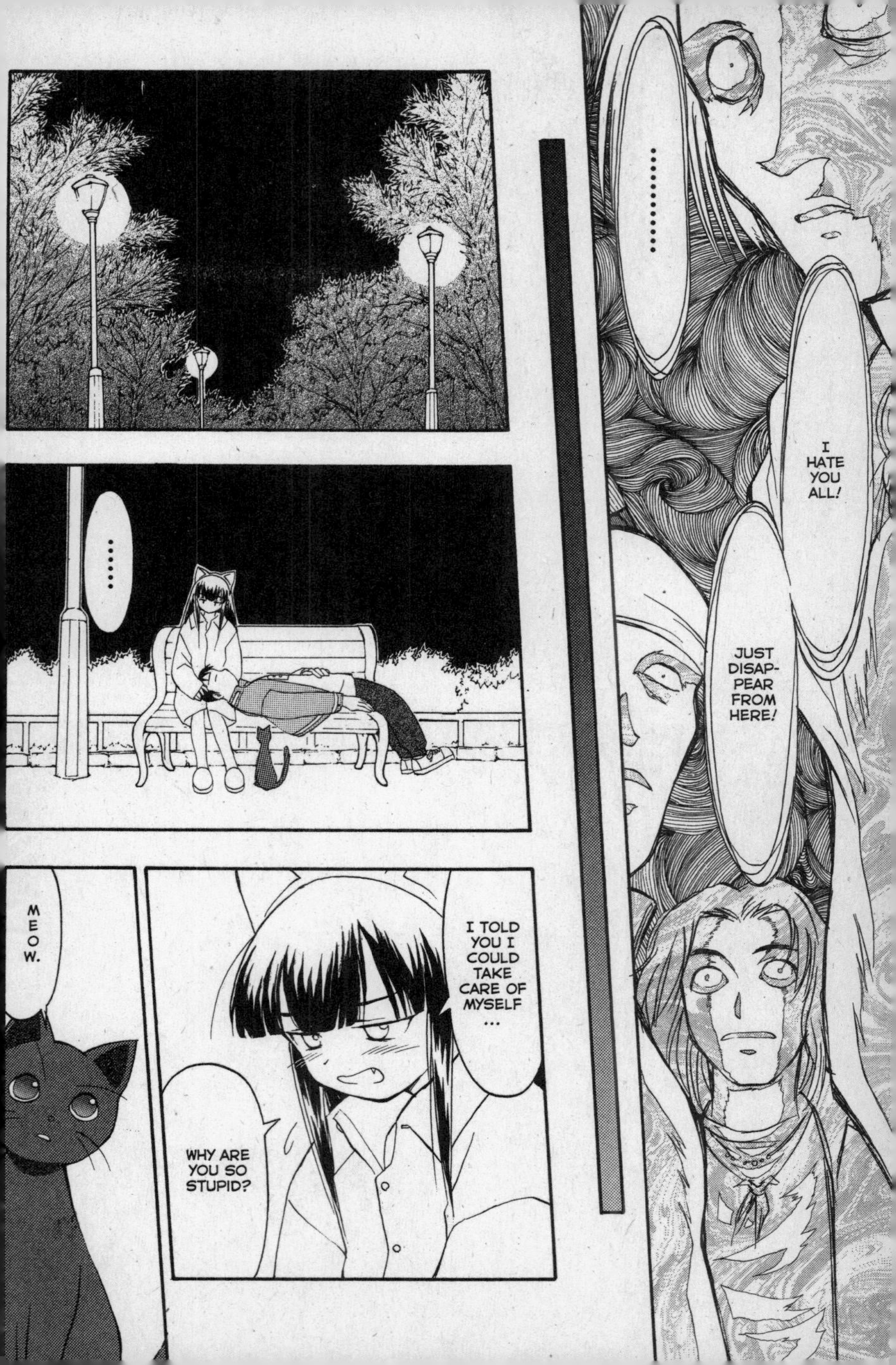
......
I HATE YOU ALL!
JUST DISAP-PEAR FROM HERE!
......
I TOLD YOU I COULD TAKE CARE OF MYSELF ...
WHY ARE YOU SO STUPID?
MEOW.

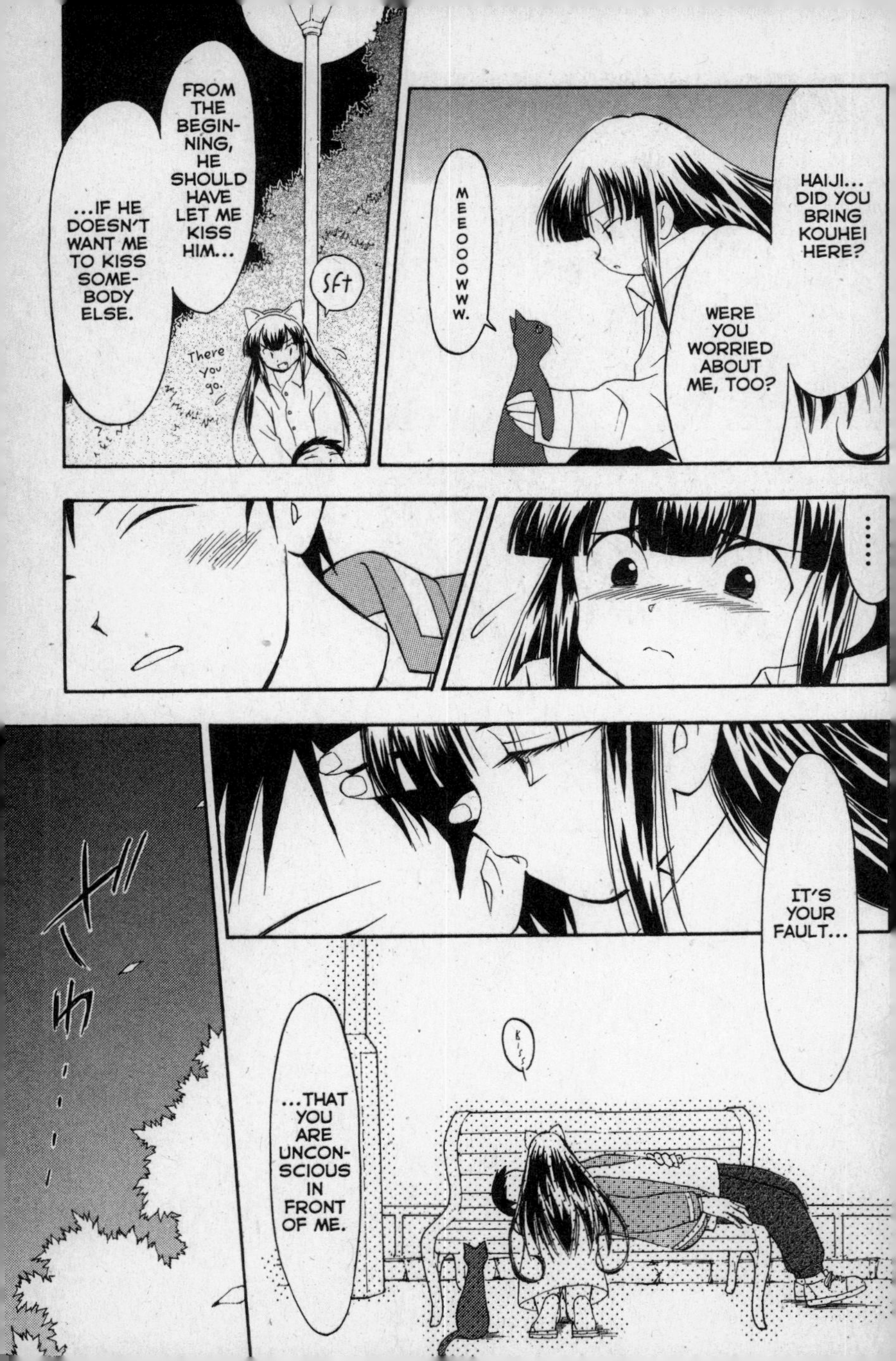
HAIJI... DID YOU BRING KOUHEI HERE?
WERE YOU WORRIED ABOUT ME, TOO?
MEEOOOOWWW.
FROM THE BEGINNING, HE SHOULD HAVE LET ME KISS HIM...
...IF HE DOESN'T WANT ME TO KISS SOMEBODY ELSE.
SFT
There you go.
......
IT'S YOUR FAULT...
...THAT YOU ARE UNCONSCIOUS IN FRONT OF ME.
KISS

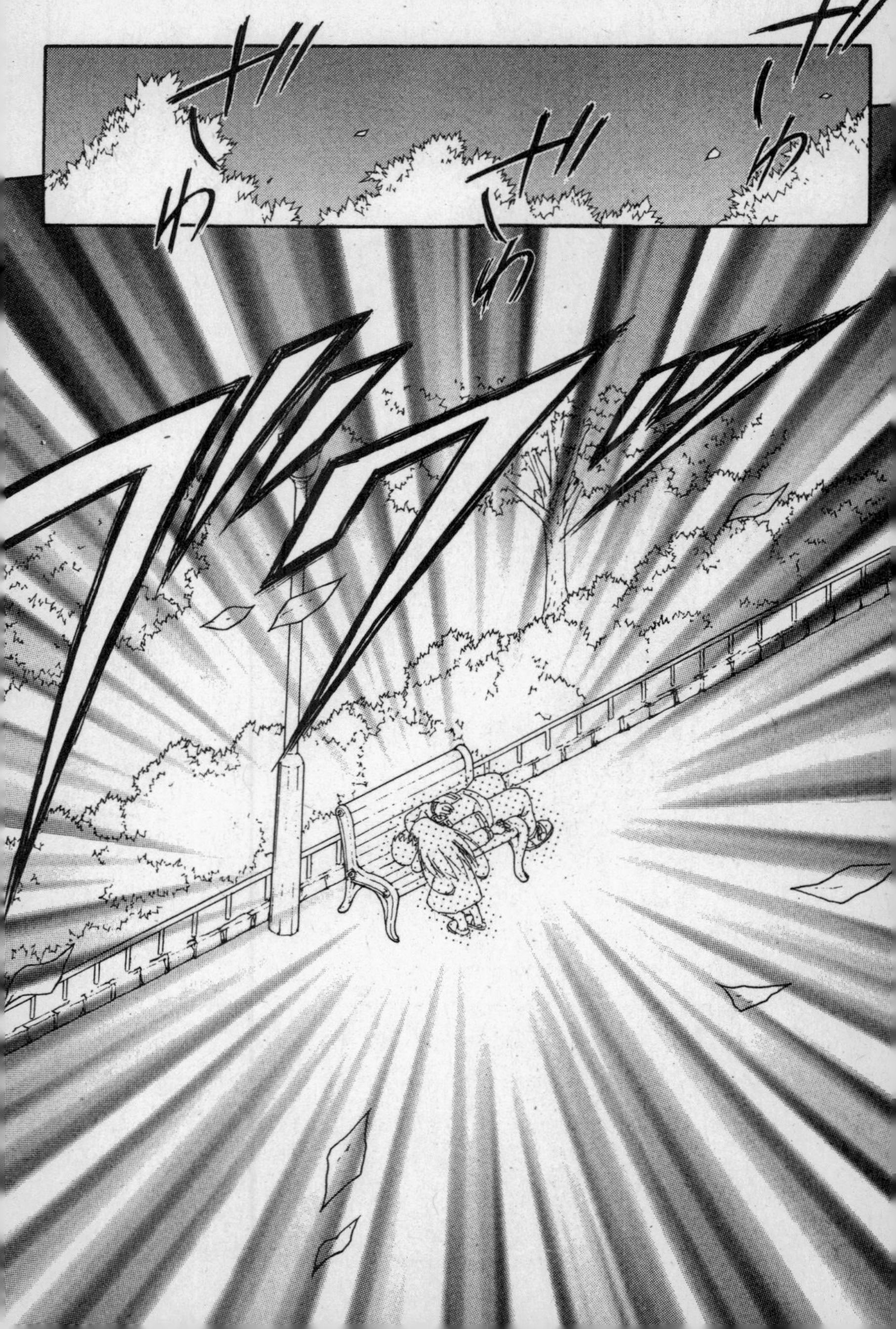
ざわ
ざわ
ざわ

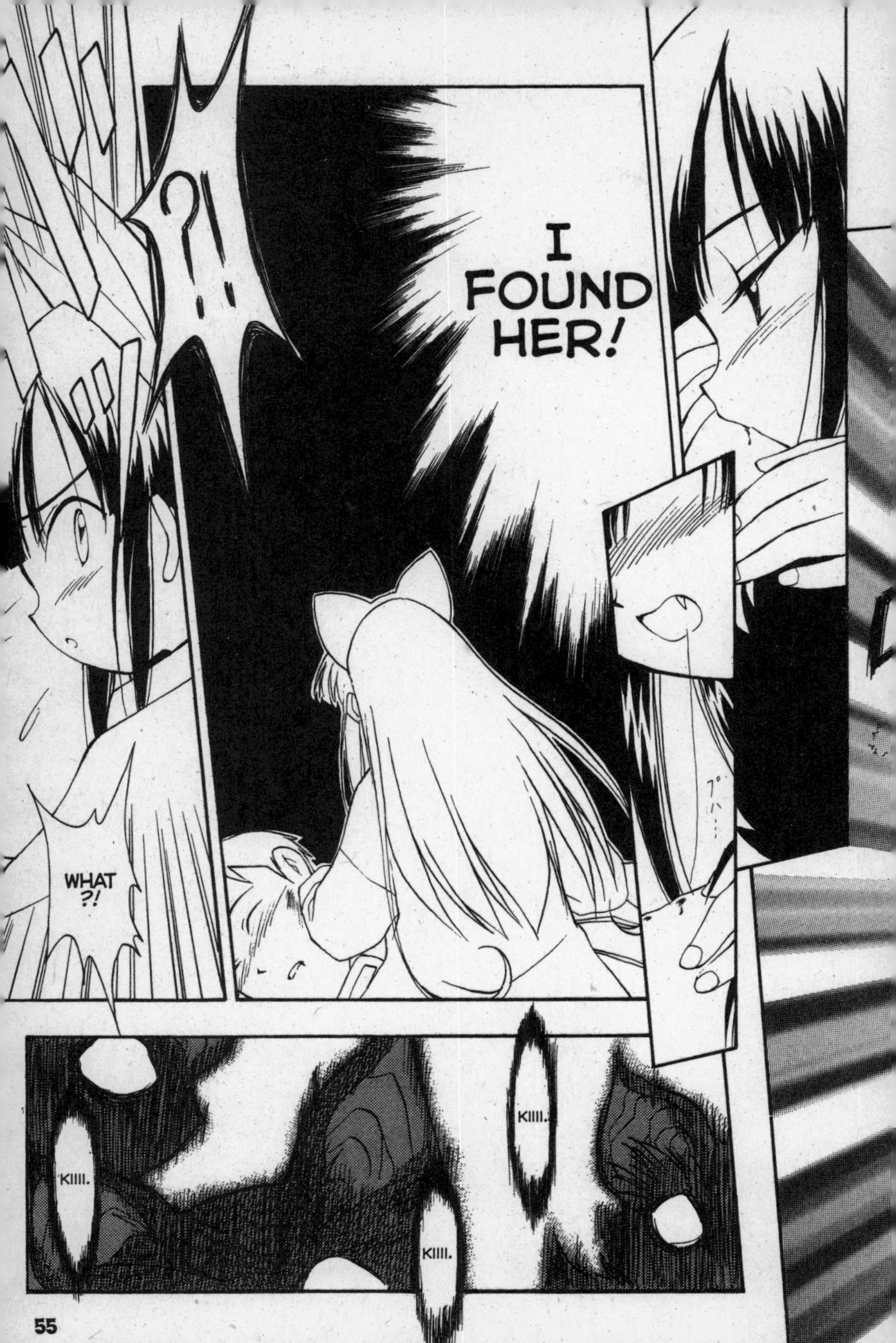
プハ…
I FOUND HER!
?!
WHAT ?!
KIIII.
KIIII.
KIIII.

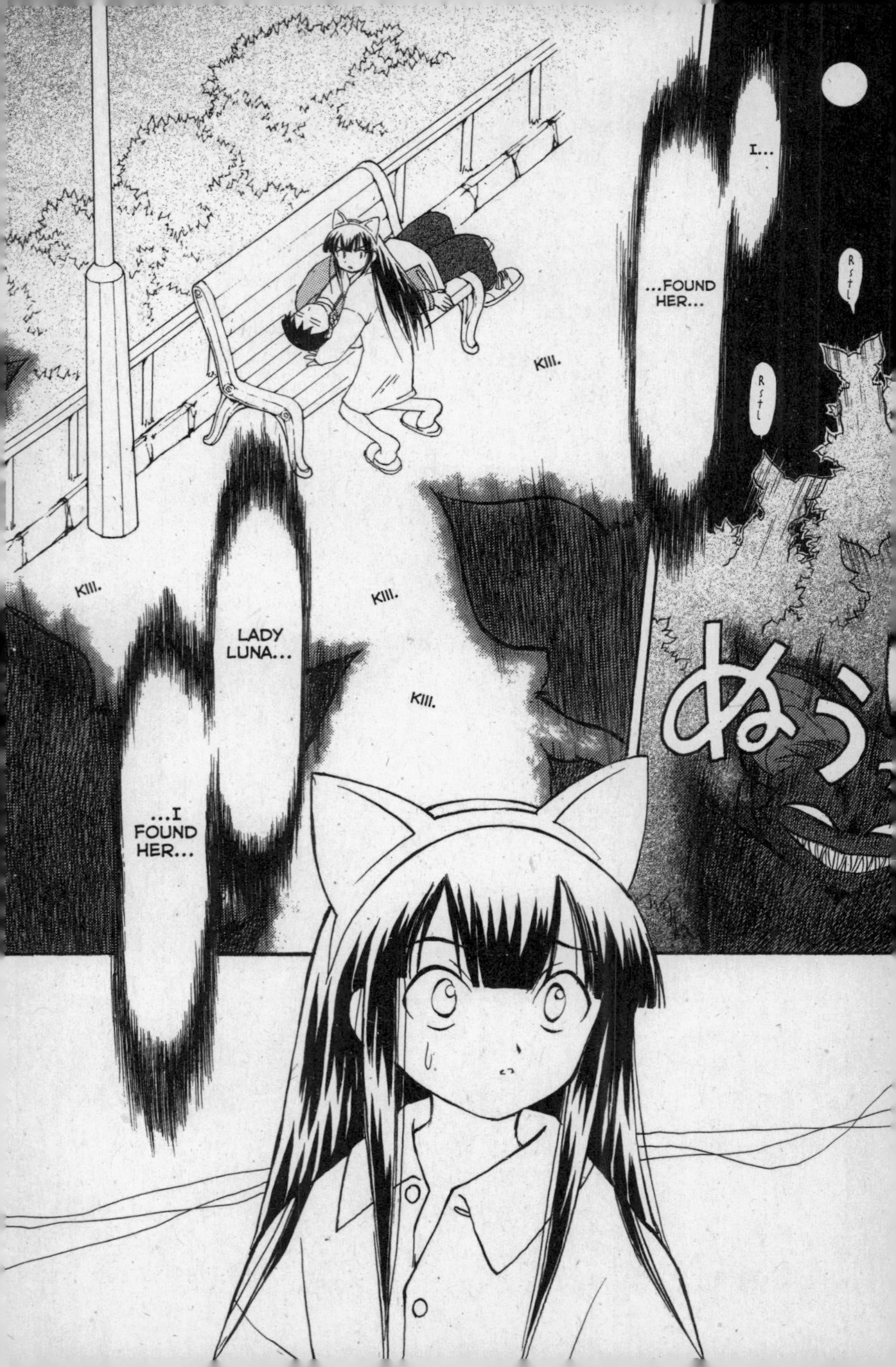
I...
...FOUND HER...
Rstl
Rstl
KIII.
ぬう
KIII.
KIII.
KIII.
LADY LUNA...
...I FOUND HER...

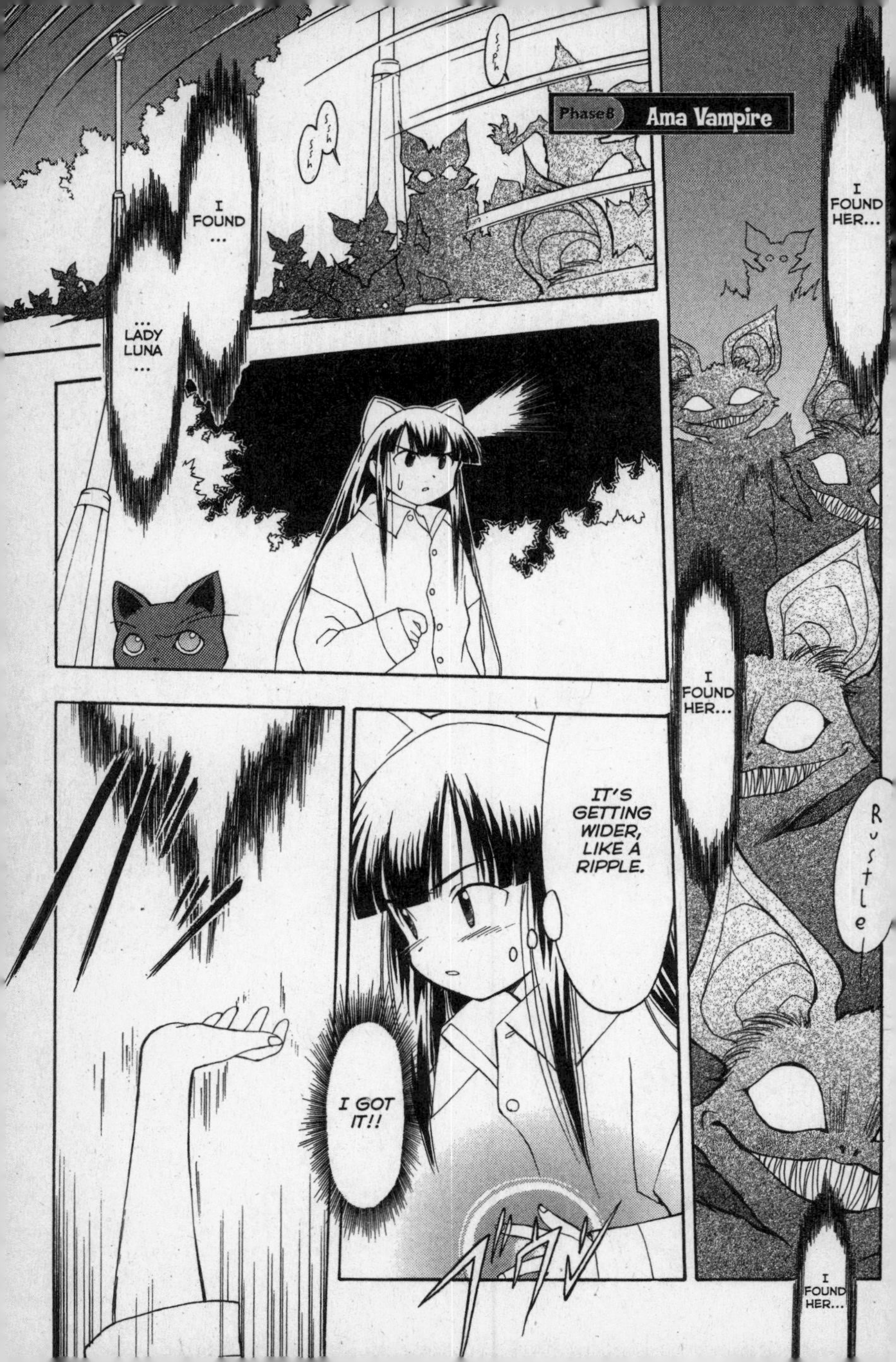
I FOUND HER...
I FOUND HER...
Rustle
I FOUND HER...
Phase 8 Ama Vampire
ssh
ssh
I FOUND ...
... LADY LUNA ...
IT'S GETTING WIDER, LIKE A RIPPLE.
I GOT IT!!

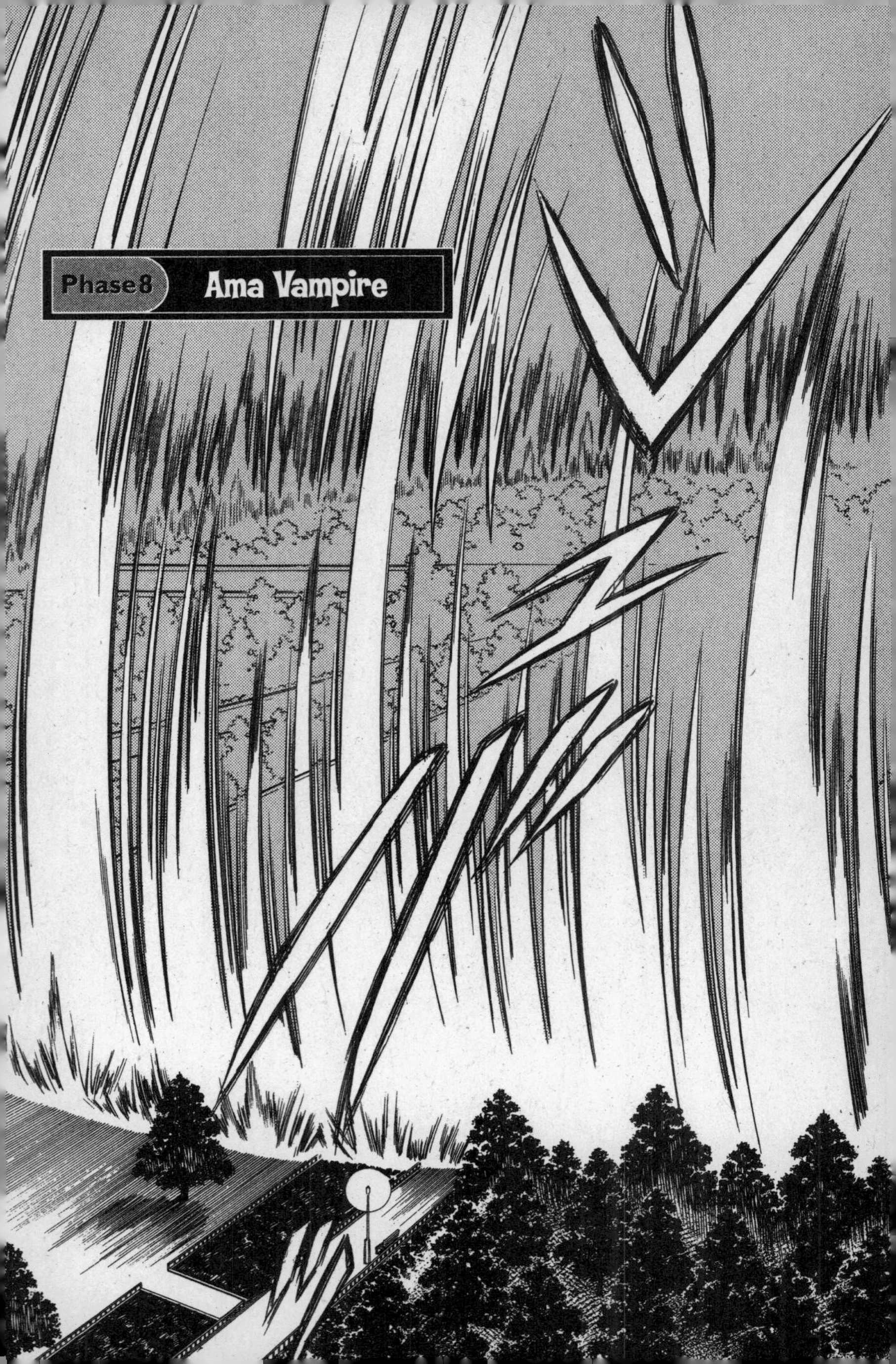
Phase 8
Ama Vampire

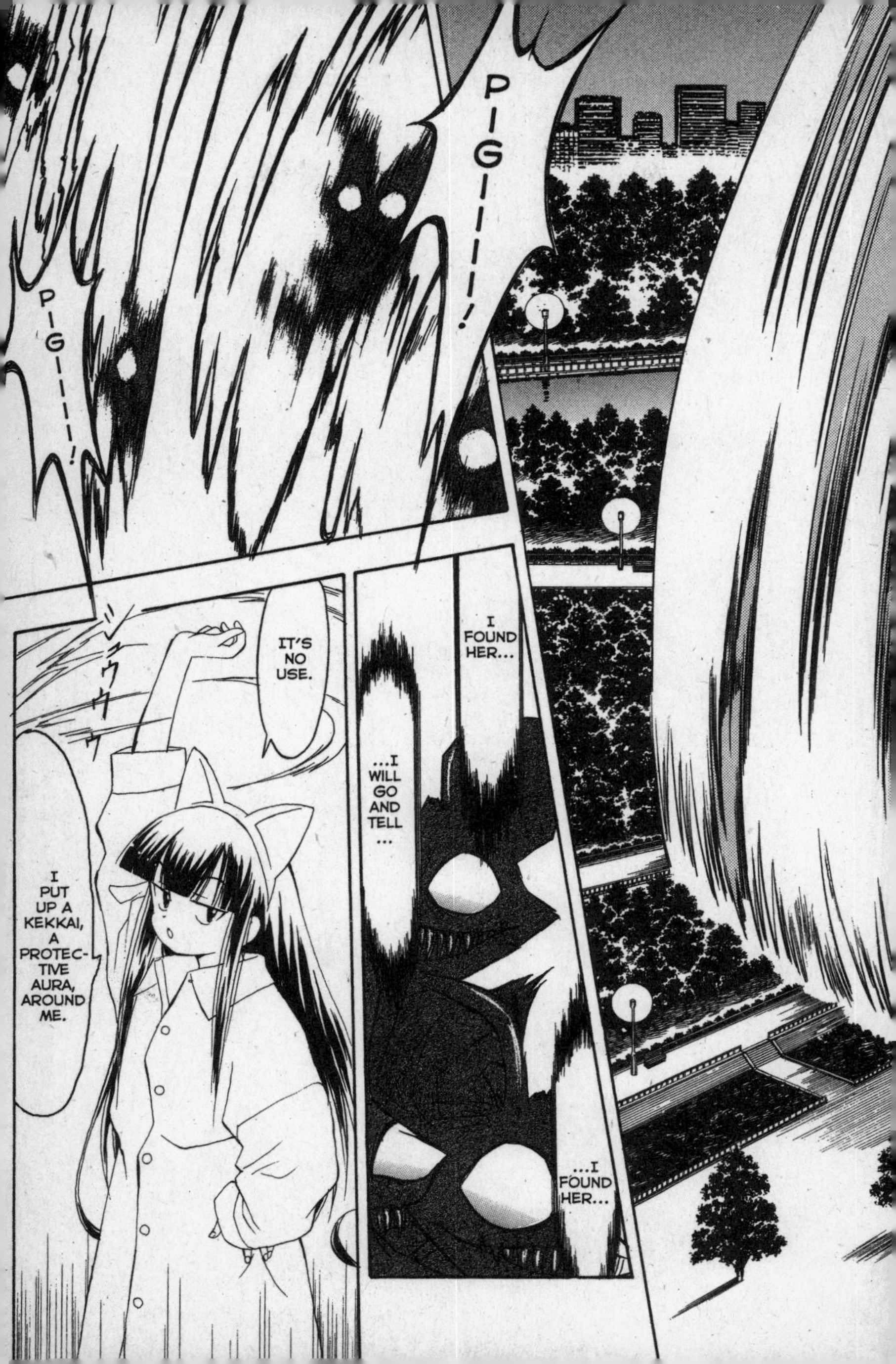
PIGI---!
PIGI---!
I FOUND HER...
...I WILL GO AND TELL...
...I FOUND HER...
IT'S NO USE.
I PUT UP A KEKKAI, A PROTECTIVE AURA, AROUND ME.

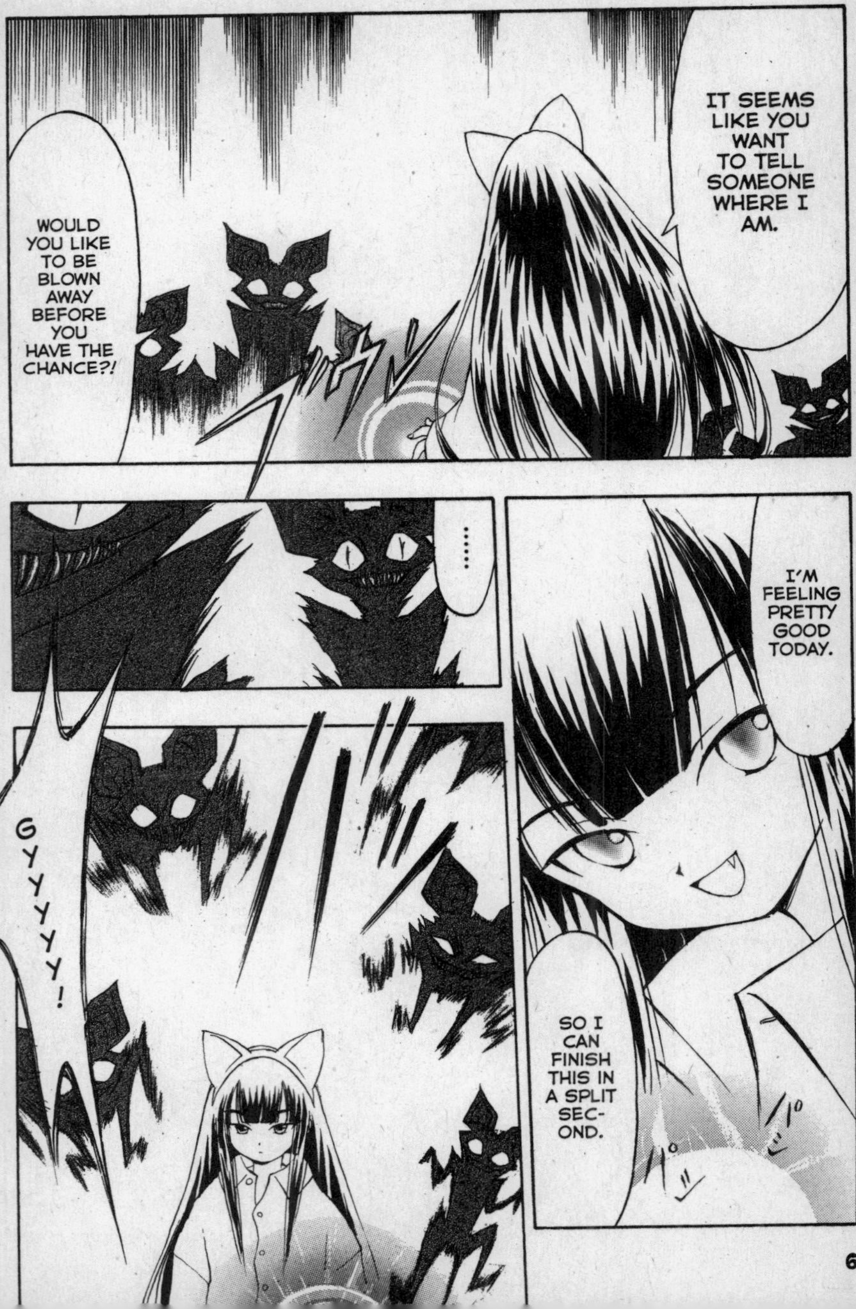
IT SEEMS LIKE YOU WANT TO TELL SOMEONE WHERE I AM.
WOULD YOU LIKE TO BE BLOWN AWAY BEFORE YOU HAVE THE CHANCE?!
I'M FEELING PRETTY GOOD TODAY.
SO I CAN FINISH THIS IN A SPLIT SEC-OND.
......
GYYYYY!

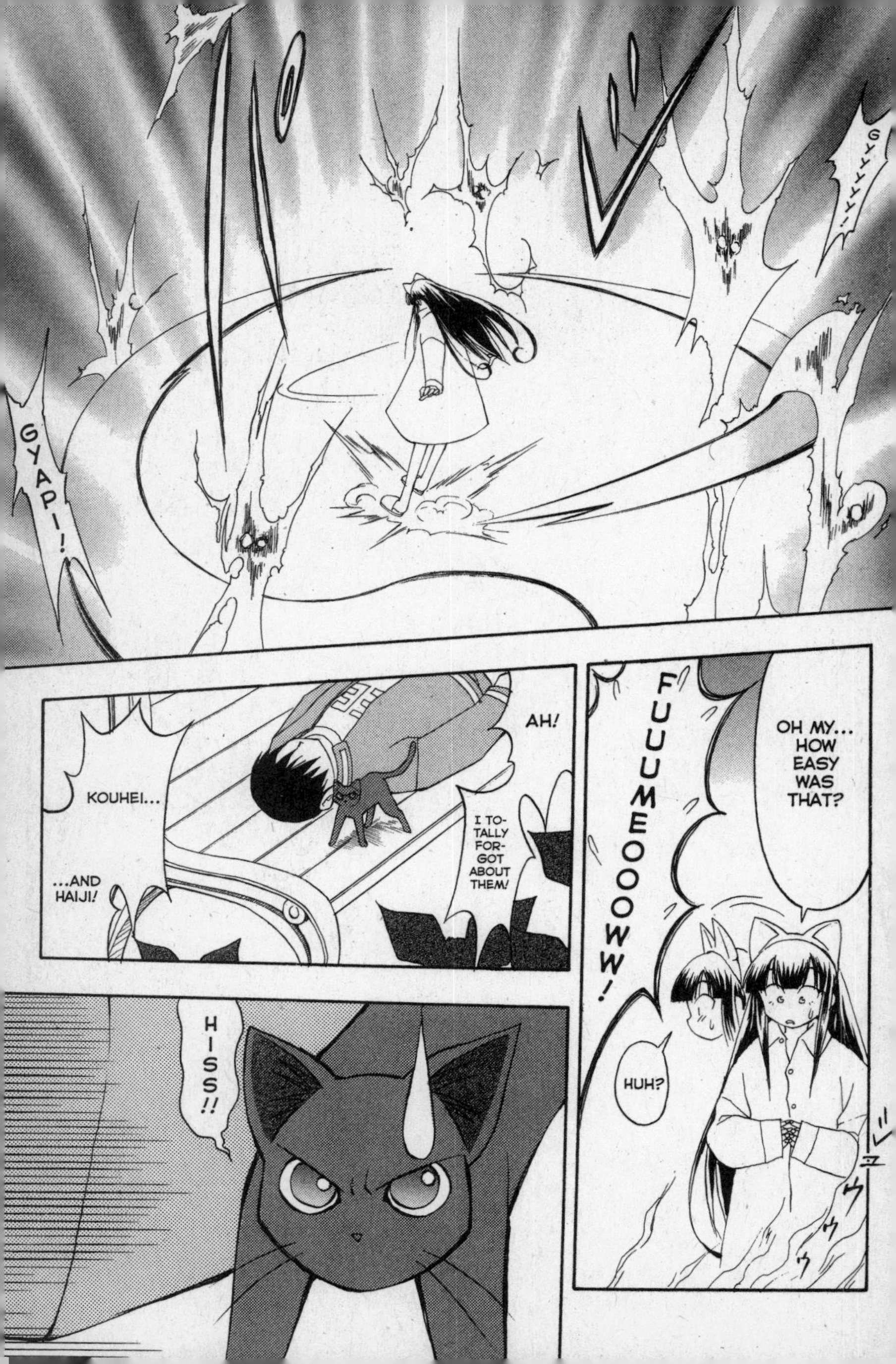
GYYYYY-!
GYAPI!
OH MY... HOW EASY WAS THAT?
FUUUMEOOOWW!
HUH?
AH!
I TOTALLY FORGOT ABOUT THEM!
KOUHEI...
...AND HAIJI!
HISS!!

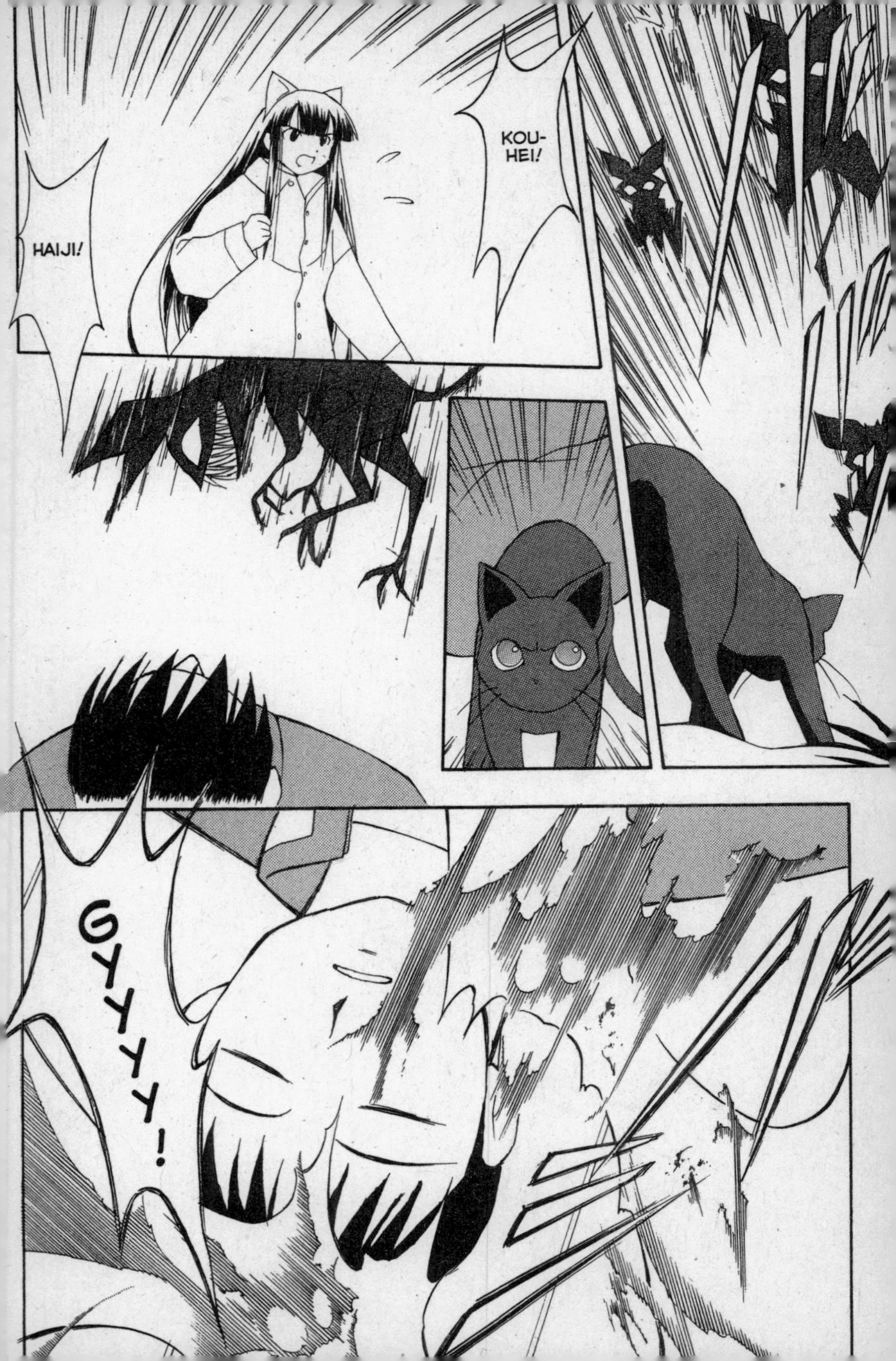
KOU-HEI!
HAIJI!
GYYYY!

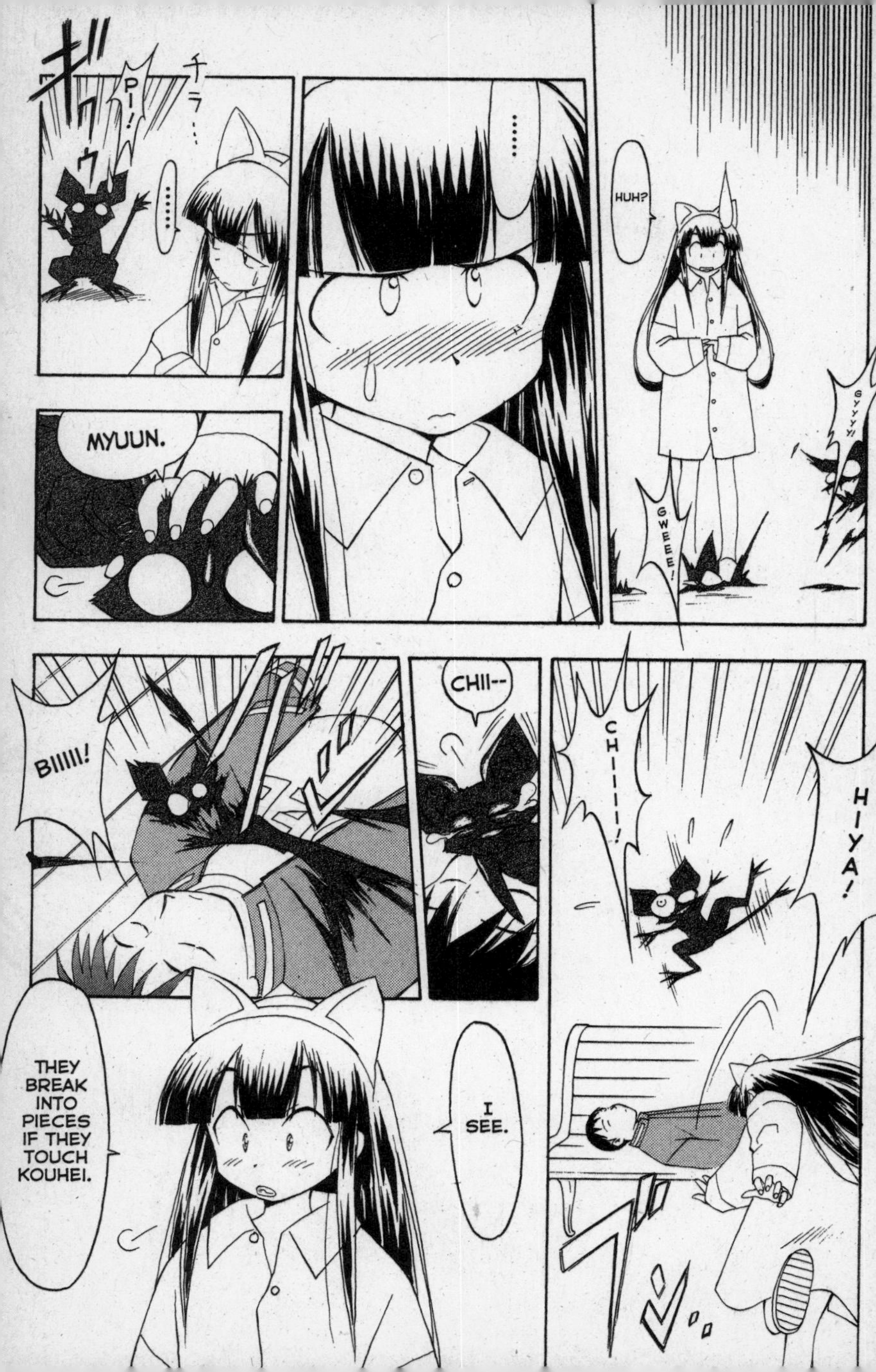
HUH?
GYYYY!
GWEEE!
......
ギュウ
PI-!
チラ...
......
MYUUN.
CHI----!
HIYA!
CHII--
BIIIII!
I SEE.
THEY BREAK INTO PIECES IF THEY TOUCH KOUHEI.

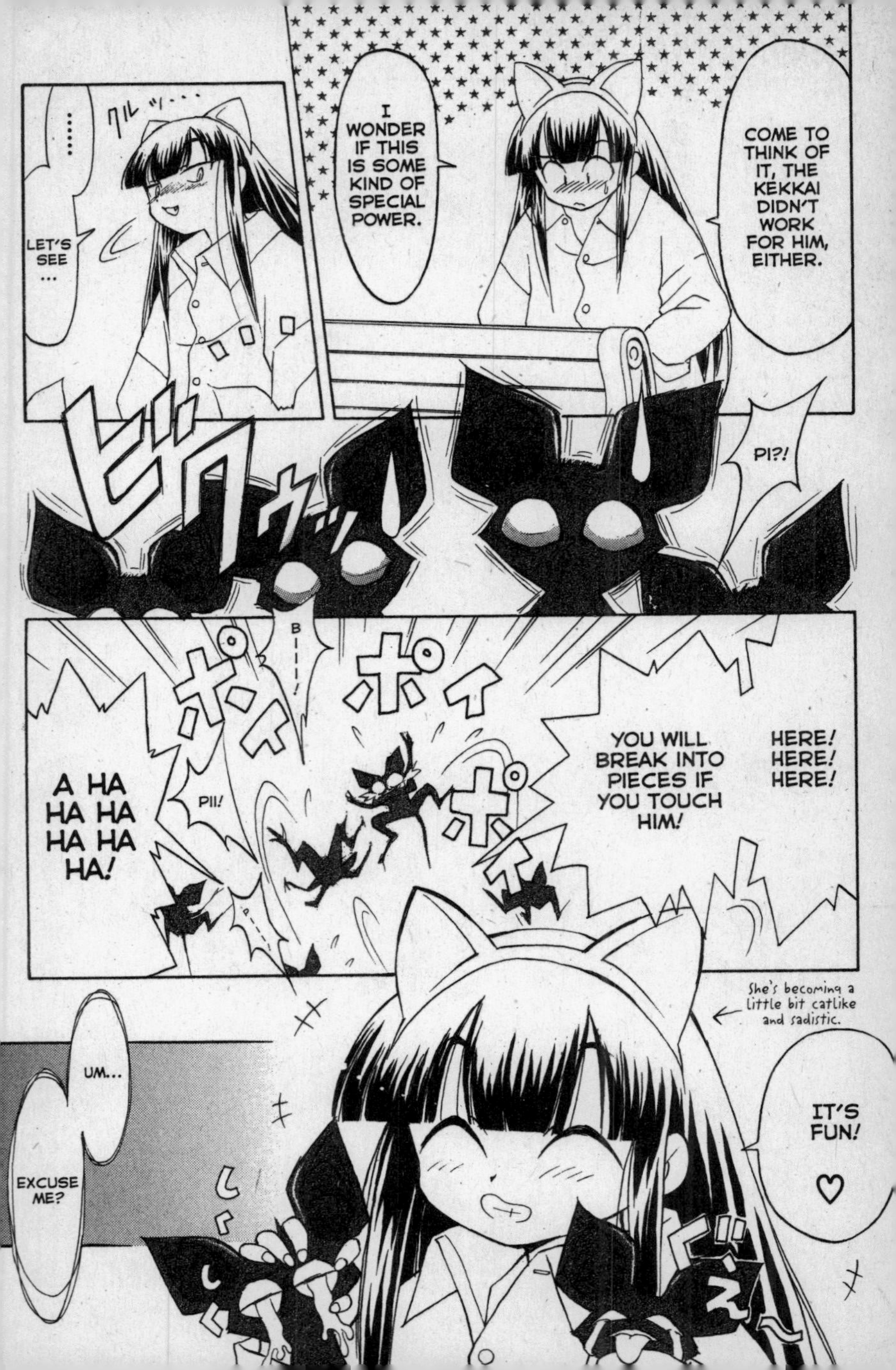

COME TO THINK OF IT, THE KEKKAI DIDN'T WORK FOR HIM, EITHER.
I WONDER IF THIS IS SOME KIND OF SPECIAL POWER.
......
LET'S SEE ...
PI?!
HERE! HERE! HERE!
YOU WILL BREAK INTO PIECES IF YOU TOUCH HIM!
B-!
PII!
A HA HA HA HA HA HA!
She's becoming a little bit catlike and sadistic.
IT'S FUN! ♥
UM... EXCUSE ME?

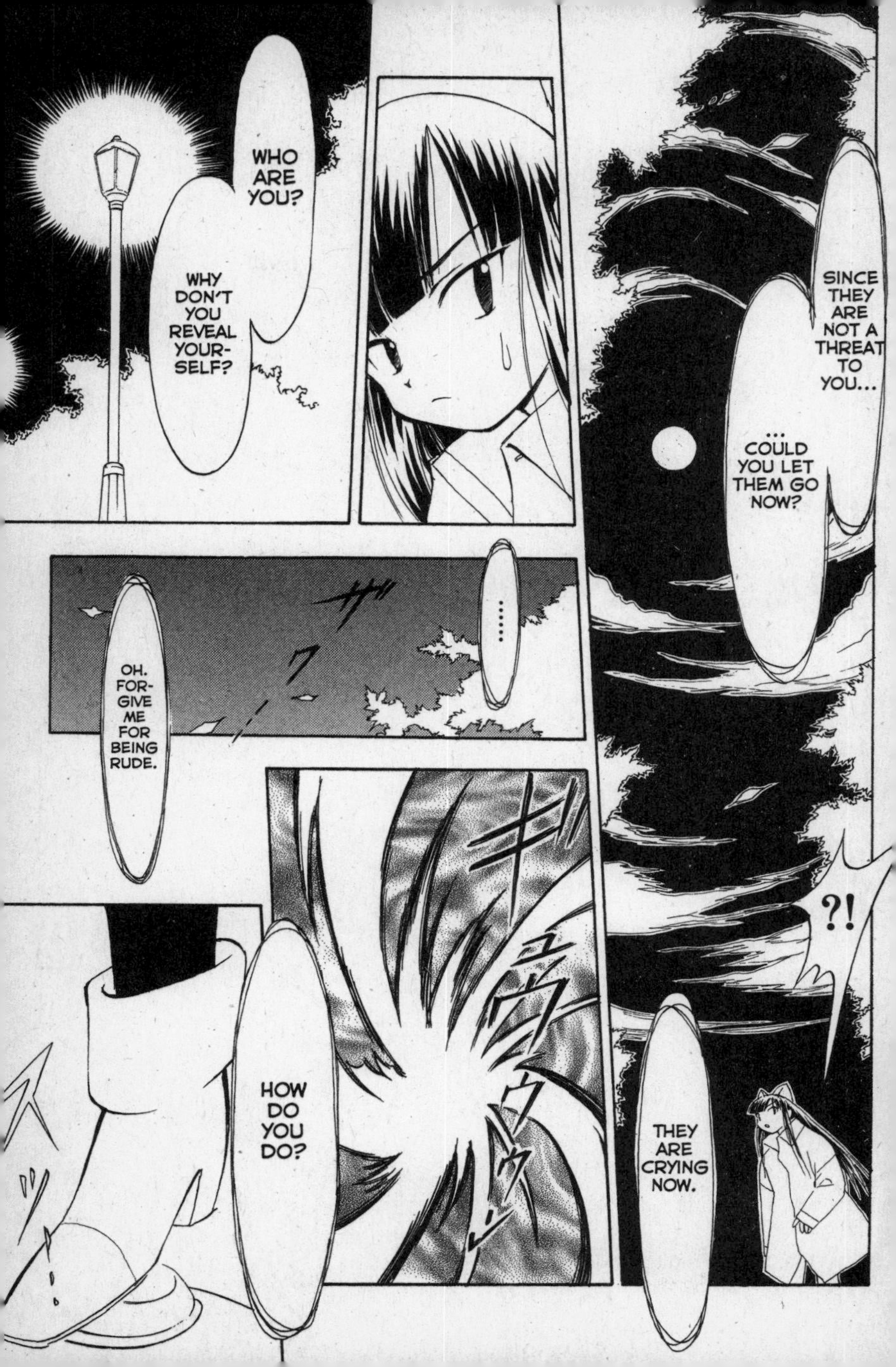
SINCE THEY ARE NOT A THREAT TO YOU...
... COULD YOU LET THEM GO NOW?
?!
THEY ARE CRYING NOW.
WHO ARE YOU?
WHY DON'T YOU REVEAL YOUR-SELF?
......
OH. FOR-GIVE ME FOR BEING RUDE.
HOW DO YOU DO?

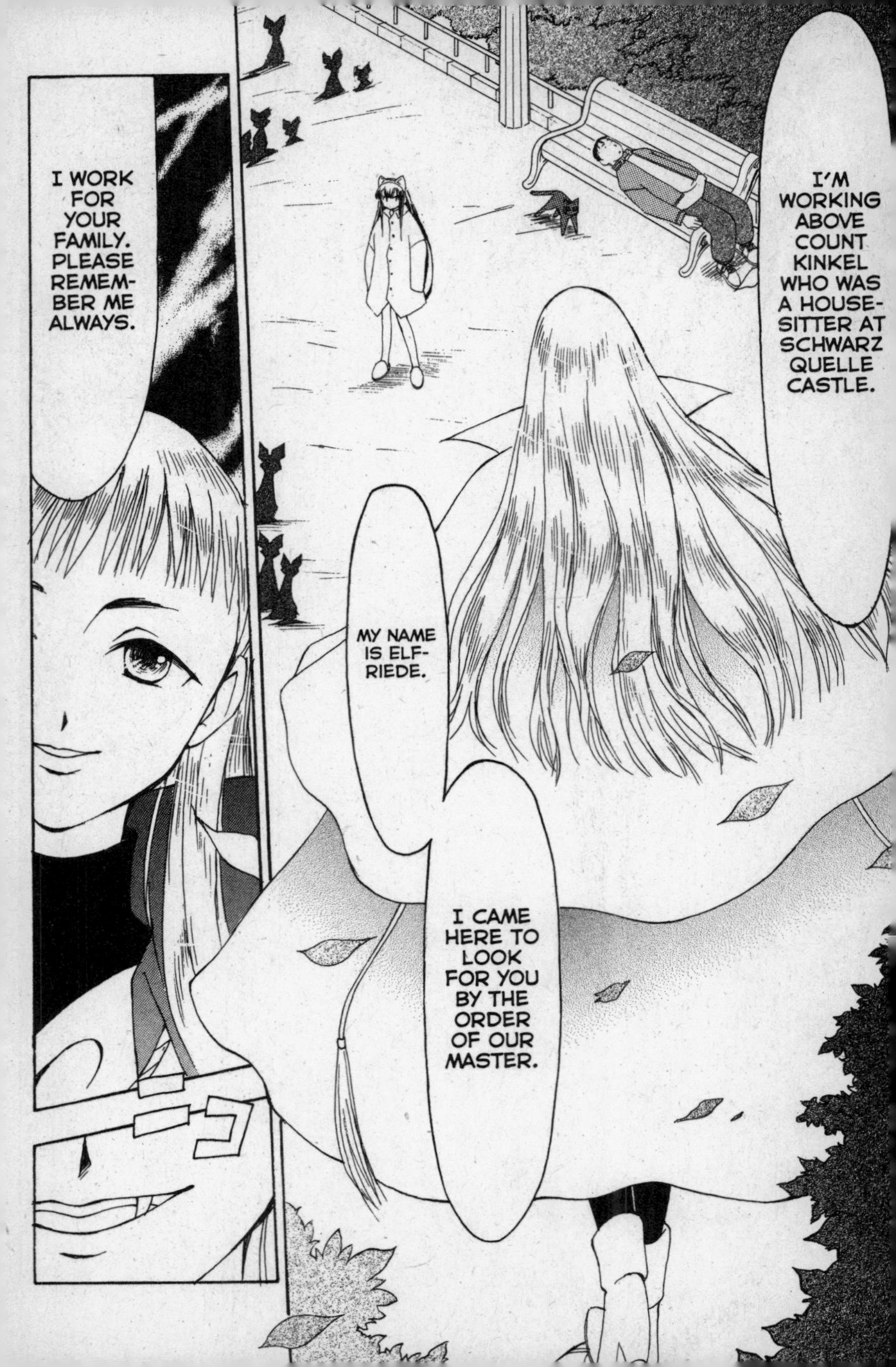
I'M WORKING ABOVE COUNT KINKEL WHO WAS A HOUSE-SITTER AT SCHWARZ QUELLE CASTLE.
MY NAME IS ELF-RIEDE.
I CAME HERE TO LOOK FOR YOU BY THE ORDER OF OUR MASTER.
I WORK FOR YOUR FAMILY. PLEASE REMEM-BER ME ALWAYS.

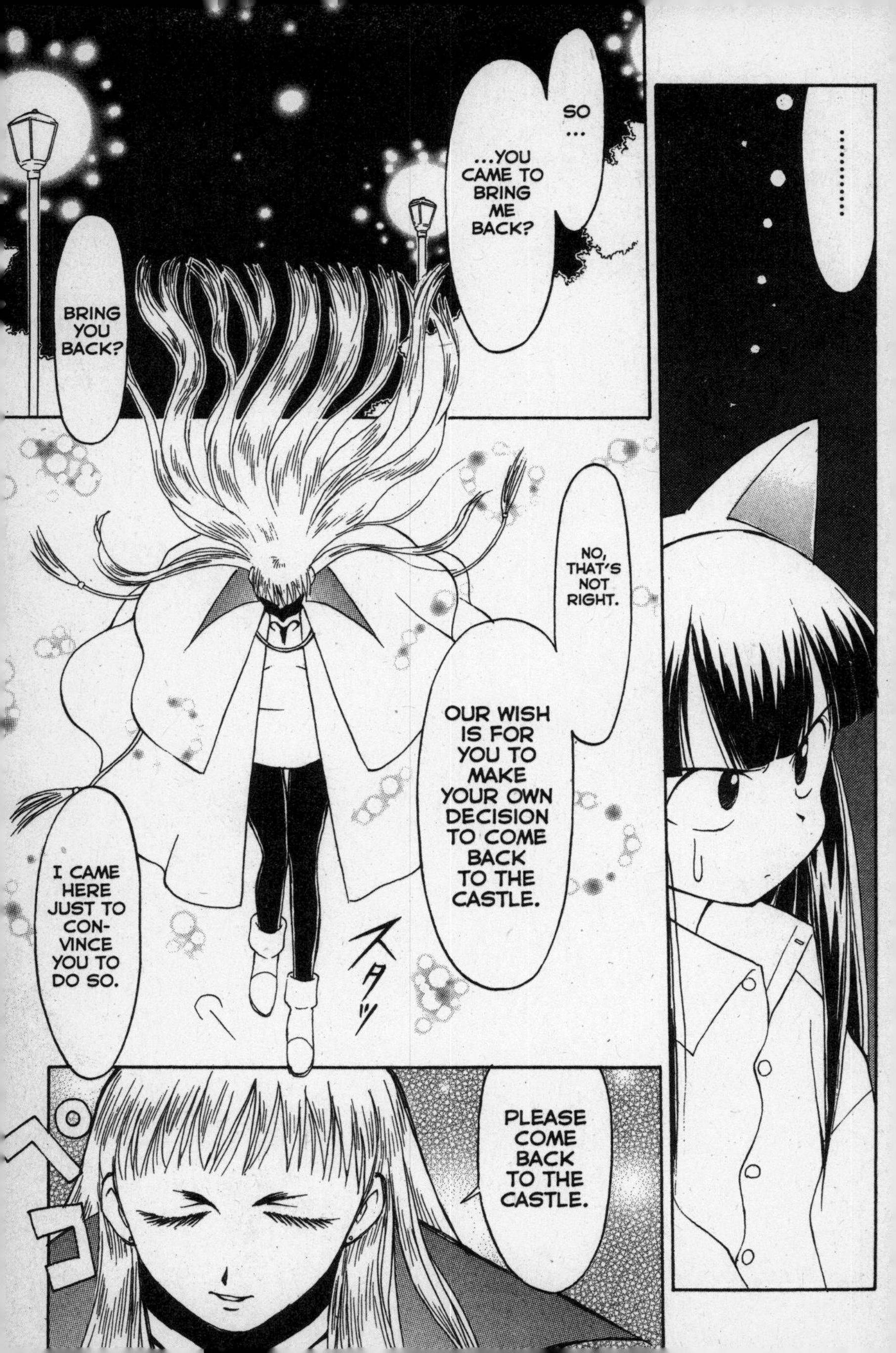

......
SO ...
...YOU CAME TO BRING ME BACK?
BRING YOU BACK?
NO, THAT'S NOT RIGHT.
OUR WISH IS FOR YOU TO MAKE YOUR OWN DECISION TO COME BACK TO THE CASTLE.
I CAME HERE JUST TO CON-VINCE YOU TO DO SO.
スタッ
PLEASE COME BACK TO THE CASTLE.
ペコ

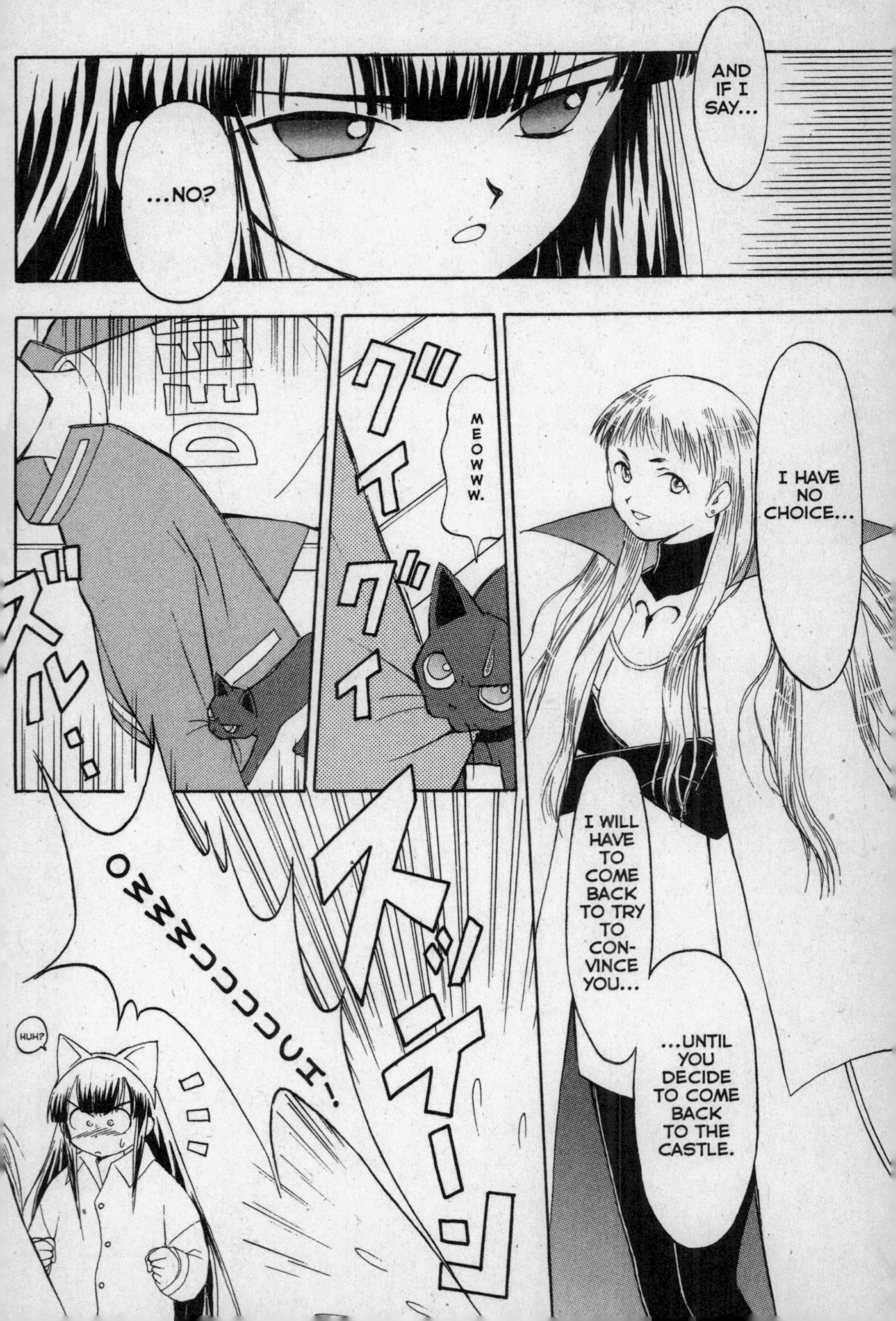
AND IF I SAY...
...NO?
I HAVE NO CHOICE...
I WILL HAVE TO COME BACK TO TRY TO CONVINCE YOU...
...UNTIL YOU DECIDE TO COME BACK TO THE CASTLE.
MEOWWW.
OWWWUUUUUUCH!!
HUH?

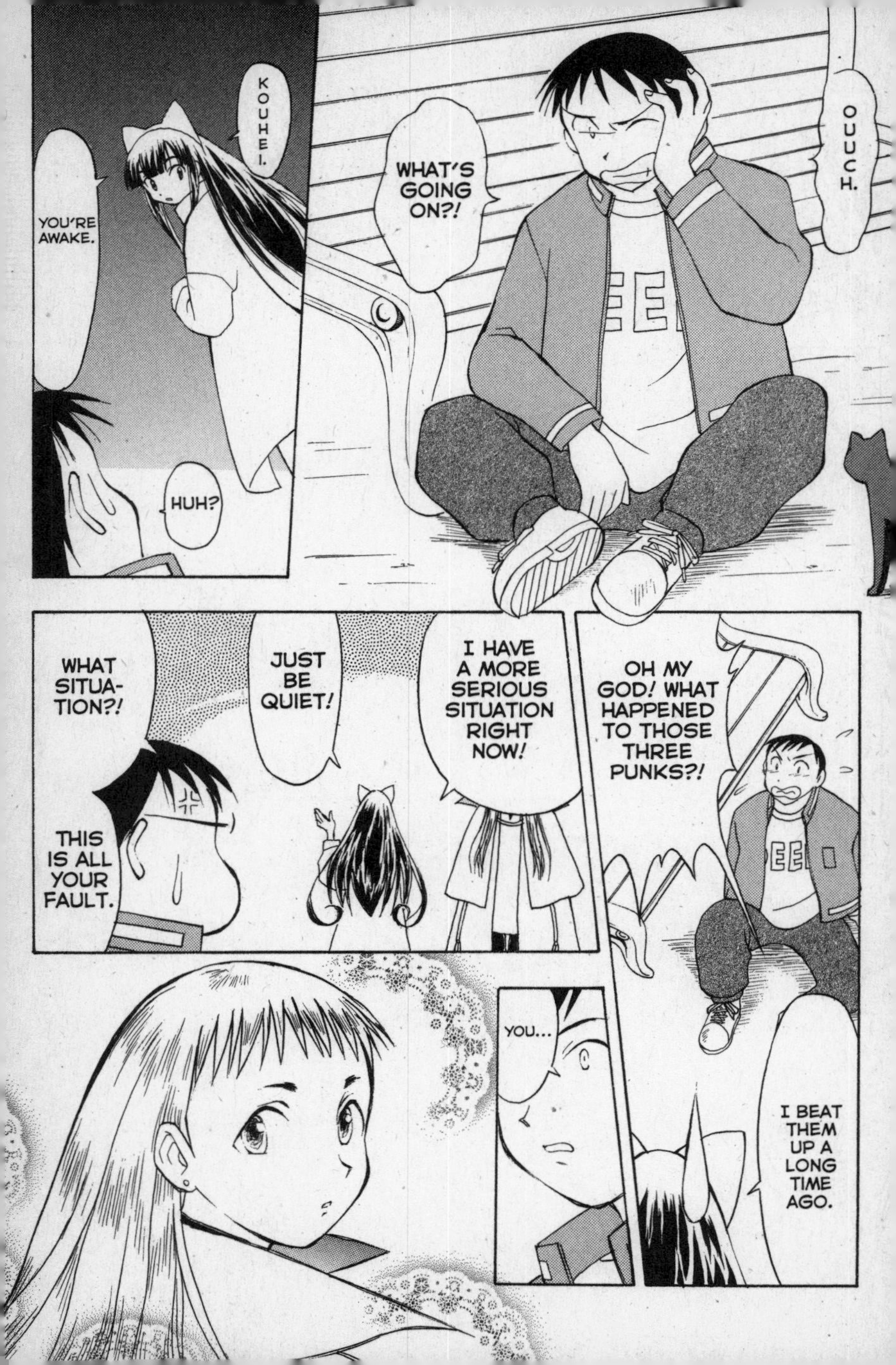

OUUCH.
WHAT'S GOING ON?!
KOUHEI.
YOU'RE AWAKE.
HUH?
OH MY GOD! WHAT HAPPENED TO THOSE THREE PUNKS?!
I BEAT THEM UP A LONG TIME AGO.
I HAVE A MORE SERIOUS SITUATION RIGHT NOW!
JUST BE QUIET!
WHAT SITUATION?!
THIS IS ALL YOUR FAULT.
YOU...

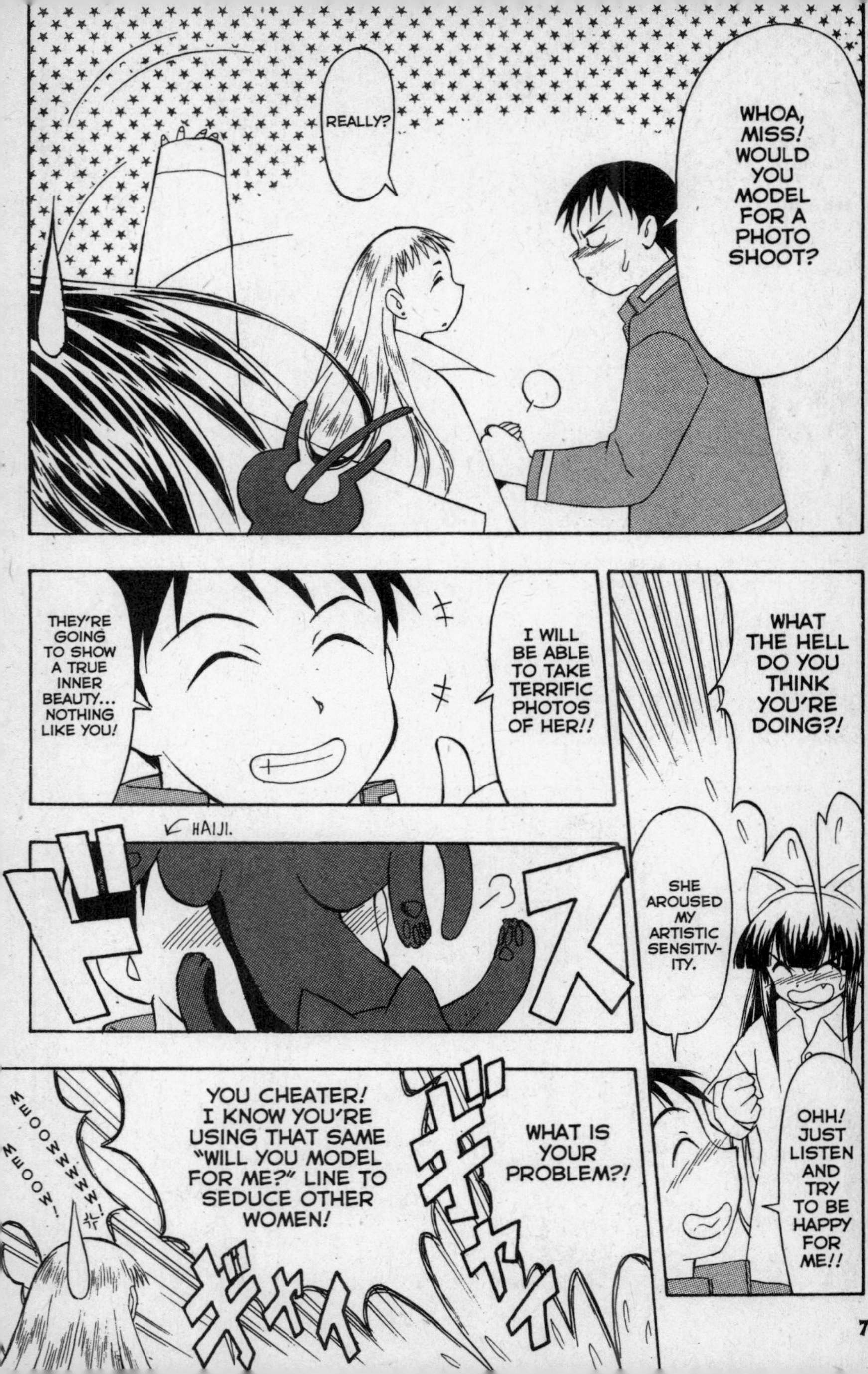
WHOA, MISS! WOULD YOU MODEL FOR A PHOTO SHOOT?
REALLY?
WHAT THE HELL DO YOU THINK YOU'RE DOING?!
SHE AROUSED MY ARTISTIC SENSITIVITY.
OHH! JUST LISTEN AND TRY TO BE HAPPY FOR ME!!
I WILL BE ABLE TO TAKE TERRIFIC PHOTOS OF HER!!
THEY'RE GOING TO SHOW A TRUE INNER BEAUTY... NOTHING LIKE YOU!
HAIJI.
ドス
WHAT IS YOUR PROBLEM?!
ギャイ
YOU CHEATER! I KNOW YOU'RE USING THAT SAME "WILL YOU MODEL FOR ME?" LINE TO SEDUCE OTHER WOMEN!
ギャイ
MEOOWWWW! MEOOW!

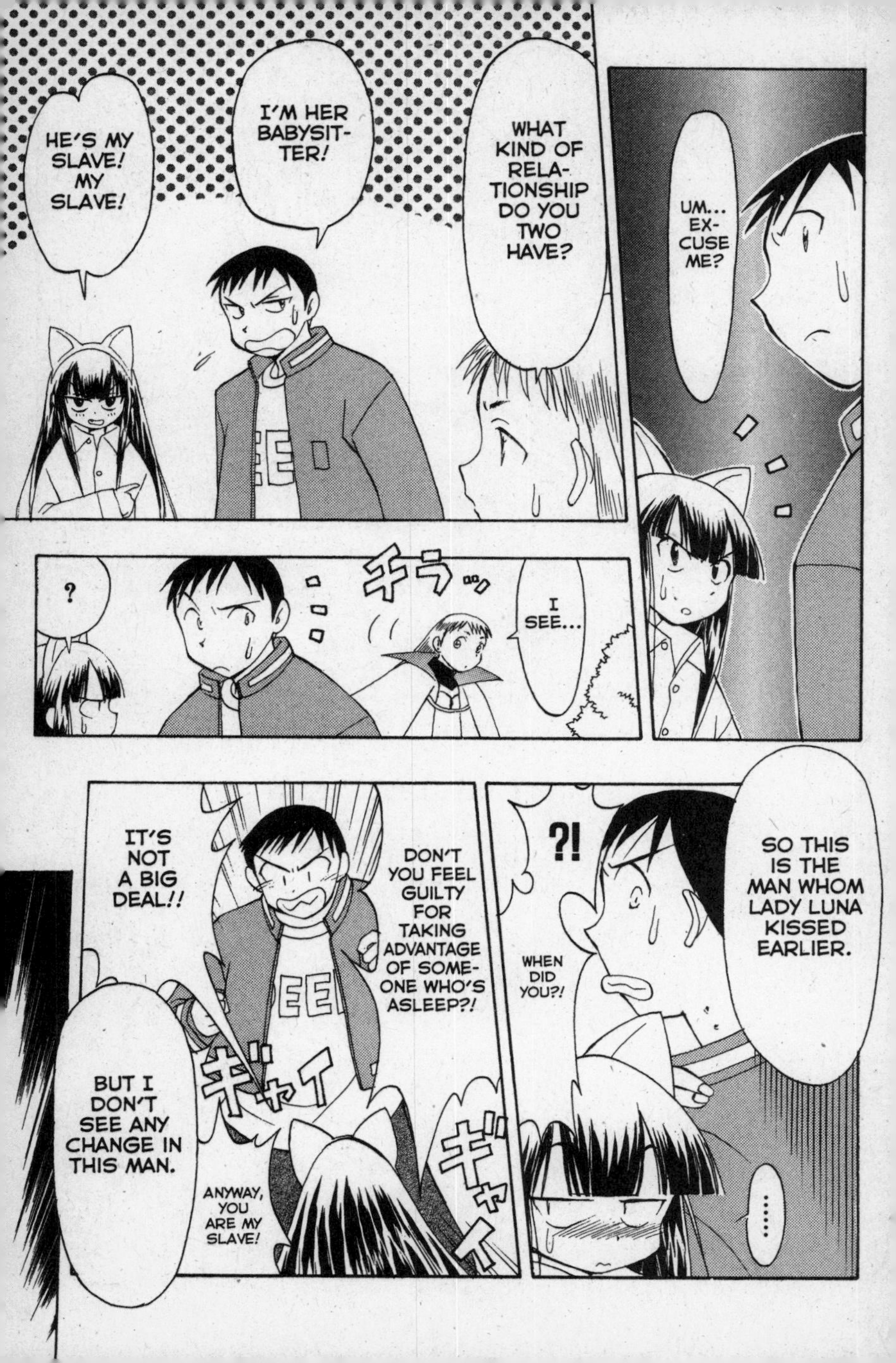
UM... EX-CUSE ME?
WHAT KIND OF RELA-TIONSHIP DO YOU TWO HAVE?
I'M HER BABYSIT-TER!
HE'S MY SLAVE! MY SLAVE!
I SEE...
チラッ
?
SO THIS IS THE MAN WHOM LADY LUNA KISSED EARLIER.
?!
WHEN DID YOU?!
......
DON'T YOU FEEL GUILTY FOR TAKING ADVANTAGE OF SOME-ONE WHO'S ASLEEP?!
IT'S NOT A BIG DEAL!!
ギャイ
ギャイ
BUT I DON'T SEE ANY CHANGE IN THIS MAN.
ANYWAY, YOU ARE MY SLAVE!

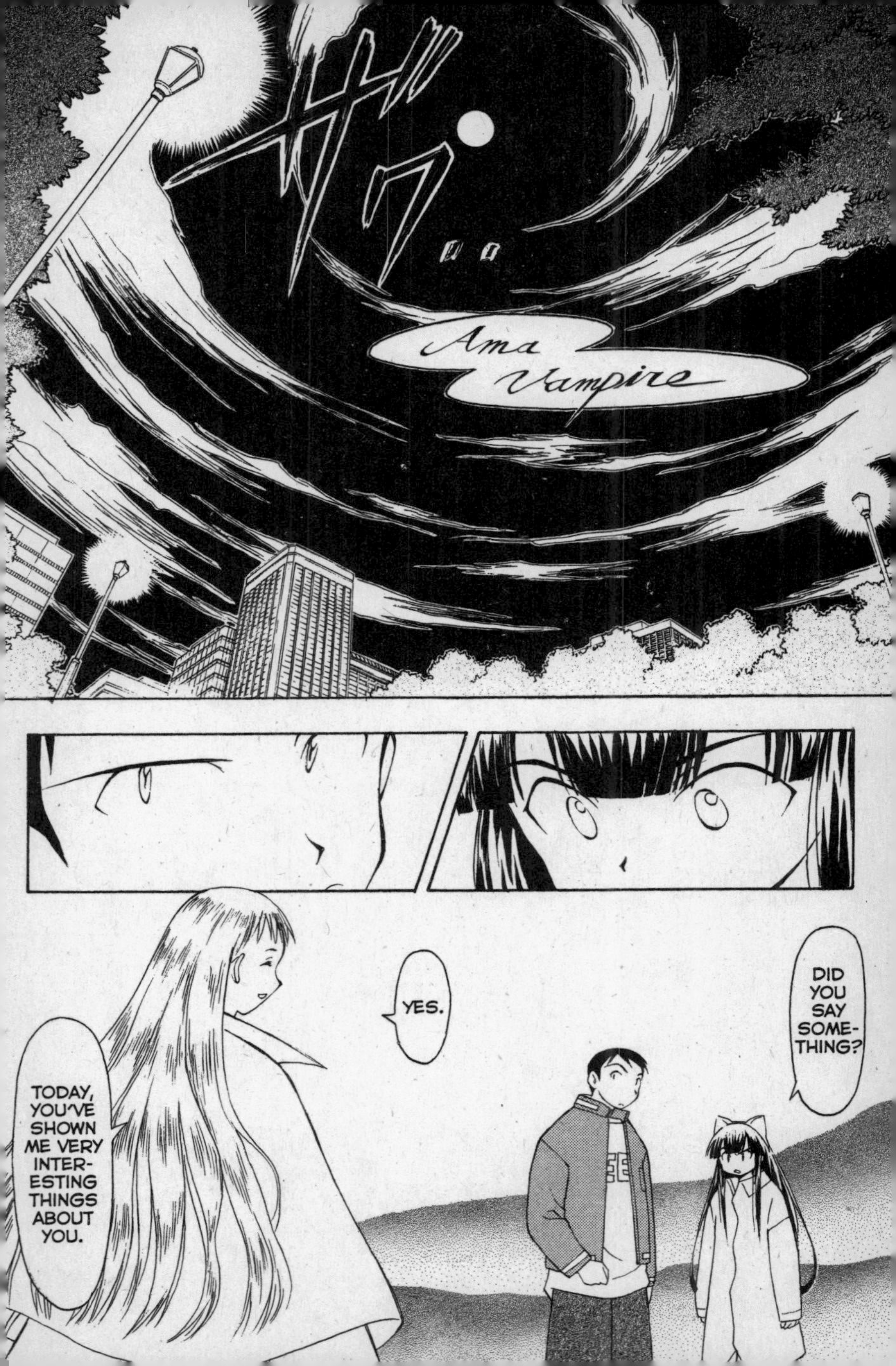
Ama Vampire
DID YOU SAY SOME-THING?
YES.
TODAY, YOU'VE SHOWN ME VERY INTER-ESTING THINGS ABOUT YOU.

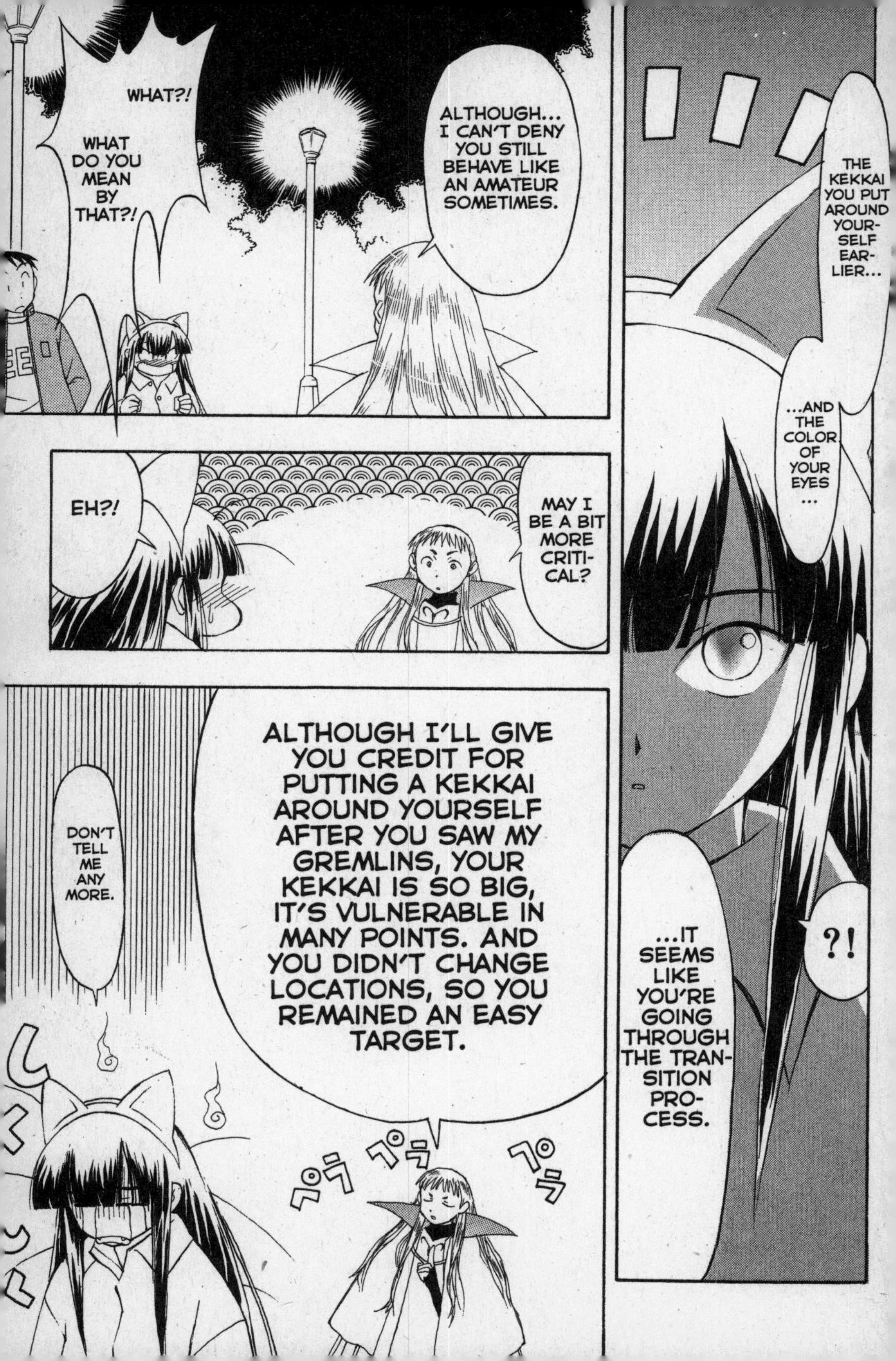
THE KEKKAI YOU PUT AROUND YOURSELF EARLIER...
...AND THE COLOR OF YOUR EYES...
?!
...IT SEEMS LIKE YOU'RE GOING THROUGH THE TRANSITION PROCESS.
ALTHOUGH... I CAN'T DENY YOU STILL BEHAVE LIKE AN AMATEUR SOMETIMES.
WHAT?!
WHAT DO YOU MEAN BY THAT?!
MAY I BE A BIT MORE CRITICAL?
EH?!
ALTHOUGH I'LL GIVE YOU CREDIT FOR PUTTING A KEKKAI AROUND YOURSELF AFTER YOU SAW MY GREMLINS, YOUR KEKKAI IS SO BIG, IT'S VULNERABLE IN MANY POINTS. AND YOU DIDN'T CHANGE LOCATIONS, SO YOU REMAINED AN EASY TARGET.
DON'T TELL ME ANY MORE.

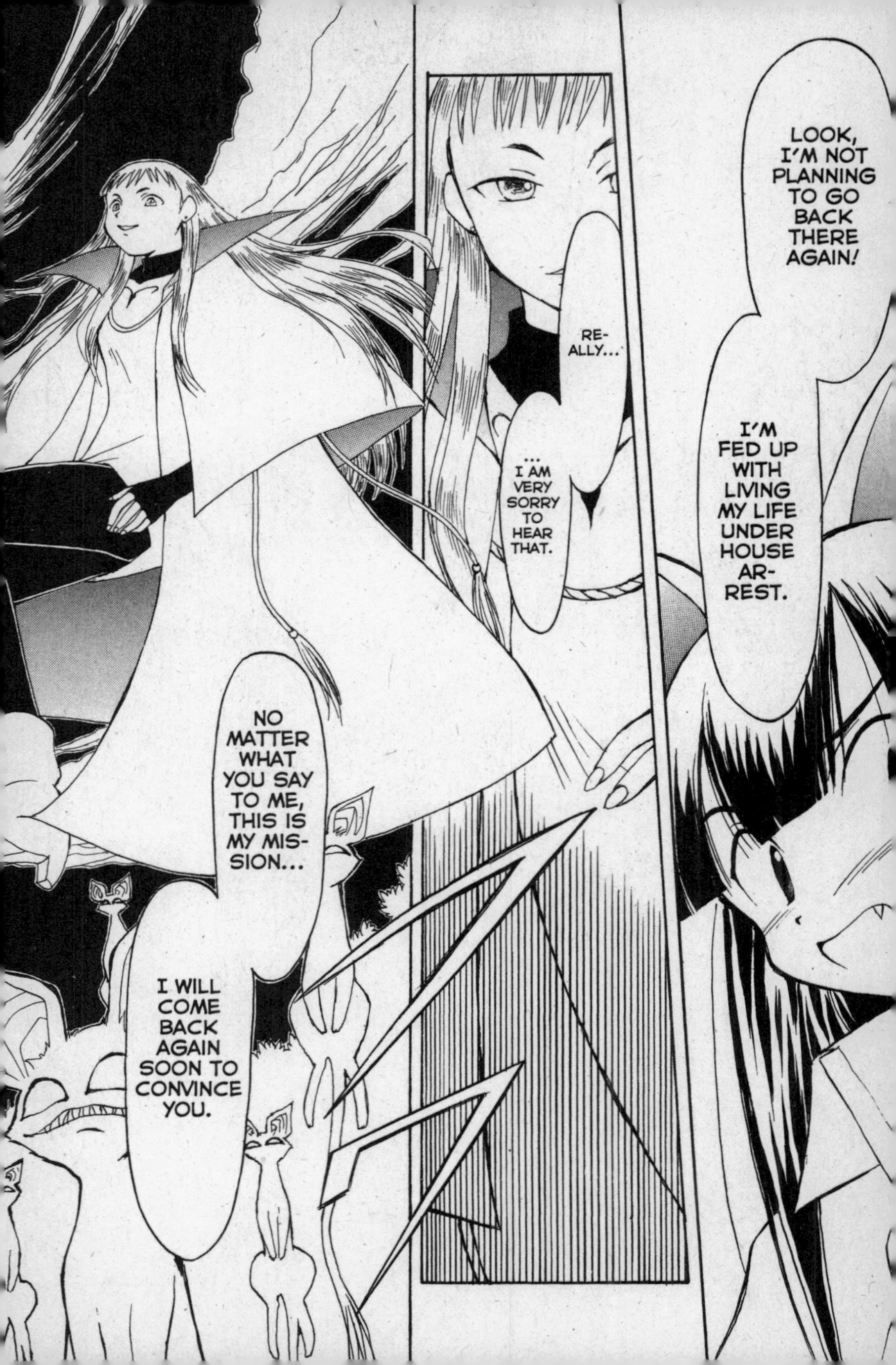
LOOK, I'M NOT PLANNING TO GO BACK THERE AGAIN!
I'M FED UP WITH LIVING MY LIFE UNDER HOUSE AR-REST.
RE-ALLY...
... I AM VERY SORRY TO HEAR THAT.
NO MATTER WHAT YOU SAY TO ME, THIS IS MY MIS-SION...
I WILL COME BACK AGAIN SOON TO CONVINCE YOU.

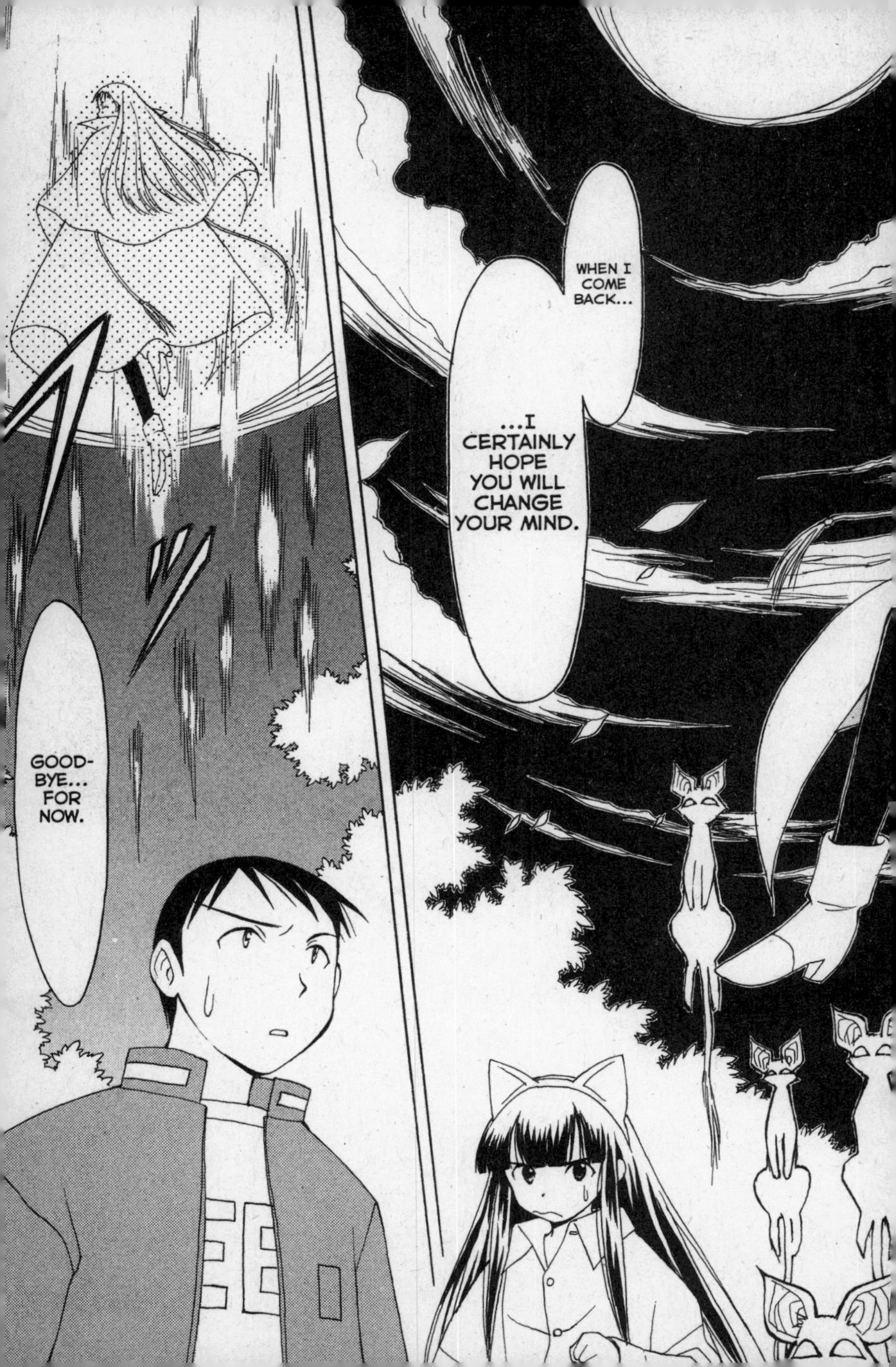
WHEN I COME BACK...
...I CERTAINLY HOPE YOU WILL CHANGE YOUR MIND.
GOOD-BYE... FOR NOW.

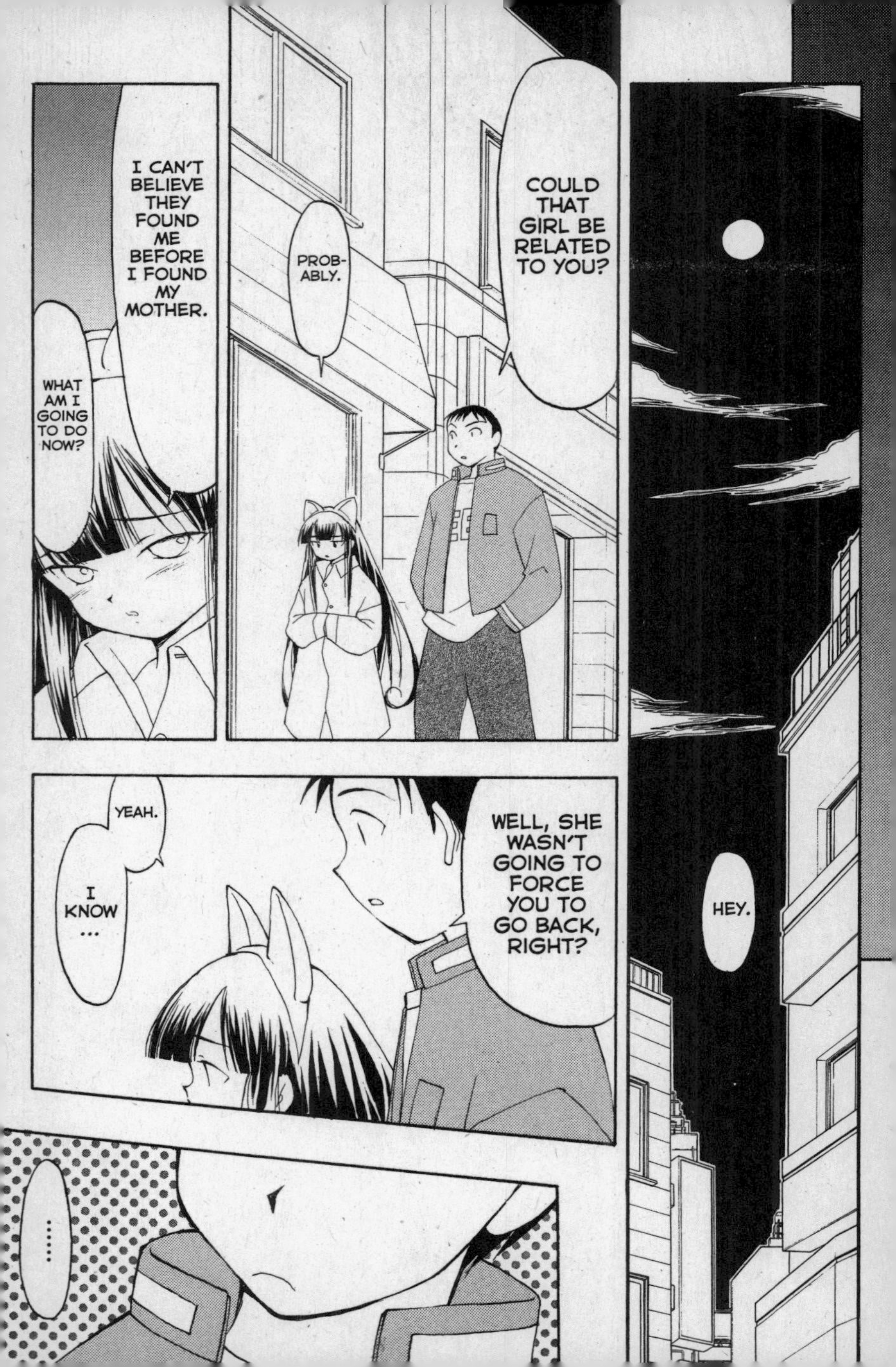
HEY.
COULD THAT GIRL BE RELATED TO YOU?
PROBABLY.
I CAN'T BELIEVE THEY FOUND ME BEFORE I FOUND MY MOTHER.
WHAT AM I GOING TO DO NOW?
WELL, SHE WASN'T GOING TO FORCE YOU TO GO BACK, RIGHT?
YEAH.
I KNOW...
......

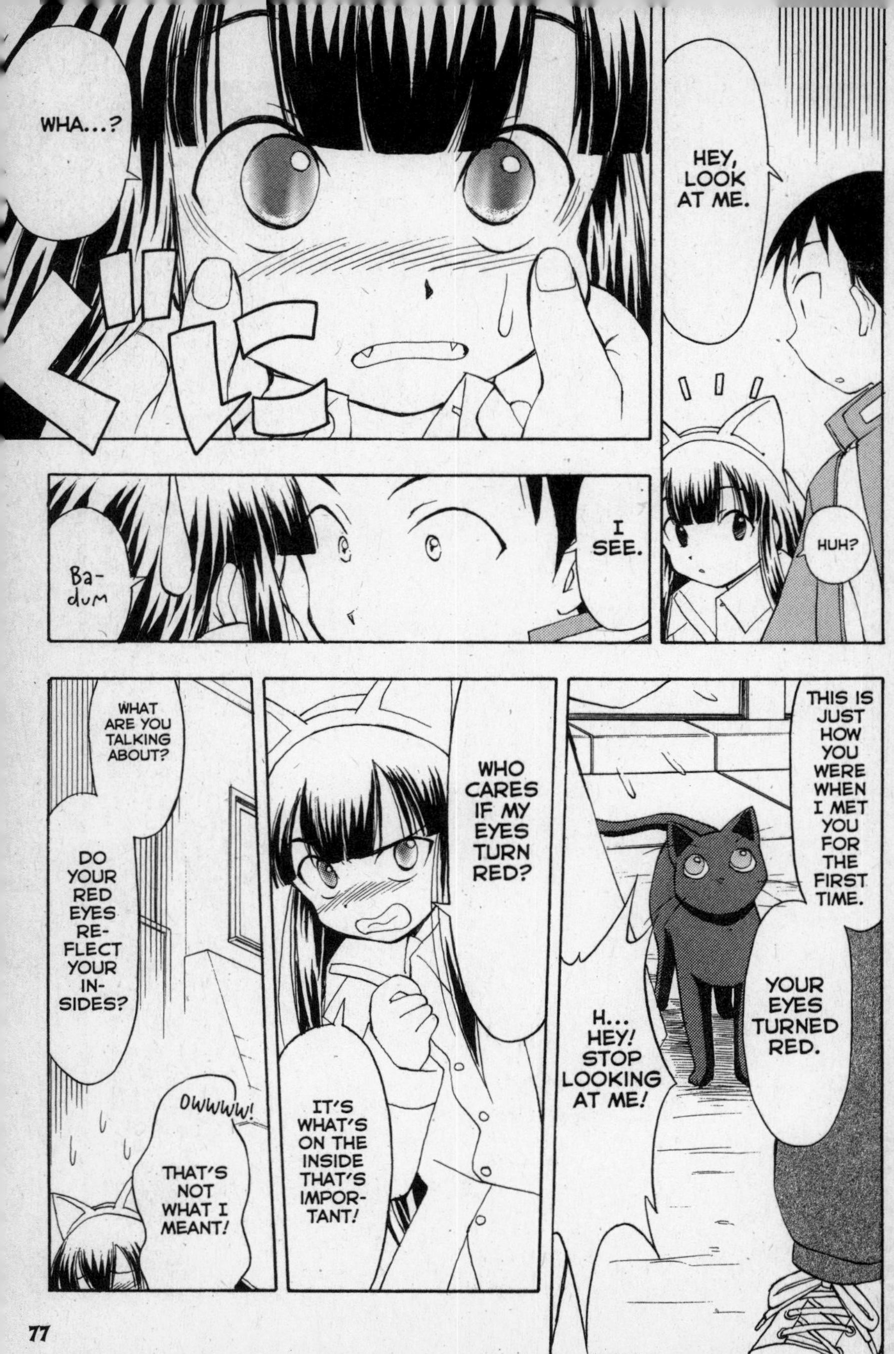

HEY, LOOK AT ME.
HUH?
WHA...?
I SEE.
Ba-dum
THIS IS JUST HOW YOU WERE WHEN I MET YOU FOR THE FIRST TIME.
YOUR EYES TURNED RED.
H... HEY! STOP LOOKING AT ME!
WHO CARES IF MY EYES TURN RED?
IT'S WHAT'S ON THE INSIDE THAT'S IMPORTANT!
WHAT ARE YOU TALKING ABOUT?
DO YOUR RED EYES REFLECT YOUR INSIDES?
OWWWW!
THAT'S NOT WHAT I MEANT!

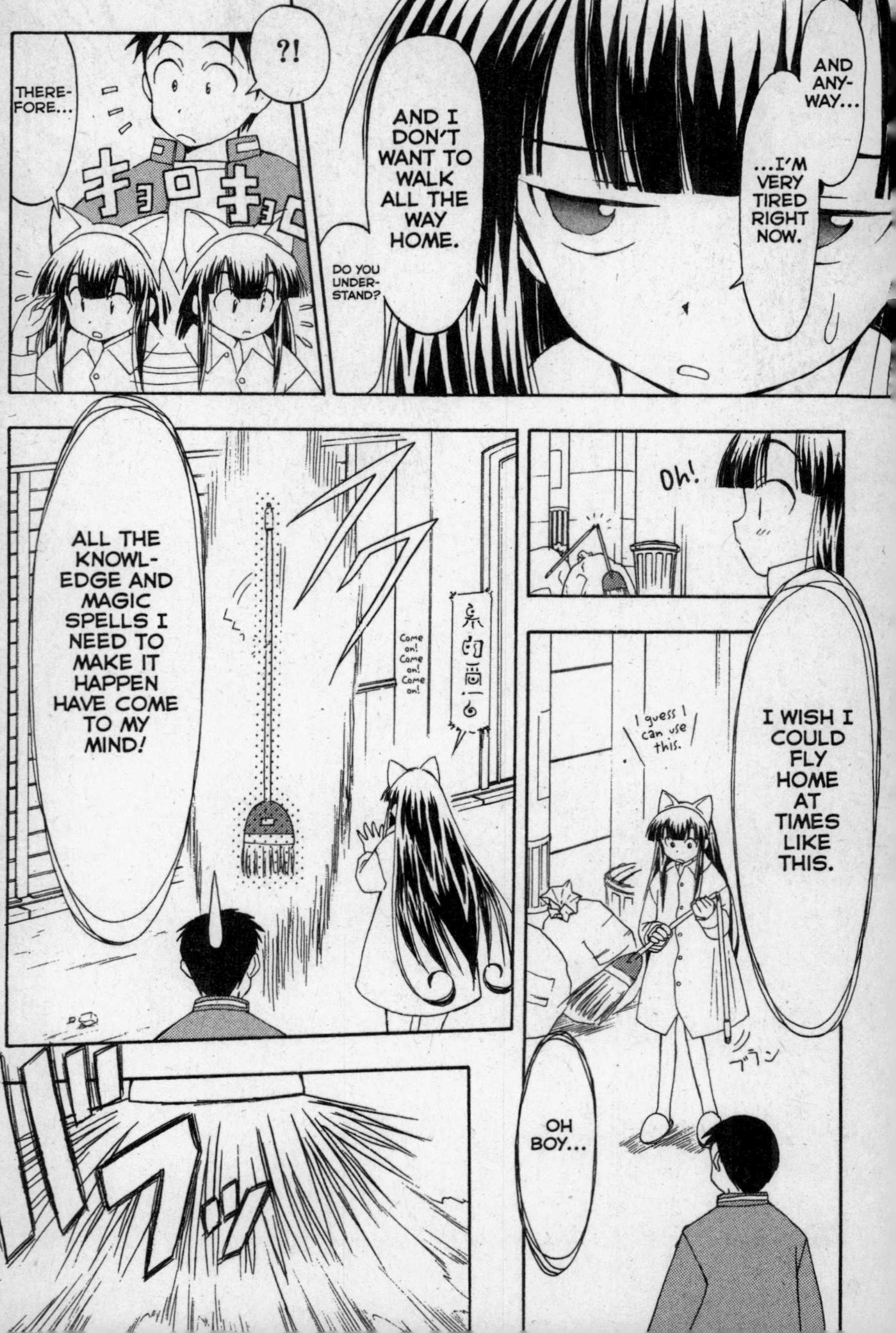

AND ANYWAY...
...I'M VERY TIRED RIGHT NOW.
AND I DON'T WANT TO WALK ALL THE WAY HOME.
DO YOU UNDERSTAND?
?!
THEREFORE...
キョロキョロ
Oh!
I WISH I COULD FLY HOME AT TIMES LIKE THIS.
I guess I can use this.
OH BOY...
ALL THE KNOWLEDGE AND MAGIC SPELLS I NEED TO MAKE IT HAPPEN HAVE COME TO MY MIND!
Come on! Come on! Come on!

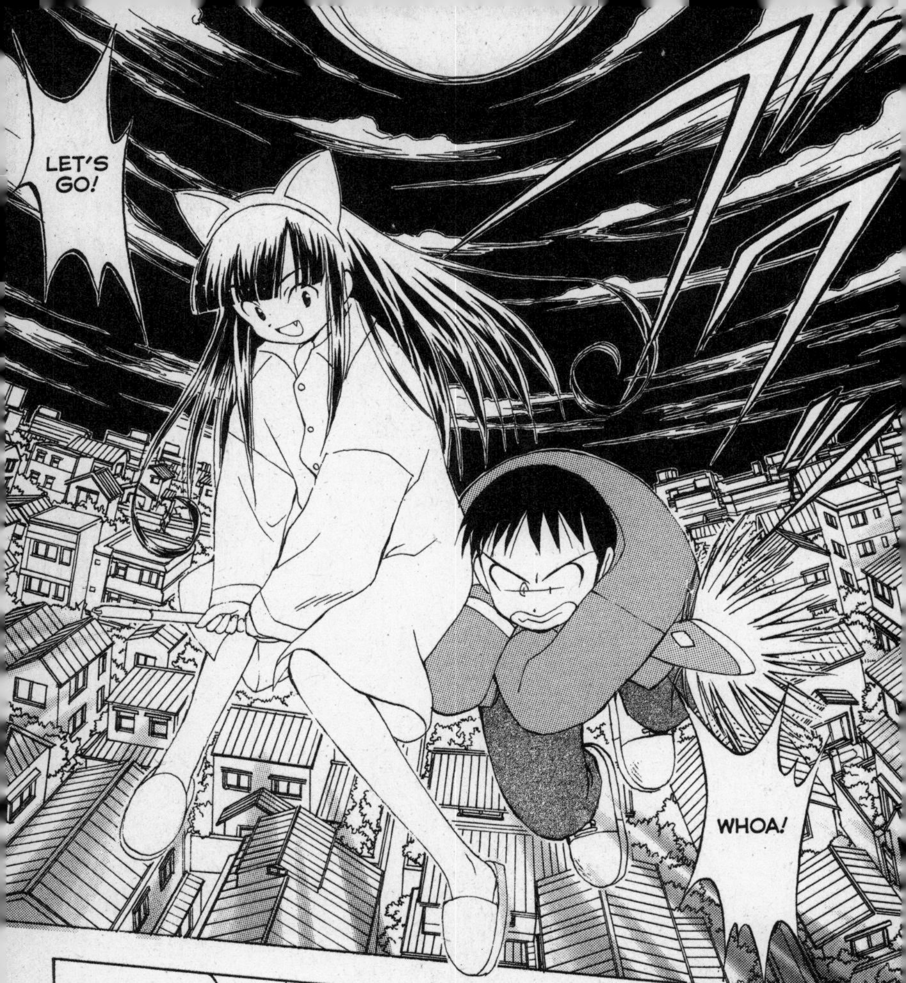
LET'S GO!
WHOA!

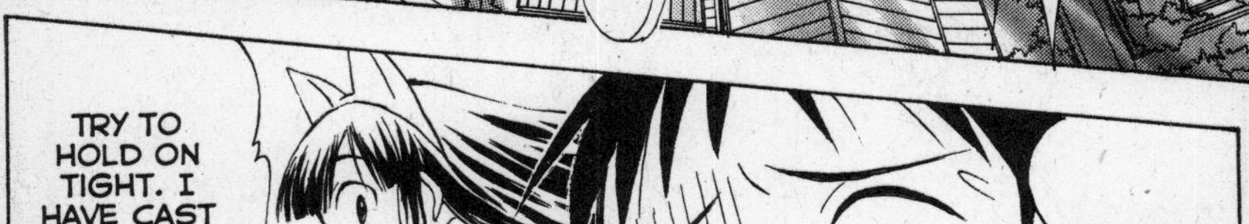
WHAT'S GOING ON HERE?
TRY TO HOLD ON TIGHT. I HAVE CAST A SPELL ON THIS BROOM.

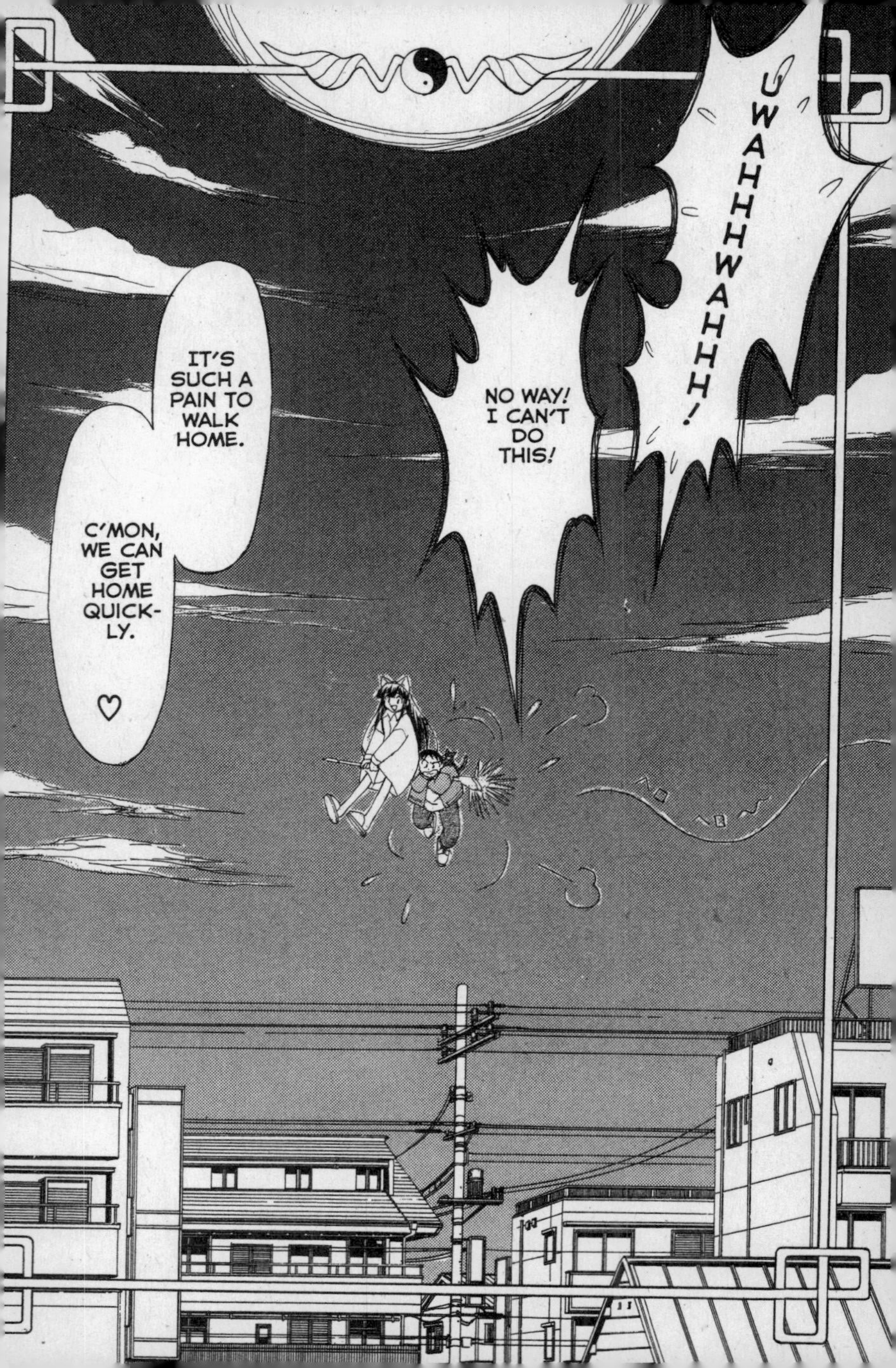
UWAHHHWAHHH!
NO WAY! I CAN'T DO THIS!
IT'S SUCH A PAIN TO WALK HOME.
C'MON, WE CAN GET HOME QUICKLY. ♥

What happened to the three punks?

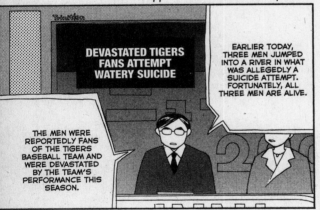

EARLIER TODAY, THREE MEN JUMPED INTO A RIVER IN WHAT WAS ALLEGEDLY A SUICIDE ATTEMPT. FORTUNATELY, ALL THREE MEN ARE ALIVE.
DEVASTATED TIGERS FANS ATTEMPT WATERY SUICIDE
THE MEN WERE REPORTEDLY FANS OF THE TIGERS BASEBALL TEAM AND WERE DEVASTATED BY THE TEAM'S PERFORMANCE THIS SEASON.

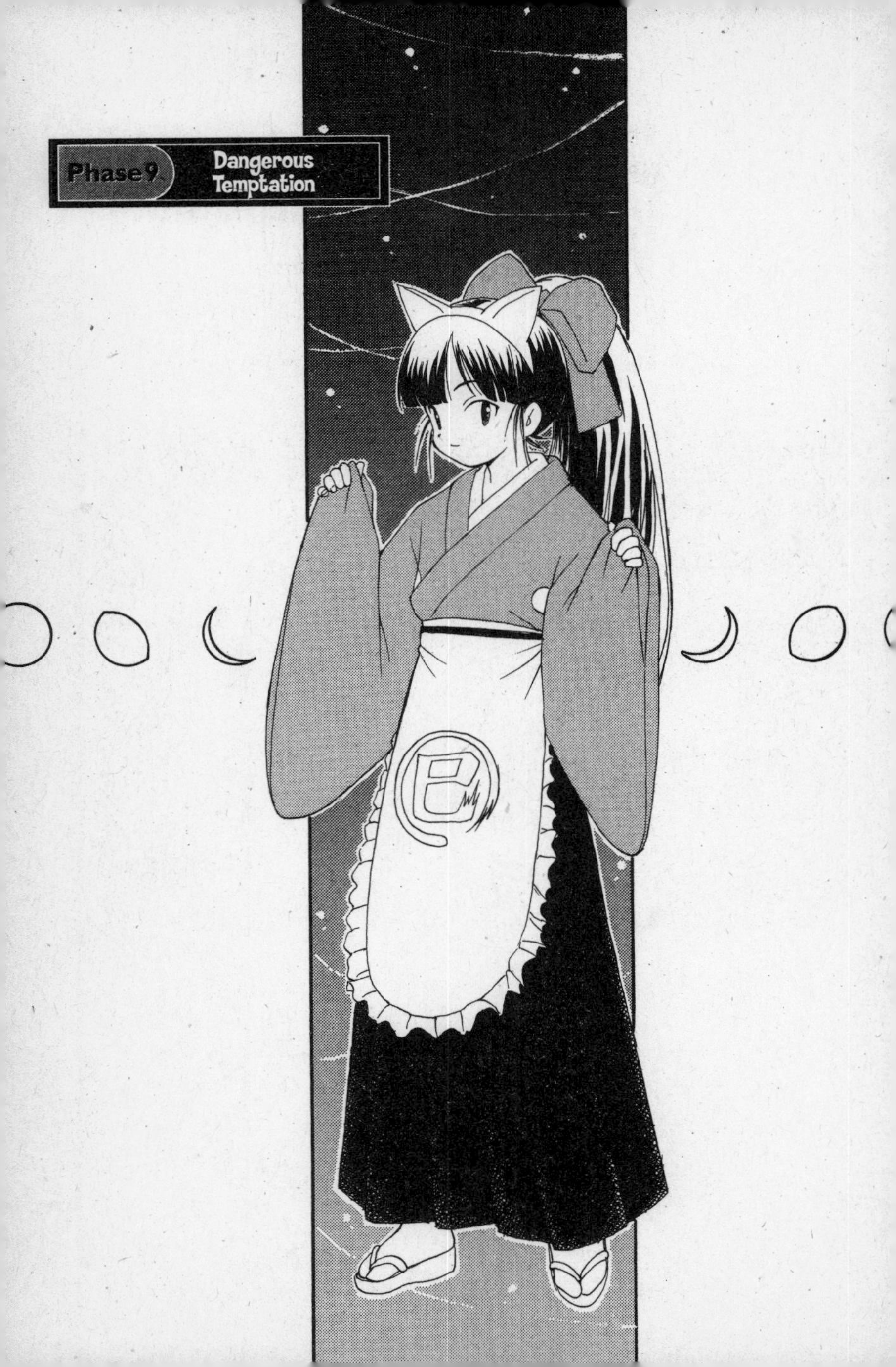
Phase 9
Dangerous Temptation

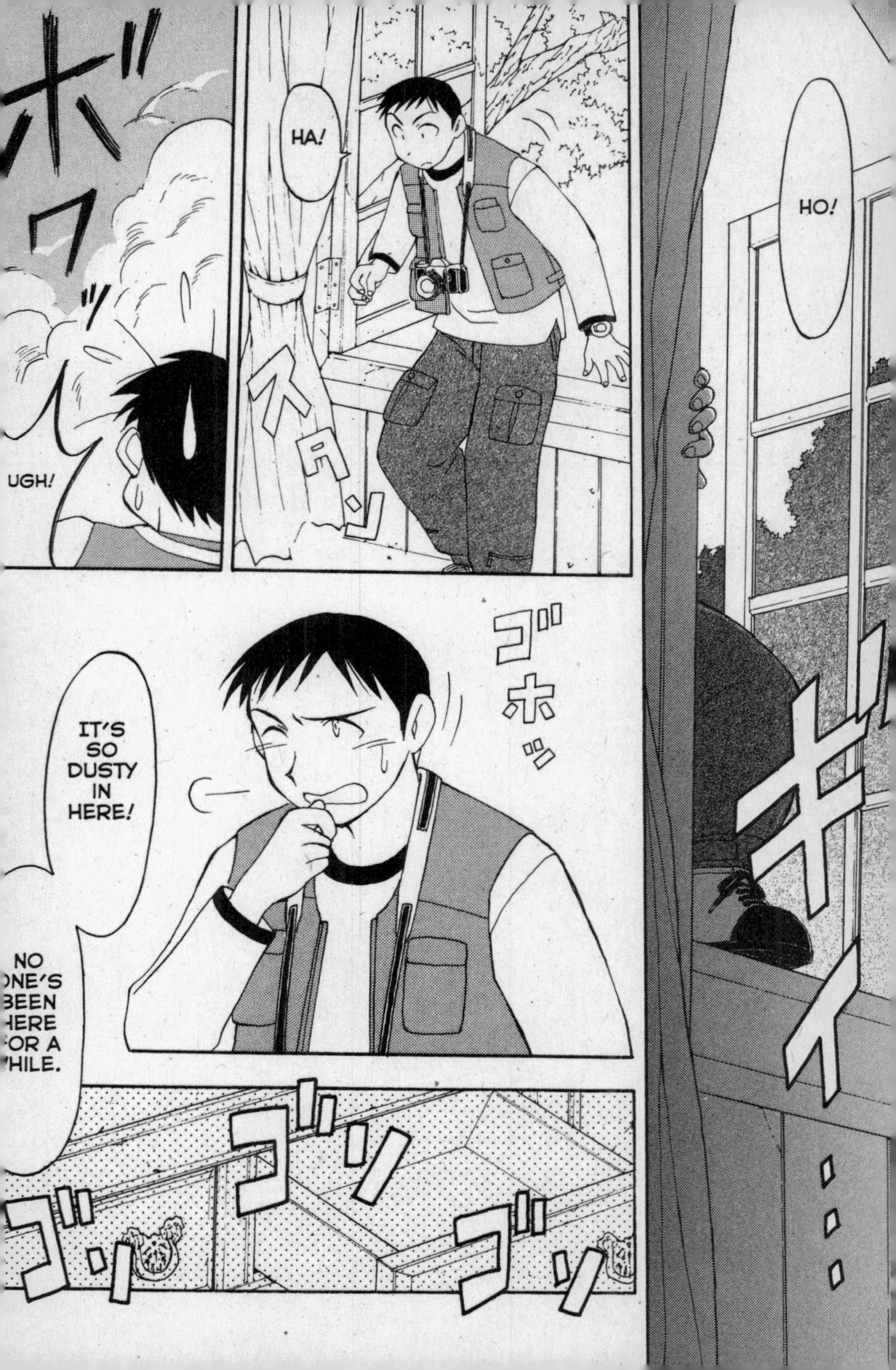
HO!
ギィ
HA!
スタン
ボワッ
UGH!
ゴホッ
IT'S SO DUSTY IN HERE!
NO ONE'S BEEN HERE FOR A WHILE.

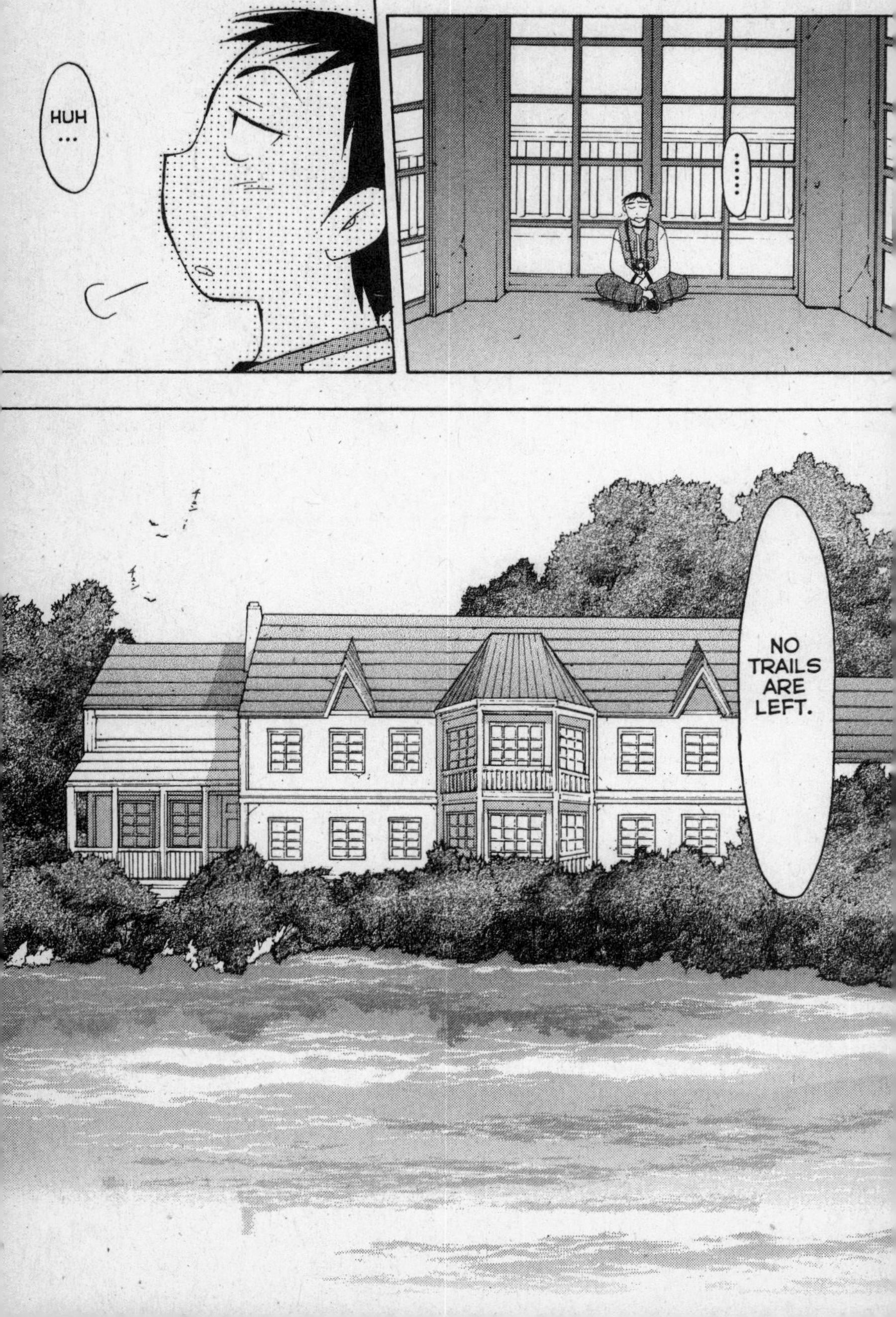
......
HUH ...
NO TRAILS ARE LEFT.

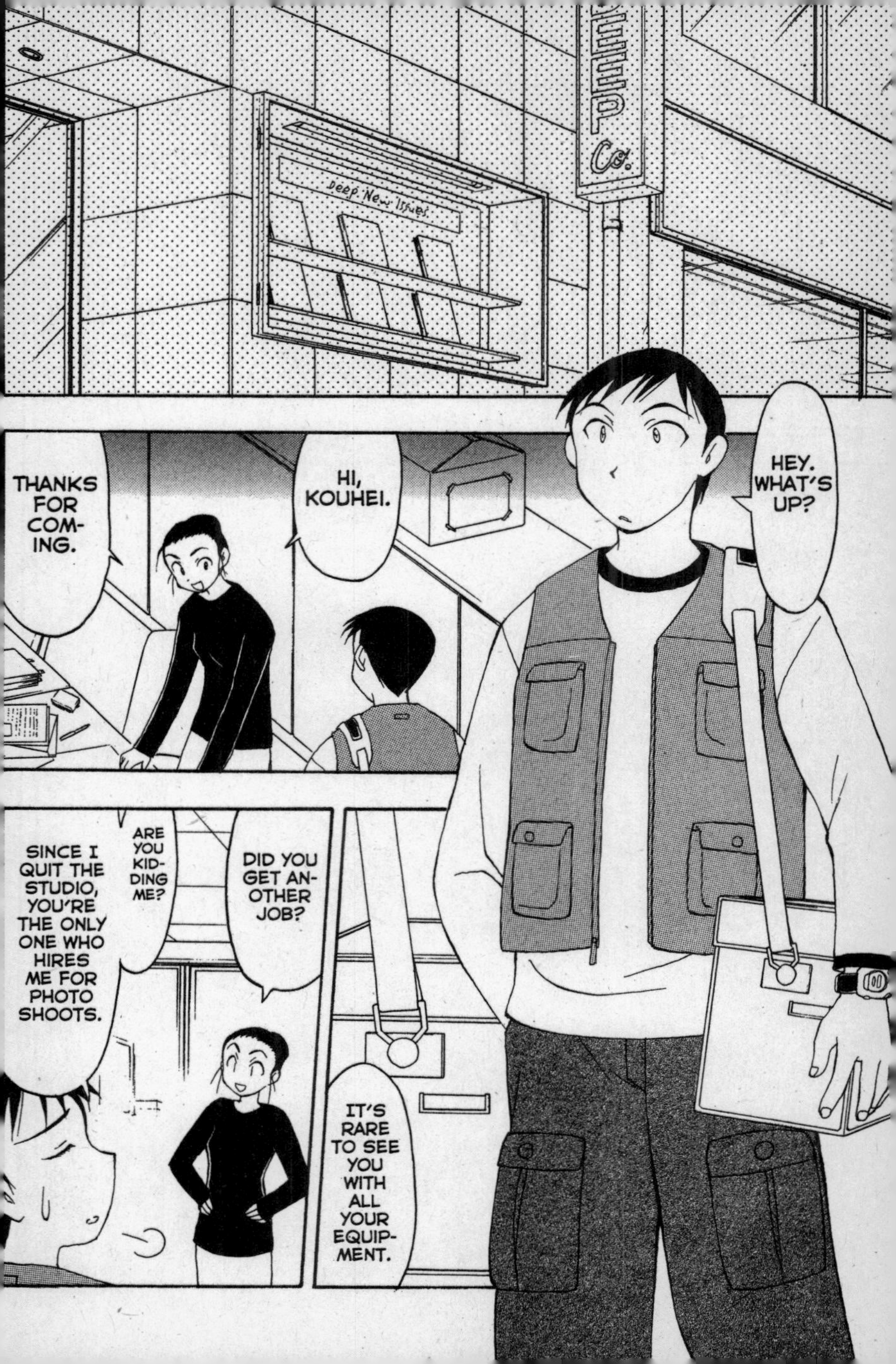
DEEP Co.
Deep New Issues
HEY. WHAT'S UP?
HI, KOUHEI.
THANKS FOR COMING.
IT'S RARE TO SEE YOU WITH ALL YOUR EQUIPMENT.
DID YOU GET ANOTHER JOB?
ARE YOU KIDDING ME?
SINCE I QUIT THE STUDIO, YOU'RE THE ONLY ONE WHO HIRES ME FOR PHOTO SHOOTS.

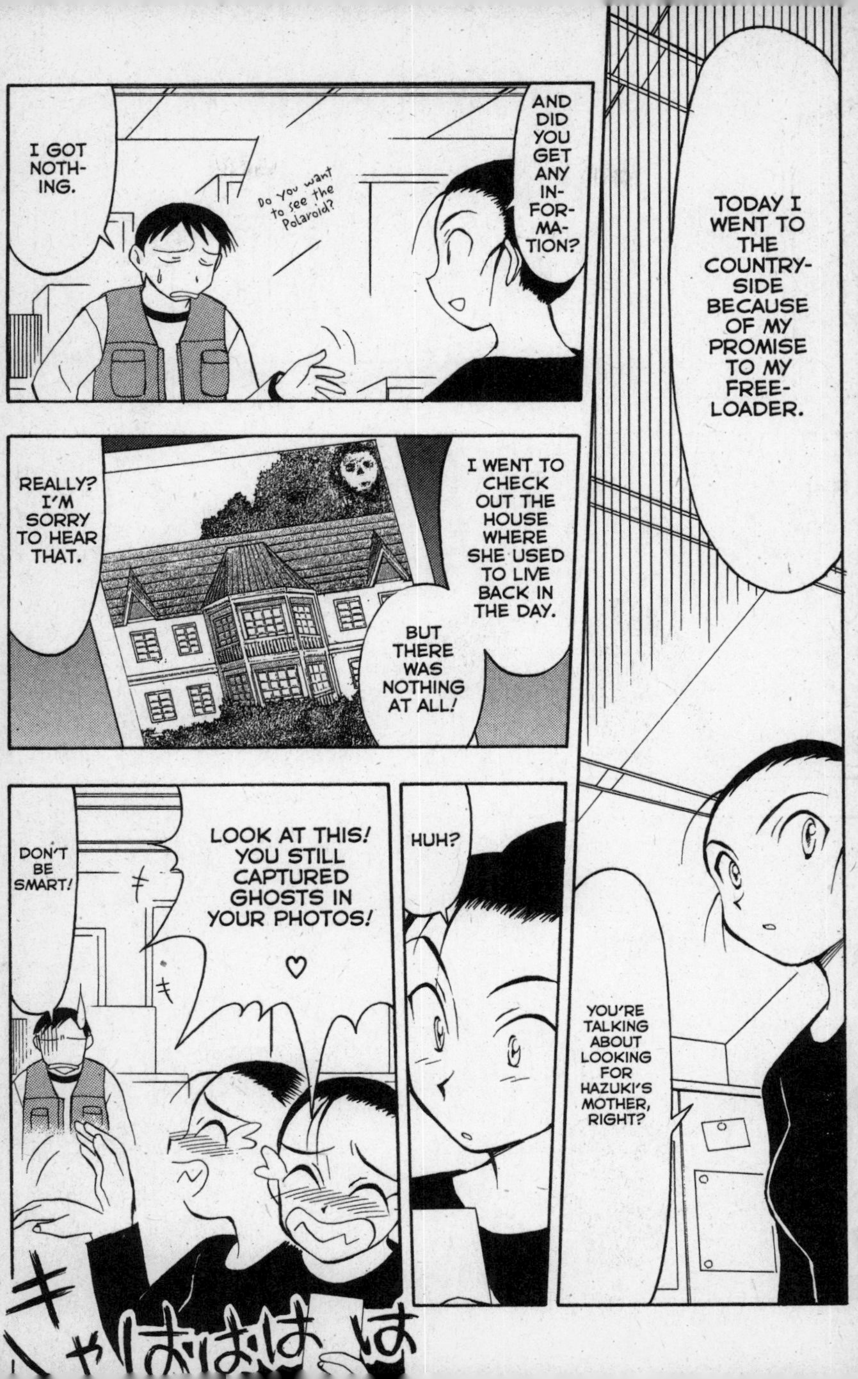
TODAY I WENT TO THE COUNTRYSIDE BECAUSE OF MY PROMISE TO MY FREELOADER.
YOU'RE TALKING ABOUT LOOKING FOR HAZUKI'S MOTHER, RIGHT?
AND DID YOU GET ANY INFORMATION?
I GOT NOTHING.
Do you want to see the Polaroid?
I WENT TO CHECK OUT THE HOUSE WHERE SHE USED TO LIVE BACK IN THE DAY.
BUT THERE WAS NOTHING AT ALL!
REALLY? I'M SORRY TO HEAR THAT.
HUH?
LOOK AT THIS! YOU STILL CAPTURED GHOSTS IN YOUR PHOTOS!
DON'T BE SMART!
キャははは は

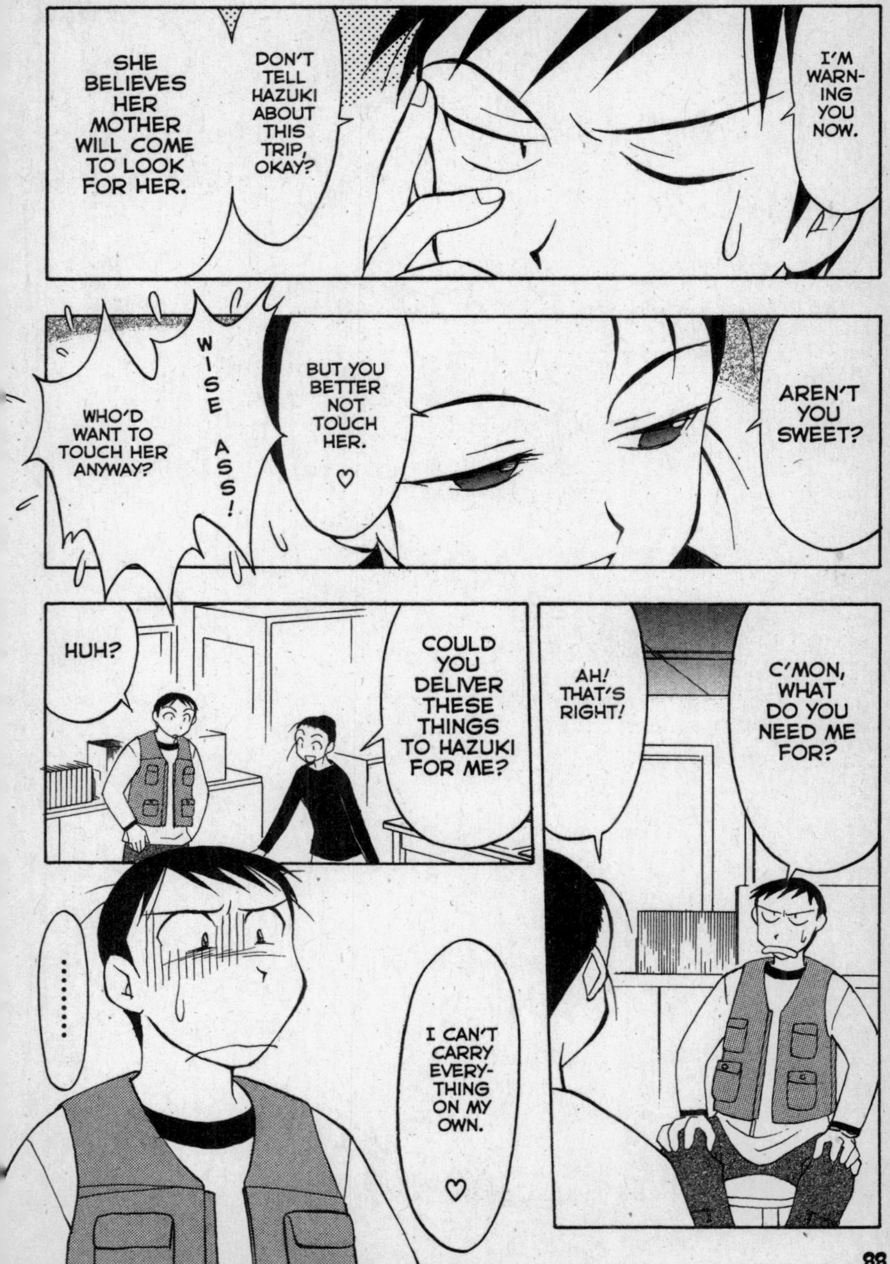
I'M WARNING YOU NOW.
DON'T TELL HAZUKI ABOUT THIS TRIP, OKAY?
SHE BELIEVES HER MOTHER WILL COME TO LOOK FOR HER.
AREN'T YOU SWEET?
BUT YOU BETTER NOT TOUCH HER. ♡
WISE ASS!
WHO'D WANT TO TOUCH HER ANYWAY?
C'MON, WHAT DO YOU NEED ME FOR?
AH! THAT'S RIGHT!
COULD YOU DELIVER THESE THINGS TO HAZUKI FOR ME?
HUH?
I CAN'T CARRY EVERYTHING ON MY OWN. ♡
....

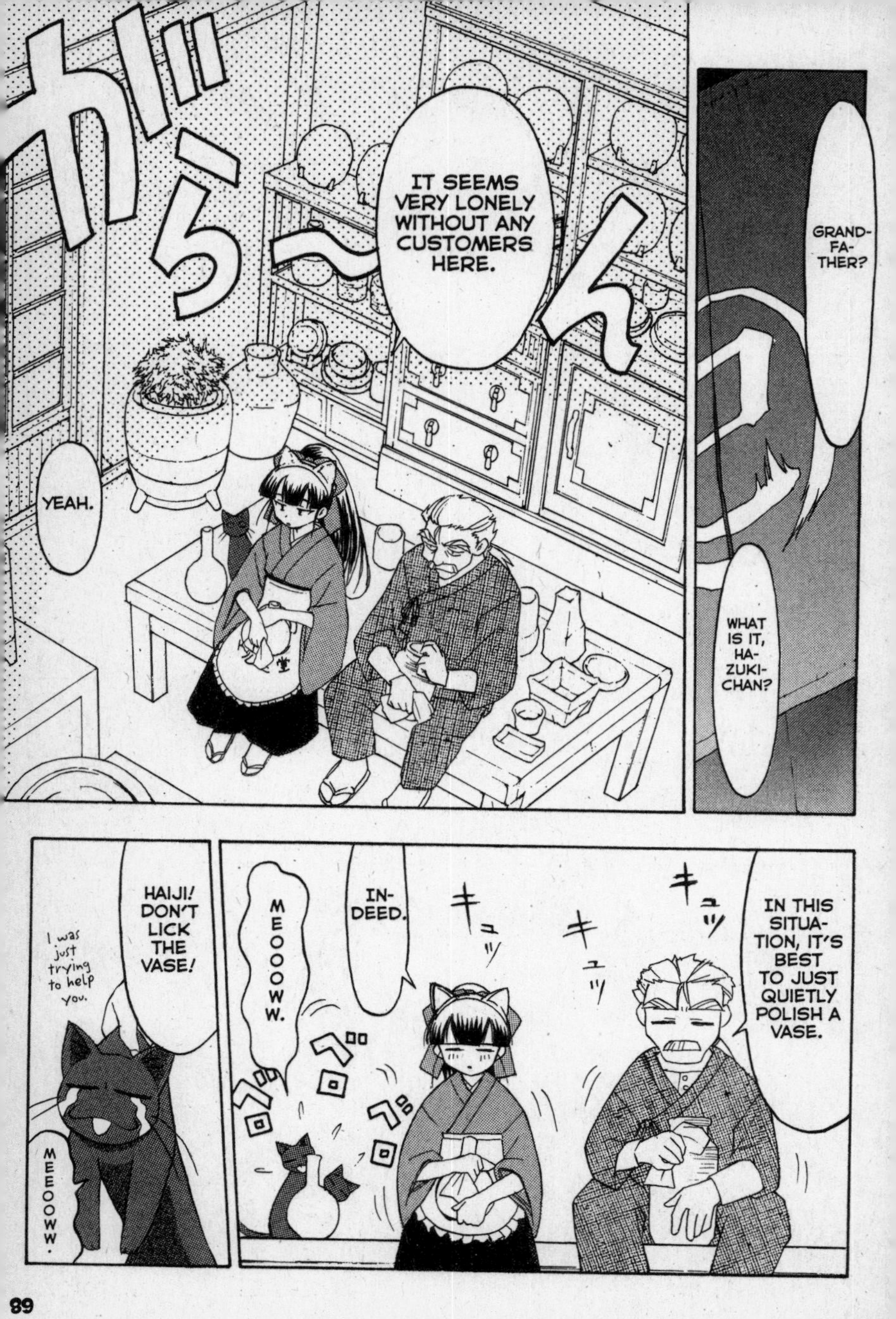
GRAND-FA-THER?
WHAT IS IT, HA-ZUKI-CHAN?
がら〜ん
IT SEEMS VERY LONELY WITHOUT ANY CUSTOMERS HERE.
YEAH.
IN THIS SITUA-TION, IT'S BEST TO JUST QUIETLY POLISH A VASE.
キュッ
キュッ
キュッ
IN-DEED.
MEOOOOWW.
ペロ
ペロ
ペロ
HAIJI! DON'T LICK THE VASE!
I was just trying to help you.
MEEOOWW.

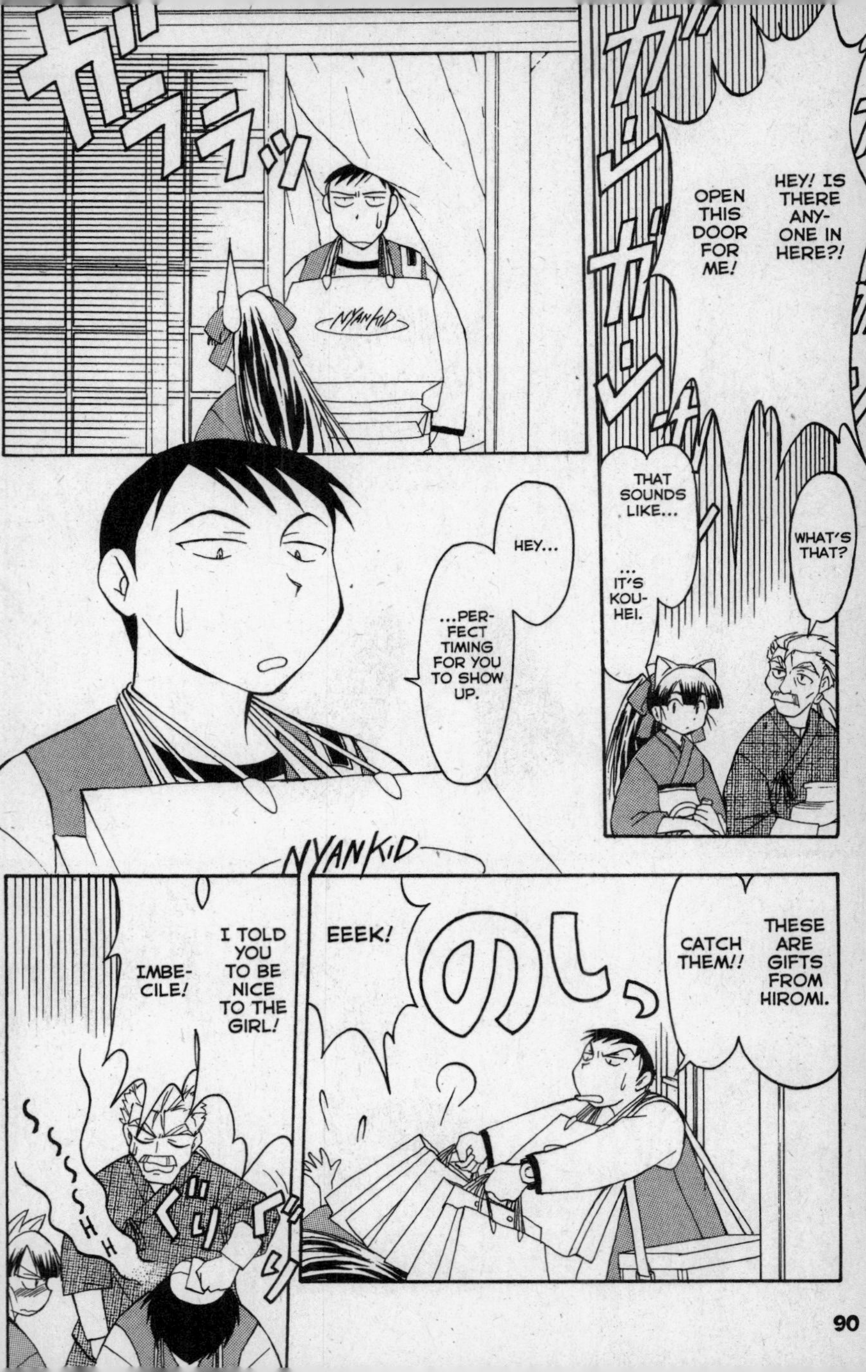
HEY! IS THERE ANY-ONE IN HERE?!
OPEN THIS DOOR FOR ME!
WHAT'S THAT?
THAT SOUNDS LIKE...
...IT'S KOU-HEI.
HEY...
...PER-FECT TIMING FOR YOU TO SHOW UP.
NYANKID
THESE ARE GIFTS FROM HIROMI.
CATCH THEM!!
のし、
EEEK!
I TOLD YOU TO BE NICE TO THE GIRL!
IMBE-CILE!

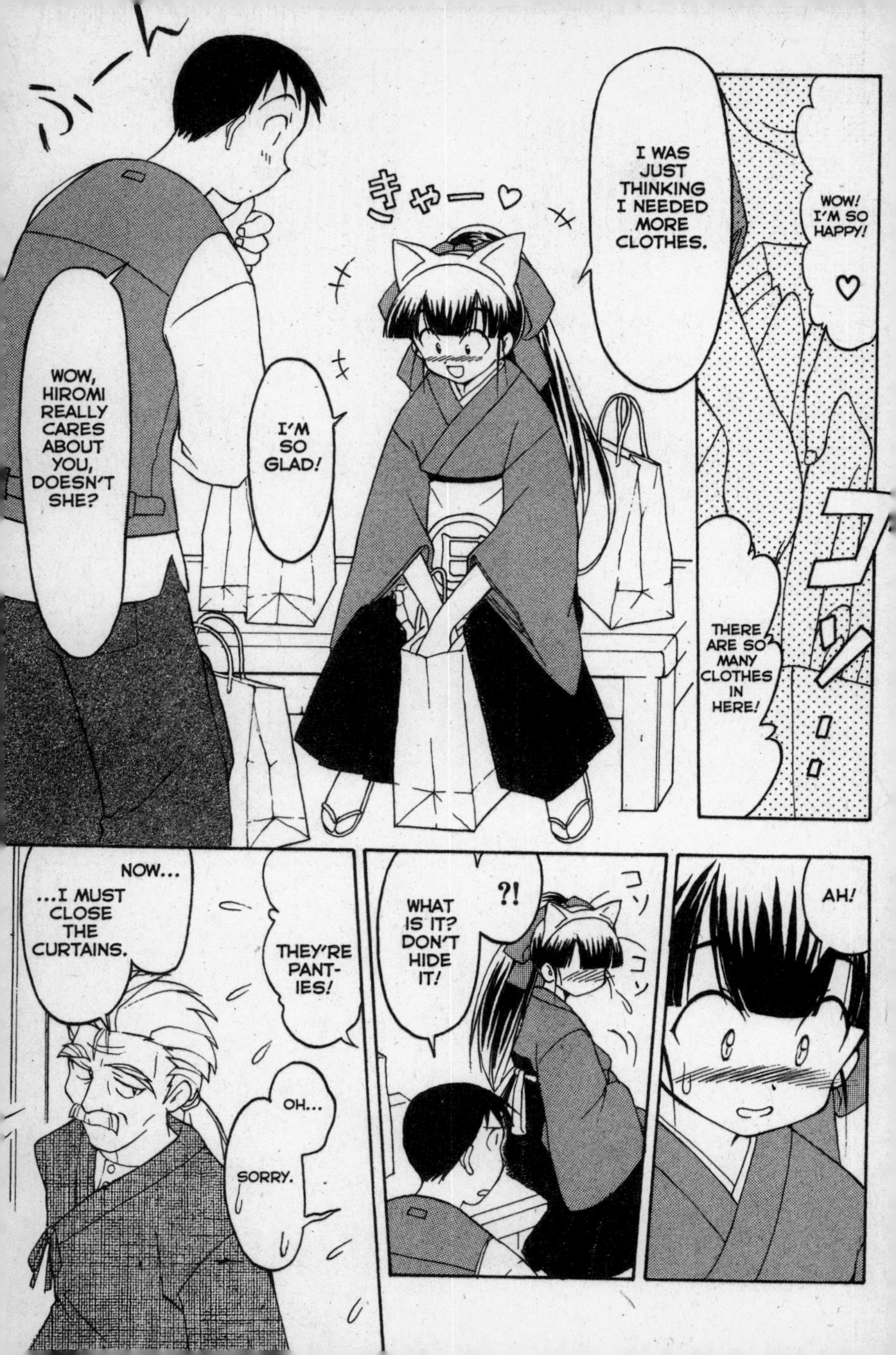
WOW! I'M SO HAPPY! ♡
THERE ARE SO MANY CLOTHES IN HERE!
I WAS JUST THINKING I NEEDED MORE CLOTHES.
きゃー♡
I'M SO GLAD!
WOW, HIROMI REALLY CARES ABOUT YOU, DOESN'T SHE?
AH!
?!
WHAT IS IT? DON'T HIDE IT!
THEY'RE PANT-IES!
NOW...
...I MUST CLOSE THE CURTAINS.
OH...
SORRY.

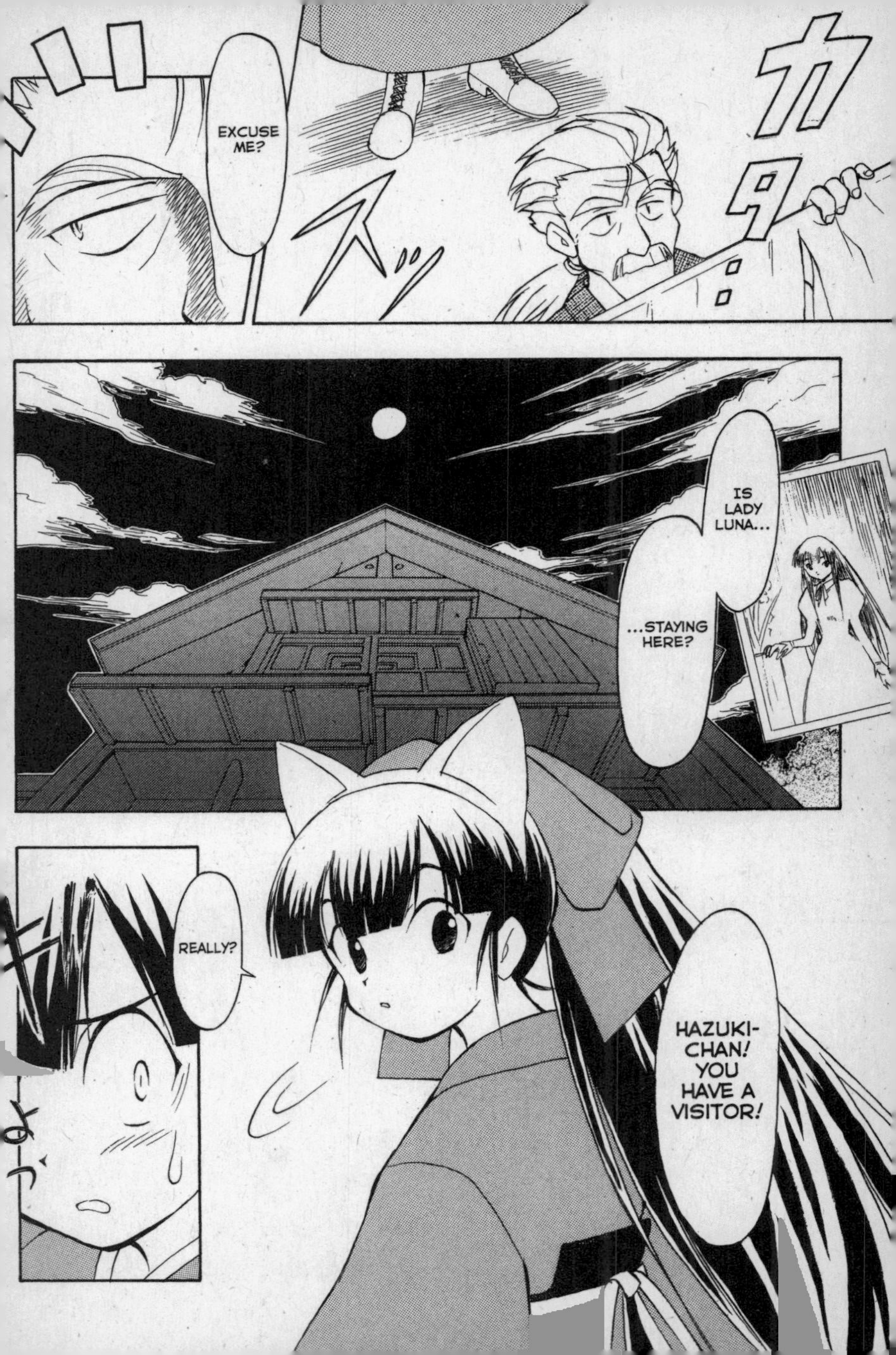
カタ
スッ
EXCUSE ME?
IS LADY LUNA...
...STAYING HERE?
HAZUKI-CHAN! YOU HAVE A VISITOR!
REALLY?

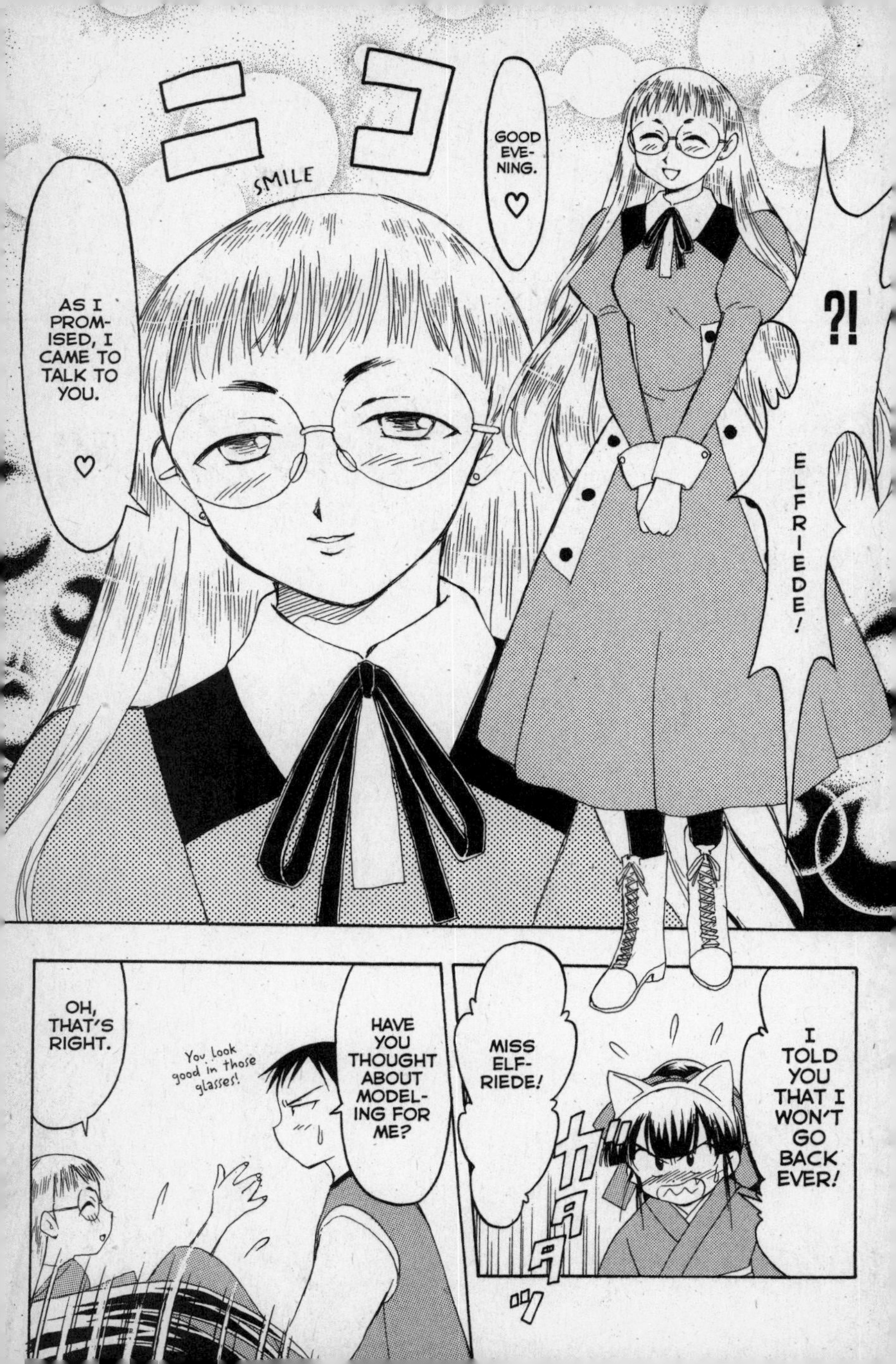
?!
ELFRIEDE!
GOOD EVE-NING. ♥
ニコ
SMILE
AS I PROM-ISED, I CAME TO TALK TO YOU. ♥
I TOLD YOU THAT I WON'T GO BACK EVER!
MISS ELF-RIEDE!
カタタッ
HAVE YOU THOUGHT ABOUT MODEL-ING FOR ME?
You look good in those glasses!
OH, THAT'S RIGHT.

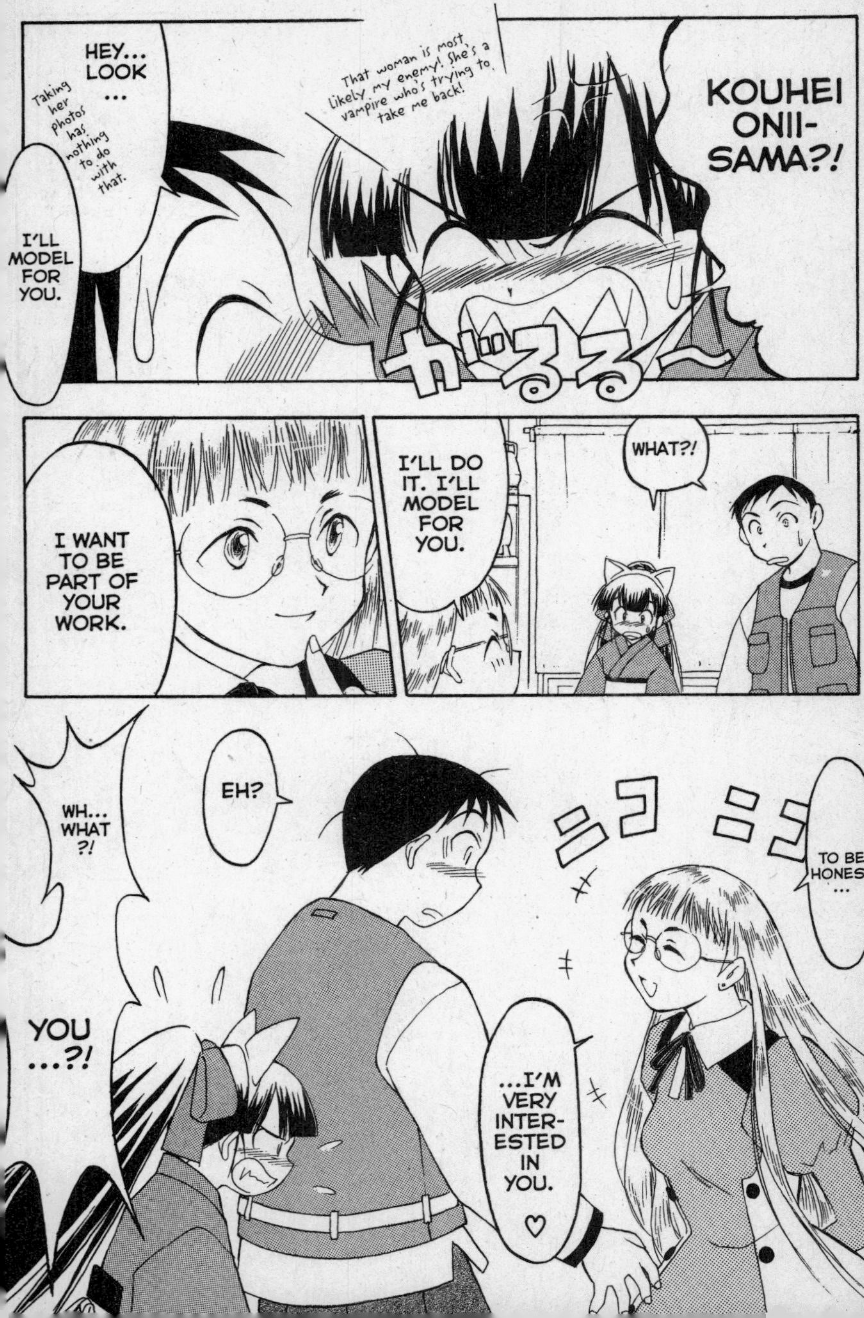
KOUHEI ONII-SAMA?!
That woman is most likely my enemy! She's a vampire who's trying to take me back!
がるる～
HEY... LOOK ...
Taking her photos has nothing to do with that.
I'LL MODEL FOR YOU.
WHAT?!
I'LL DO IT. I'LL MODEL FOR YOU.
I WANT TO BE PART OF YOUR WORK.
TO BE HONEST ...
ニコ ニコ
...I'M VERY INTERESTED IN YOU. ♥
EH?
WH... WHAT ?!
YOU ...?!

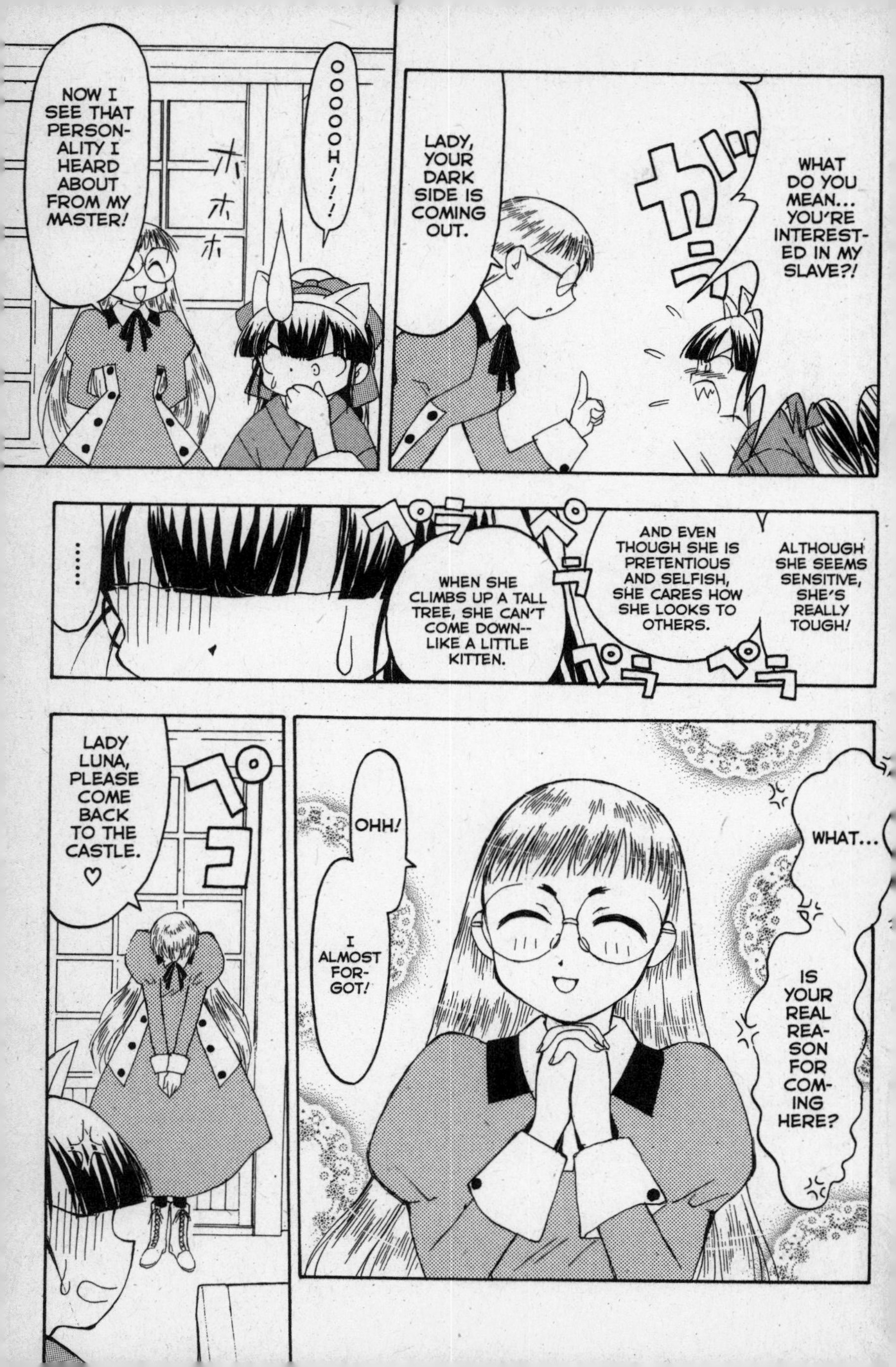

WHAT DO YOU MEAN... YOU'RE INTEREST-ED IN MY SLAVE?!
カッ
LADY, YOUR DARK SIDE IS COMING OUT.
OOOOOOH!!!
ホホホ
NOW I SEE THAT PERSON-ALITY I HEARD ABOUT FROM MY MASTER!
ALTHOUGH SHE SEEMS SENSITIVE, SHE'S REALLY TOUGH!
AND EVEN THOUGH SHE IS PRETENTIOUS AND SELFISH, SHE CARES HOW SHE LOOKS TO OTHERS.
WHEN SHE CLIMBS UP A TALL TREE, SHE CAN'T COME DOWN-- LIKE A LITTLE KITTEN.
......
WHAT...
IS YOUR REAL REA-SON FOR COM-ING HERE?
OHH!
I ALMOST FOR-GOT!
LADY LUNA, PLEASE COME BACK TO THE CASTLE. ♡

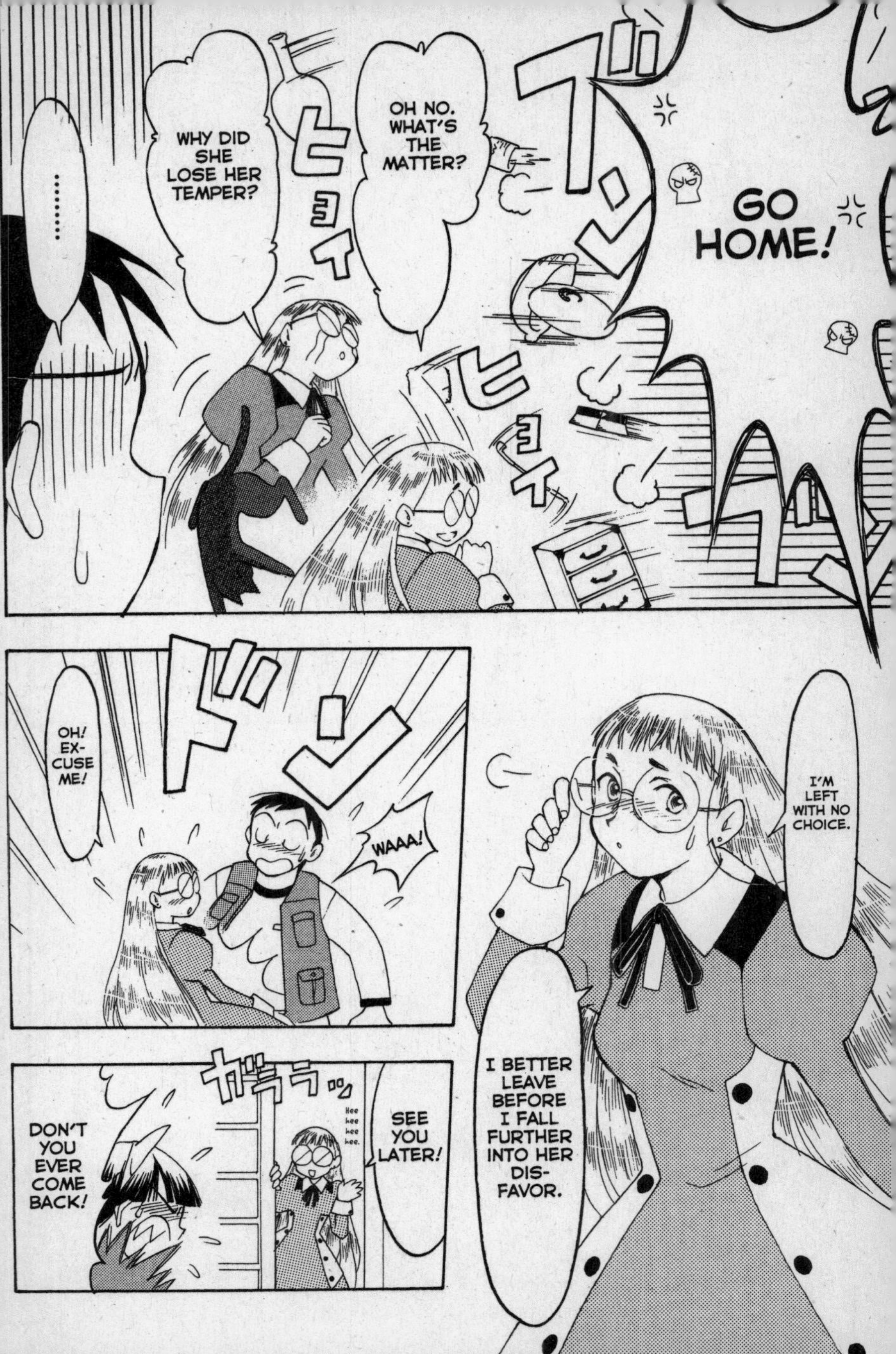
GO HOME!
ドン
ヒョイ
OH NO. WHAT'S THE MATTER?
ヒョイ
WHY DID SHE LOSE HER TEMPER?
......
I'M LEFT WITH NO CHOICE.
I BETTER LEAVE BEFORE I FALL FURTHER INTO HER DIS-FAVOR.
ドン
WAAA!
OH! EX-CUSE ME!
ガララ
SEE YOU LATER!
Hee hee hee hee.
DON'T YOU EVER COME BACK!

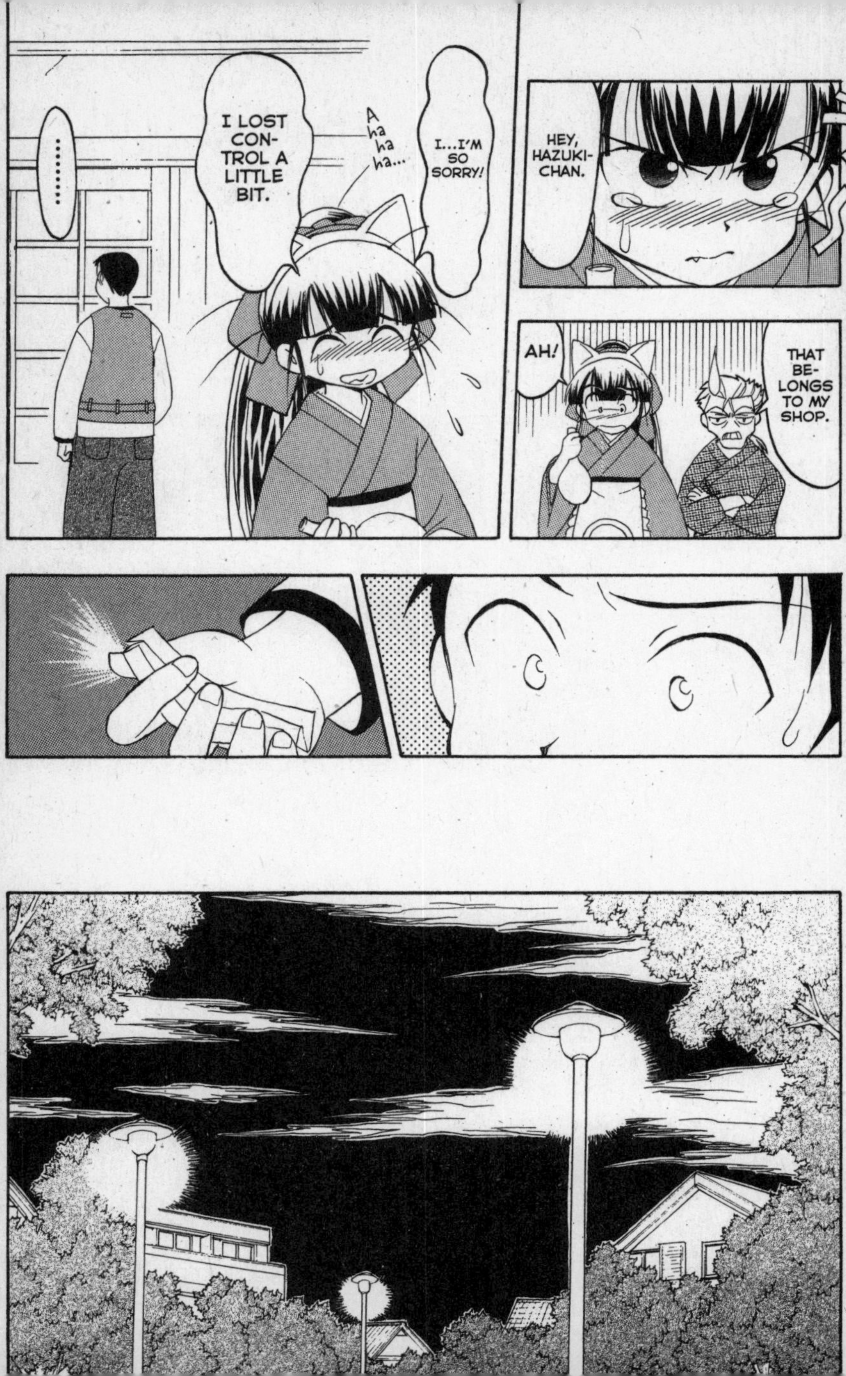

HEY, HAZUKI-CHAN.
THAT BE-LONGS TO MY SHOP.
AH!
I...I'M SO SORRY!
A ha ha ha...
I LOST CON-TROL A LITTLE BIT.
......

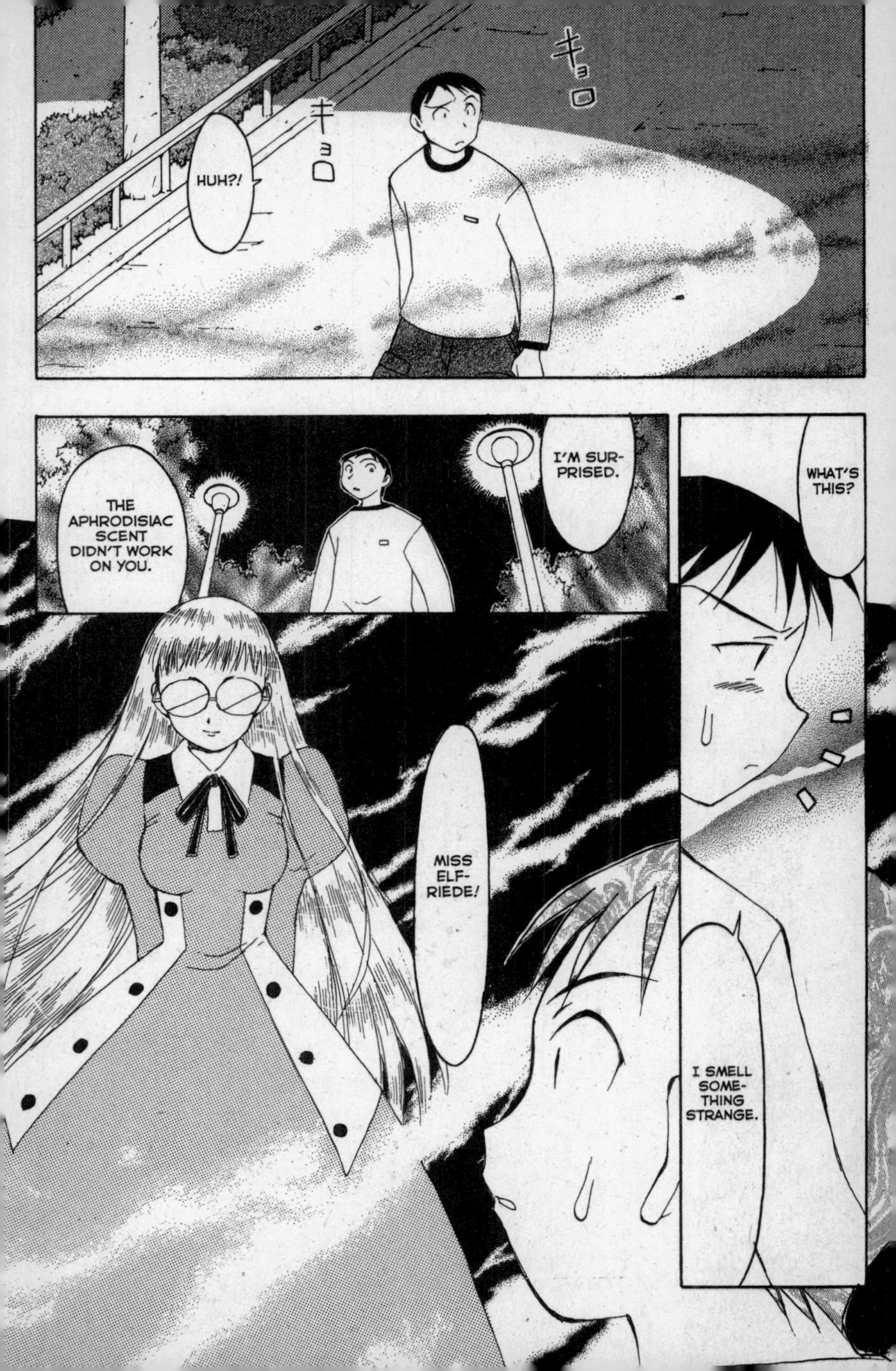
キョロ
キョロ
HUH?!
WHAT'S THIS?
I SMELL SOME-THING STRANGE.
I'M SUR-PRISED.
THE APHRODISIAC SCENT DIDN'T WORK ON YOU.
MISS ELF-RIEDE!

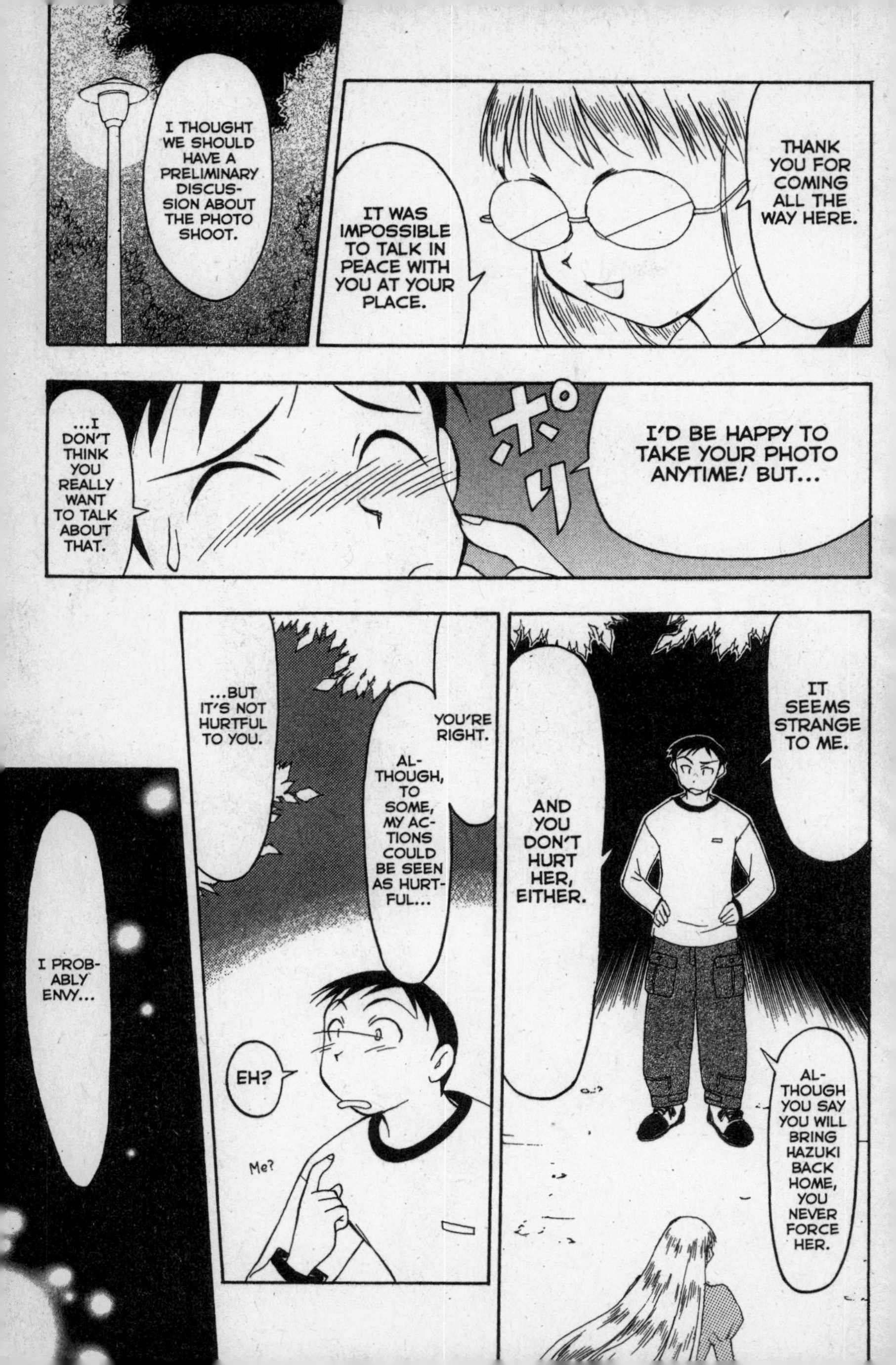
THANK YOU FOR COMING ALL THE WAY HERE.
IT WAS IMPOSSIBLE TO TALK IN PEACE WITH YOU AT YOUR PLACE.
I THOUGHT WE SHOULD HAVE A PRELIMINARY DISCUSSION ABOUT THE PHOTO SHOOT.
I'D BE HAPPY TO TAKE YOUR PHOTO ANYTIME! BUT...
...I DON'T THINK YOU REALLY WANT TO TALK ABOUT THAT.
IT SEEMS STRANGE TO ME.
ALTHOUGH YOU SAY YOU WILL BRING HAZUKI BACK HOME, YOU NEVER FORCE HER.
AND YOU DON'T HURT HER, EITHER.
YOU'RE RIGHT.
ALTHOUGH, TO SOME, MY ACTIONS COULD BE SEEN AS HURTFUL...
...BUT IT'S NOT HURTFUL TO YOU.
EH?
Me?
I PROBABLY ENVY...

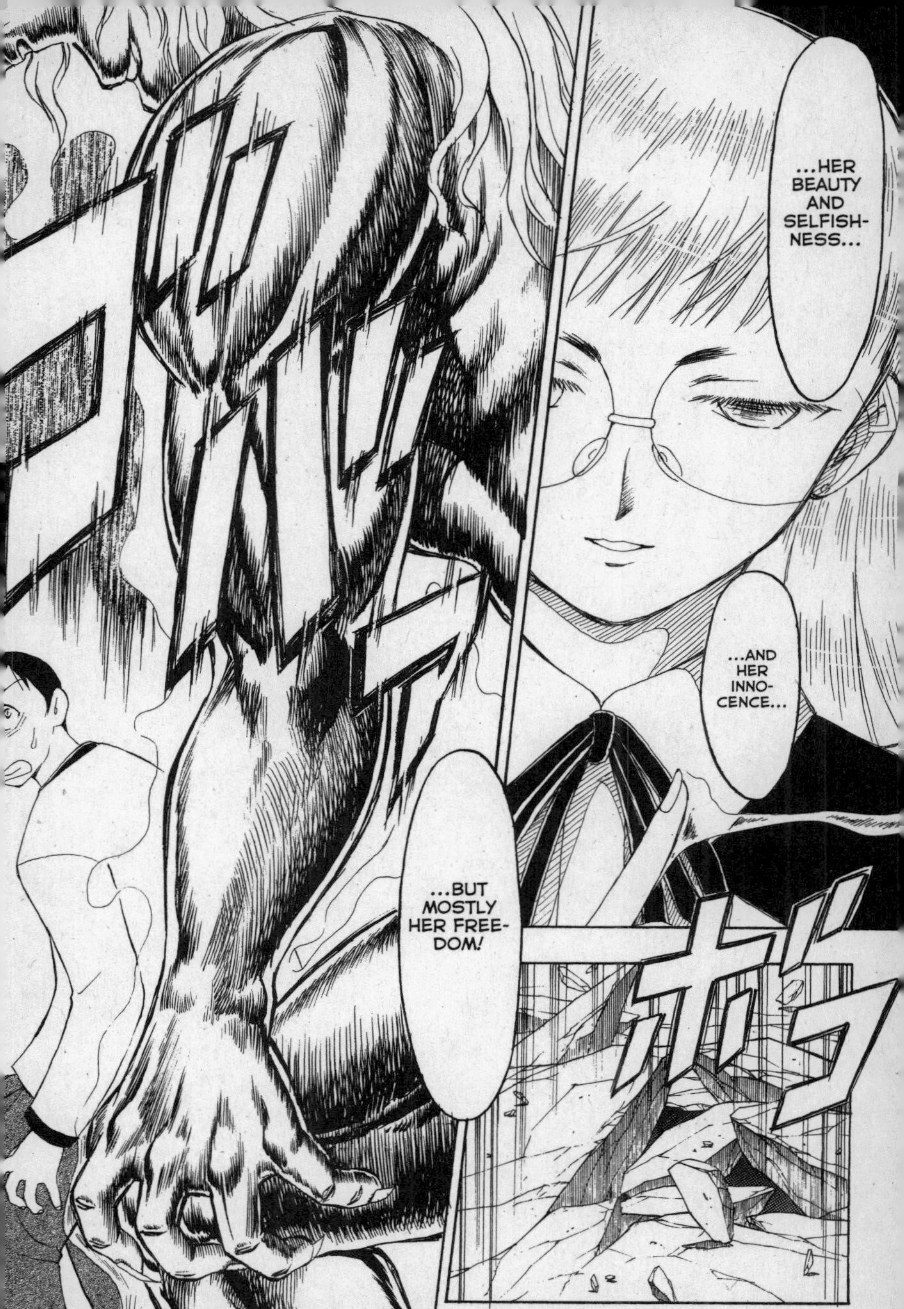
...HER BEAUTY AND SELFISHNESS...
...AND HER INNOCENCE...
...BUT MOSTLY HER FREEDOM!
← This creature may be too much...

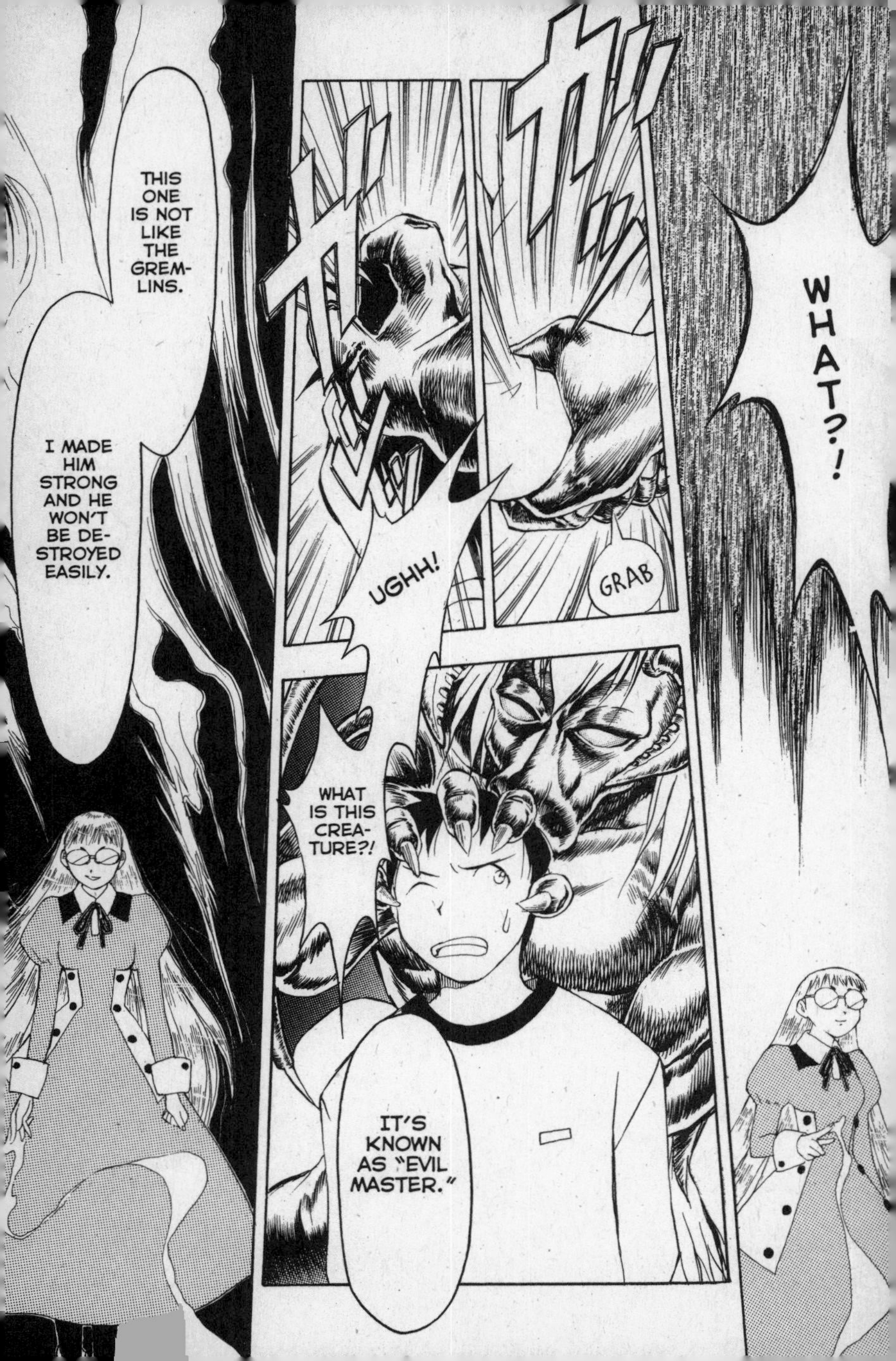
WHAT?!
GRAB
UGHH!
WHAT IS THIS CREATURE?!
IT'S KNOWN AS "EVIL MASTER."
THIS ONE IS NOT LIKE THE GREMLINS.
I MADE HIM STRONG AND HE WON'T BE DESTROYED EASILY.

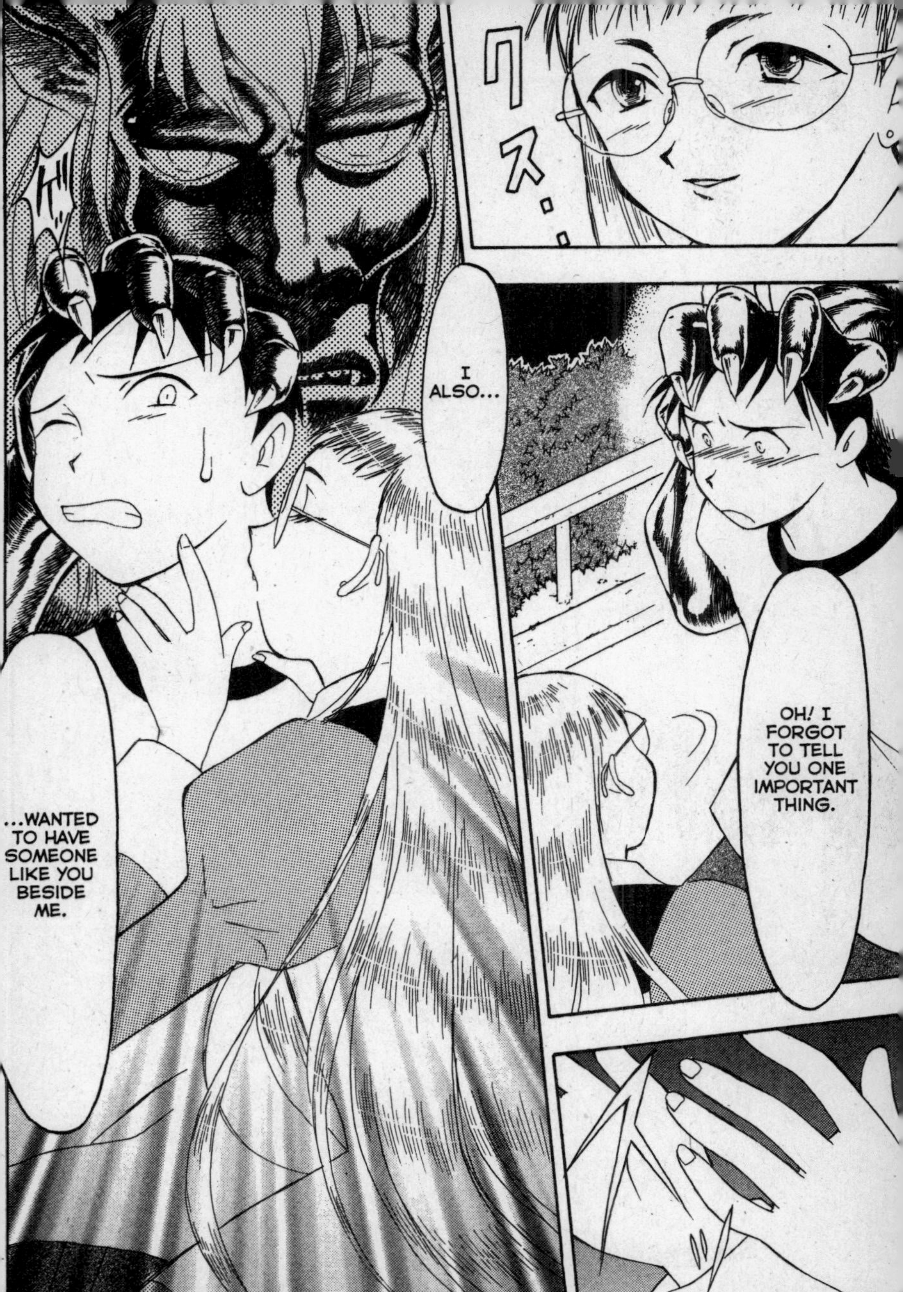
クス…
OH! I FORGOT TO TELL YOU ONE IMPORTANT THING.
I ALSO...
...WANTED TO HAVE SOMEONE LIKE YOU BESIDE ME.

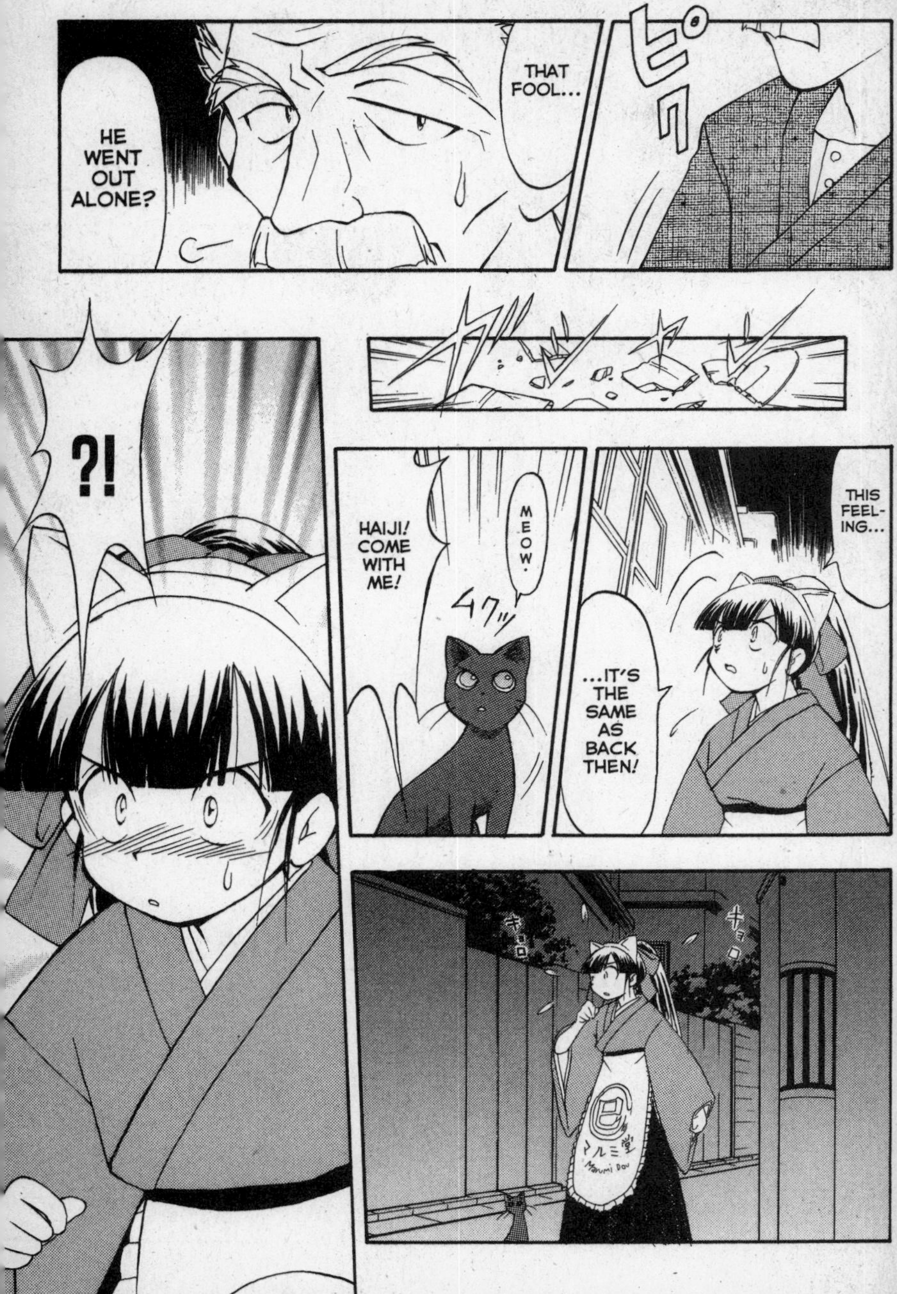
ピク
THAT FOOL...
HE WENT OUT ALONE?
THIS FEELING...
...IT'S THE SAME AS BACK THEN!
HAIJI! COME WITH ME!
MEOW.
ムクッ
キョロ
キョロ
マルミ堂
Marumi Dou
?!

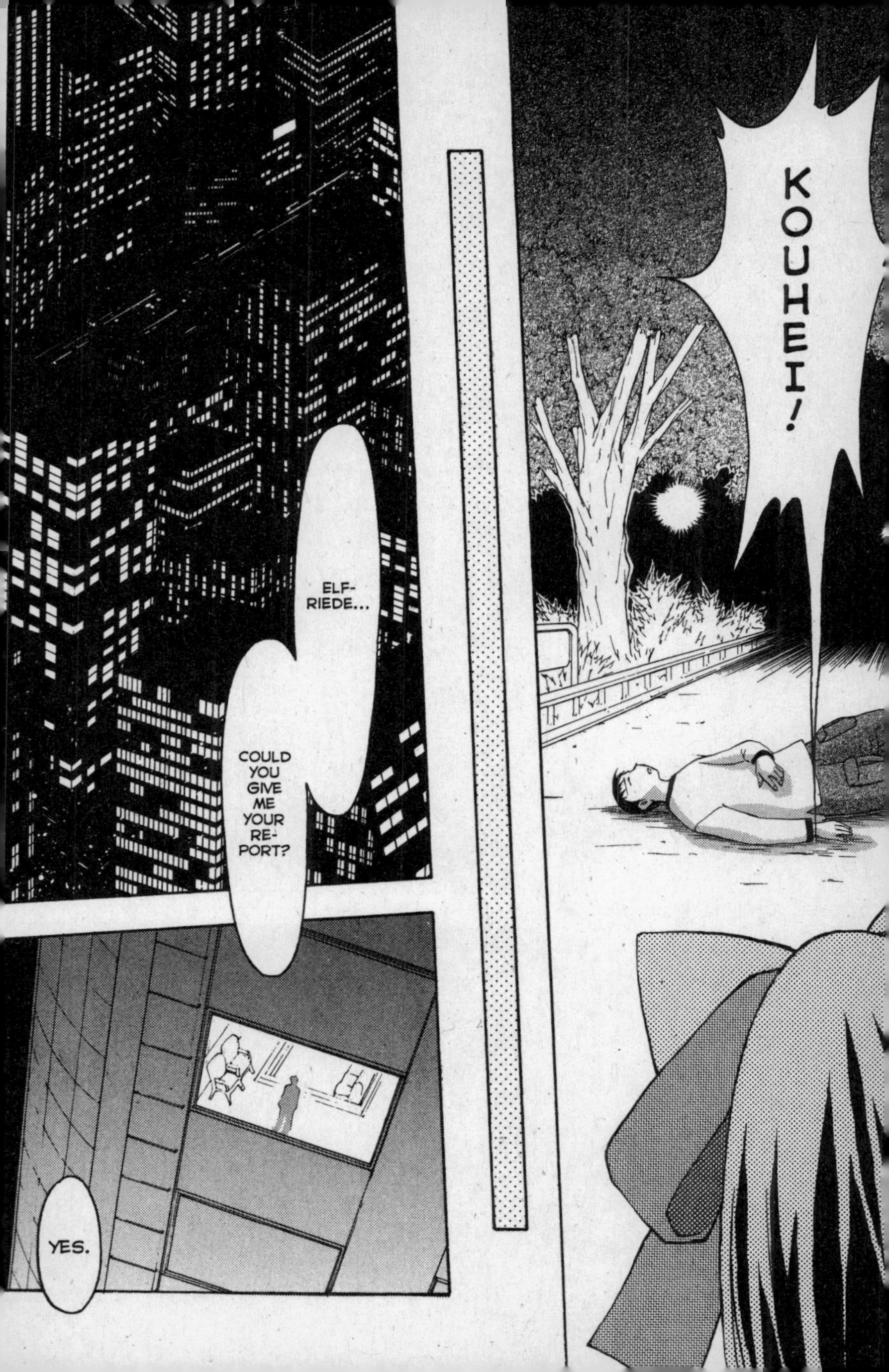
KOUHEI!
ELF-RIEDE...
COULD YOU GIVE ME YOUR RE-PORT?
YES.

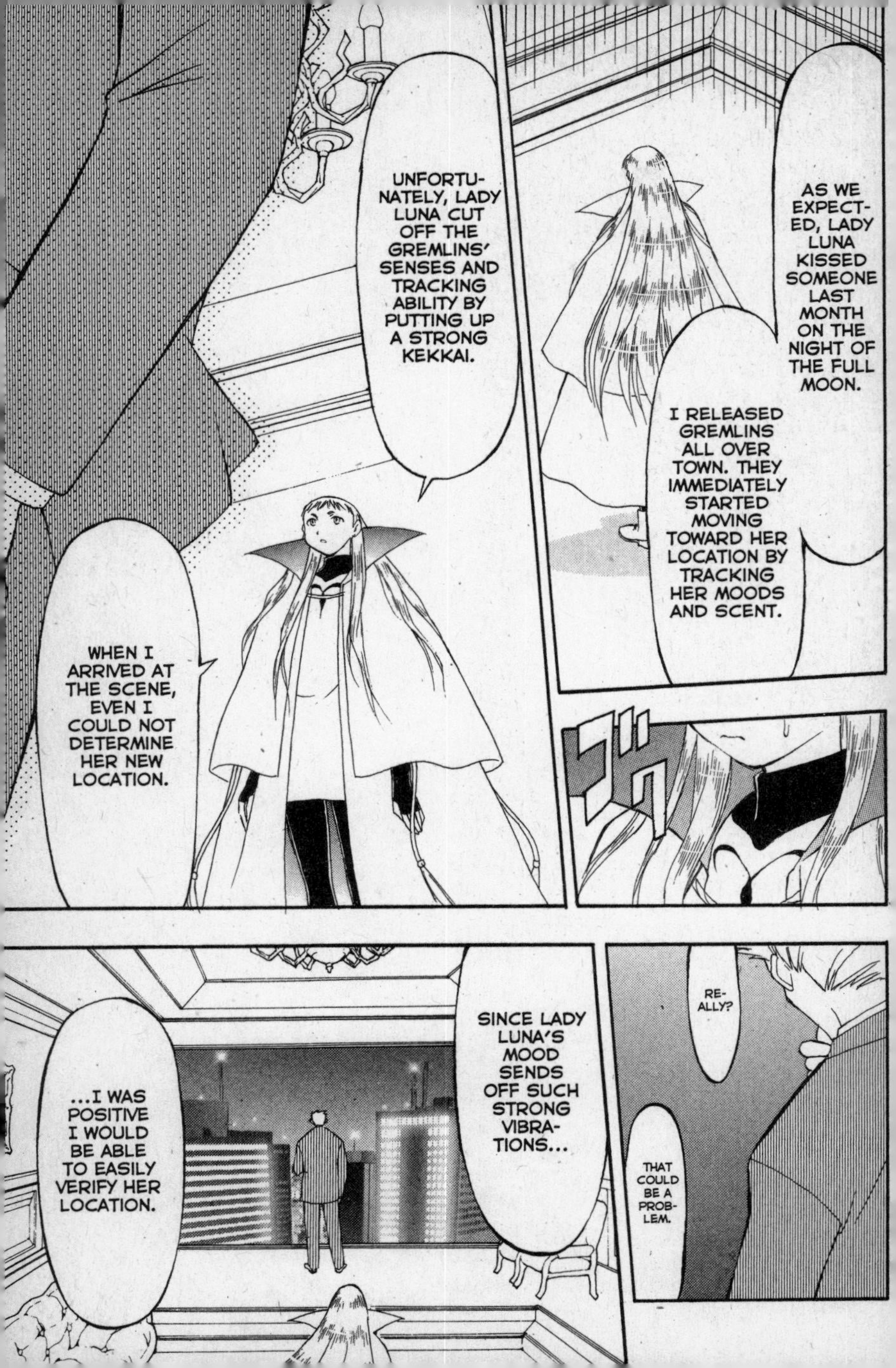
AS WE EXPECTED, LADY LUNA KISSED SOMEONE LAST MONTH ON THE NIGHT OF THE FULL MOON.
I RELEASED GREMLINS ALL OVER TOWN. THEY IMMEDIATELY STARTED MOVING TOWARD HER LOCATION BY TRACKING HER MOODS AND SCENT.
UNFORTUNATELY, LADY LUNA CUT OFF THE GREMLINS' SENSES AND TRACKING ABILITY BY PUTTING UP A STRONG KEKKAI.
WHEN I ARRIVED AT THE SCENE, EVEN I COULD NOT DETERMINE HER NEW LOCATION.
REALLY?
THAT COULD BE A PROBLEM.
SINCE LADY LUNA'S MOOD SENDS OFF SUCH STRONG VIBRATIONS...
...I WAS POSITIVE I WOULD BE ABLE TO EASILY VERIFY HER LOCATION.

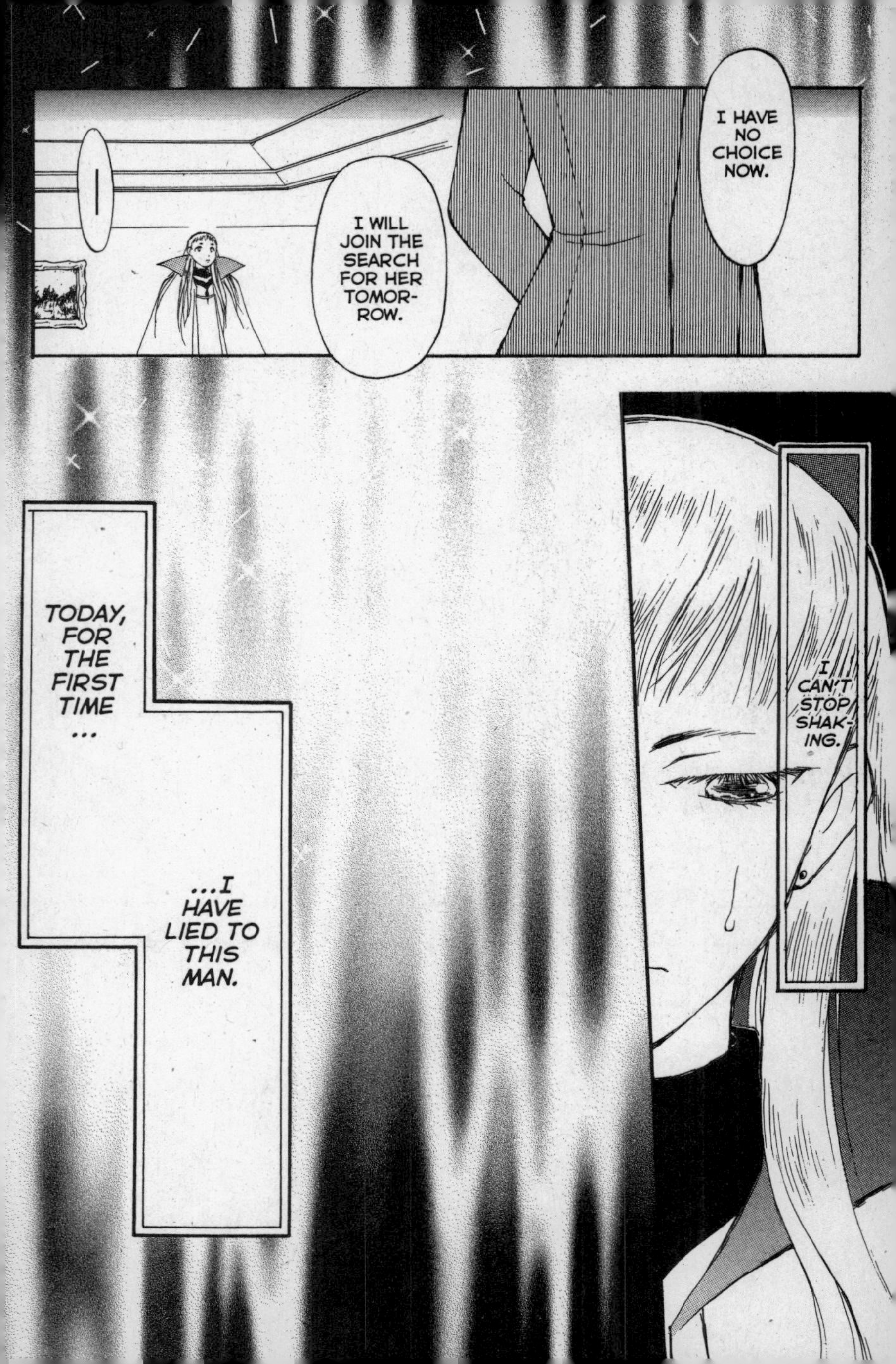
I HAVE NO CHOICE NOW.
I WILL JOIN THE SEARCH FOR HER TOMORROW.
I CAN'T STOP SHAKING.
TODAY, FOR THE FIRST TIME ...
...I HAVE LIED TO THIS MAN.

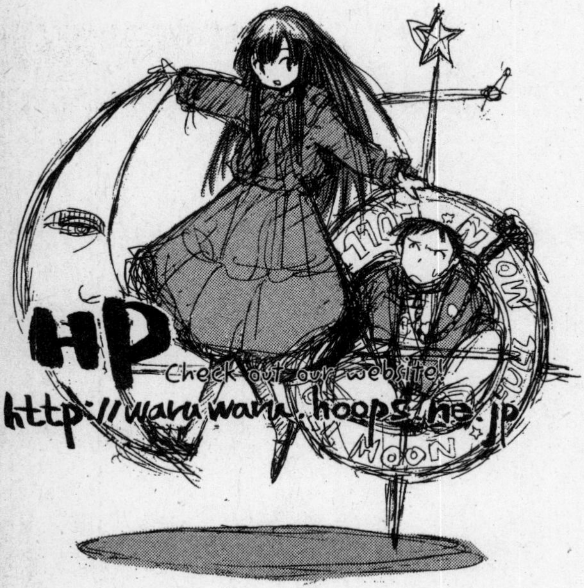
HP
Check out our website!
http://waruwaru.hoops.ne.jp
MOON

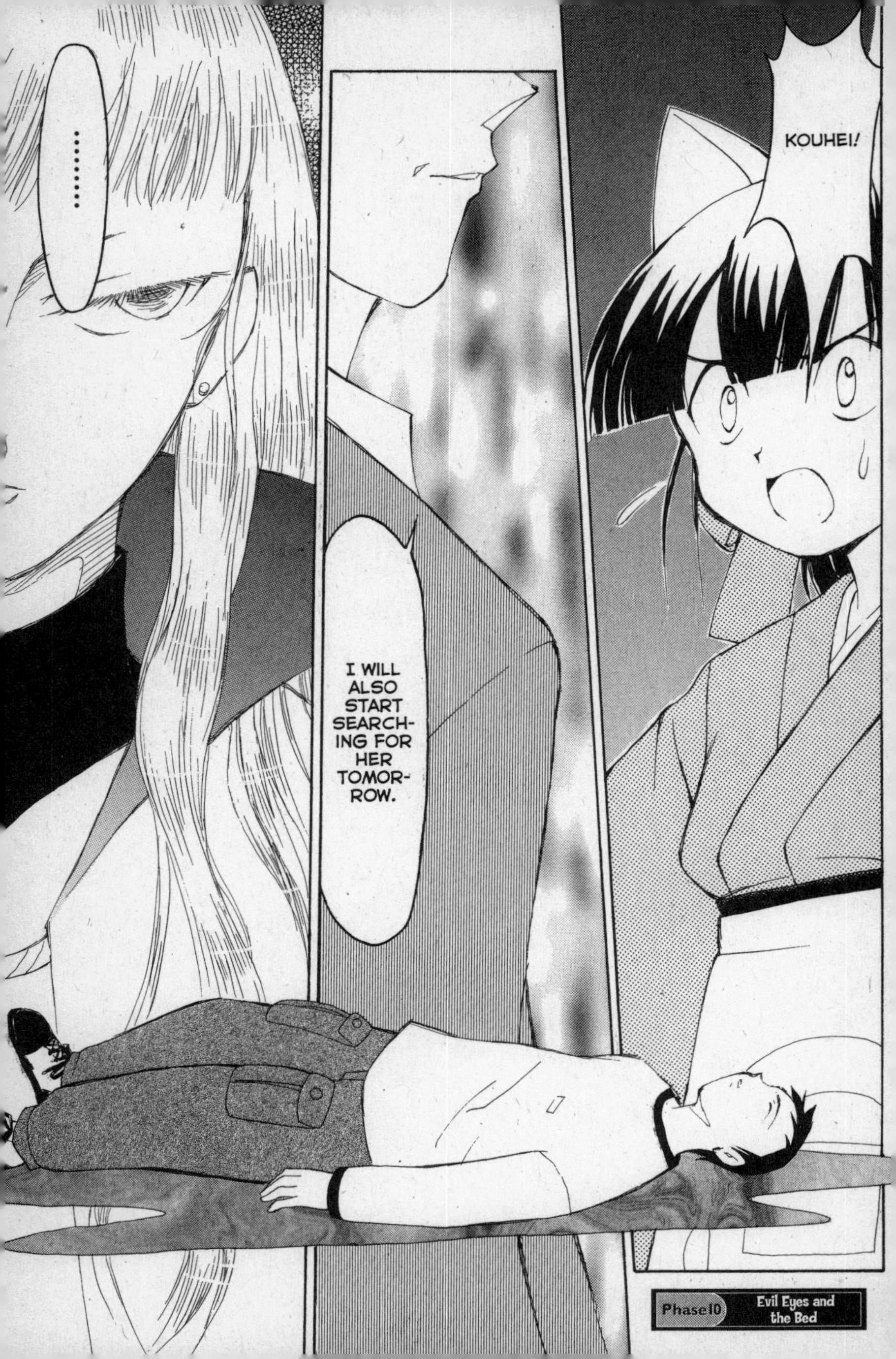
KOUHEI!
I WILL ALSO START SEARCHING FOR HER TOMORROW.
……

Phase 10 Evil Eyes and the Bed

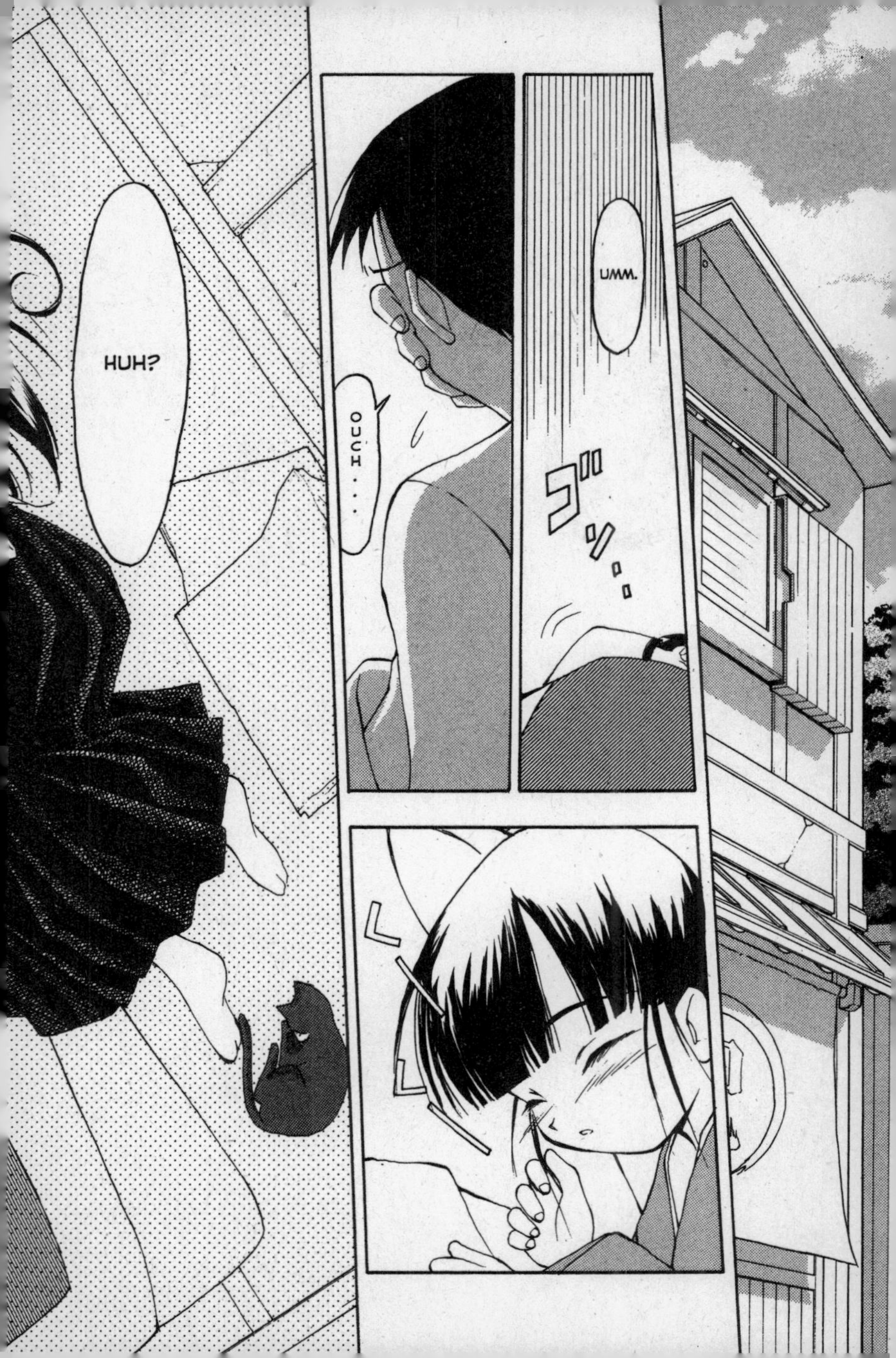
UMM.
OUCH...
HUH?

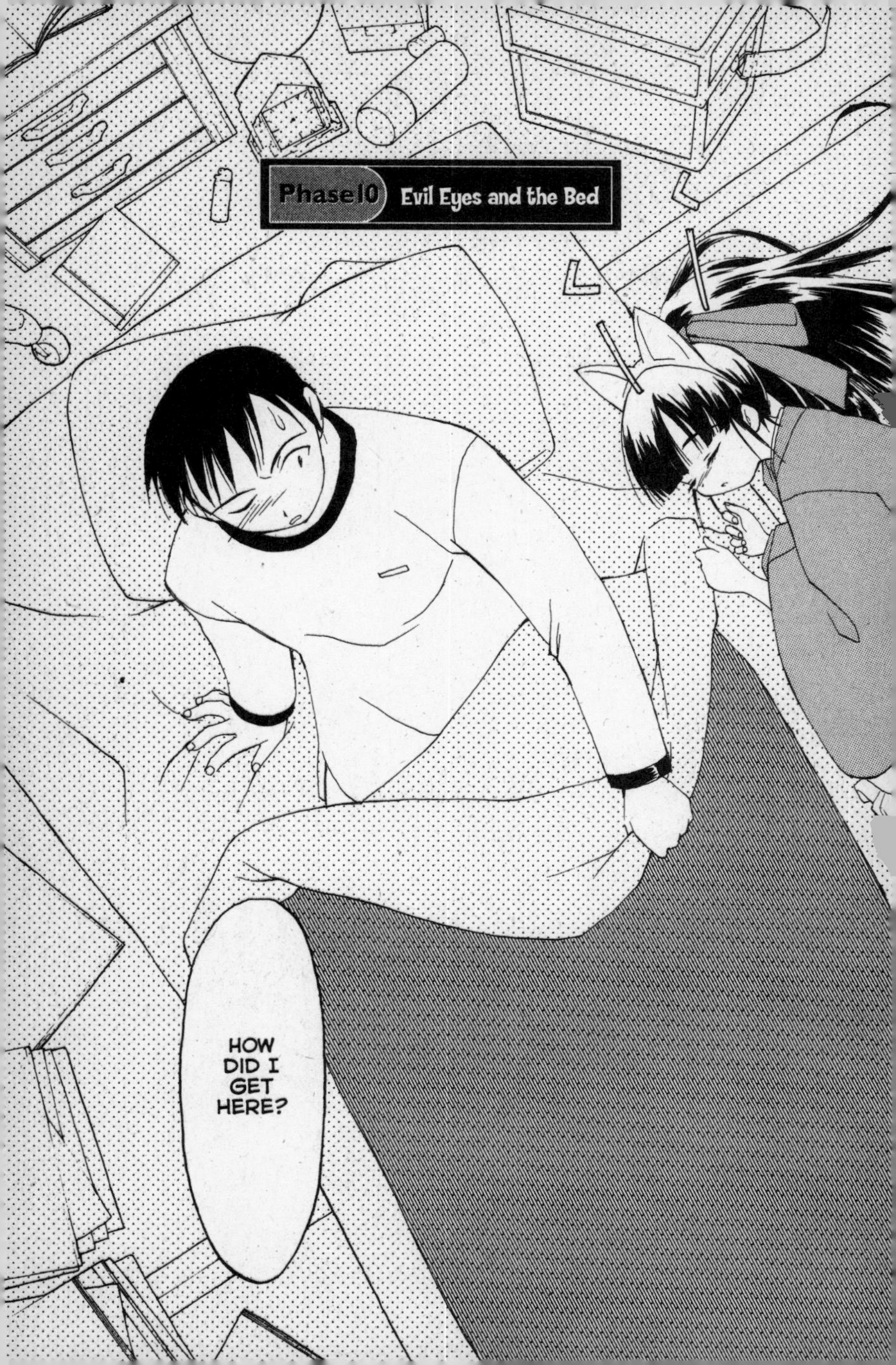
Phase 10 Evil Eyes and the Bed
HOW DID I GET HERE?

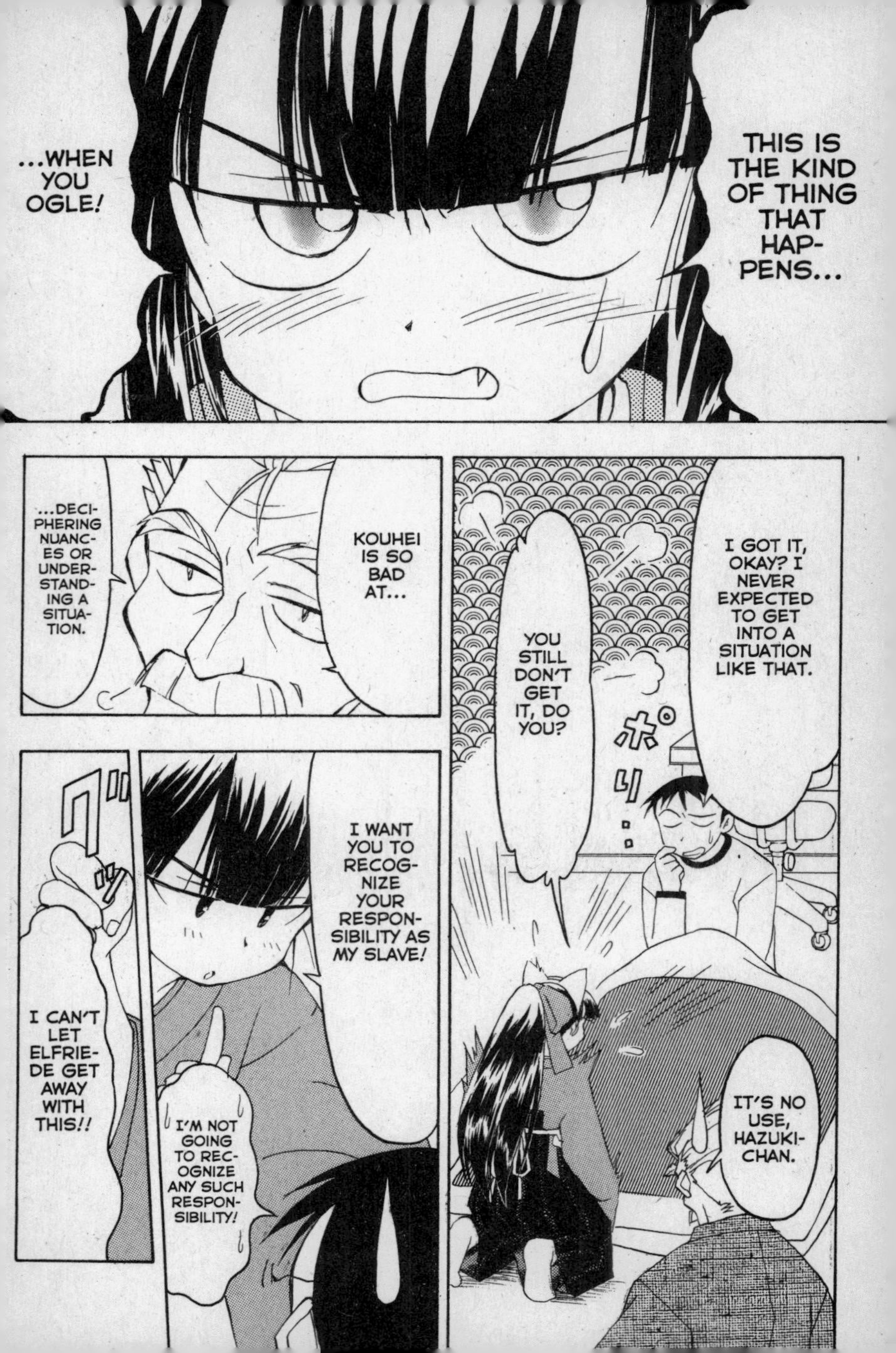
THIS IS THE KIND OF THING THAT HAP-PENS...
...WHEN YOU OGLE!
I GOT IT, OKAY? I NEVER EXPECTED TO GET INTO A SITUATION LIKE THAT.
YOU STILL DON'T GET IT, DO YOU?
ポリ
IT'S NO USE, HAZUKI-CHAN.
KOUHEI IS SO BAD AT...
...DECI-PHERING NUANC-ES OR UNDER-STAND-ING A SITUA-TION.
I WANT YOU TO RECOG-NIZE YOUR RESPON-SIBILITY AS MY SLAVE!
I'M NOT GOING TO REC-OGNIZE ANY SUCH RESPON-SIBILITY!
I CAN'T LET ELFRIE-DE GET AWAY WITH THIS!!

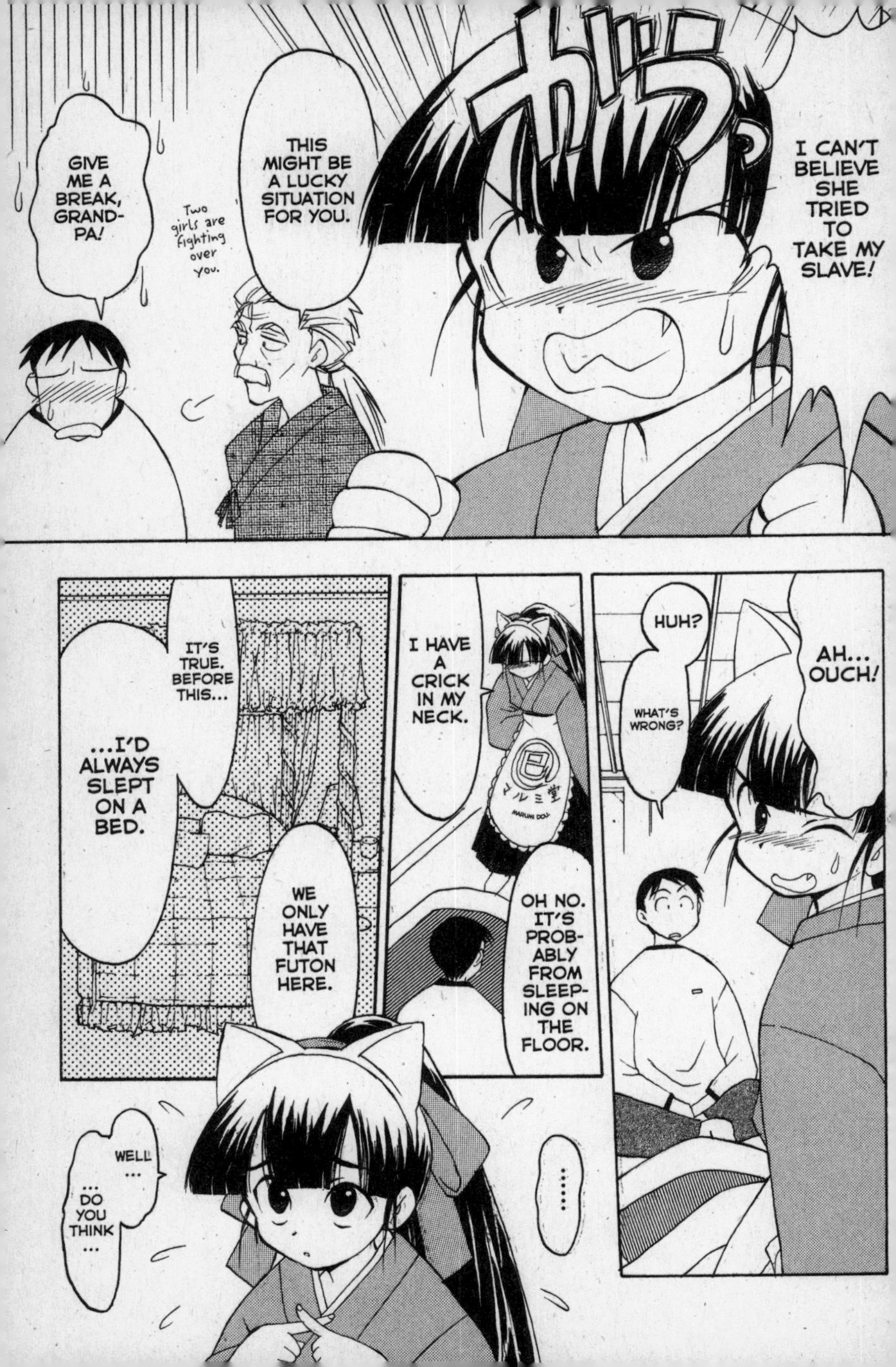
I CAN'T BELIEVE SHE TRIED TO TAKE MY SLAVE!
THIS MIGHT BE A LUCKY SITUATION FOR YOU.
Two girls are fighting over you.
GIVE ME A BREAK, GRAND-PA!
AH... OUCH!
HUH?
WHAT'S WRONG?
I HAVE A CRICK IN MY NECK.
マルミ堂
MARUMI DOU
OH NO. IT'S PROBABLY FROM SLEEPING ON THE FLOOR.
IT'S TRUE. BEFORE THIS...
...I'D ALWAYS SLEPT ON A BED.
WE ONLY HAVE THAT FUTON HERE.
......
WELL ... ... DO YOU THINK ...

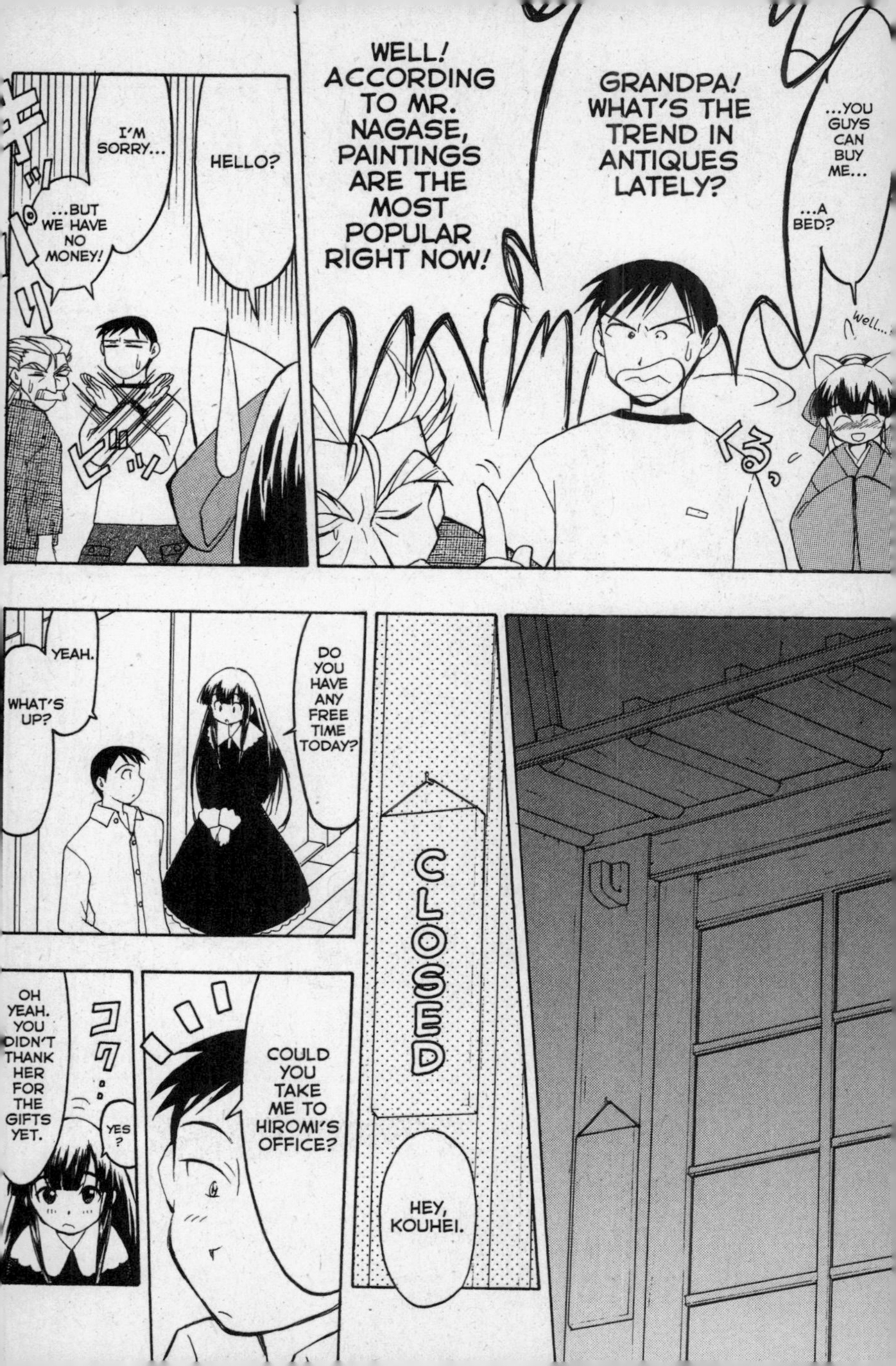

...YOU GUYS CAN BUY ME...
...A BED?
Well...
GRANDPA! WHAT'S THE TREND IN ANTIQUES LATELY?
くる
WELL! ACCORDING TO MR. NAGASE, PAINTINGS ARE THE MOST POPULAR RIGHT NOW!
HELLO?
I'M SORRY...
...BUT WE HAVE NO MONEY!
CLOSED
HEY, KOUHEI.
DO YOU HAVE ANY FREE TIME TODAY?
YEAH.
WHAT'S UP?
COULD YOU TAKE ME TO HIROMI'S OFFICE?
YES?
OH YEAH. YOU DIDN'T THANK HER FOR THE GIFTS YET.

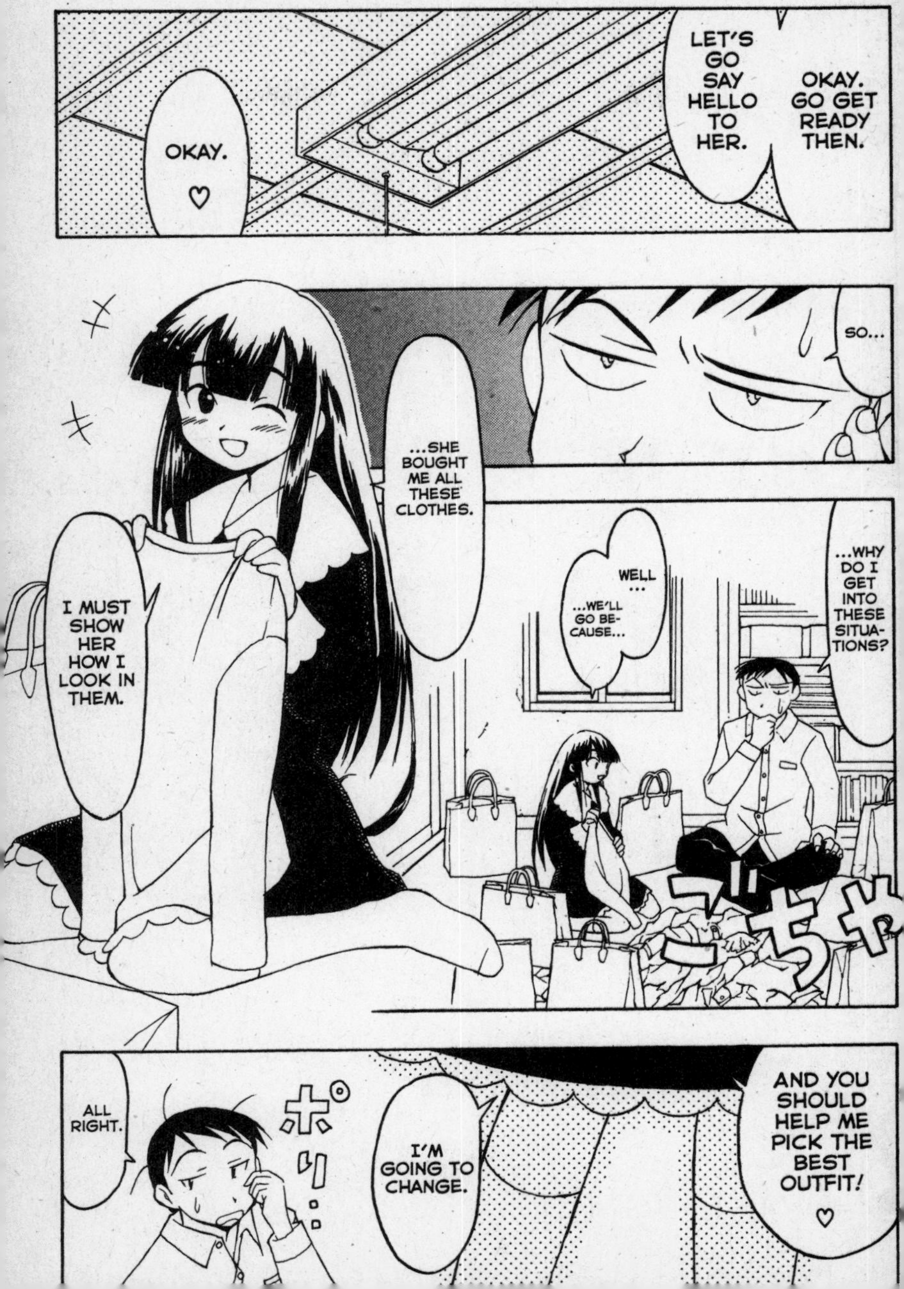
OKAY. GO GET READY THEN.
LET'S GO SAY HELLO TO HER.
OKAY. ♡
SO...
...WHY DO I GET INTO THESE SITUATIONS?
WELL ...
...WE'LL GO BE-CAUSE...
ごちゃ
...SHE BOUGHT ME ALL THESE CLOTHES.
I MUST SHOW HER HOW I LOOK IN THEM.
AND YOU SHOULD HELP ME PICK THE BEST OUTFIT! ♡
I'M GOING TO CHANGE.
ALL RIGHT.

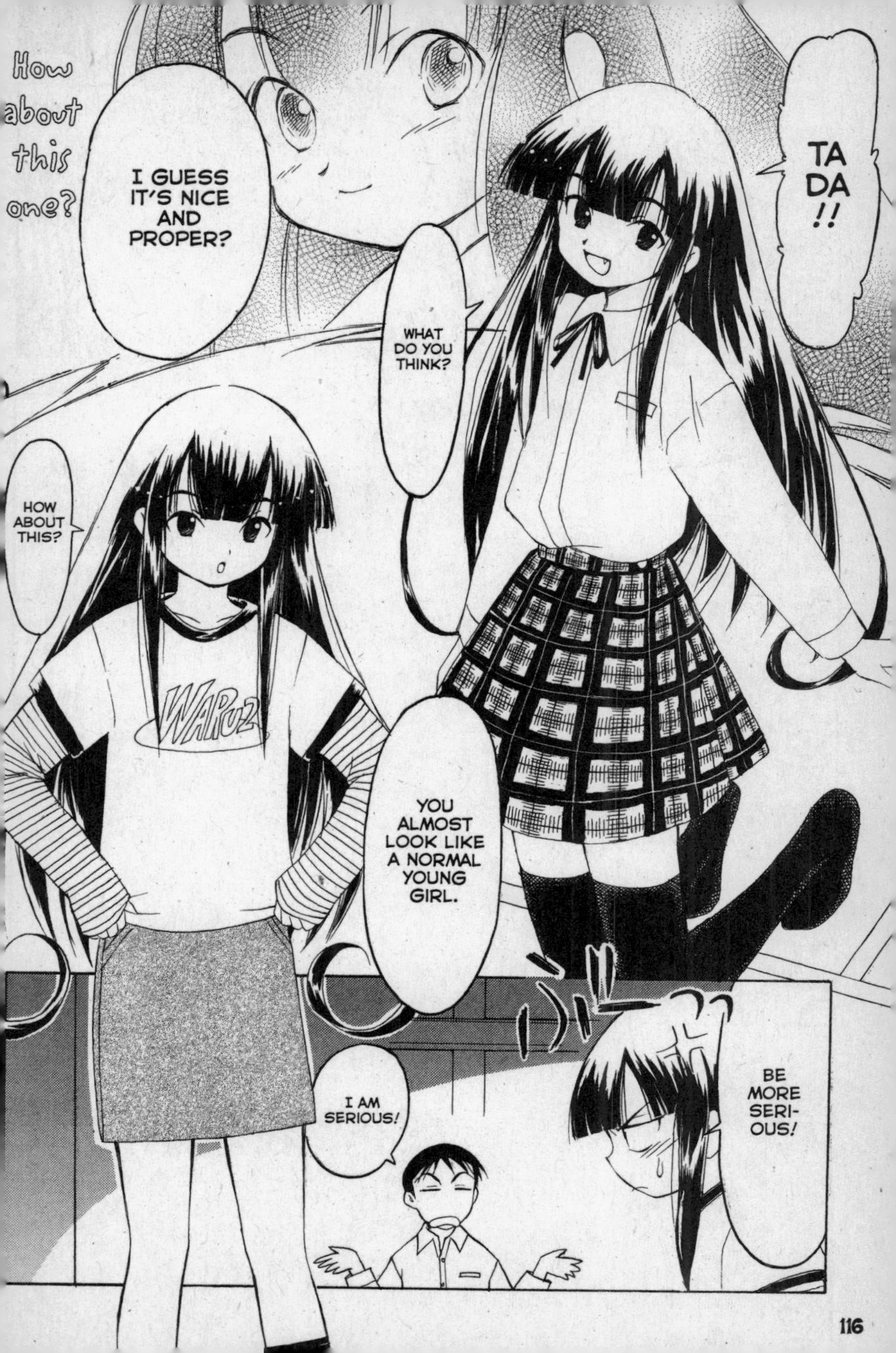
TA DA!!
WHAT DO YOU THINK?
I GUESS IT'S NICE AND PROPER?
How about this one?
HOW ABOUT THIS?
YOU ALMOST LOOK LIKE A NORMAL YOUNG GIRL.
BE MORE SERI-OUS!
I AM SERIOUS!

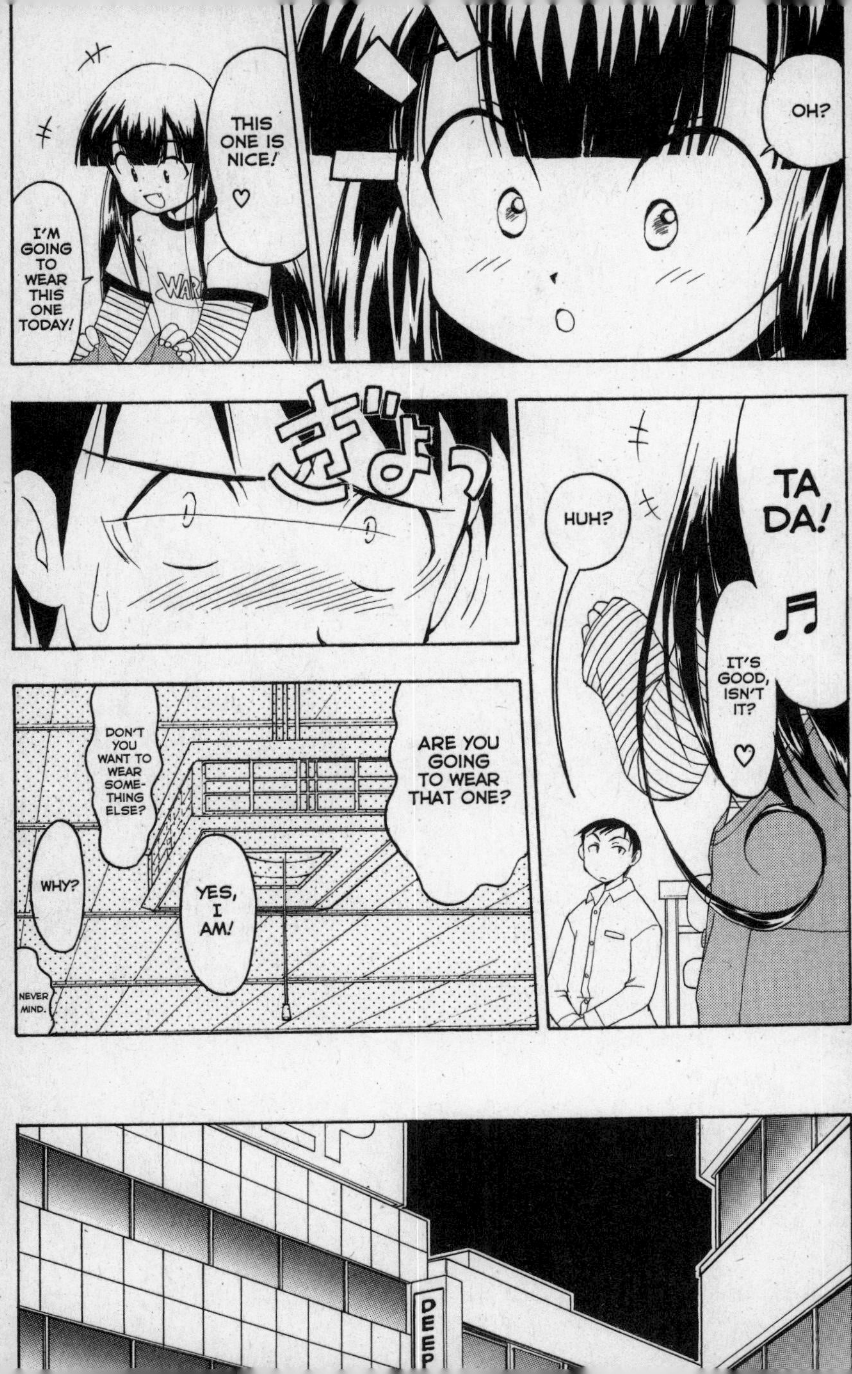
OH?
THIS ONE IS NICE! ♡
I'M GOING TO WEAR THIS ONE TODAY!
TA DA!
IT'S GOOD, ISN'T IT? ♡
HUH?
ぎょっ
ARE YOU GOING TO WEAR THAT ONE?
YES, I AM!
DON'T YOU WANT TO WEAR SOME-THING ELSE?
WHY?
NEVER MIND.
DEEP

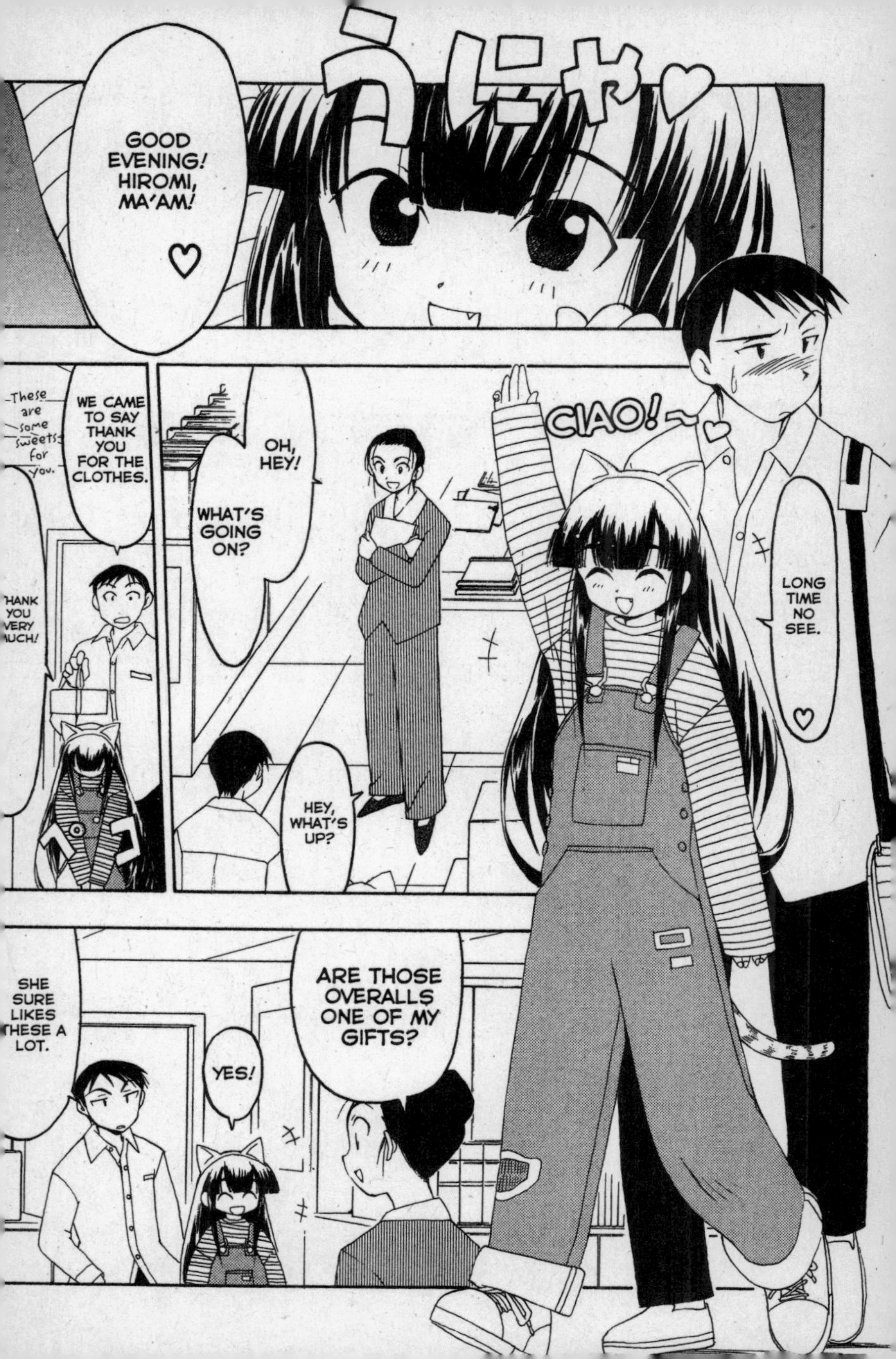
うにゃ♡
GOOD EVENING! HIROMI, MA'AM! ♡
CIAO!~♡
LONG TIME NO SEE. ♡
OH, HEY!
WHAT'S GOING ON?
HEY, WHAT'S UP?
WE CAME TO SAY THANK YOU FOR THE CLOTHES.
These are some sweets for you.
HANK YOU VERY UCH!
ARE THOSE OVERALLS ONE OF MY GIFTS?
YES!
SHE SURE LIKES HESE A LOT.

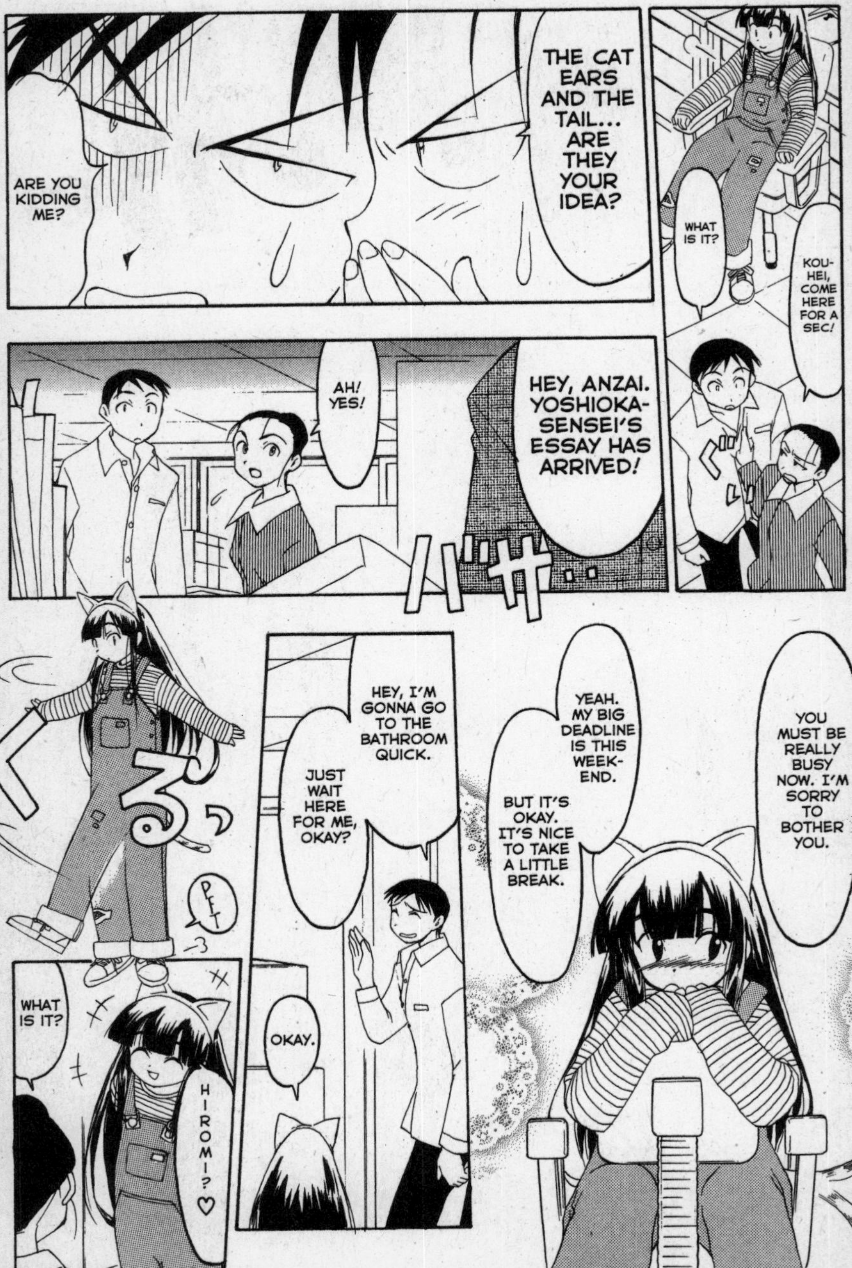
KOU-HEI, COME HERE FOR A SEC!
WHAT IS IT?
THE CAT EARS AND THE TAIL... ARE THEY YOUR IDEA?
ARE YOU KIDDING ME?
HEY, ANZAI. YOSHIOKA-SENSEI'S ESSAY HAS ARRIVED!
AH! YES!
バッ..
YOU MUST BE REALLY BUSY NOW. I'M SORRY TO BOTHER YOU.
YEAH. MY BIG DEADLINE IS THIS WEEKEND.
BUT IT'S OKAY. IT'S NICE TO TAKE A LITTLE BREAK.
HEY, I'M GONNA GO TO THE BATHROOM QUICK.
JUST WAIT HERE FOR ME, OKAY?
OKAY.
PET
HIROMI?♡
WHAT IS IT?

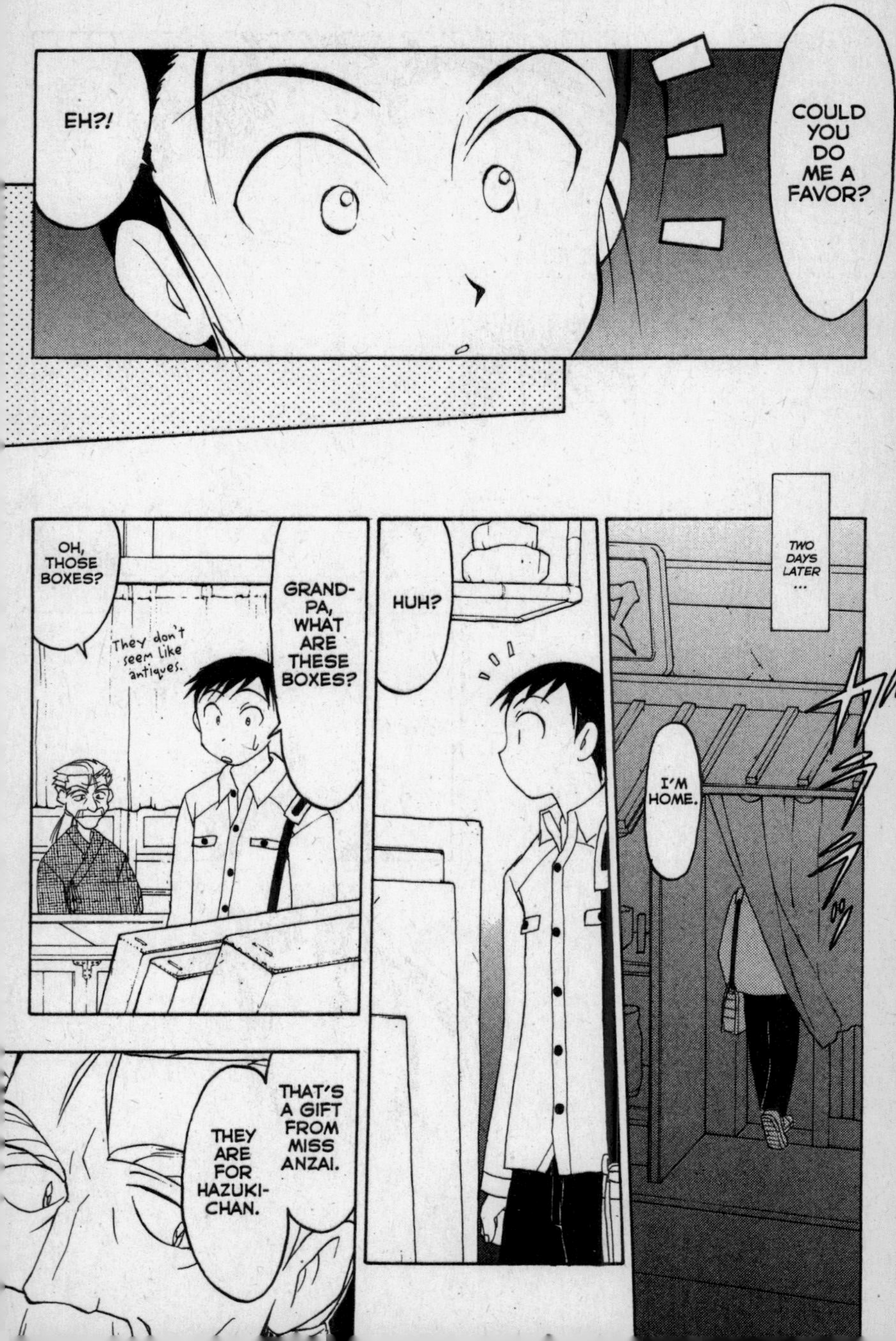
COULD YOU DO ME A FAVOR?
EH?!
TWO DAYS LATER...
I'M HOME.
HUH?
GRANDPA, WHAT ARE THESE BOXES?
OH, THOSE BOXES?
They don't seem like antiques.
THAT'S A GIFT FROM MISS ANZAI.
THEY ARE FOR HAZUKI-CHAN.

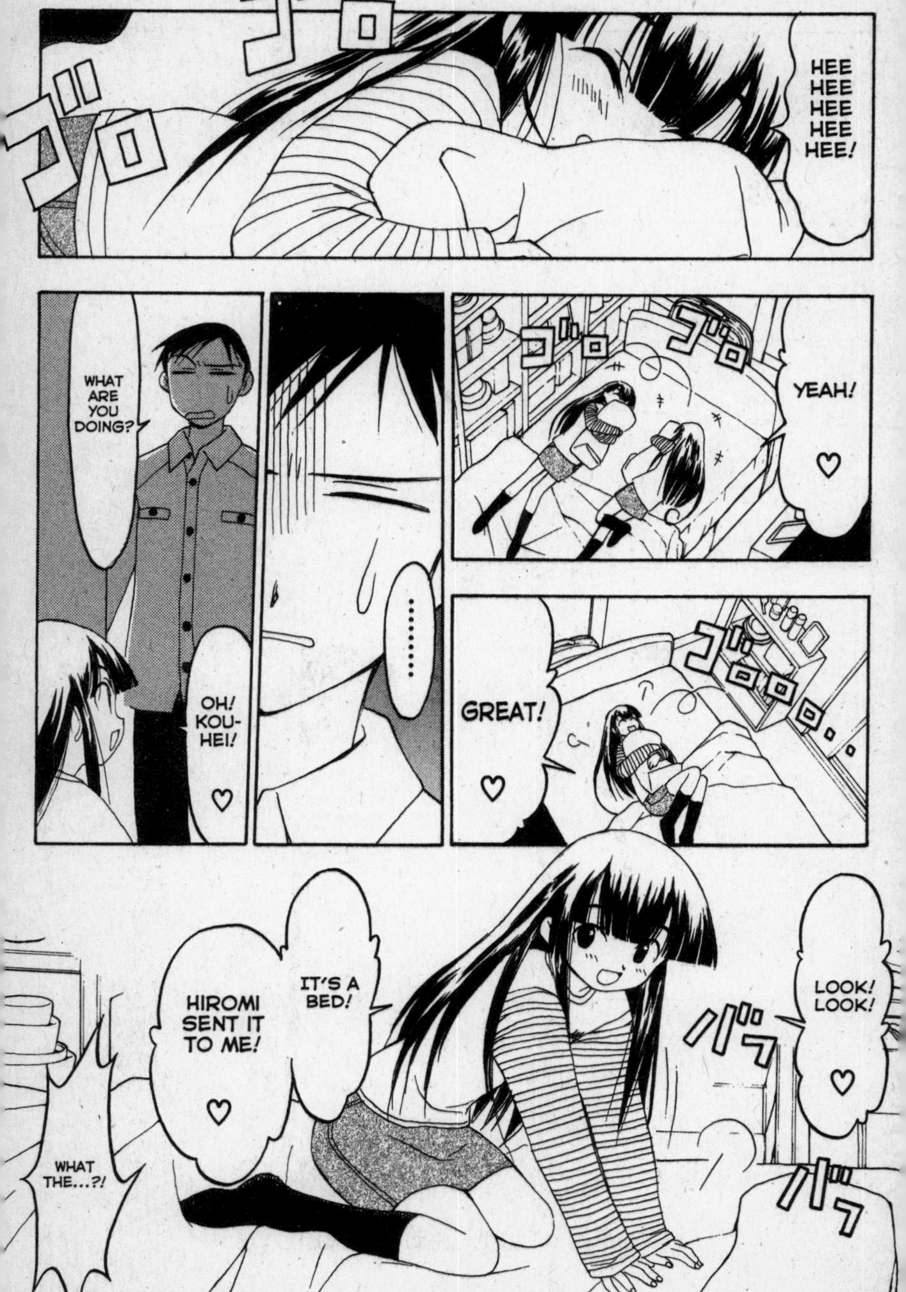

HEE HEE HEE HEE HEE!
ゴロ
ゴロ
YEAH! ♡
ゴロ
ゴロ
GREAT! ♡
ゴロロロロ。。
......
WHAT ARE YOU DOING?
OH! KOU-HEI! ♡
LOOK! LOOK! ♡
バフ
バフ
IT'S A BED!
HIROMI SENT IT TO ME! ♡
WHAT THE...?!

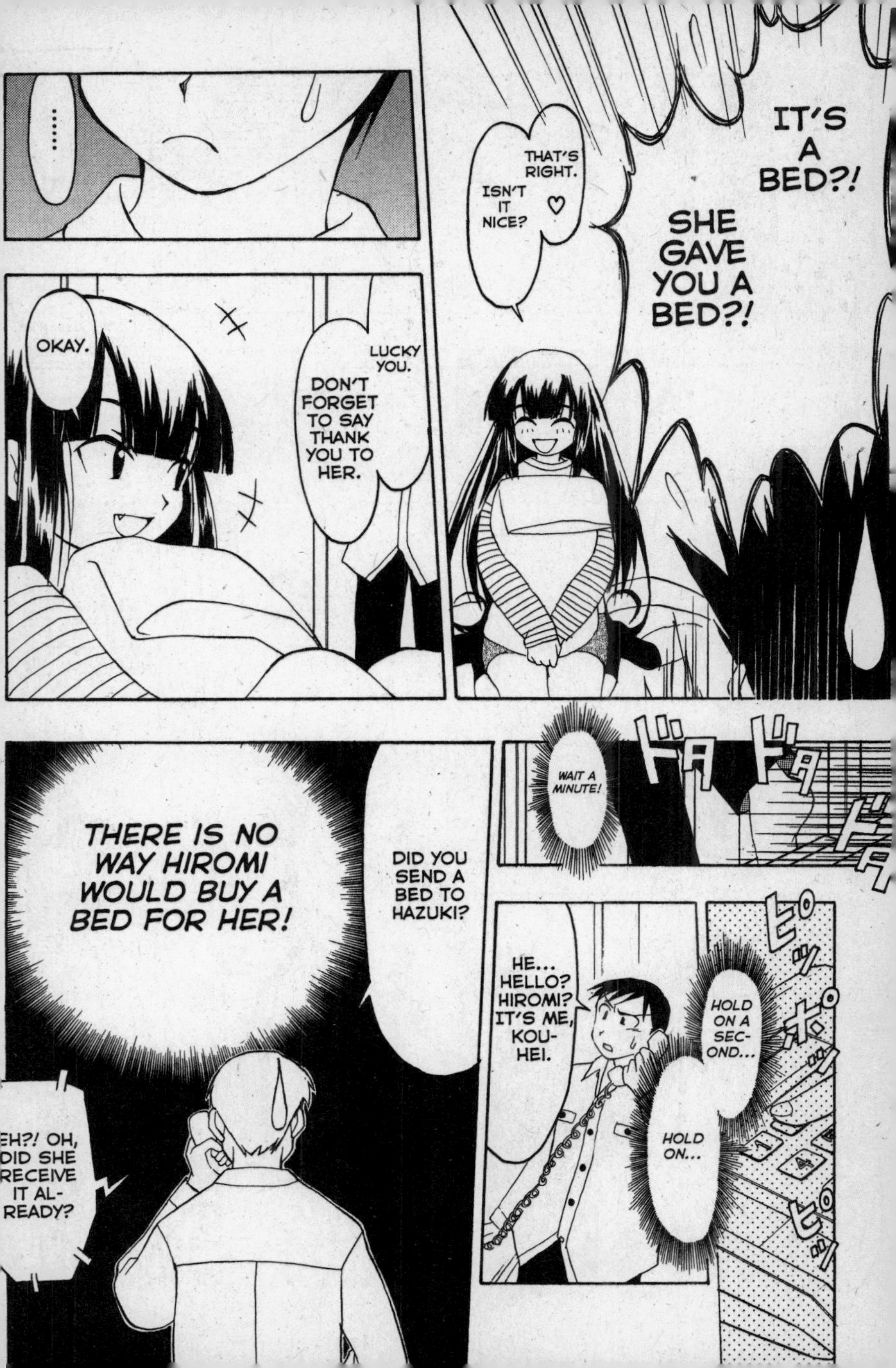

IT'S A BED?!
SHE GAVE YOU A BED?!
THAT'S RIGHT. ISN'T IT NICE? ♡
......
LUCKY YOU.
DON'T FORGET TO SAY THANK YOU TO HER.
OKAY.
ドタ ドタ ドタ
WAIT A MINUTE!
HOLD ON A SECOND...
HOLD ON...
HE... HELLO? HIROMI? IT'S ME, KOU-HEI.
DID YOU SEND A BED TO HAZUKI?
THERE IS NO WAY HIROMI WOULD BUY A BED FOR HER!
EH?! OH, DID SHE RECEIVE IT AL-READY?

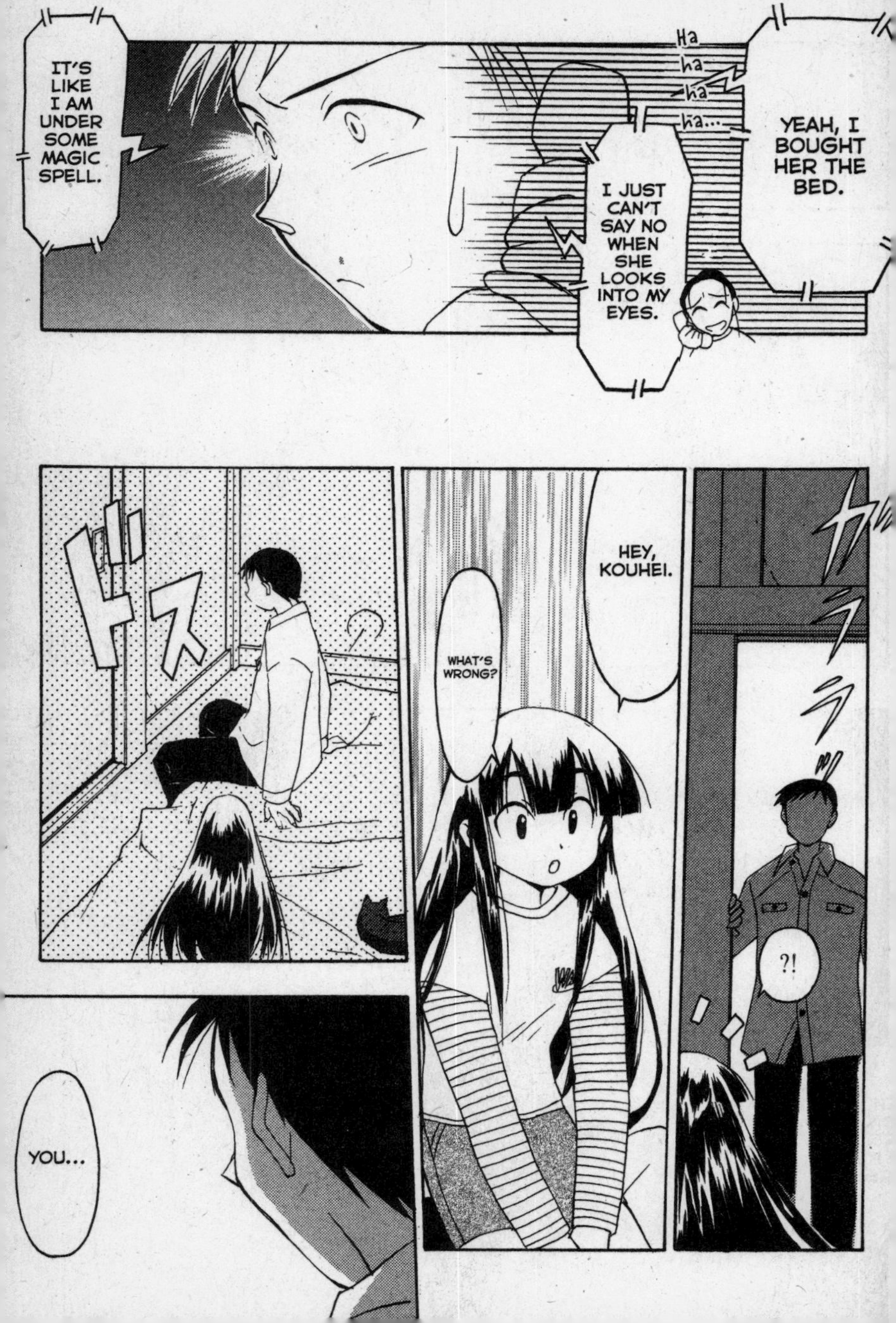
YEAH, I BOUGHT HER THE BED.
Ha ha ha ha...
I JUST CAN'T SAY NO WHEN SHE LOOKS INTO MY EYES.
IT'S LIKE I AM UNDER SOME MAGIC SPELL.
ガララ
?!
HEY, KOUHEI.
WHAT'S WRONG?
ドス
YOU...

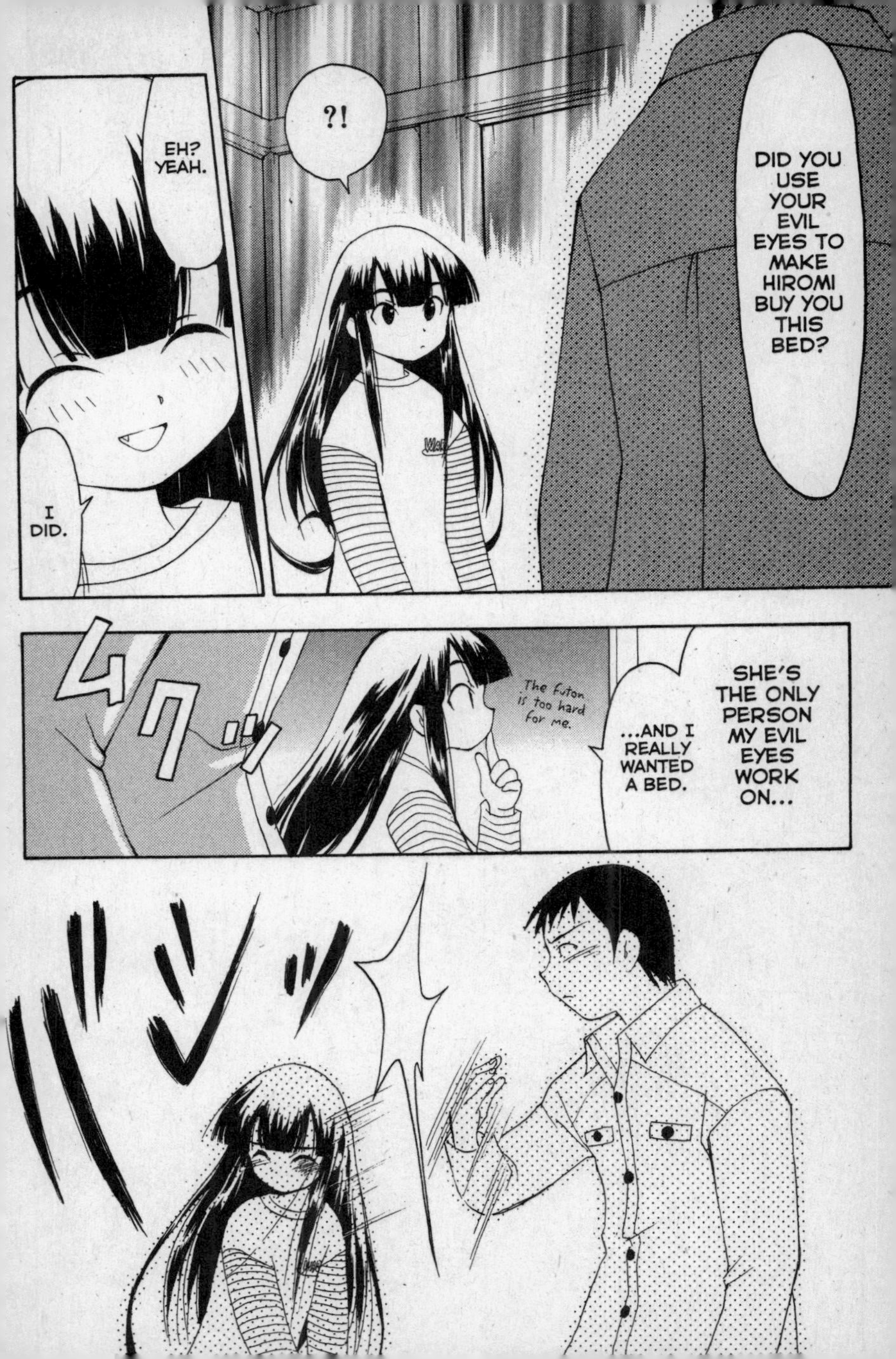
DID YOU USE YOUR EVIL EYES TO MAKE HIROMI BUY YOU THIS BED?
?!
EH? YEAH.
I DID.
SHE'S THE ONLY PERSON MY EVIL EYES WORK ON...
...AND I REALLY WANTED A BED.
The futon is too hard for me.
ムクッ

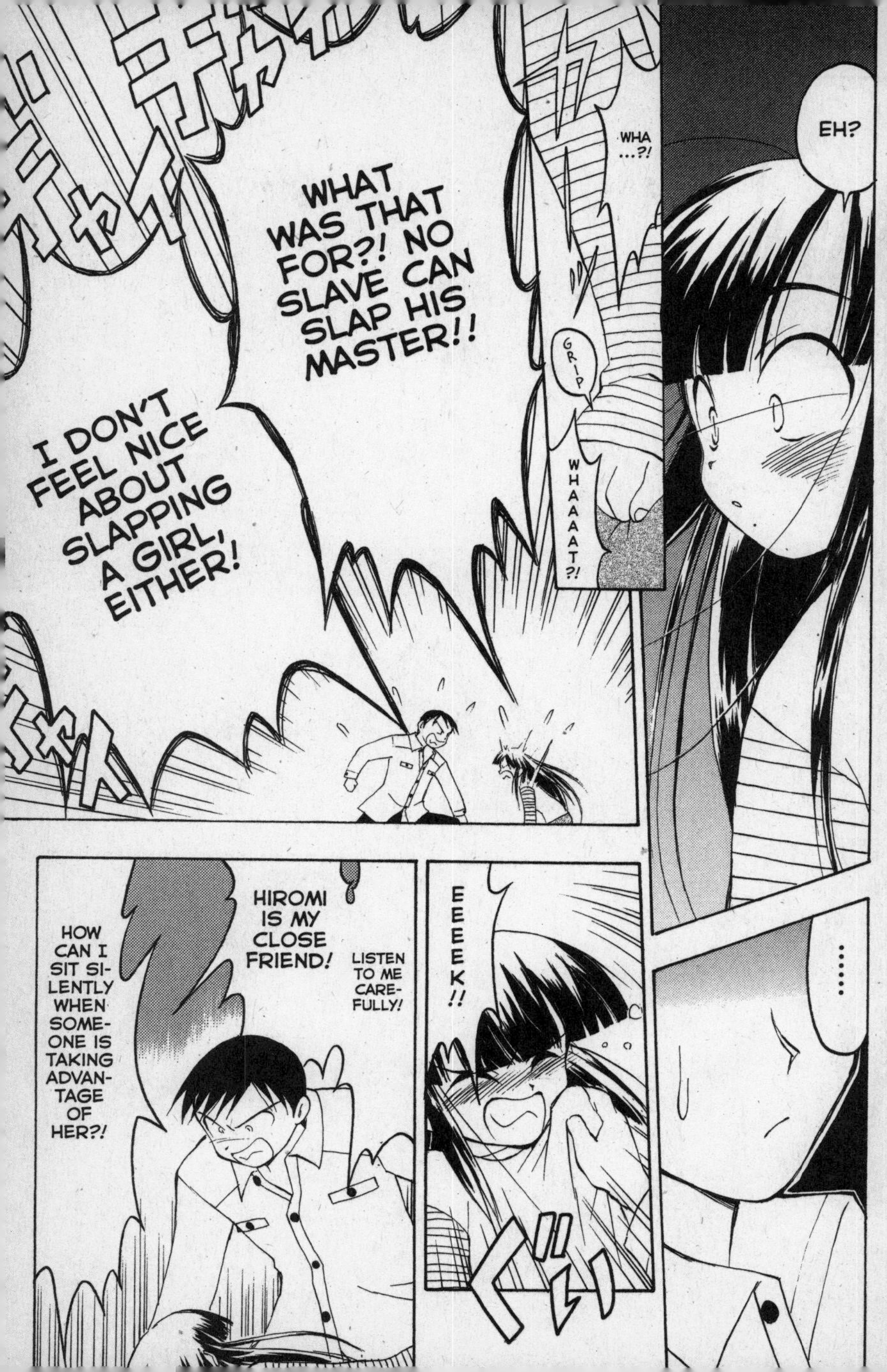
EH?
WHA ...?!
GRIP
WHAAAAAT?!
WHAT WAS THAT FOR?! NO SLAVE CAN SLAP HIS MASTER!!
I DON'T FEEL NICE ABOUT SLAPPING A GIRL, EITHER!
......
EEEEK!!
HIROMI IS MY CLOSE FRIEND!
LISTEN TO ME CARE-FULLY!
HOW CAN I SIT SI-LENTLY WHEN SOME-ONE IS TAKING ADVAN-TAGE OF HER?!

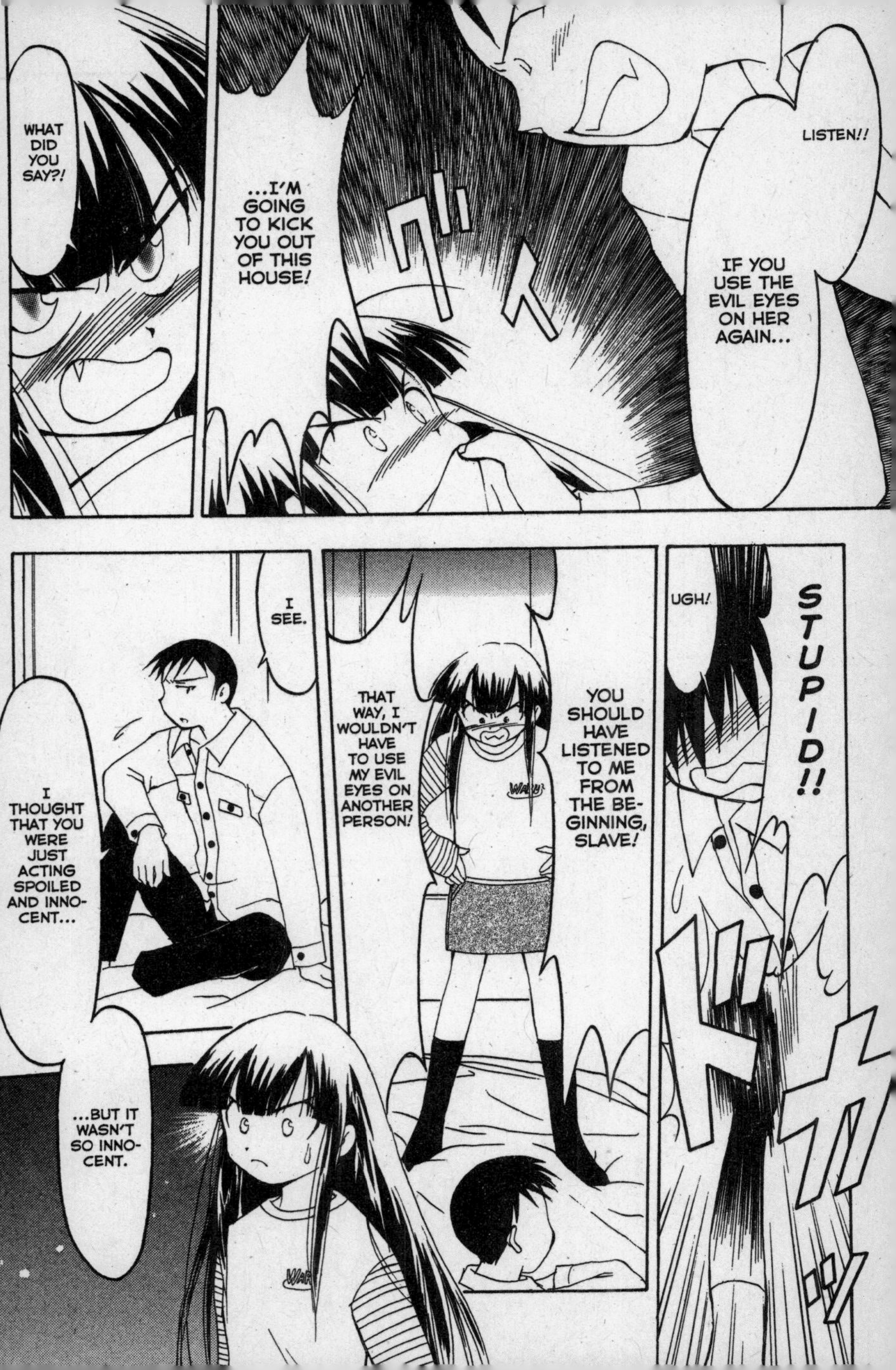
LISTEN!!
IF YOU USE THE EVIL EYES ON HER AGAIN...
...I'M GOING TO KICK YOU OUT OF THIS HOUSE!
WHAT DID YOU SAY?!
STUPID!!
UGH!
YOU SHOULD HAVE LISTENED TO ME FROM THE BE-GINNING, SLAVE!
THAT WAY, I WOULDN'T HAVE TO USE MY EVIL EYES ON ANOTHER PERSON!
I SEE.
I THOUGHT THAT YOU WERE JUST ACTING SPOILED AND INNO-CENT...
...BUT IT WASN'T SO INNO-CENT.

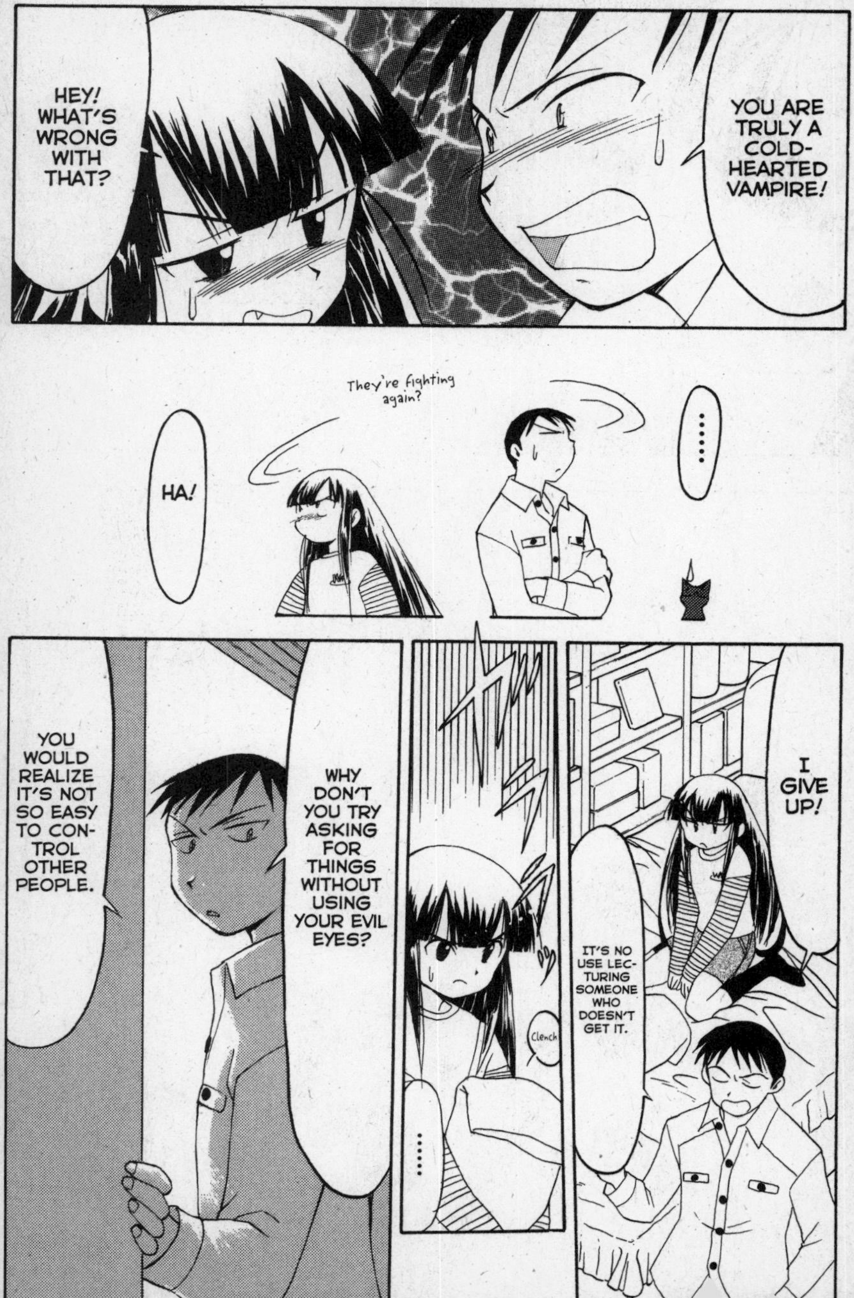
YOU ARE TRULY A COLD-HEARTED VAMPIRE!
HEY! WHAT'S WRONG WITH THAT?
......
They're fighting again?
HA!
I GIVE UP!
IT'S NO USE LECTURING SOMEONE WHO DOESN'T GET IT.
Clench
......
WHY DON'T YOU TRY ASKING FOR THINGS WITHOUT USING YOUR EVIL EYES?
YOU WOULD REALIZE IT'S NOT SO EASY TO CONTROL OTHER PEOPLE.

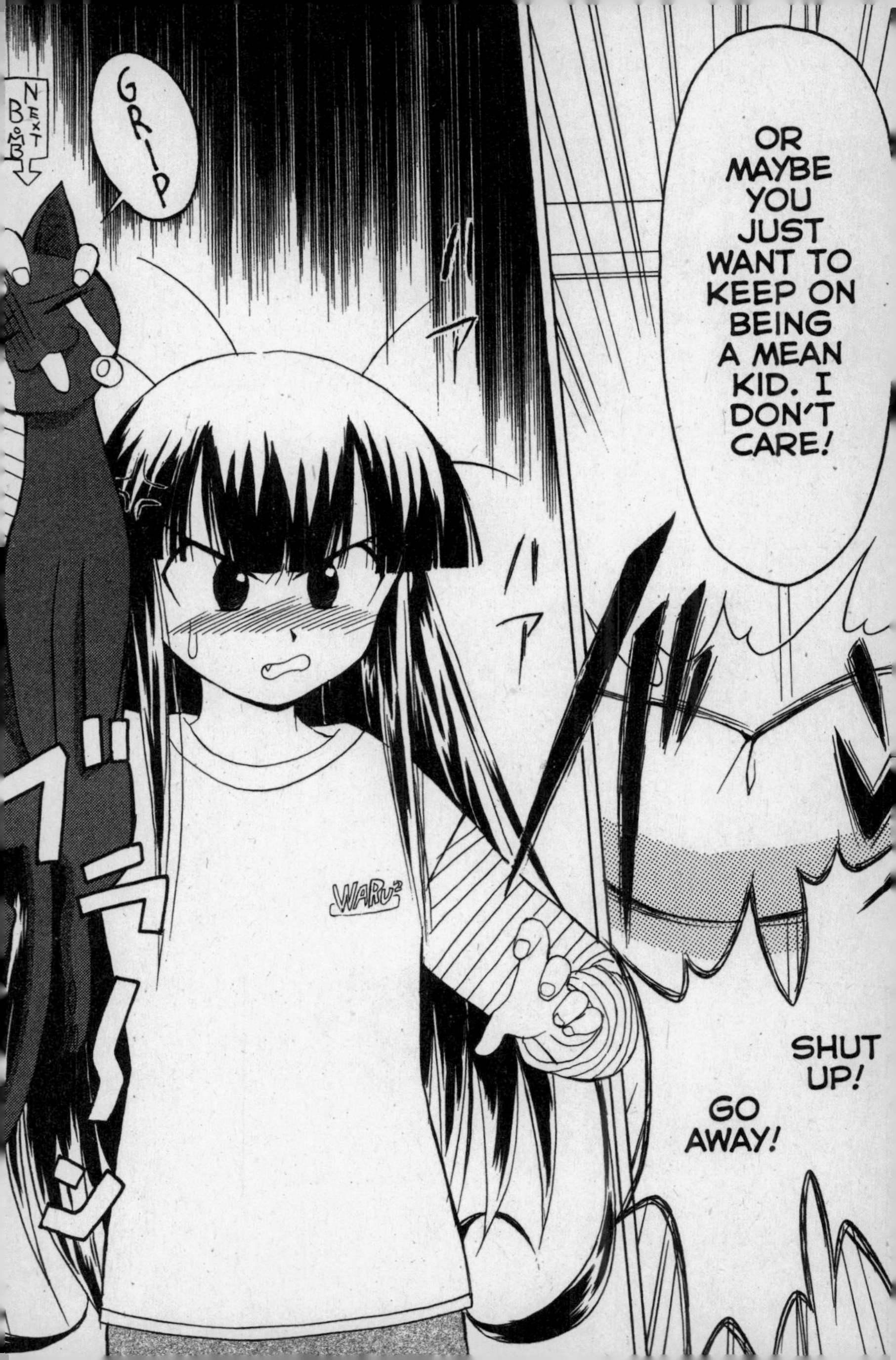
OR MAYBE YOU JUST WANT TO KEEP ON BEING A MEAN KID. I DON'T CARE!
SHUT UP!
GO AWAY!
GRIP
NEXT BOMB

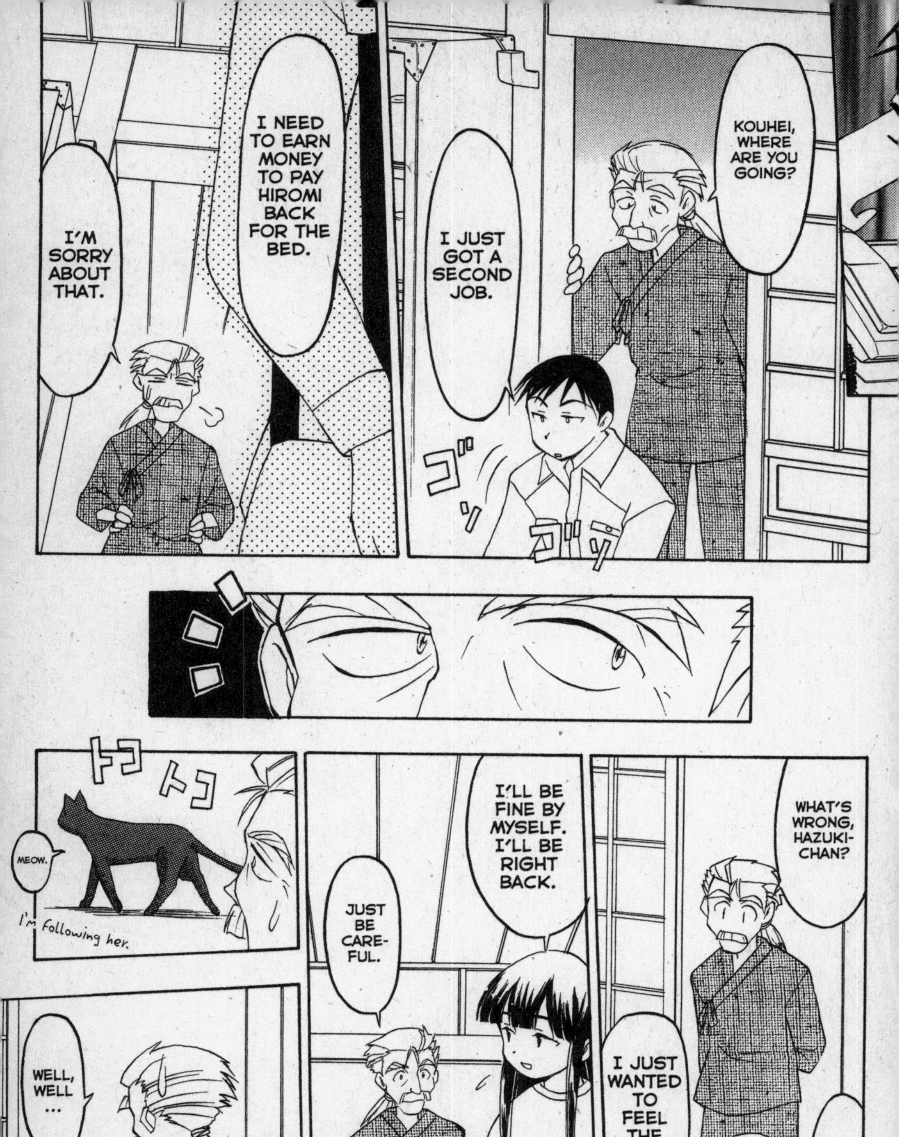
KOUHEI, WHERE ARE YOU GOING?
I JUST GOT A SECOND JOB.
ゴソ ゴソ
I NEED TO EARN MONEY TO PAY HIROMI BACK FOR THE BED.
I'M SORRY ABOUT THAT.
WHAT'S WRONG, HAZUKI-CHAN?
HI, GRAND-FA-THER.
I JUST WANTED TO FEEL THE COOL NIGHT AIR.
I'LL BE FINE BY MYSELF. I'LL BE RIGHT BACK.
JUST BE CARE-FUL.
トコ トコ
MEOW.
I'm following her.
WELL, WELL ...

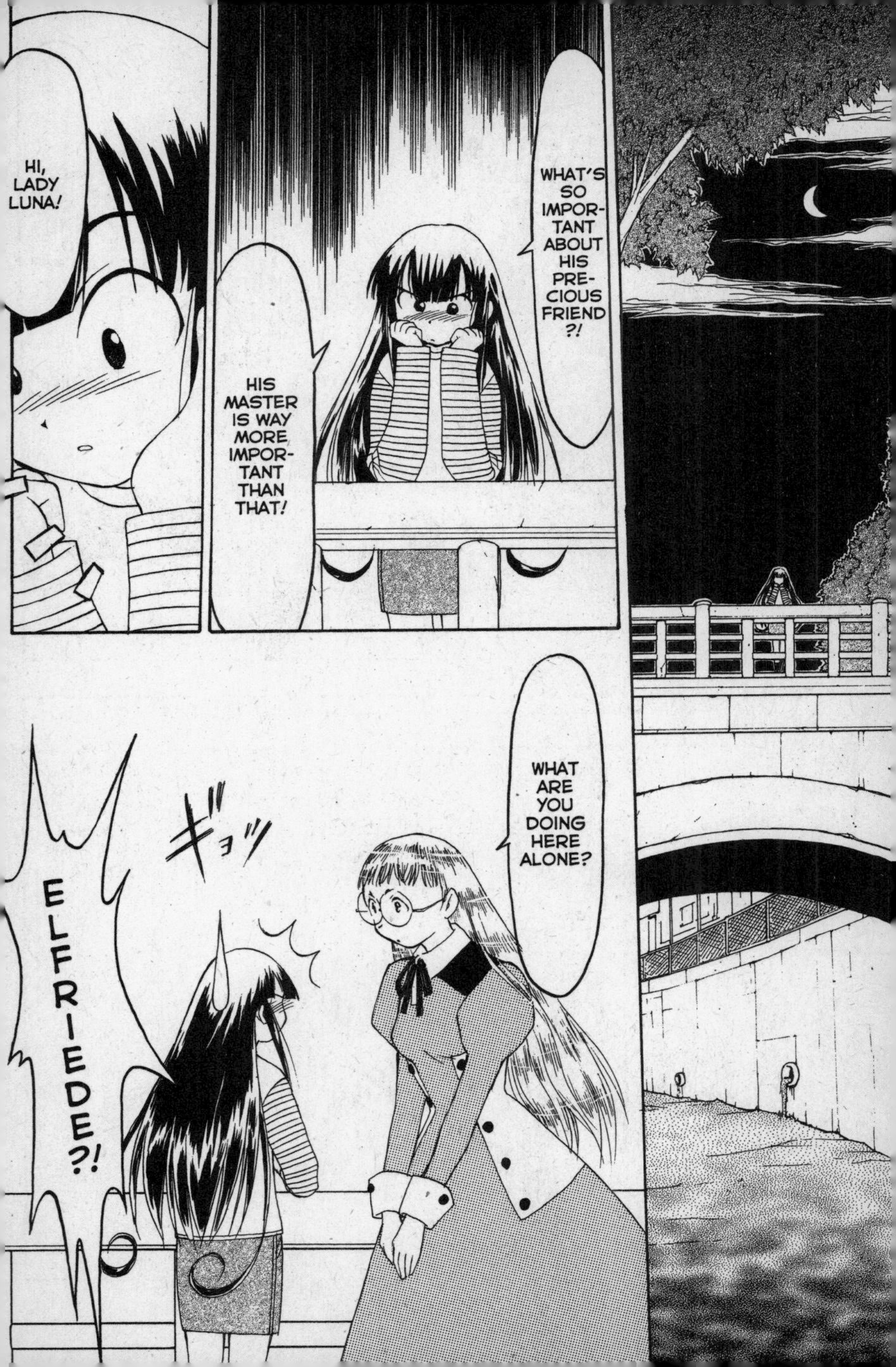
WHAT'S SO IMPORTANT ABOUT HIS PRECIOUS FRIEND?!
HIS MASTER IS WAY MORE IMPORTANT THAN THAT!
HI, LADY LUNA!
WHAT ARE YOU DOING HERE ALONE?
ギョッ
ELFRIEDE?!

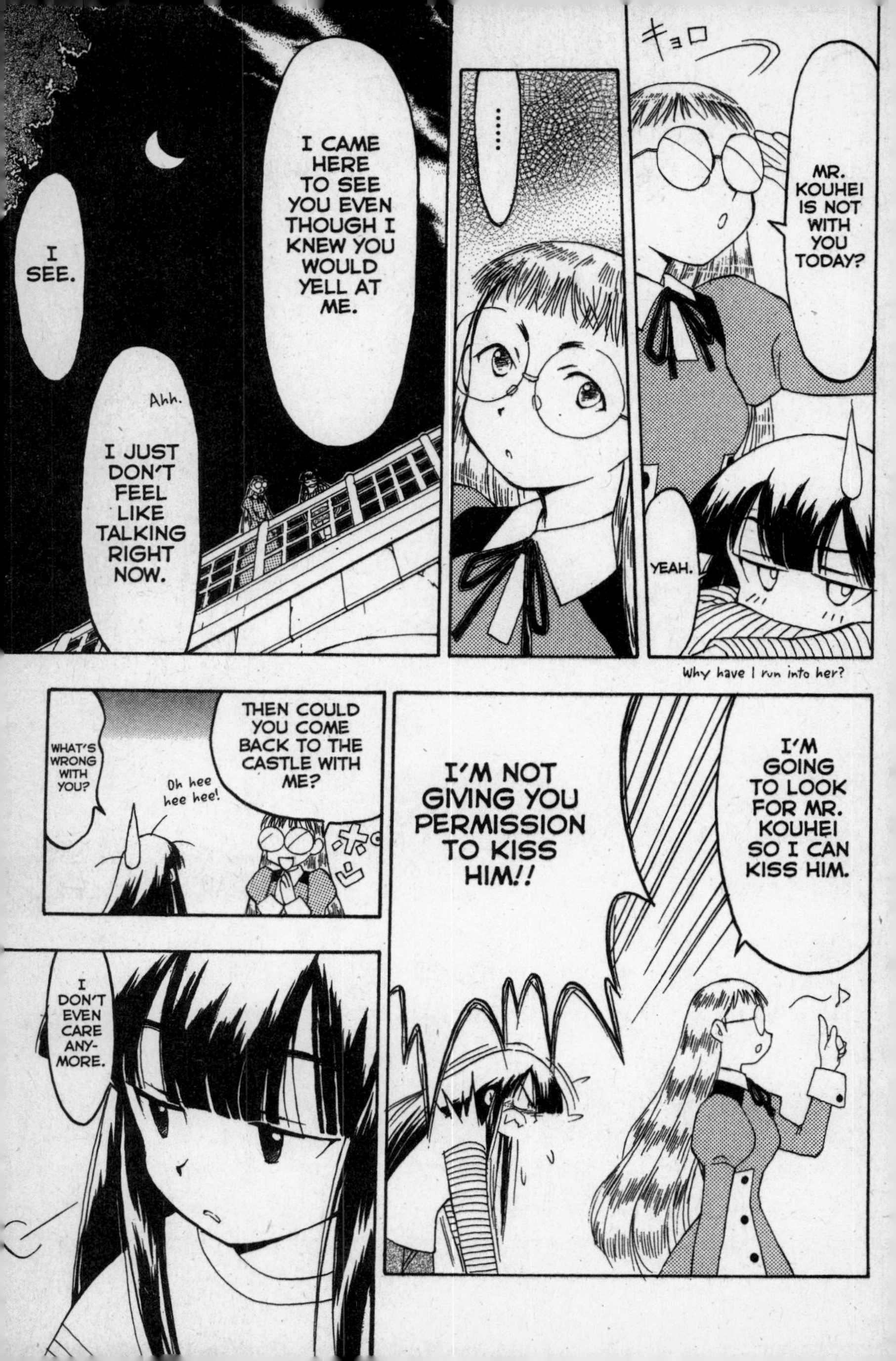
キョロ
MR. KOUHEI IS NOT WITH YOU TODAY?
YEAH.
Why have I run into her?
......
I CAME HERE TO SEE YOU EVEN THOUGH I KNEW YOU WOULD YELL AT ME.
I SEE.
Ahh.
I JUST DON'T FEEL LIKE TALKING RIGHT NOW.
I'M GOING TO LOOK FOR MR. KOUHEI SO I CAN KISS HIM.
I'M NOT GIVING YOU PERMISSION TO KISS HIM!!
THEN COULD YOU COME BACK TO THE CASTLE WITH ME?
Oh hee hee hee!
WHAT'S WRONG WITH YOU?
I DON'T EVEN CARE ANYMORE.

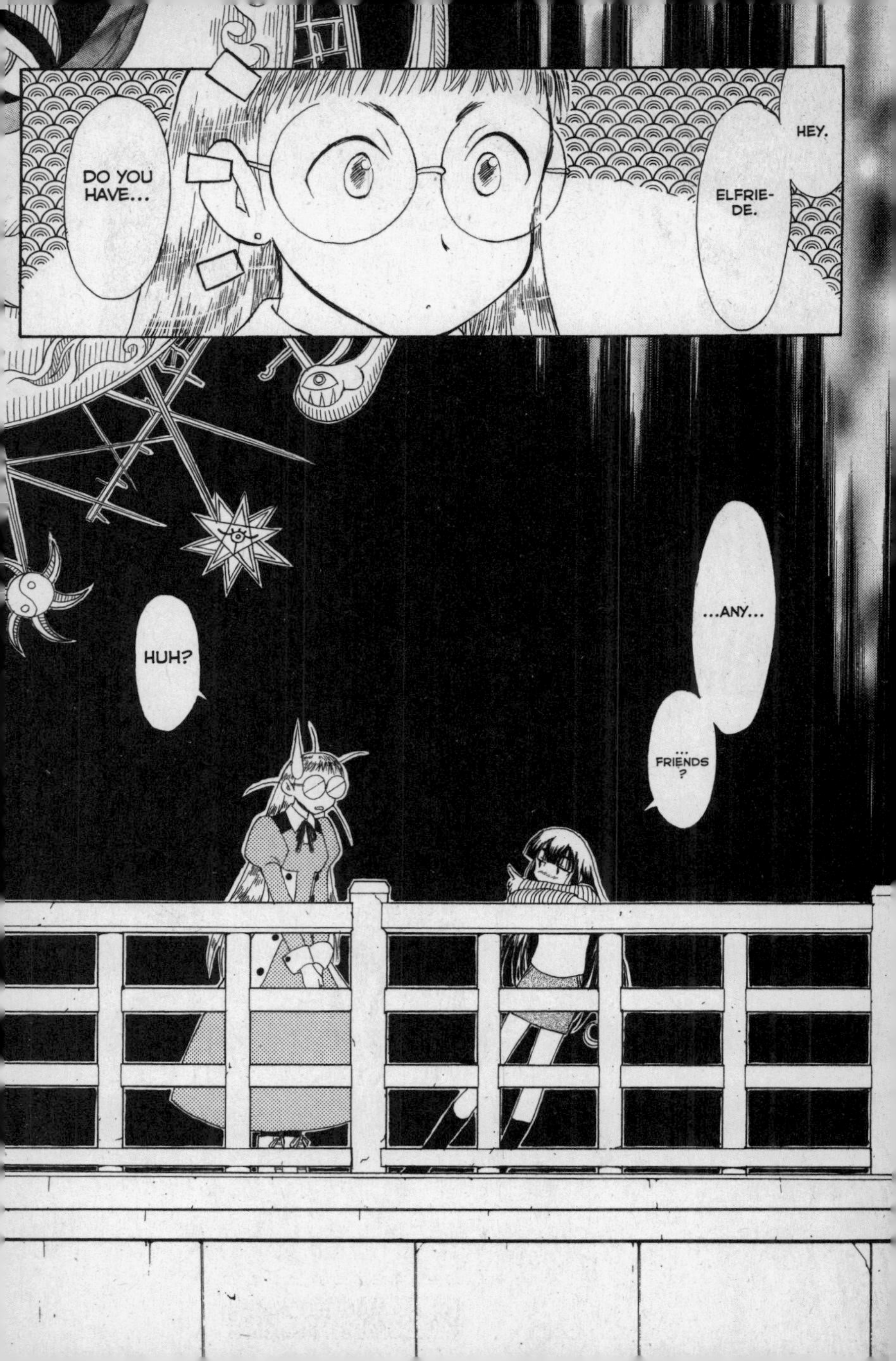
HEY.
ELFRIEDE.
DO YOU HAVE...
...ANY...
...FRIENDS?
HUH?

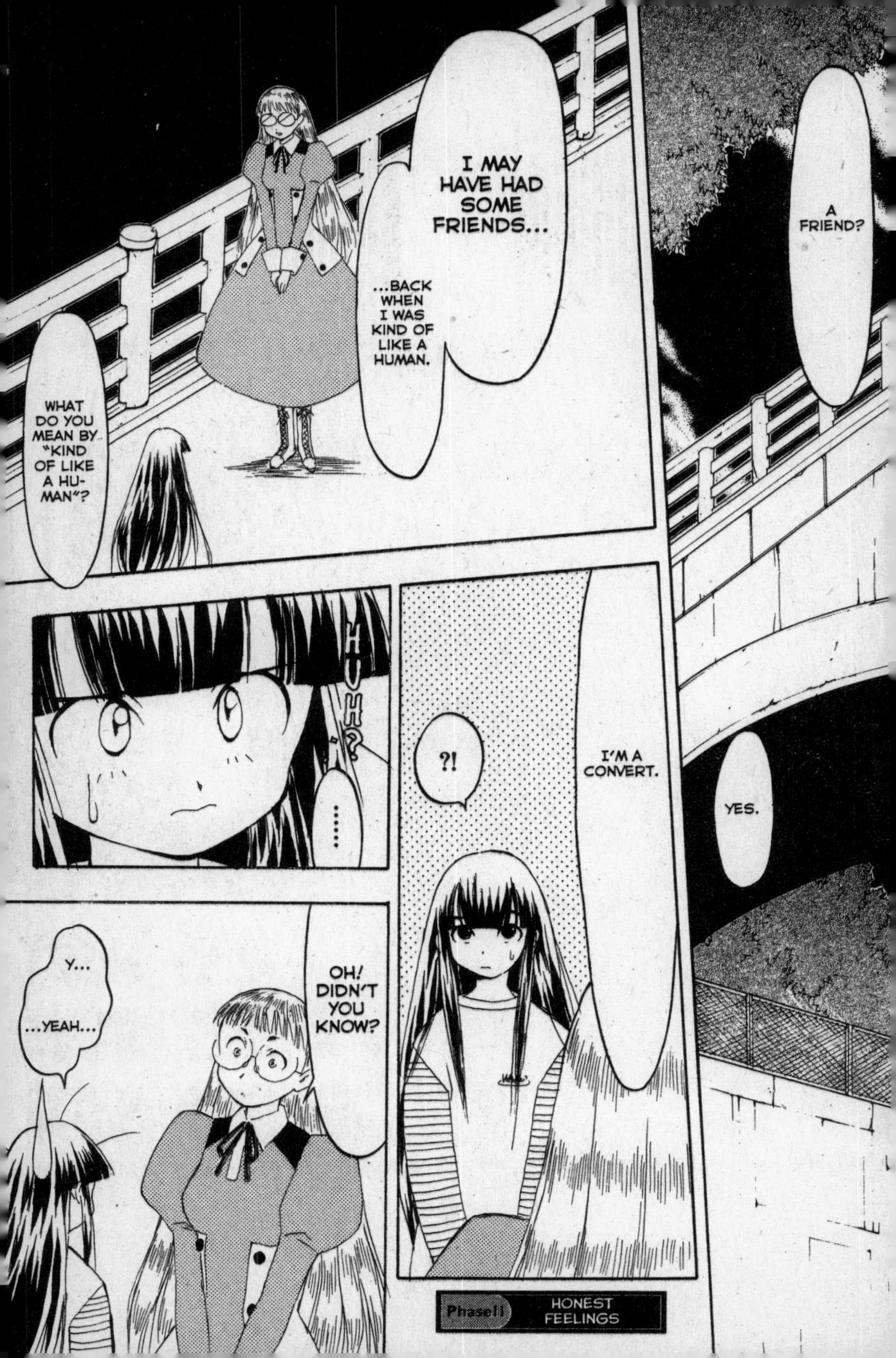
A FRIEND?
YES.
I MAY HAVE HAD SOME FRIENDS...
...BACK WHEN I WAS KIND OF LIKE A HUMAN.
WHAT DO YOU MEAN BY "KIND OF LIKE A HU-MAN"?
I'M A CONVERT.
?!
HUH?
......
OH! DIDN'T YOU KNOW?
Y... ...YEAH...
Phase11 HONEST FEELINGS

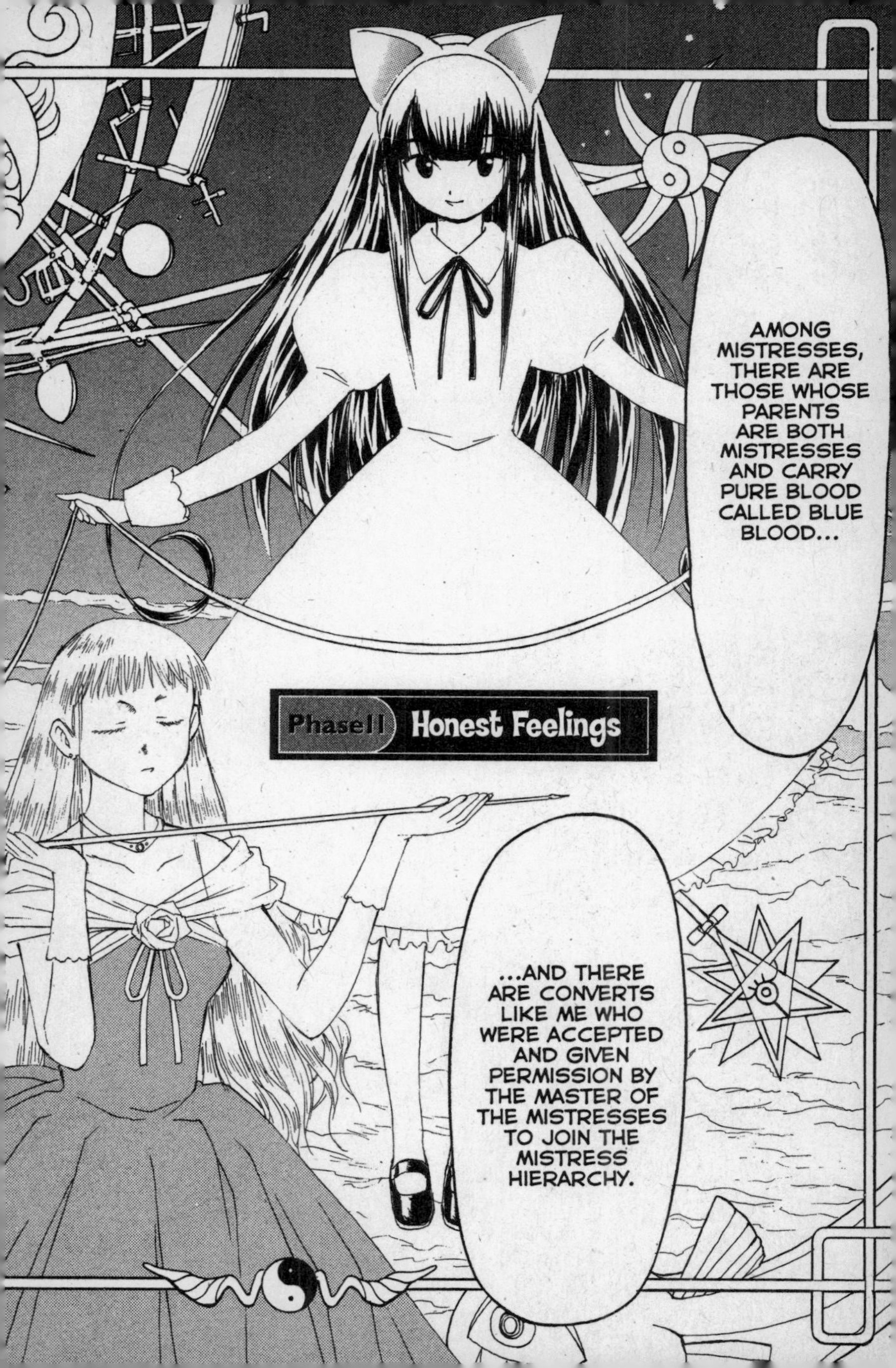
AMONG MISTRESSES, THERE ARE THOSE WHOSE PARENTS ARE BOTH MISTRESSES AND CARRY PURE BLOOD CALLED BLUE BLOOD...
Phase11 Honest Feelings
...AND THERE ARE CONVERTS LIKE ME WHO WERE ACCEPTED AND GIVEN PERMISSION BY THE MASTER OF THE MISTRESSES TO JOIN THE MISTRESS HIERARCHY.

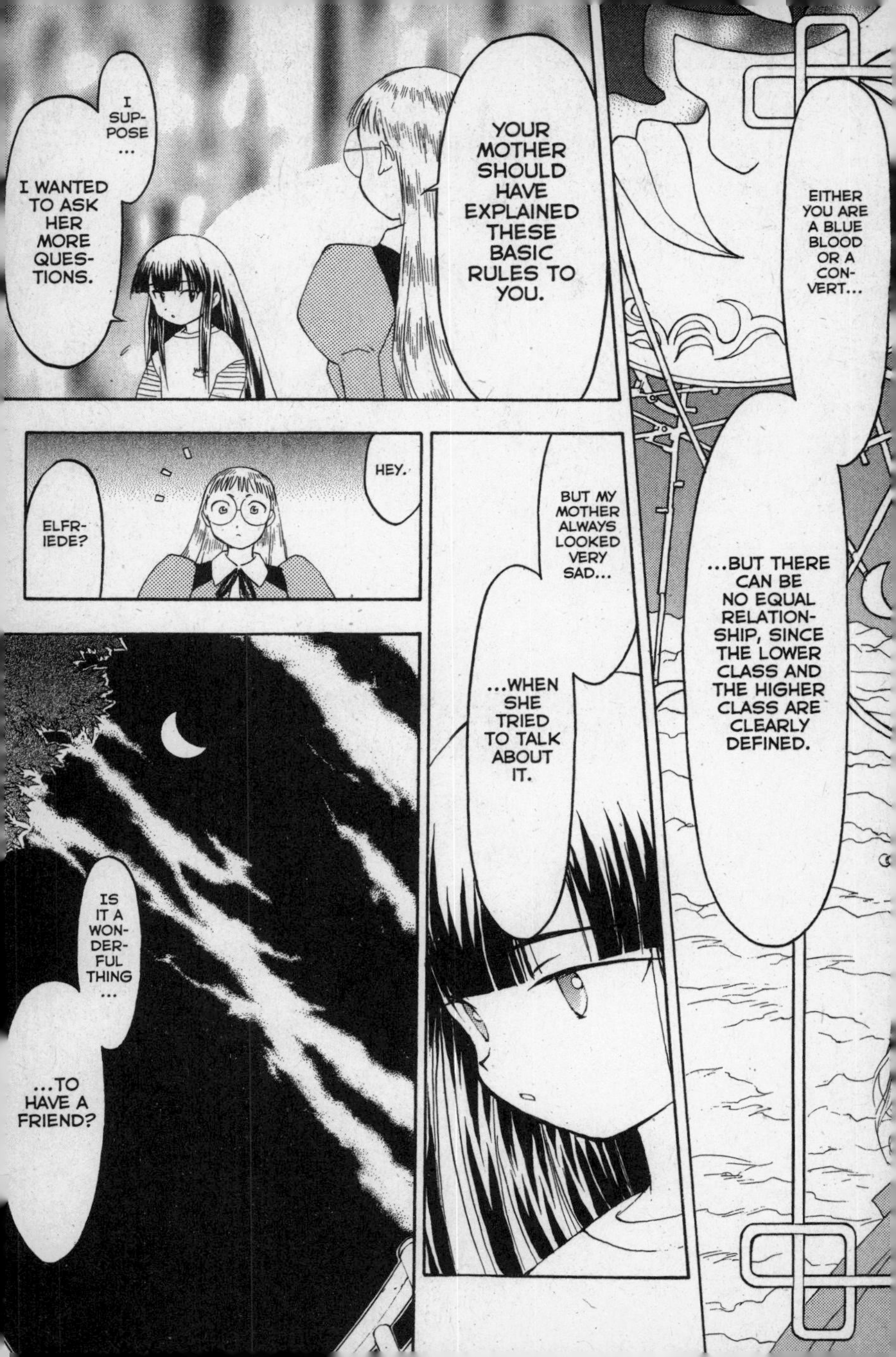
EITHER YOU ARE A BLUE BLOOD OR A CONVERT...
...BUT THERE CAN BE NO EQUAL RELATIONSHIP, SINCE THE LOWER CLASS AND THE HIGHER CLASS ARE CLEARLY DEFINED.
YOUR MOTHER SHOULD HAVE EXPLAINED THESE BASIC RULES TO YOU.
I SUPPOSE...
I WANTED TO ASK HER MORE QUESTIONS.
BUT MY MOTHER ALWAYS LOOKED VERY SAD...
...WHEN SHE TRIED TO TALK ABOUT IT.
HEY.
ELFRIEDE?
IS IT A WONDERFUL THING...
...TO HAVE A FRIEND?

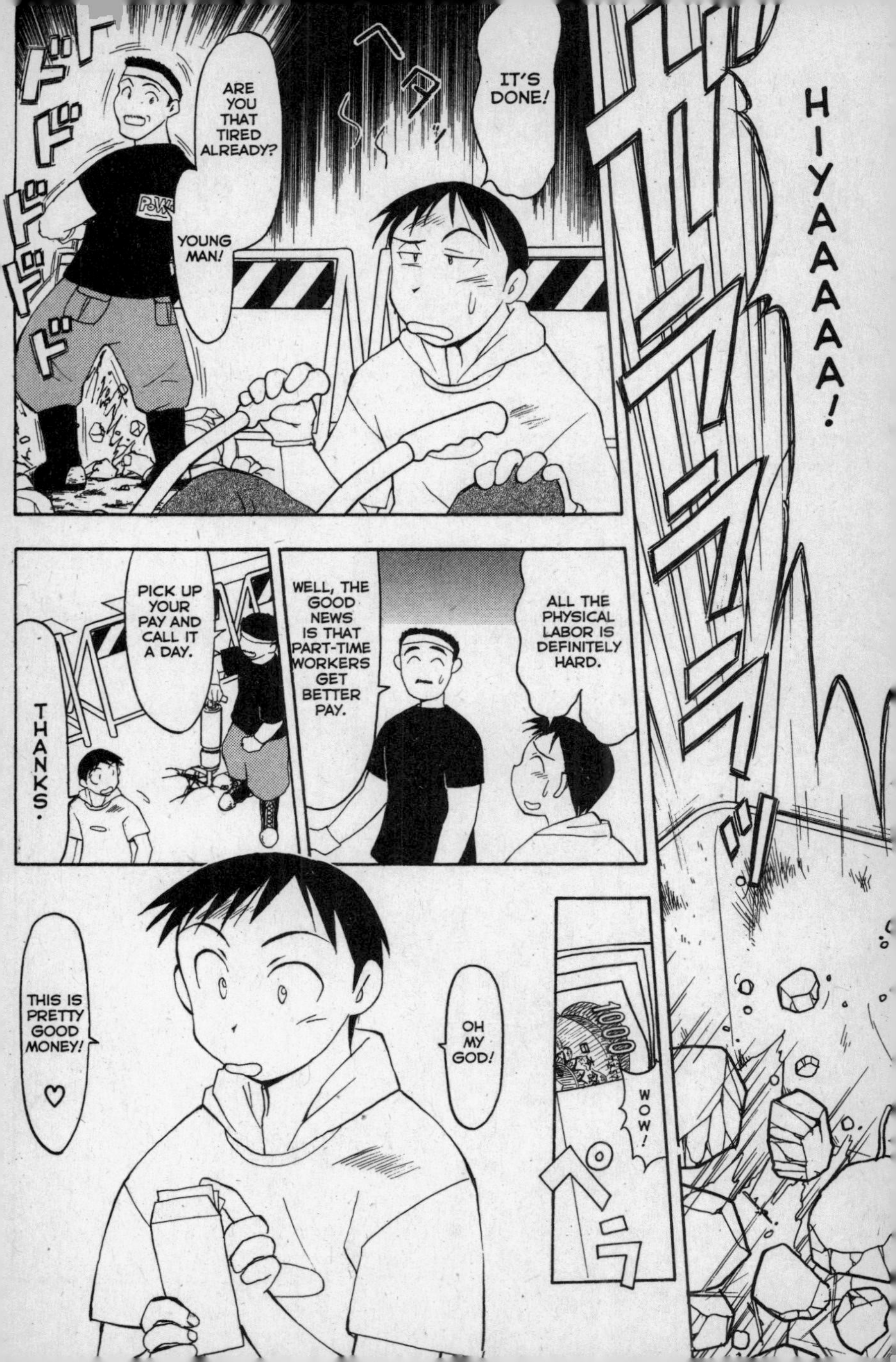
HIYAAAAAA!
IT'S DONE!
ARE YOU THAT TIRED ALREADY?
YOUNG MAN!
ALL THE PHYSICAL LABOR IS DEFINITELY HARD.
WELL, THE GOOD NEWS IS THAT PART-TIME WORKERS GET BETTER PAY.
PICK UP YOUR PAY AND CALL IT A DAY.
THANKS.
WOW!
OH MY GOD!
THIS IS PRETTY GOOD MONEY! ♥

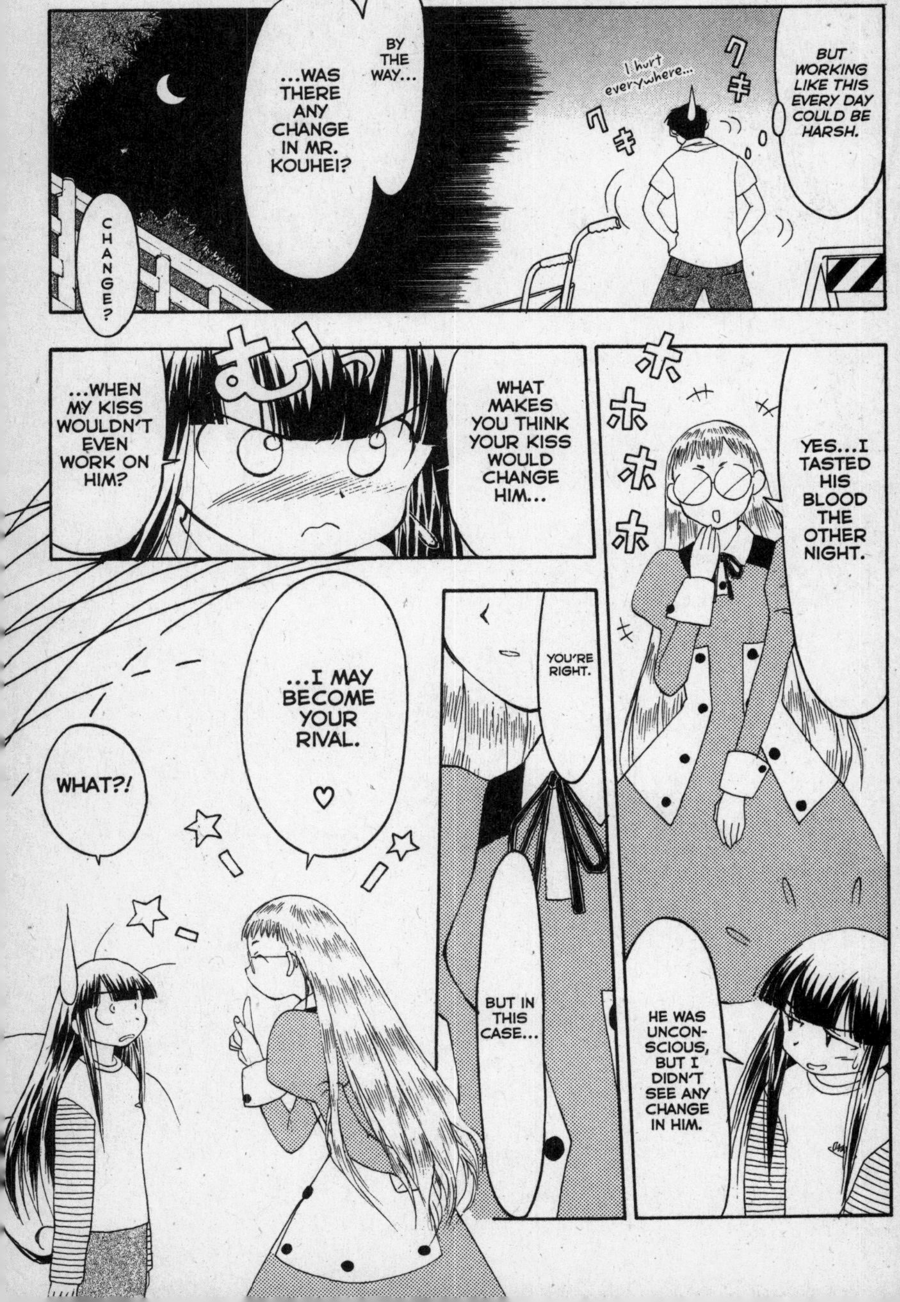
BUT WORKING LIKE THIS EVERY DAY COULD BE HARSH.
I hurt everywhere...
クキ
クキ
BY THE WAY...
...WAS THERE ANY CHANGE IN MR. KOUHEI?
CHANGE?
ホホホホ
YES...I TASTED HIS BLOOD THE OTHER NIGHT.
HE WAS UNCONSCIOUS, BUT I DIDN'T SEE ANY CHANGE IN HIM.
むっ
WHAT MAKES YOU THINK YOUR KISS WOULD CHANGE HIM...
...WHEN MY KISS WOULDN'T EVEN WORK ON HIM?
YOU'RE RIGHT.
BUT IN THIS CASE...
...I MAY BECOME YOUR RIVAL. ♡
WHAT?!

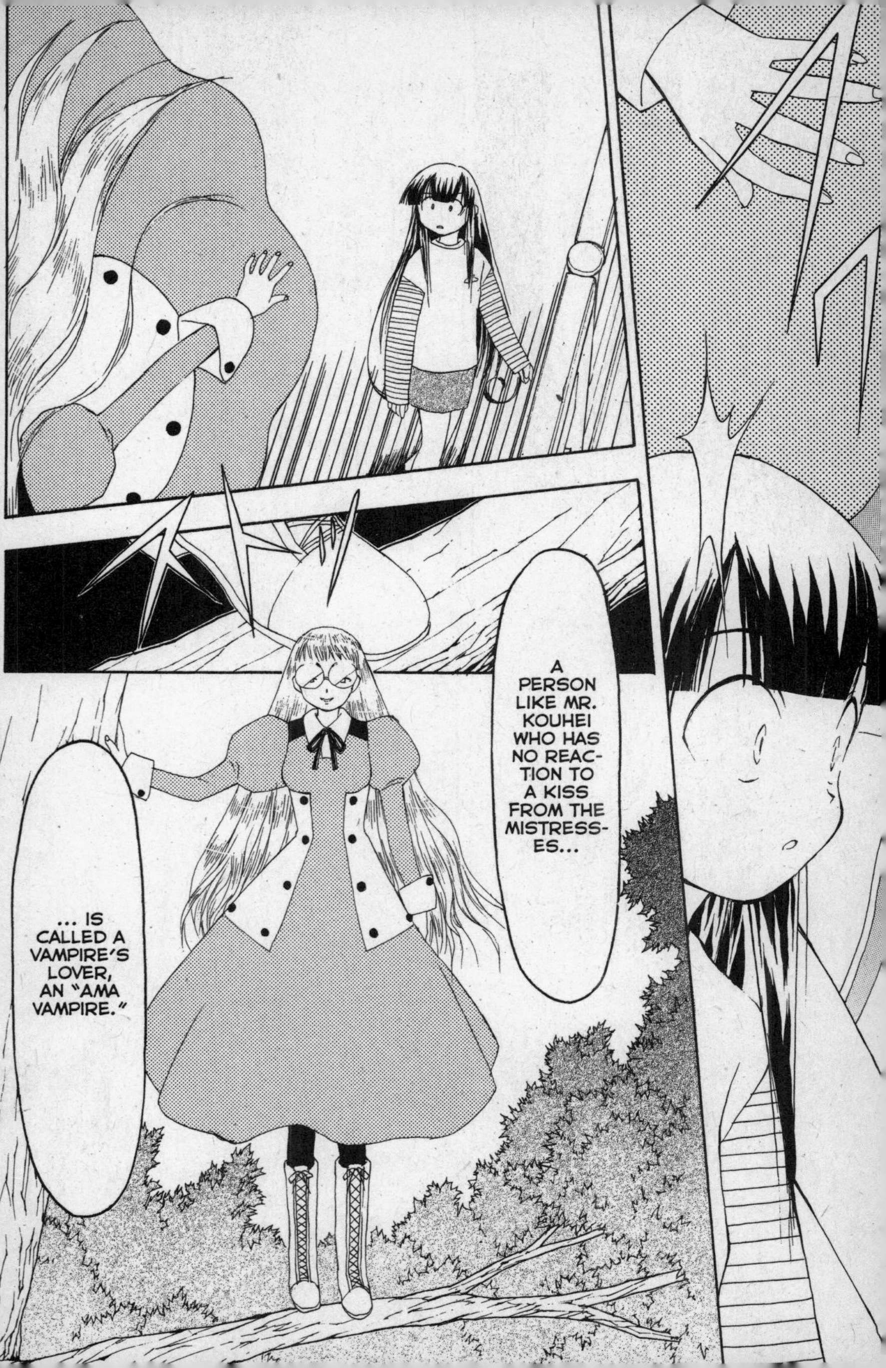
A PERSON LIKE MR. KOUHEI WHO HAS NO REACTION TO A KISS FROM THE MISTRESSES...
... IS CALLED A VAMPIRE'S LOVER, AN "AMA VAMPIRE."

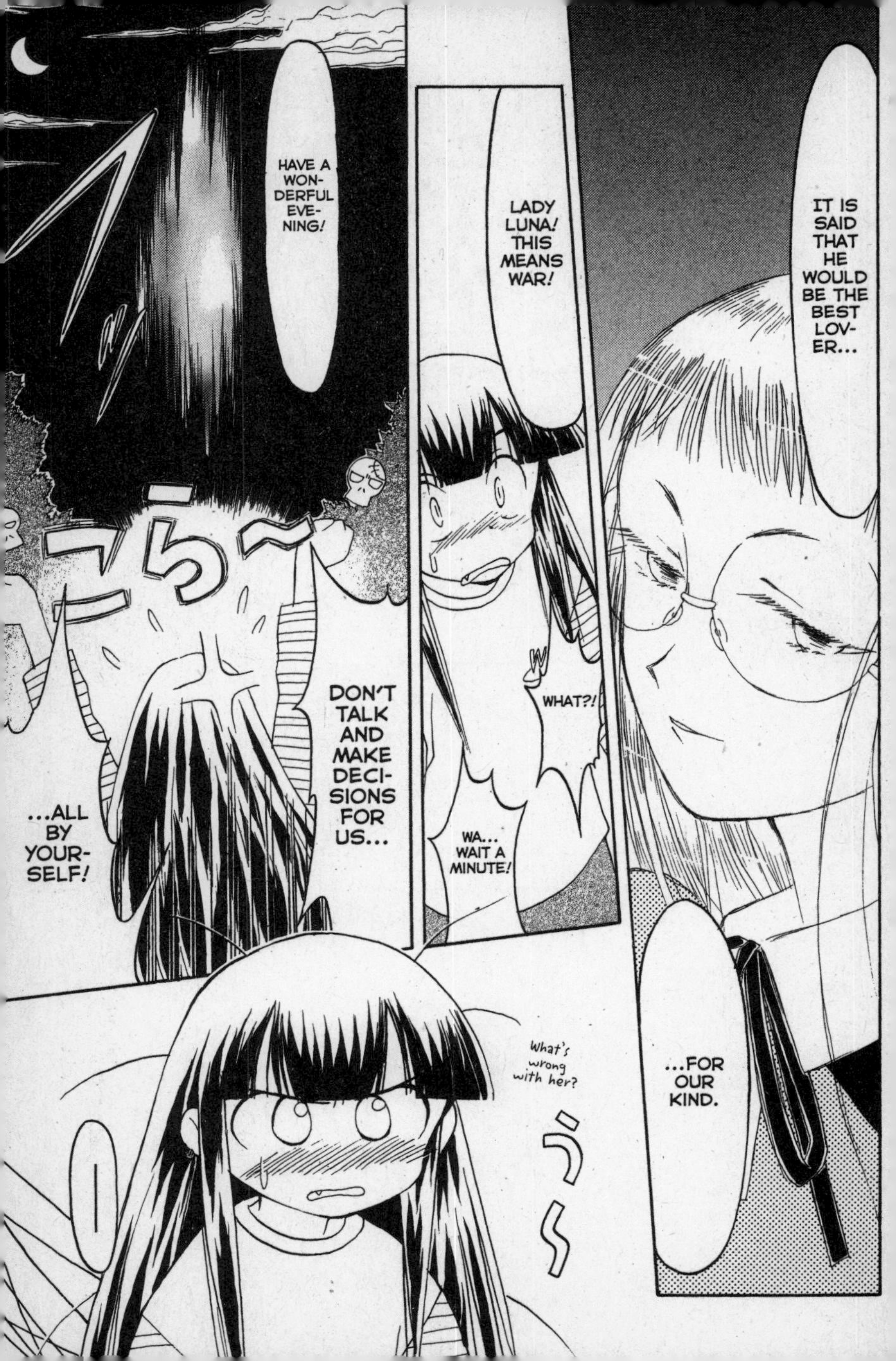
IT IS SAID THAT HE WOULD BE THE BEST LOV-ER...
...FOR OUR KIND.
LADY LUNA! THIS MEANS WAR!
WHAT?!
WA... WAIT A MINUTE!
HAVE A WON-DERFUL EVE-NING!
DON'T TALK AND MAKE DECI-SIONS FOR US...
...ALL BY YOUR-SELF!
What's wrong with her?

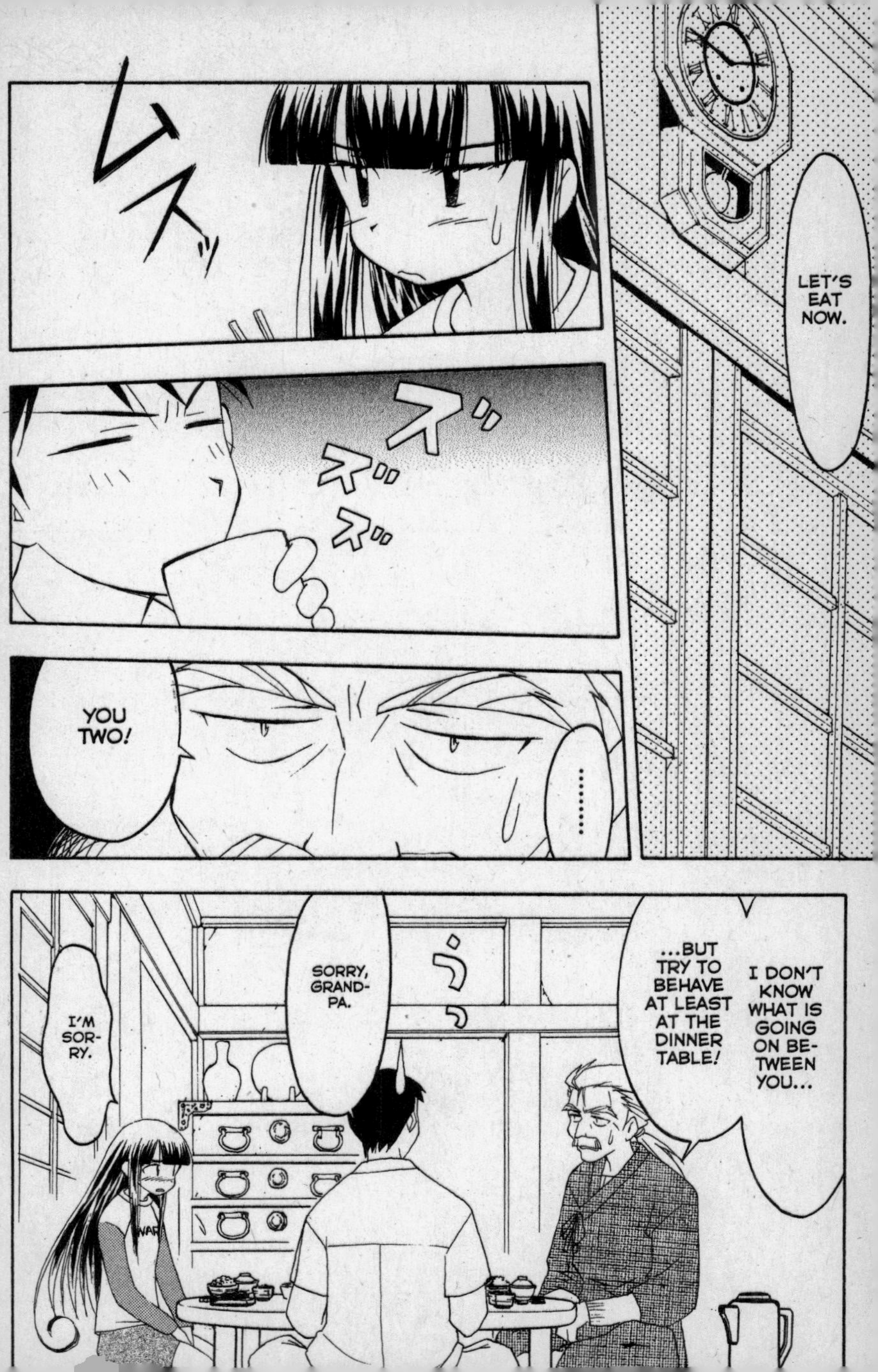
LET'S EAT NOW.
YOU TWO!
......
I DON'T KNOW WHAT IS GOING ON BETWEEN YOU...
...BUT TRY TO BEHAVE AT LEAST AT THE DINNER TABLE!
SORRY, GRANDPA.
I'M SORRY.

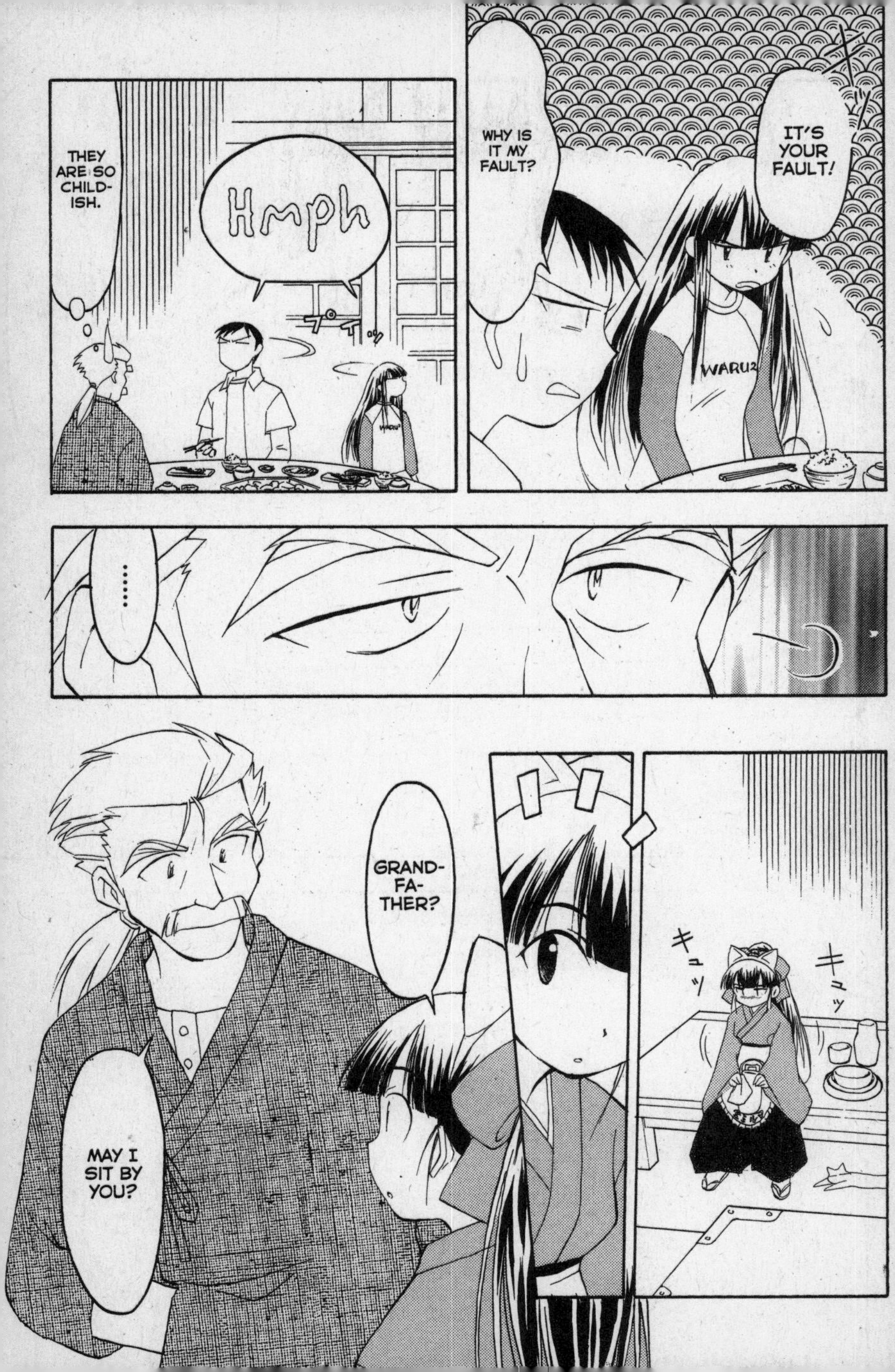
IT'S YOUR FAULT!
WHY IS IT MY FAULT?
Hmph
プイッ
THEY ARE SO CHILD-ISH.
......
キュッ
キュッ
GRAND-FA-THER?
MAY I SIT BY YOU?

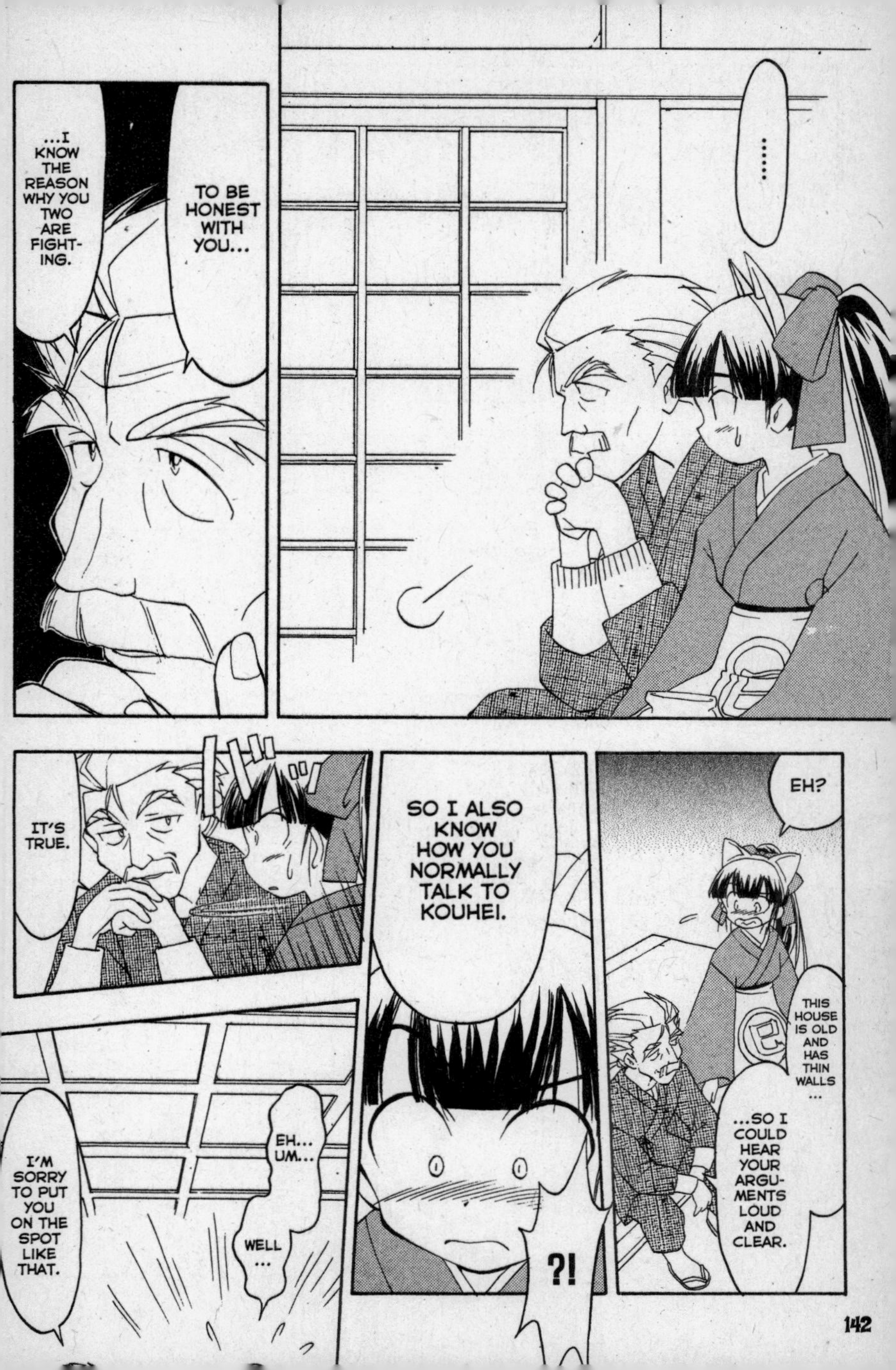
......
TO BE HONEST WITH YOU...
...I KNOW THE REASON WHY YOU TWO ARE FIGHTING.
EH?
THIS HOUSE IS OLD AND HAS THIN WALLS...
...SO I COULD HEAR YOUR ARGUMENTS LOUD AND CLEAR.
SO I ALSO KNOW HOW YOU NORMALLY TALK TO KOUHEI.
?!
IT'S TRUE.
EH... UM...
WELL...
I'M SORRY TO PUT YOU ON THE SPOT LIKE THAT.

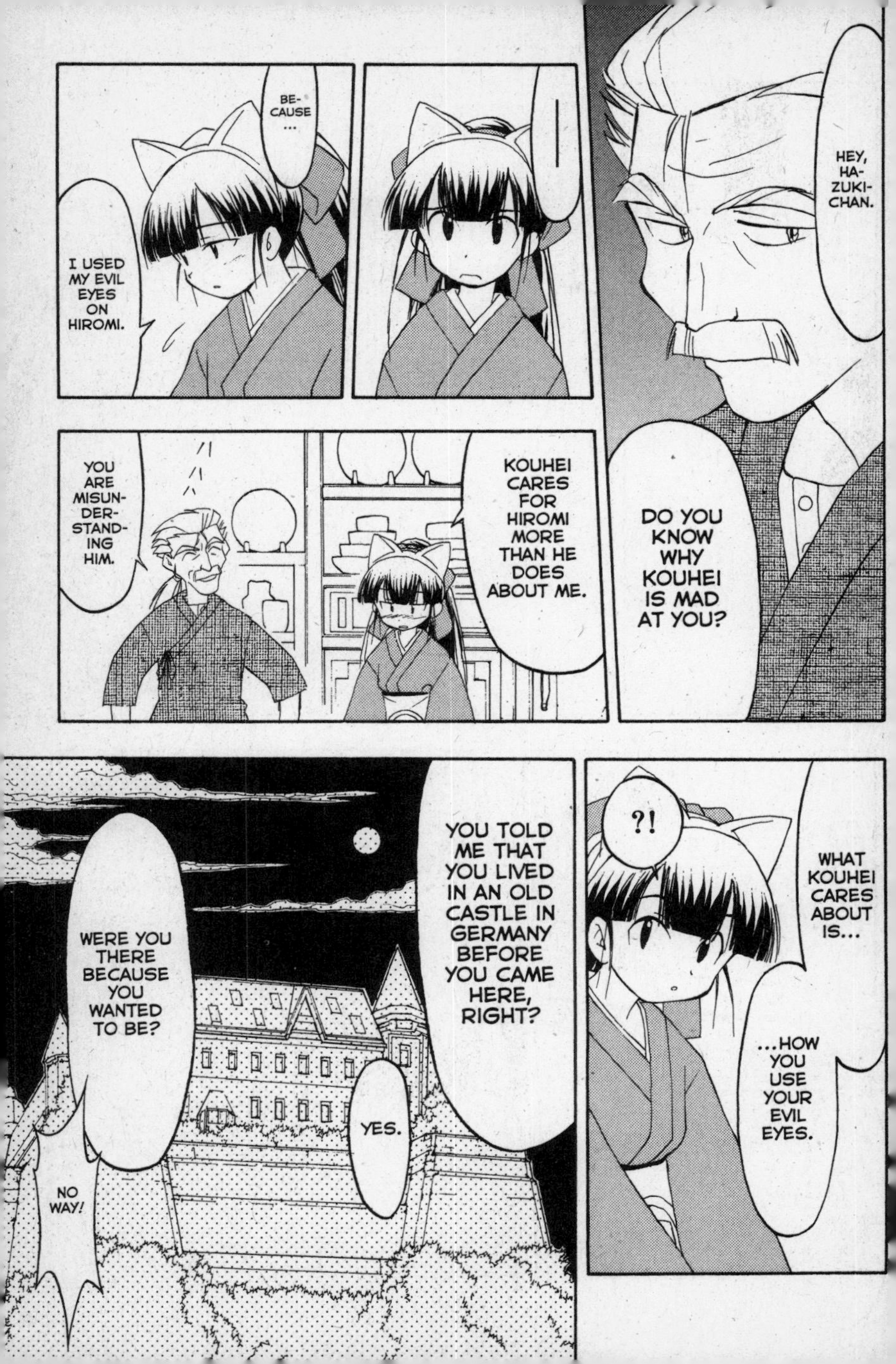
HEY, HA-ZUKI-CHAN.
DO YOU KNOW WHY KOUHEI IS MAD AT YOU?
BE-CAUSE ...
I USED MY EVIL EYES ON HIROMI.
KOUHEI CARES FOR HIROMI MORE THAN HE DOES ABOUT ME.
YOU ARE MISUN-DER-STAND-ING HIM.
?!
WHAT KOUHEI CARES ABOUT IS...
...HOW YOU USE YOUR EVIL EYES.
YOU TOLD ME THAT YOU LIVED IN AN OLD CASTLE IN GERMANY BEFORE YOU CAME HERE, RIGHT?
YES.
WERE YOU THERE BECAUSE YOU WANTED TO BE?
NO WAY!

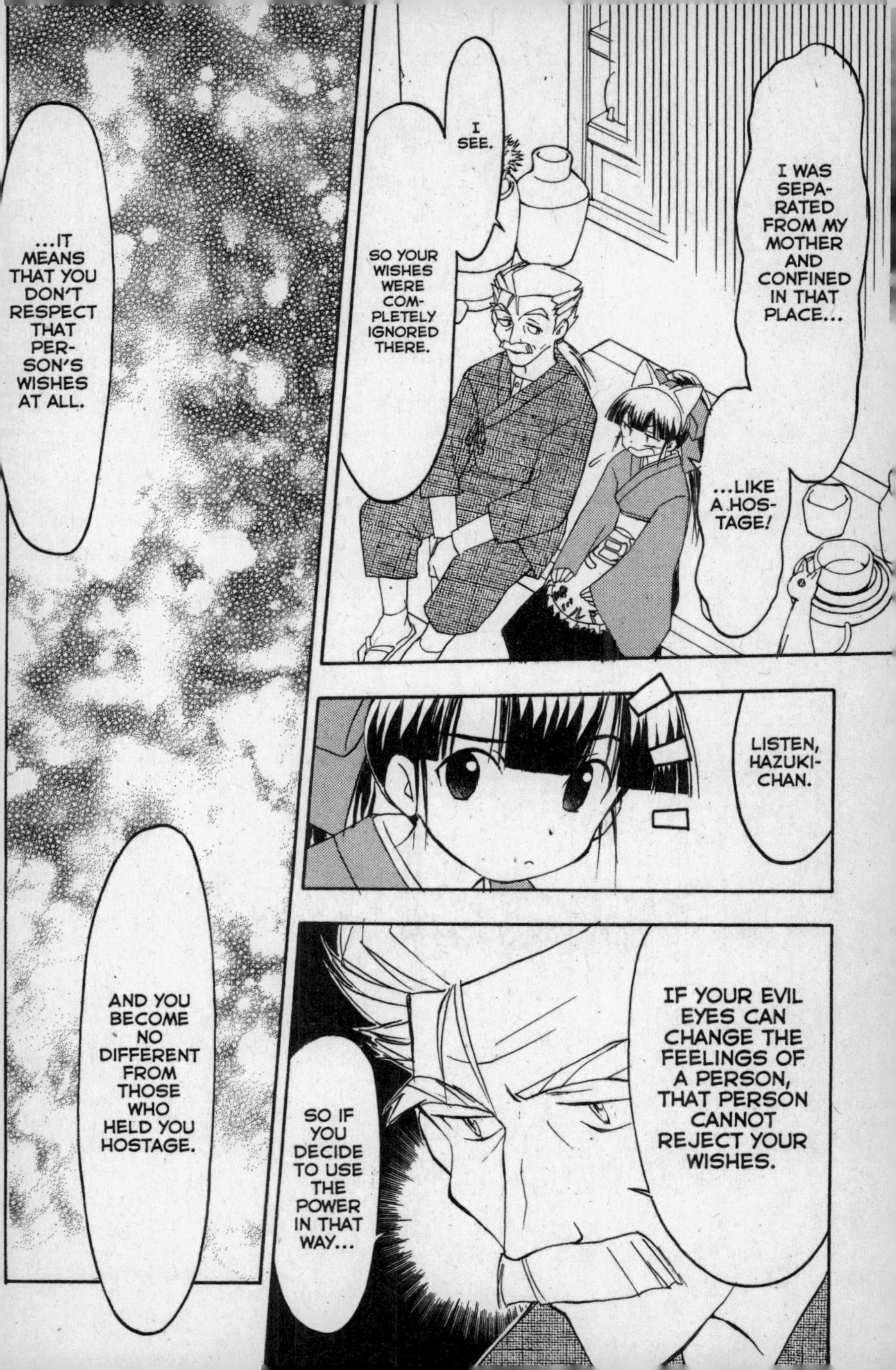
I WAS SEPARATED FROM MY MOTHER AND CONFINED IN THAT PLACE...
...LIKE A HOSTAGE!
I SEE.
SO YOUR WISHES WERE COMPLETELY IGNORED THERE.
LISTEN, HAZUKI-CHAN.
IF YOUR EVIL EYES CAN CHANGE THE FEELINGS OF A PERSON, THAT PERSON CANNOT REJECT YOUR WISHES.
SO IF YOU DECIDE TO USE THE POWER IN THAT WAY...
...IT MEANS THAT YOU DON'T RESPECT THAT PERSON'S WISHES AT ALL.
AND YOU BECOME NO DIFFERENT FROM THOSE WHO HELD YOU HOSTAGE.

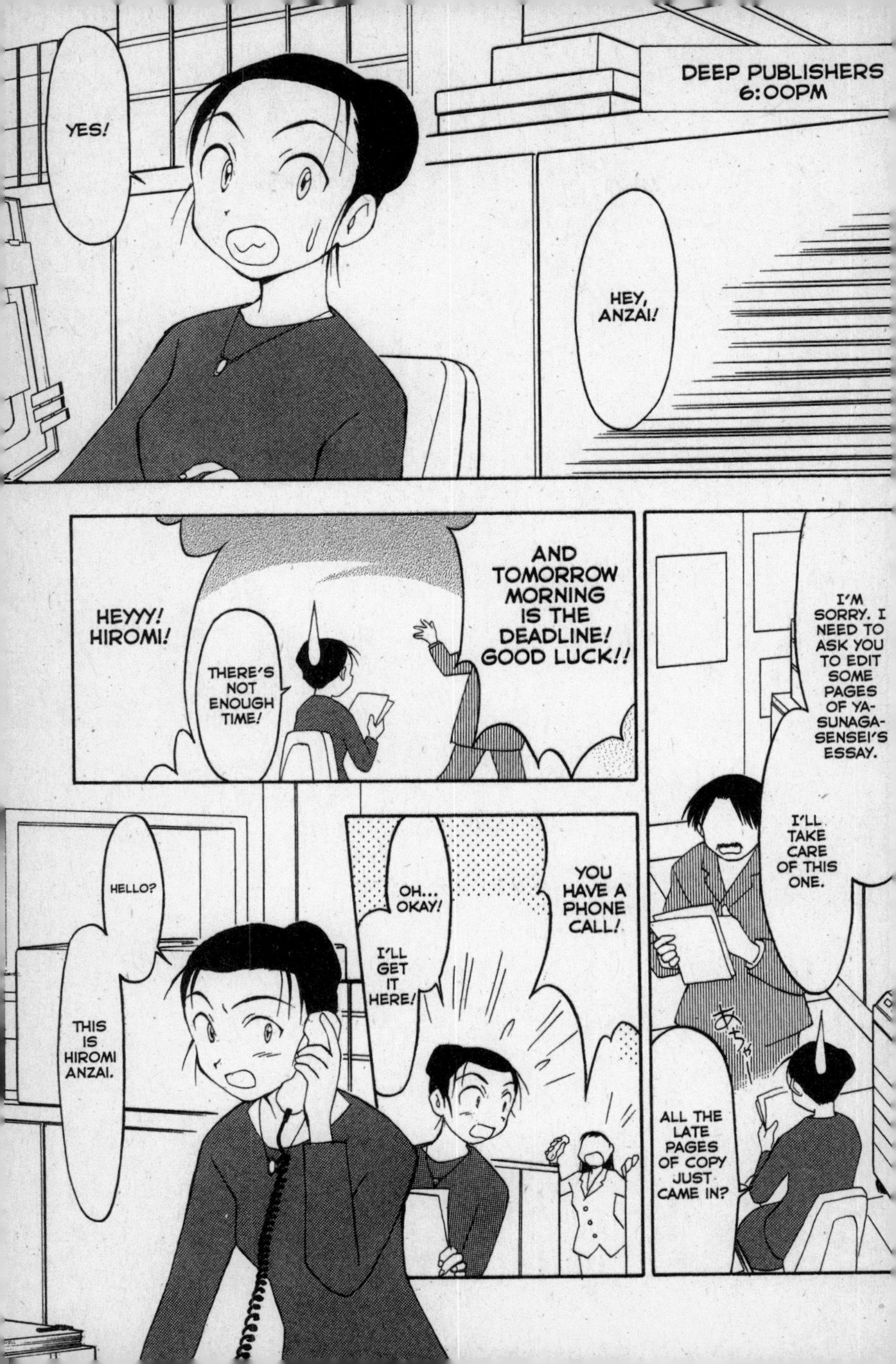
DEEP PUBLISHERS 6:00PM
HEY, ANZAI!
YES!
I'M SORRY. I NEED TO ASK YOU TO EDIT SOME PAGES OF YA-SUNAGA-SENSEI'S ESSAY.
I'LL TAKE CARE OF THIS ONE.
ALL THE LATE PAGES OF COPY JUST CAME IN?
AND TOMORROW MORNING IS THE DEADLINE! GOOD LUCK!!
HEYYY! HIROMI!
THERE'S NOT ENOUGH TIME!
YOU HAVE A PHONE CALL!
OH... OKAY!
I'LL GET IT HERE!
HELLO?
THIS IS HIROMI ANZAI.

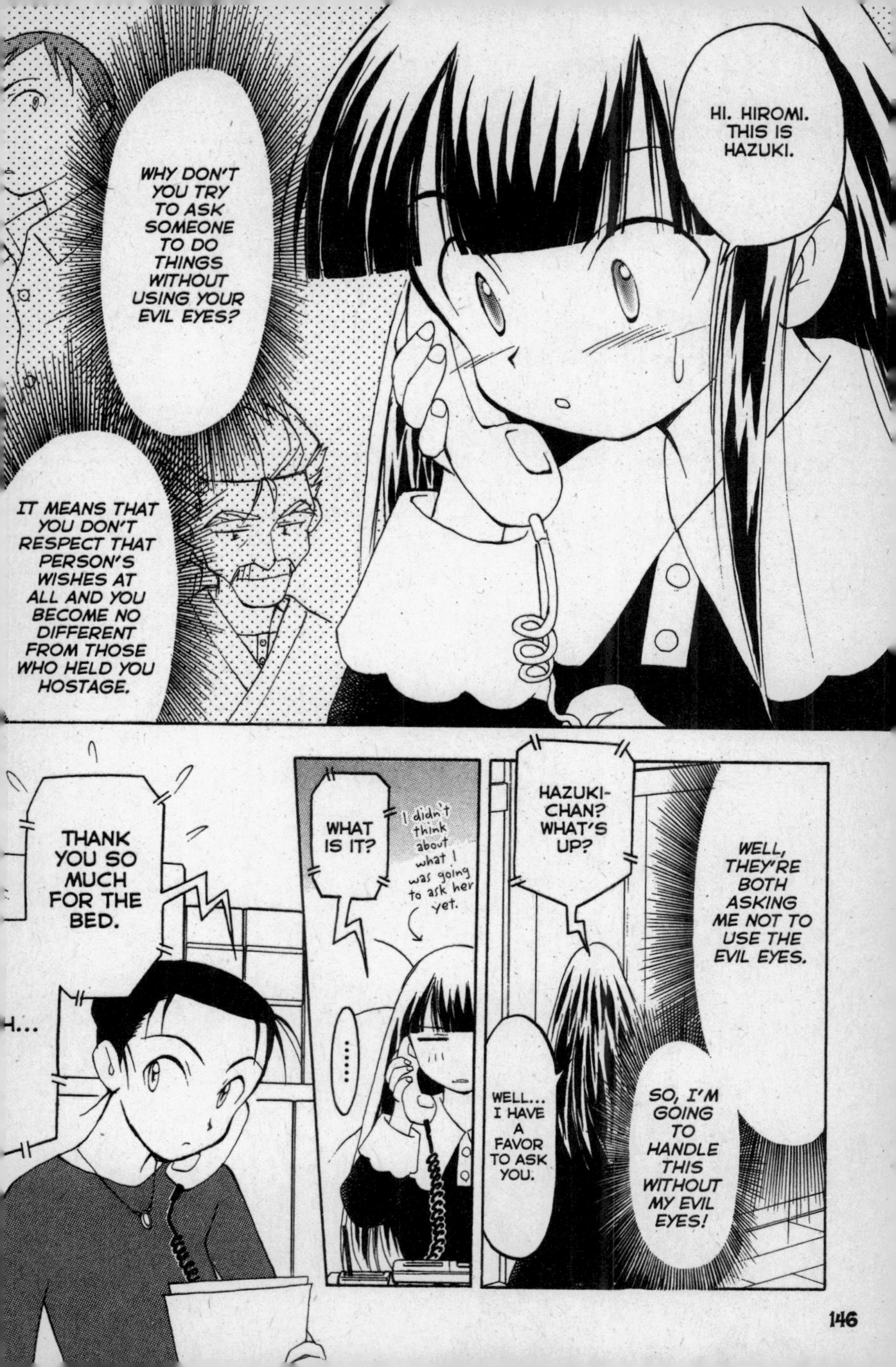

HI. HIROMI. THIS IS HAZUKI.
WHY DON'T YOU TRY TO ASK SOMEONE TO DO THINGS WITHOUT USING YOUR EVIL EYES?
IT MEANS THAT YOU DON'T RESPECT THAT PERSON'S WISHES AT ALL AND YOU BECOME NO DIFFERENT FROM THOSE WHO HELD YOU HOSTAGE.
WELL, THEY'RE BOTH ASKING ME NOT TO USE THE EVIL EYES.
HAZUKI-CHAN? WHAT'S UP?
SO, I'M GOING TO HANDLE THIS WITHOUT MY EVIL EYES!
WELL... I HAVE A FAVOR TO ASK YOU.
I didn't think about what I was going to ask her yet.
WHAT IS IT?
......
THANK YOU SO MUCH FOR THE BED.
H...

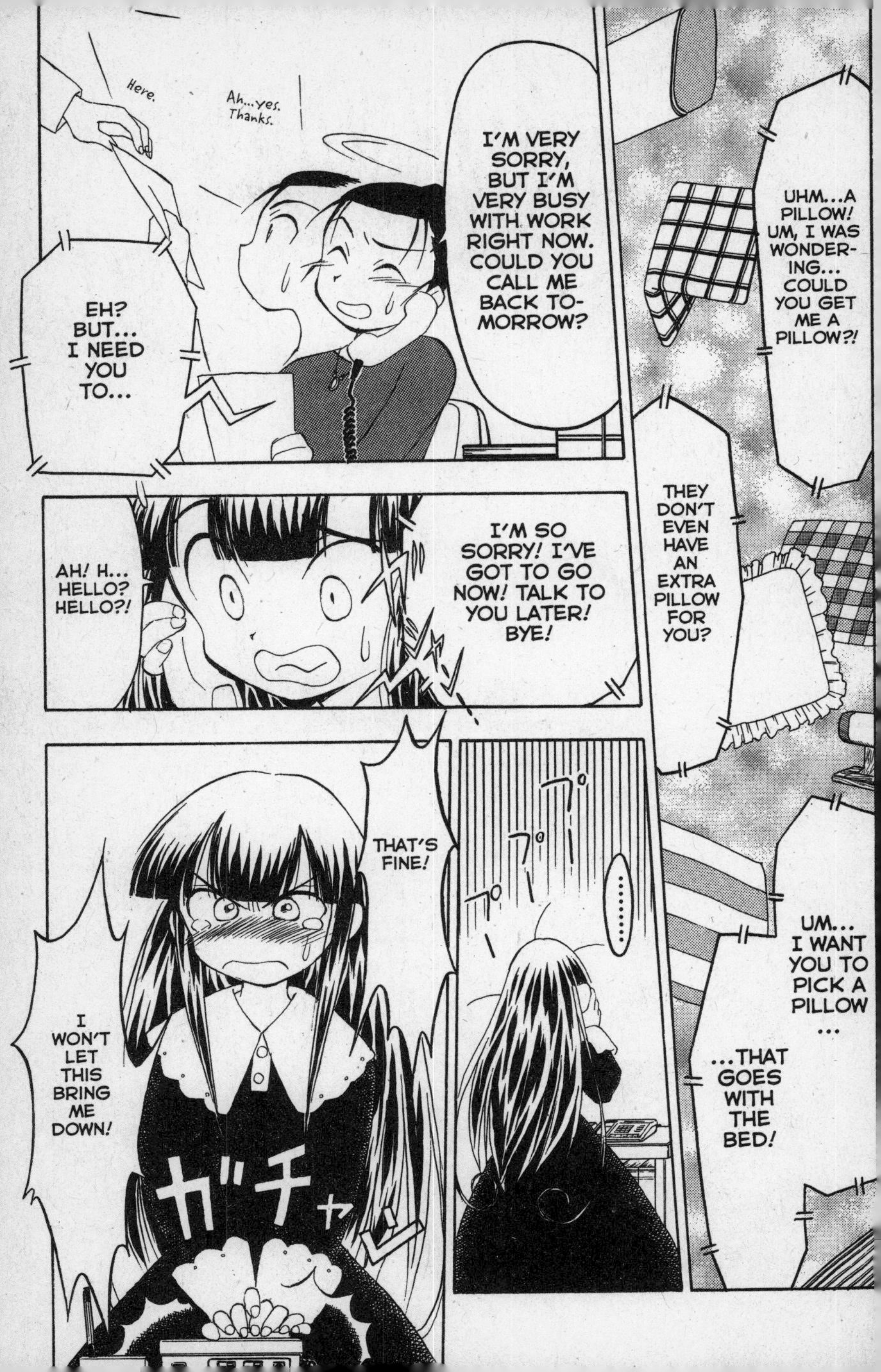
UHM...A PILLOW! UM, I WAS WONDERING... COULD YOU GET ME A PILLOW?!
THEY DON'T EVEN HAVE AN EXTRA PILLOW FOR YOU?
UM... I WANT YOU TO PICK A PILLOW ...
...THAT GOES WITH THE BED!
I'M VERY SORRY, BUT I'M VERY BUSY WITH WORK RIGHT NOW. COULD YOU CALL ME BACK TO-MORROW?
Ah...yes. Thanks.
Here.
EH? BUT... I NEED YOU TO...
I'M SO SORRY! I'VE GOT TO GO NOW! TALK TO YOU LATER! BYE!
AH! H... HELLO? HELLO?!
......
プ
プ
プ
THAT'S FINE!
I WON'T LET THIS BRING ME DOWN!
ガチャン

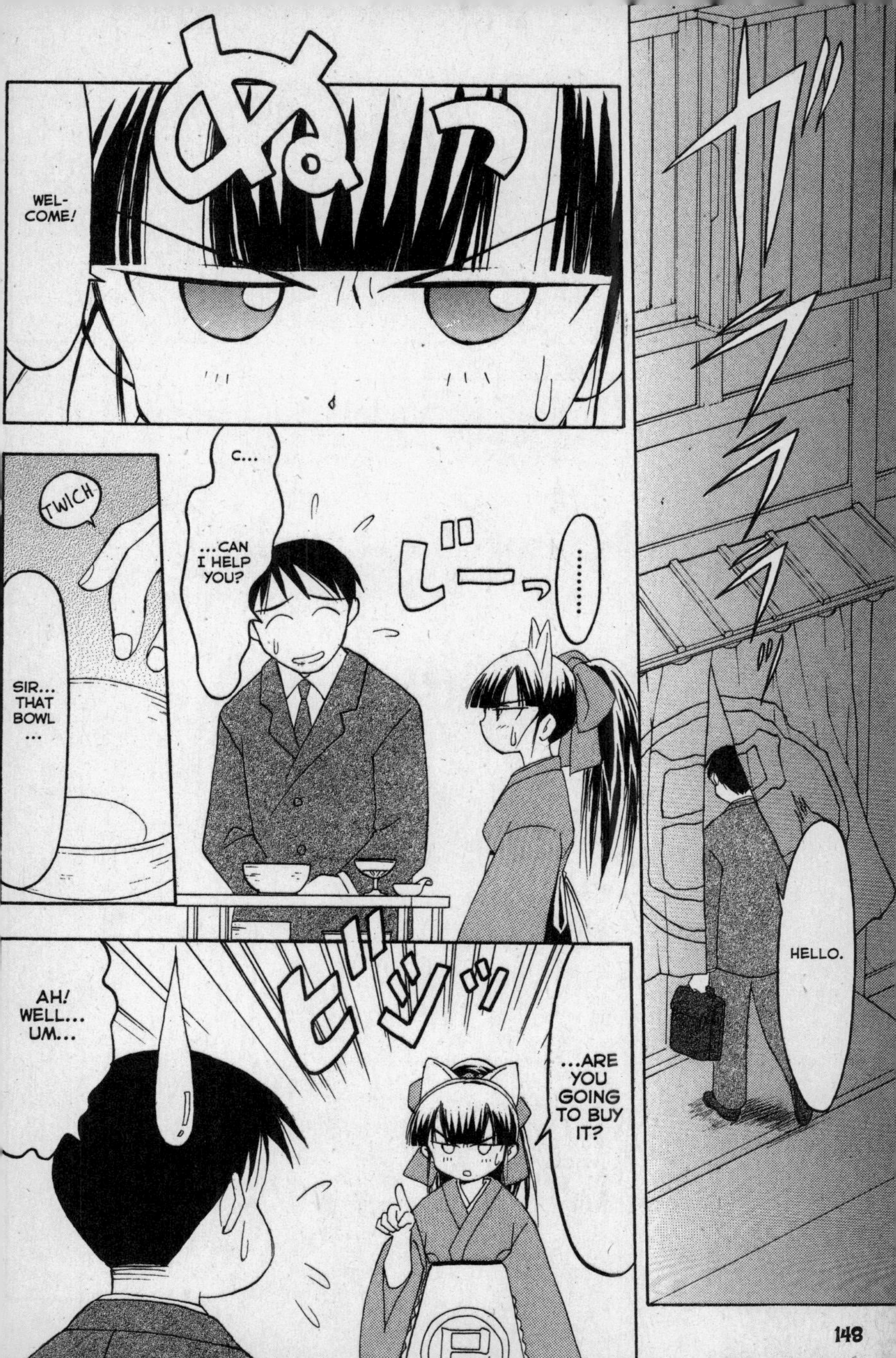
ガラララ
HELLO.
ぬっ
WEL-
COME!
C...
...CAN I HELP YOU?
じーっ
......
TWICH
SIR... THAT BOWL ...
...ARE YOU GOING TO BUY IT?
ビクッ
AH! WELL... UM...

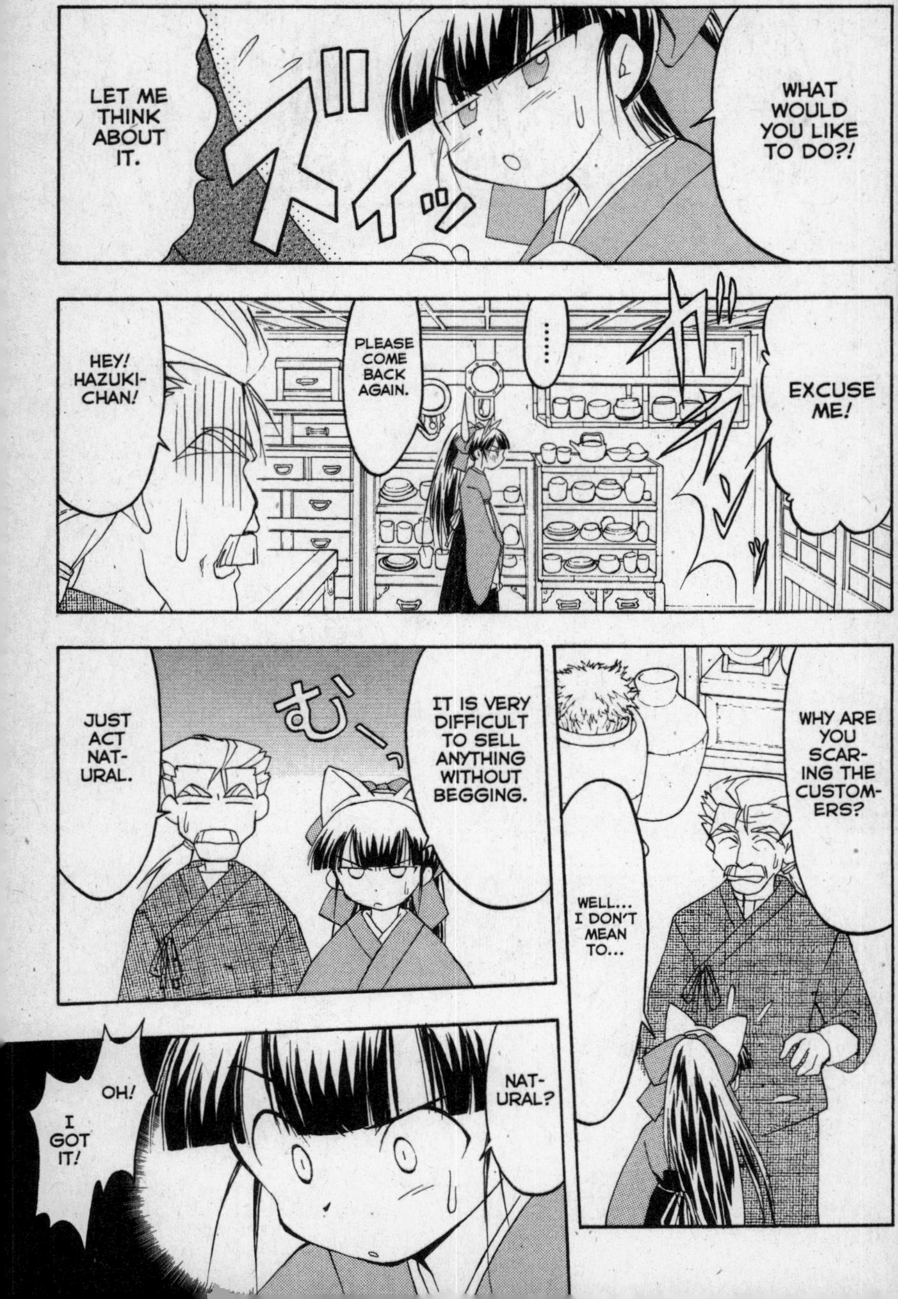
WHAT WOULD YOU LIKE TO DO?!
LET ME THINK ABOUT IT.
EXCUSE ME!
......
PLEASE COME BACK AGAIN.
HEY! HAZUKI-CHAN!
WHY ARE YOU SCARING THE CUSTOMERS?
WELL... I DON'T MEAN TO...
IT IS VERY DIFFICULT TO SELL ANYTHING WITHOUT BEGGING.
むー
JUST ACT NATURAL.
NATURAL?
OH! I GOT IT!

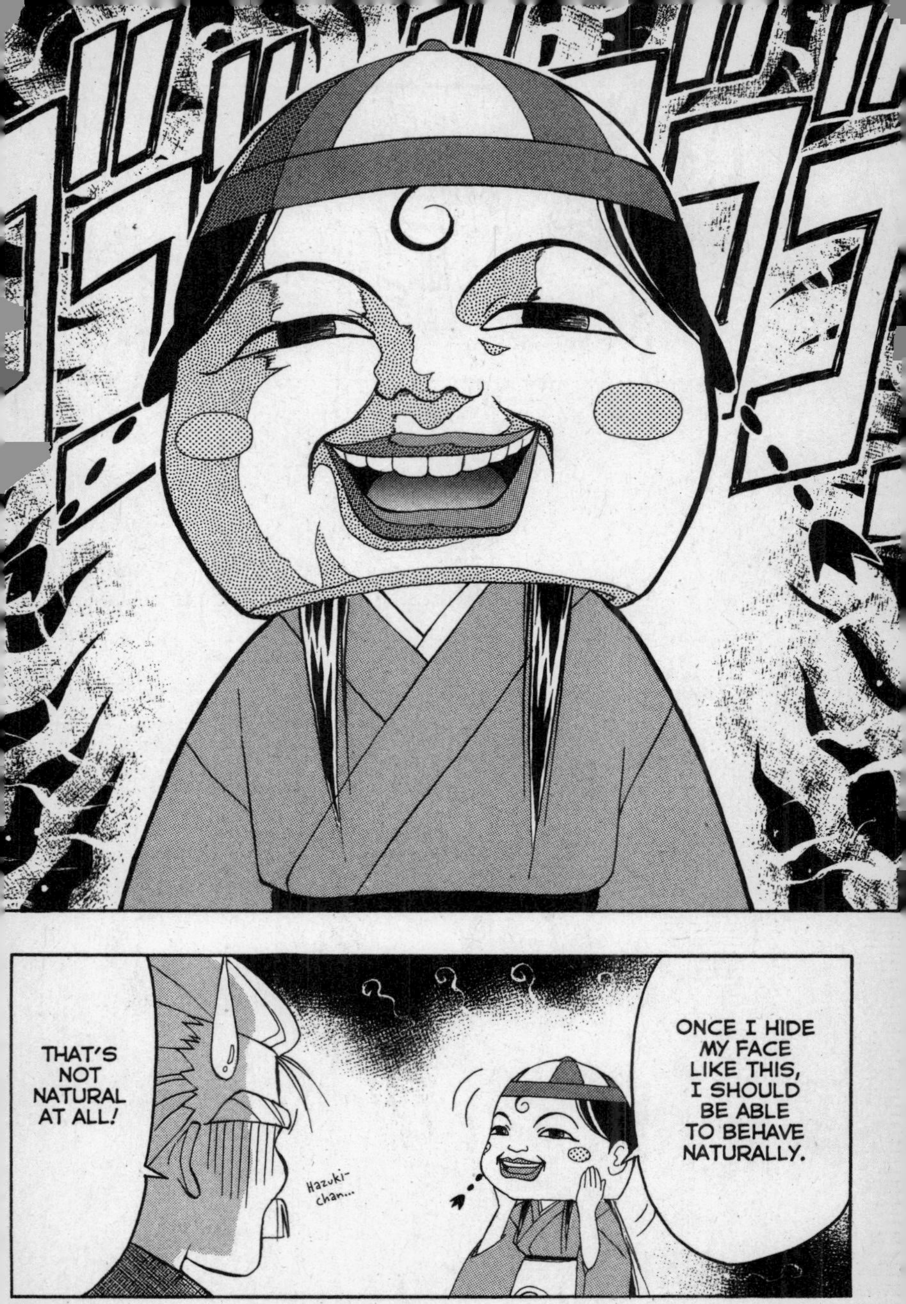
ONCE I HIDE MY FACE LIKE THIS, I SHOULD BE ABLE TO BEHAVE NATURALLY.
Hazuki-chan...
THAT'S NOT NATURAL AT ALL!

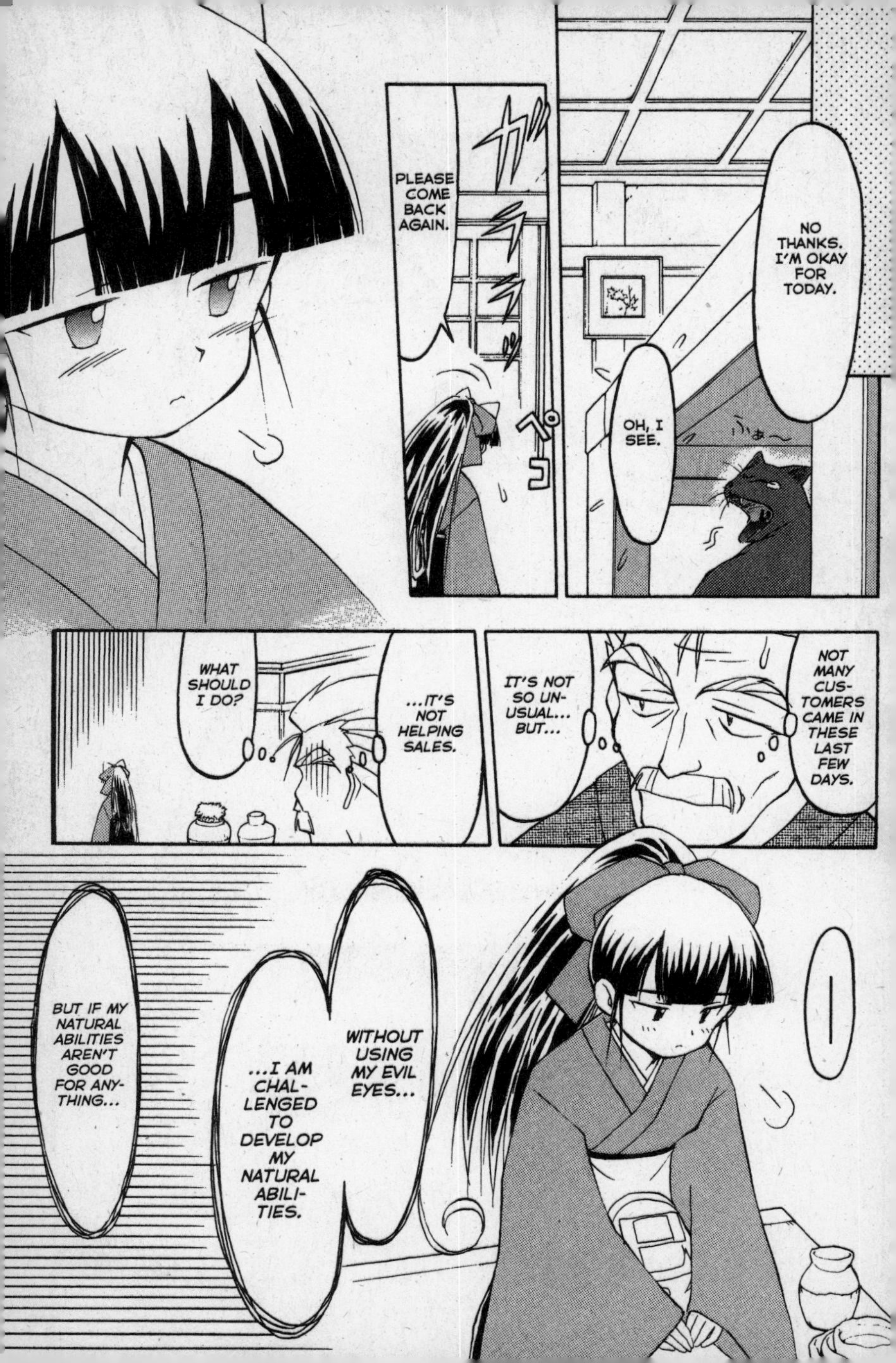
NO THANKS. I'M OKAY FOR TODAY.
OH, I SEE.
ふぁ〜
PLEASE COME BACK AGAIN.
ペコ
NOT MANY CUS-TOMERS CAME IN THESE LAST FEW DAYS.
IT'S NOT SO UN-USUAL... BUT...
...IT'S NOT HELPING SALES.
WHAT SHOULD I DO?
WITHOUT USING MY EVIL EYES...
...I AM CHAL-LENGED TO DEVELOP MY NATURAL ABILI-TIES.
BUT IF MY NATURAL ABILITIES AREN'T GOOD FOR ANY-THING...

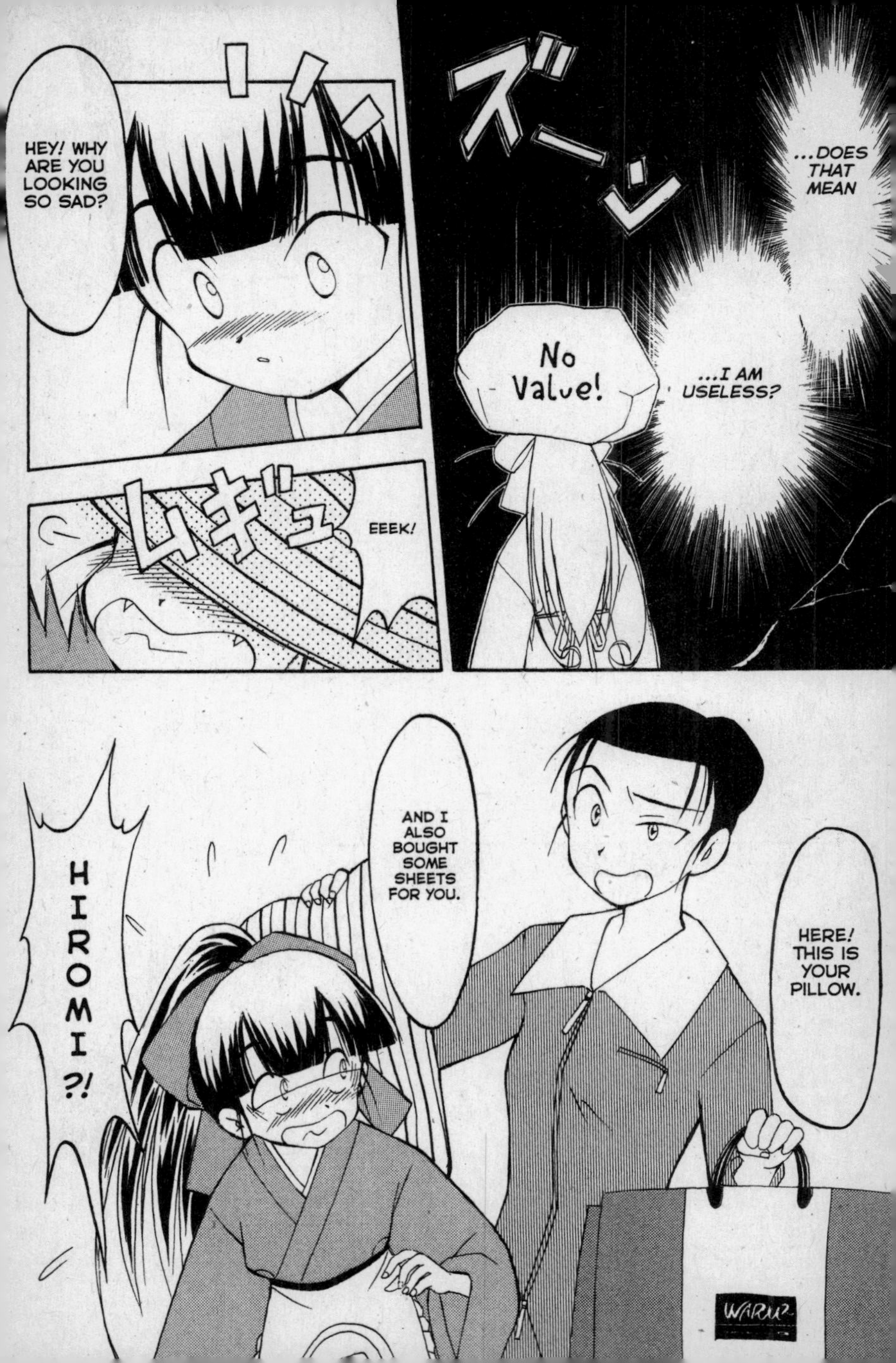
ズーン
...DOES THAT MEAN
No Value!
...I AM USELESS?
HEY! WHY ARE YOU LOOKING SO SAD?
ムぎュ
EEEK!
HERE! THIS IS YOUR PILLOW.
AND I ALSO BOUGHT SOME SHEETS FOR YOU.
HIROMI?!

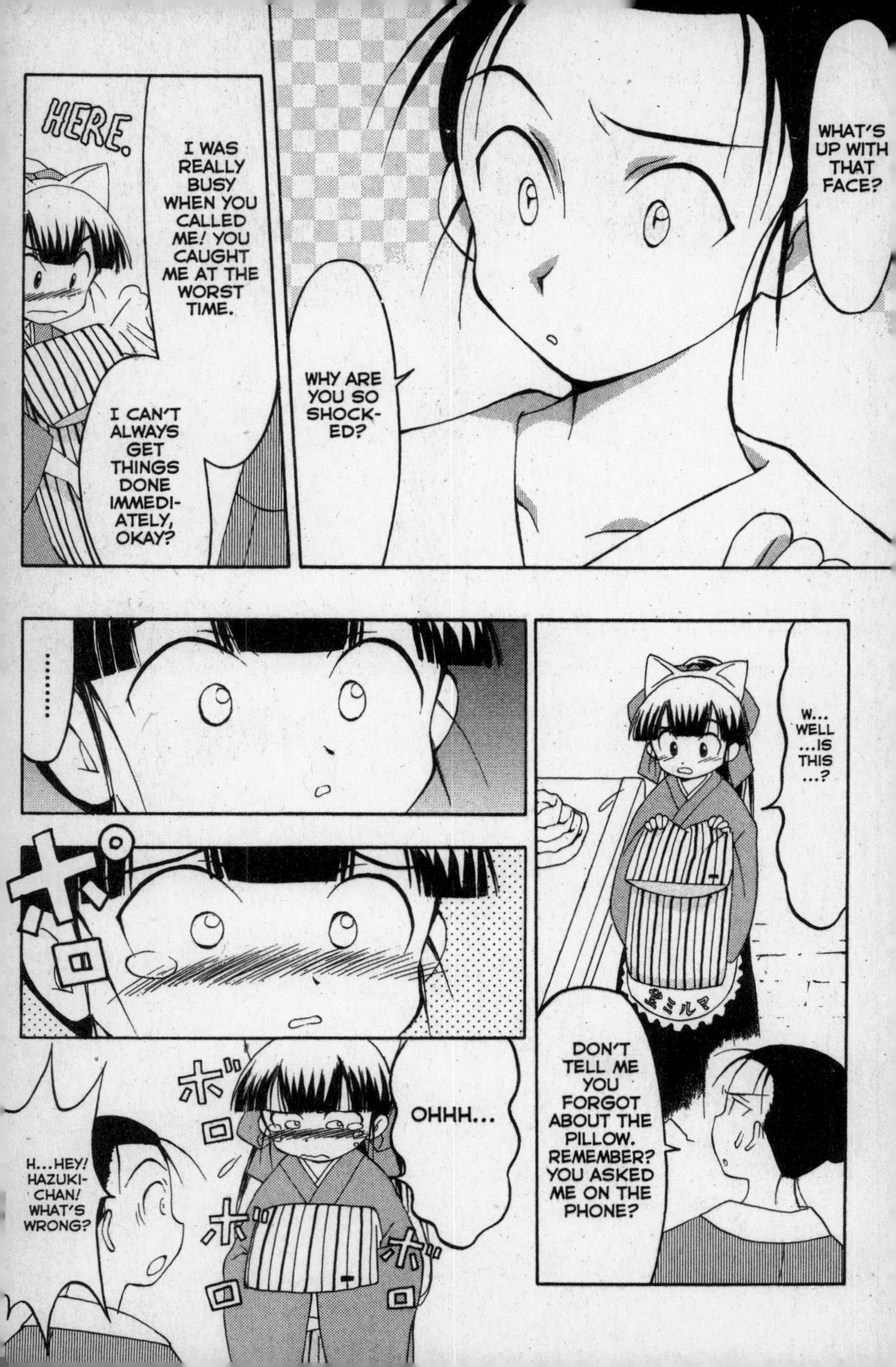
WHAT'S UP WITH THAT FACE?
WHY ARE YOU SO SHOCKED?
HERE.
I WAS REALLY BUSY WHEN YOU CALLED ME! YOU CAUGHT ME AT THE WORST TIME.
I CAN'T ALWAYS GET THINGS DONE IMMEDIATELY, OKAY?
W... WELL ...IS THIS ...?
DON'T TELL ME YOU FORGOT ABOUT THE PILLOW. REMEMBER? YOU ASKED ME ON THE PHONE?
......
OHHH...
ボロ
ボロ
ボロ
H...HEY! HAZUKI-CHAN! WHAT'S WRONG?

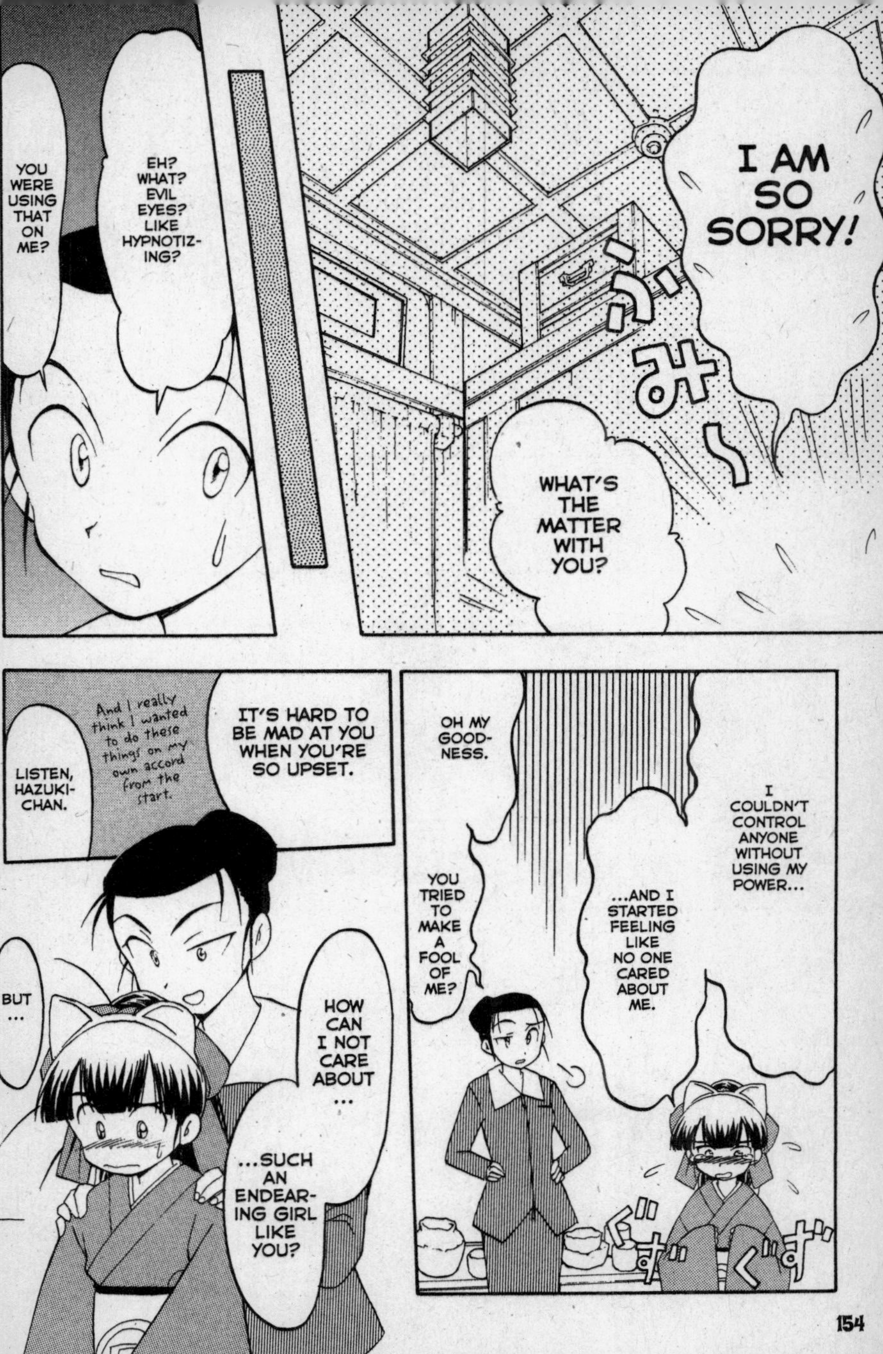
I AM SO SORRY!
ふみ〜
WHAT'S THE MATTER WITH YOU?
EH? WHAT? EVIL EYES? LIKE HYPNOTIZ-ING?
YOU WERE USING THAT ON ME?
I COULDN'T CONTROL ANYONE WITHOUT USING MY POWER...
...AND I STARTED FEELING LIKE NO ONE CARED ABOUT ME.
OH MY GOOD-NESS.
YOU TRIED TO MAKE A FOOL OF ME?
ぐずぐず
IT'S HARD TO BE MAD AT YOU WHEN YOU'RE SO UPSET.
And I really think I wanted to do these things on my own accord from the start.
LISTEN, HAZUKI-CHAN.
HOW CAN I NOT CARE ABOUT...
...SUCH AN ENDEAR-ING GIRL LIKE YOU?
BUT...

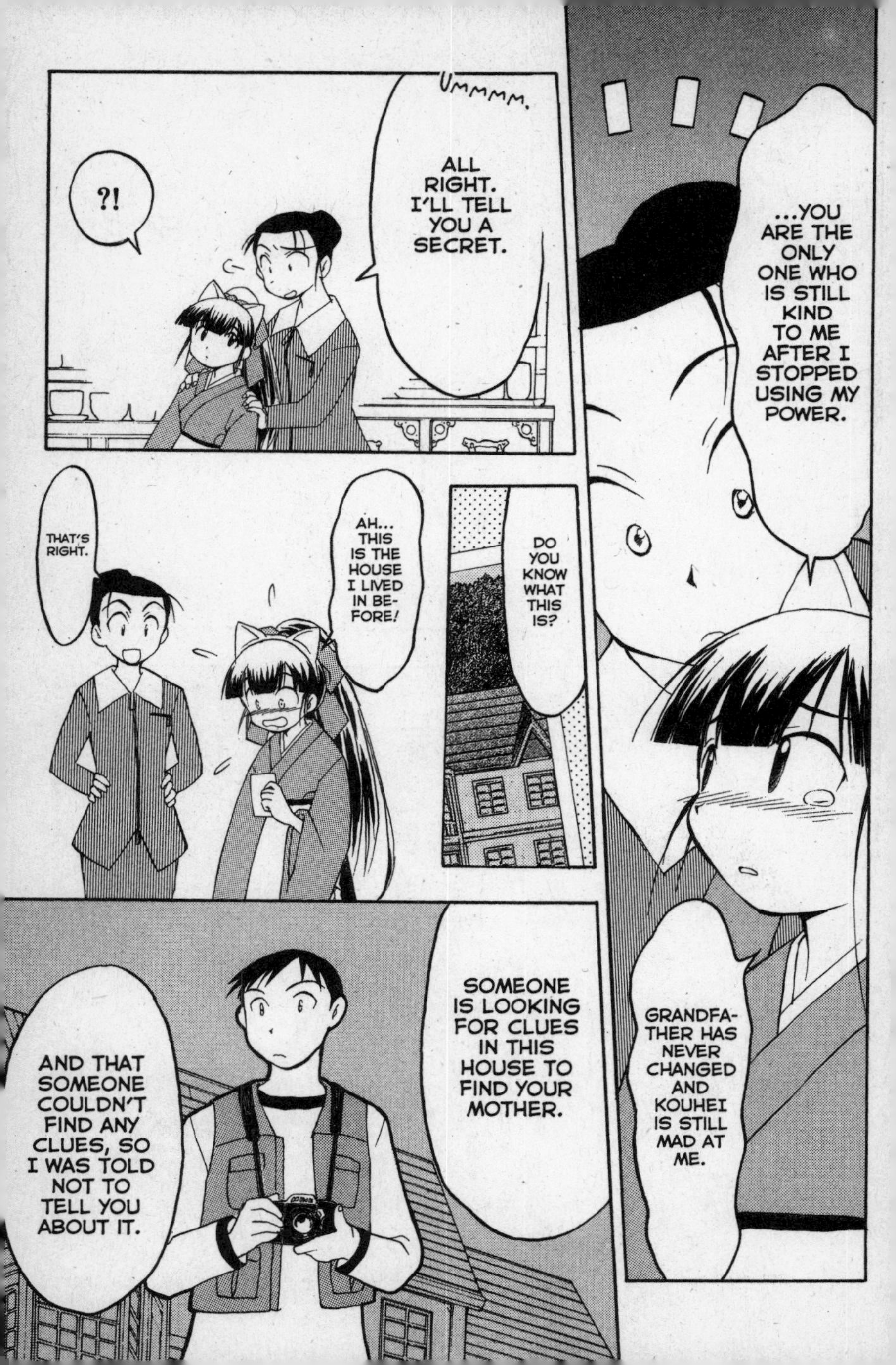
...YOU ARE THE ONLY ONE WHO IS STILL KIND TO ME AFTER I STOPPED USING MY POWER.
GRANDFATHER HAS NEVER CHANGED AND KOUHEI IS STILL MAD AT ME.
UMMMM.
ALL RIGHT. I'LL TELL YOU A SECRET.
?!
DO YOU KNOW WHAT THIS IS?
AH... THIS IS THE HOUSE I LIVED IN BE-FORE!
THAT'S RIGHT.
SOMEONE IS LOOKING FOR CLUES IN THIS HOUSE TO FIND YOUR MOTHER.
AND THAT SOMEONE COULDN'T FIND ANY CLUES, SO I WAS TOLD NOT TO TELL YOU ABOUT IT.

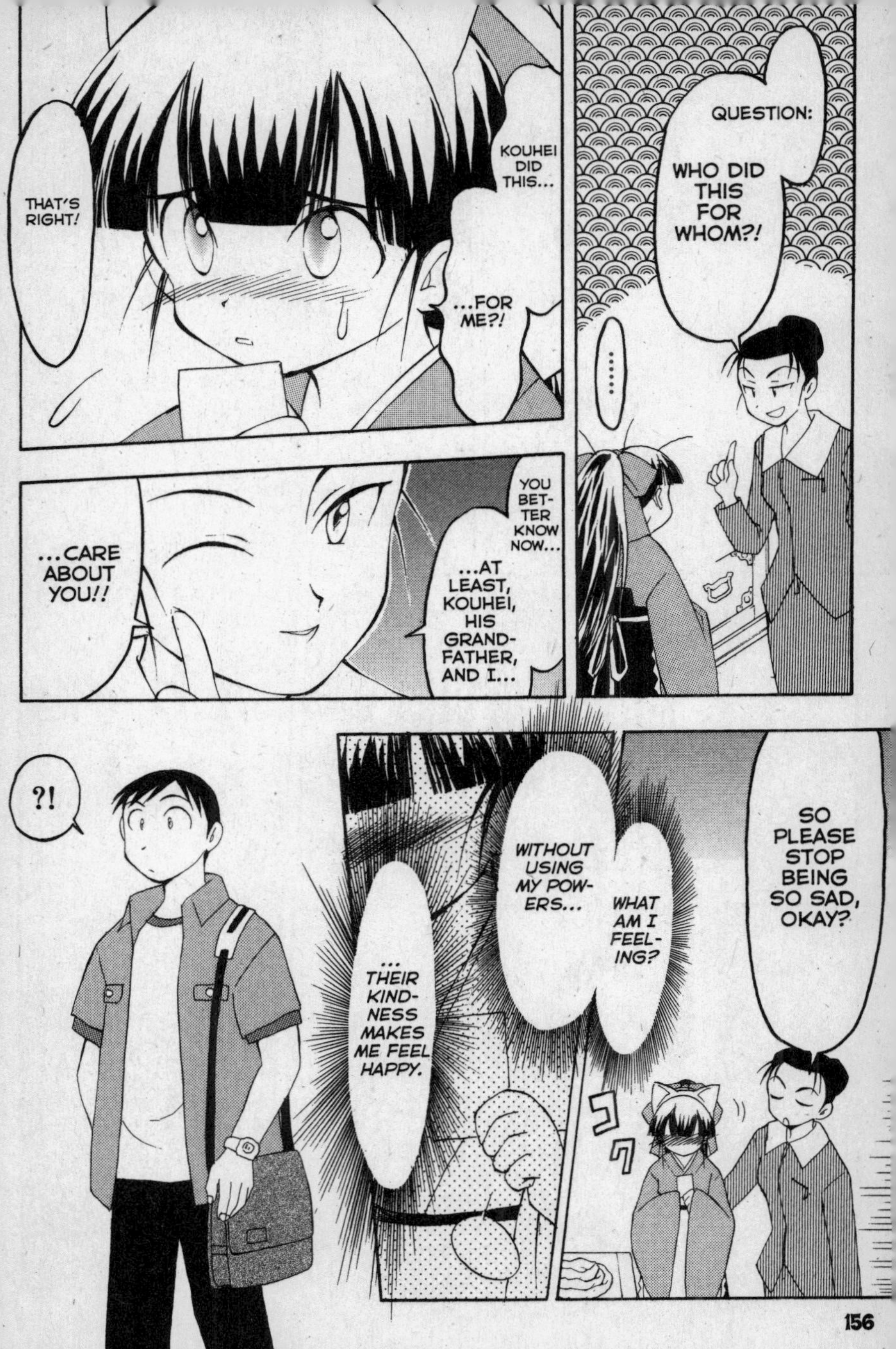
QUESTION:
WHO DID THIS FOR WHOM?!
......
KOUHEI DID THIS...
...FOR ME?!
THAT'S RIGHT!
YOU BETTER KNOW NOW...
...AT LEAST, KOUHEI, HIS GRANDFATHER, AND I...
...CARE ABOUT YOU!!
SO PLEASE STOP BEING SO SAD, OKAY?
WHAT AM I FEELING?
WITHOUT USING MY POWERS...
...THEIR KINDNESS MAKES ME FEEL HAPPY.
?!

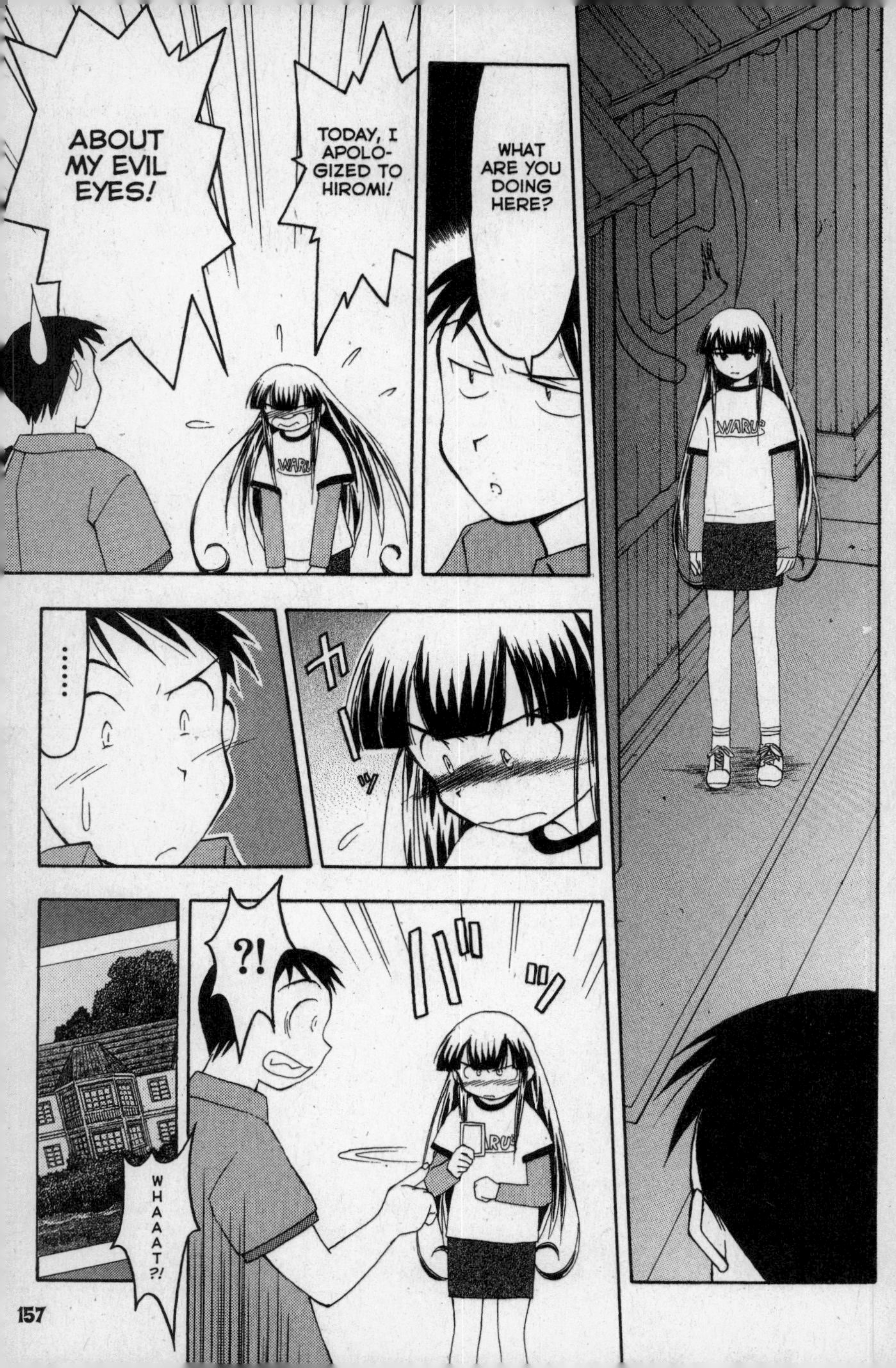
WHAT ARE YOU DOING HERE?
TODAY, I APOLOGIZED TO HIROMI!
ABOUT MY EVIL EYES!
......
?!
WHAAAT?!

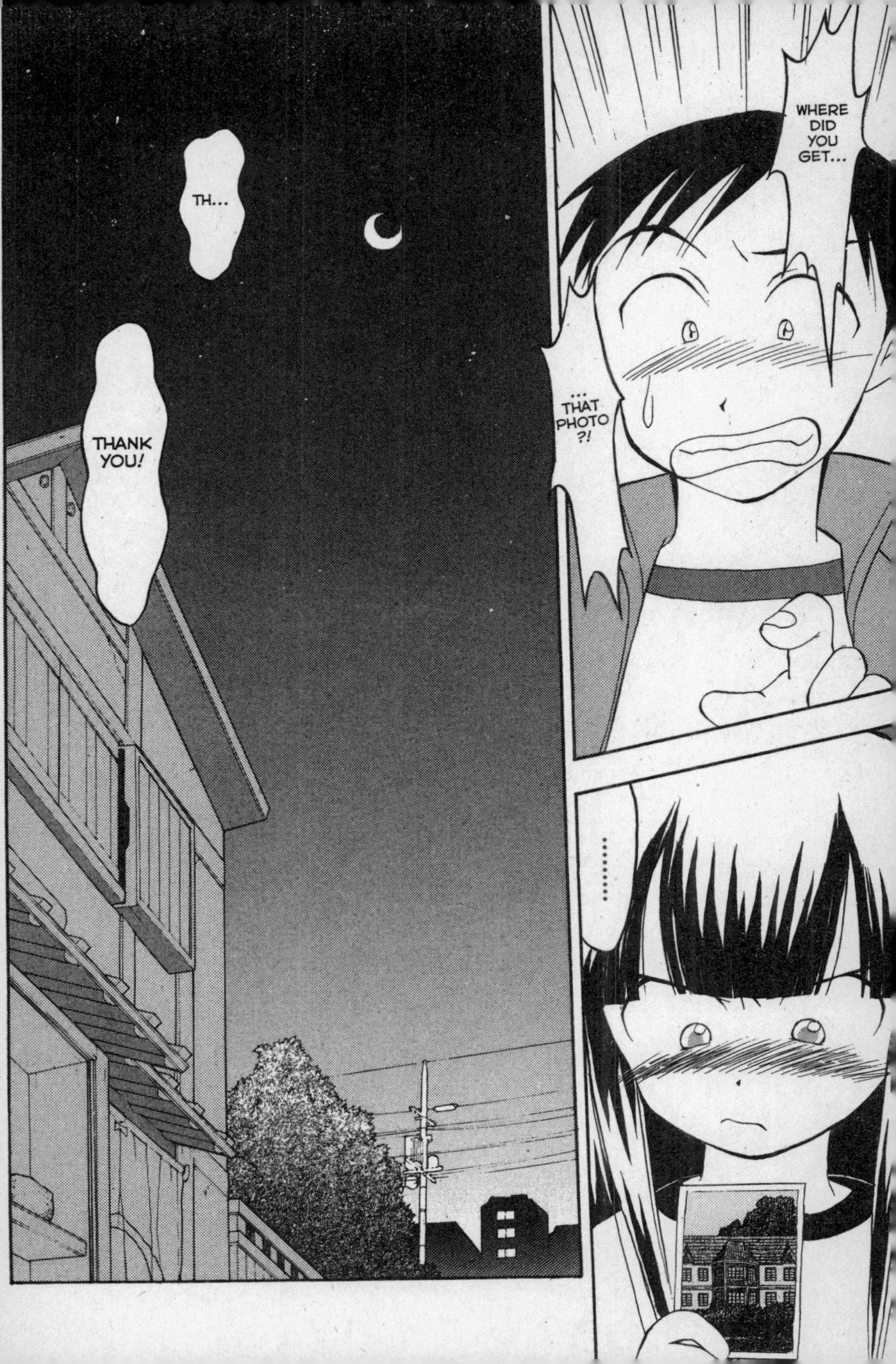
WHERE DID YOU GET...
...THAT PHOTO ?!
....
TH...
THANK YOU!

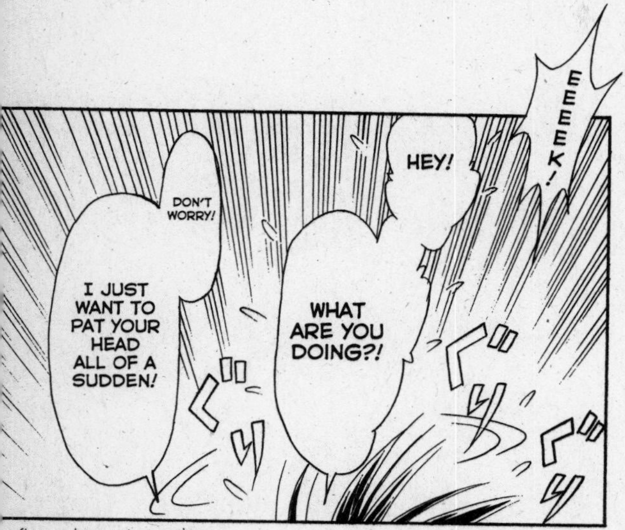
EEEEK!
HEY!
WHAT ARE YOU DOING?!
DON'T WORRY!
I JUST WANT TO PAT YOUR HEAD ALL OF A SUDDEN!
She can be so cute sometimes.

~ ORIGINAL UNUSED ROUGH SKETCHES AND TRASHED CONTENTS ~

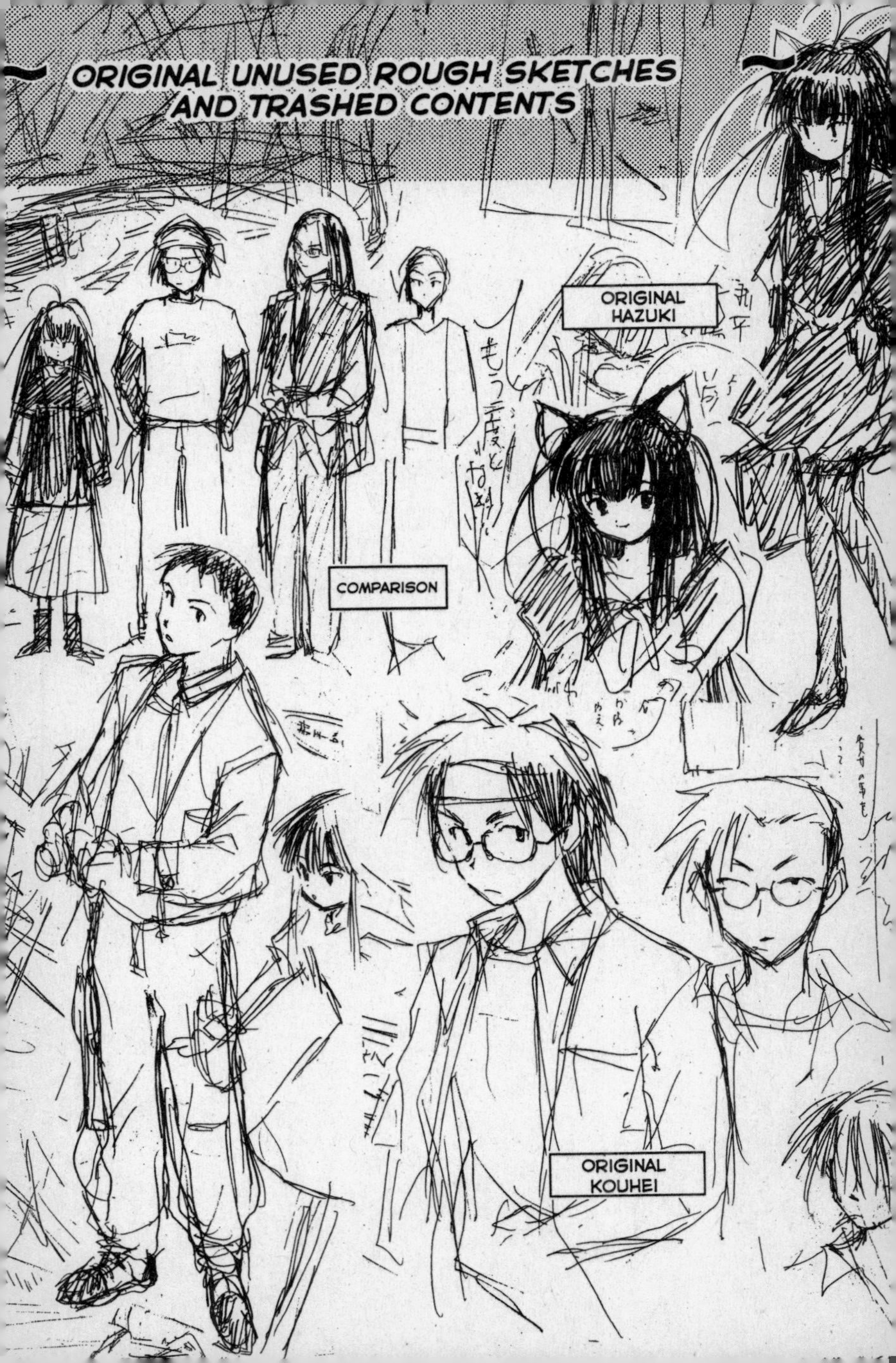
ORIGINAL HAZUKI
COMPARISON
ORIGINAL KOUHEI

MOON PHASE-- YOMOYAMA STORY

SOME PEOPLE MIGHT KNOW ALREADY THAT THE MAIN CHARACTERS OF THIS BOOK ARE BASED ON THE CHARACTERS OF MY OTHER STORY IN THE SAME MAGAZINE. ALTHOUGH AT FIRST I WAS GOING TO CREATE TOTALLY DIFFERENT CHARACTERS, I ENDED UP DESIGNING THEM WITH LITTLE CHANGES. ON THE RIGHT PAGE, ALL THREE ILLUSTRATIONS OF "ORIGINAL KOUHEI" ARE THE BASICS OF KOUHEI'S CHARACTER. HAZUKI'S IMAGE HASN'T BEEN CHANGED MUCH. JUST HER MESSY HAIR BECAME NORMAL STRAIGHT HAIR. I WAS ALSO JOKING ABOUT PUTTING CAT EARS ON HER AT THAT TIME.

TRASHED CONTENTS---ALL THE WAY TO THE RIGHT, THEY ARE THE FIRST VARIATIONS OF CHARACTERS THAT I DIDN'T USE FOR THE FIRST EPISODE. I DON'T EVEN KNOW WHAT THE TEXT EVEN SAYS. (LAUGH) THE LEFT SIDE WAS ALSO OMITTED FROM THE FIRST EPISODE. I WAS DRAWING AS I WAS STUDYING ABOUT FENG SHUI AND HANGING OUT WITH MY FRIENDS.

TRASHED CONTENTS

22

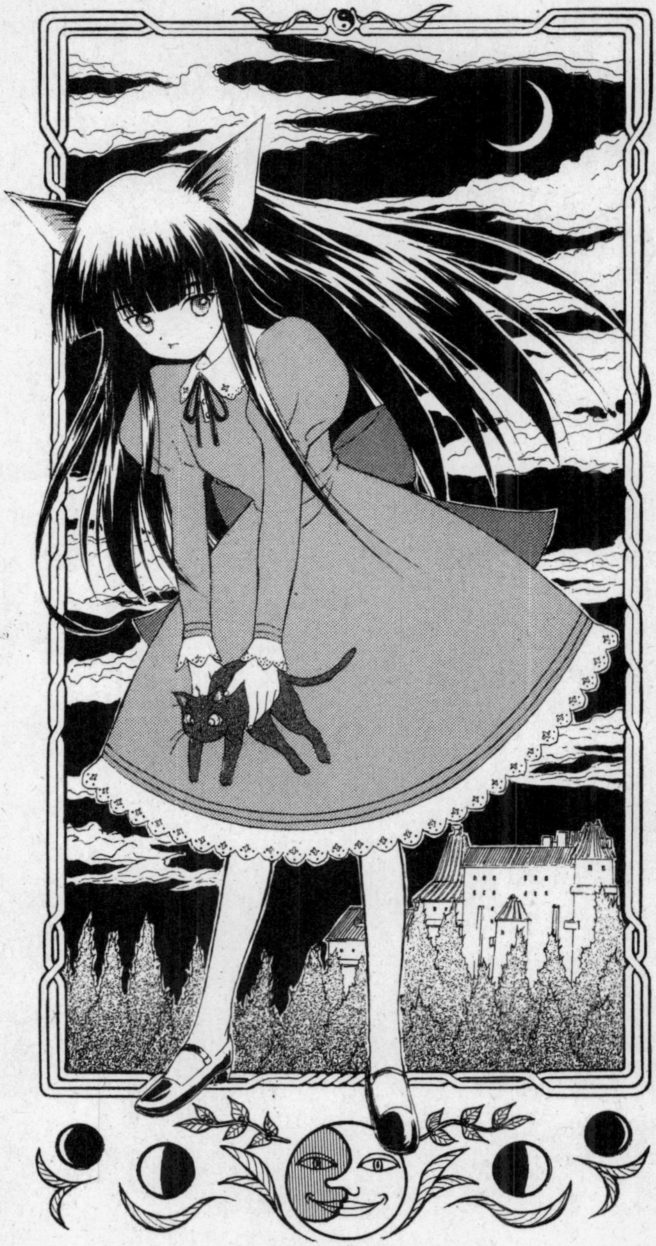

To Be Continued...

IN THE NEXT

TSUKUYOMI
Moon Phase 月詠
VOLUME 3

WHEN THE DEVIOUS
COUNT KINKEL LURES
HAZUKI AWAY, KOUHEI
AND HIS GRANDFATHER
DO EVERYTHING IN THEIR
POWER TO SEARCH
FOR HER. A TRAIL OF
CLUES LEADS THEM TO A
HOTEL, WHERE THEY ARE
CONFRONTED BY A FIERCE
MONSTER! BUT SUDDENLY,
ELFRIEDE APPEARS AND
HELPS THEM DEFEAT THE
BEAST. THE TWO MEN ARE
THANKFUL…AND PUZZLED--
WHY WOULD SHE HELP AN
"ENEMY"?

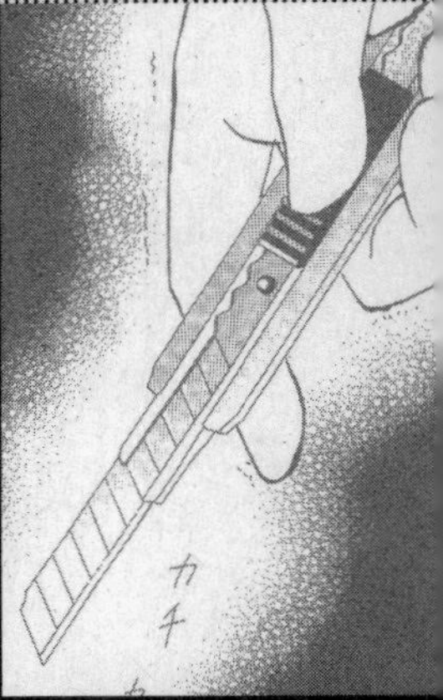
カチ

Ayumu struggles with her studies, and the all-important high school entrance exams are approaching. Fortunately, she has help from her best bud Shii-chan, who is at the top of the class. But when the test results come back, the friends are surprised: Ayumu surpasses Shii-chan's scores and gets into the school of her choice—without Shii-chan! Losing her friend is so painful for Ayumu that she starts cutting herself to ease her sorrow. Finally, Ayumu seeks comfort in a new friend, Manami. But will Manami prove to be the friend that Ayumu truly needs? Or will Ayumu continue down a dark path?

It's about real teenagers...

It's about real high school...

It's about real life.

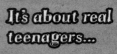

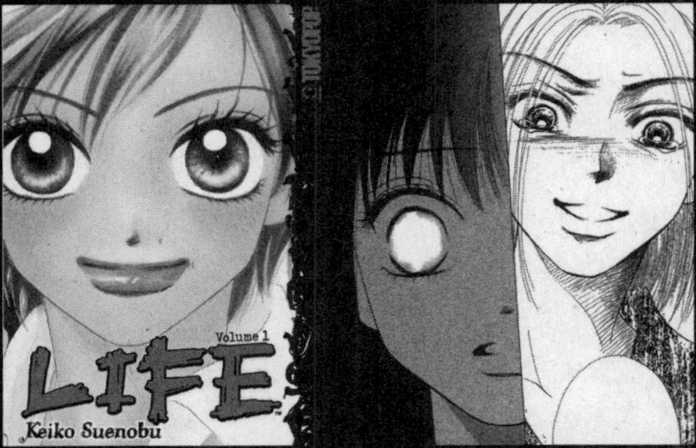
Volume 1
LIFE
Keiko Suenobu

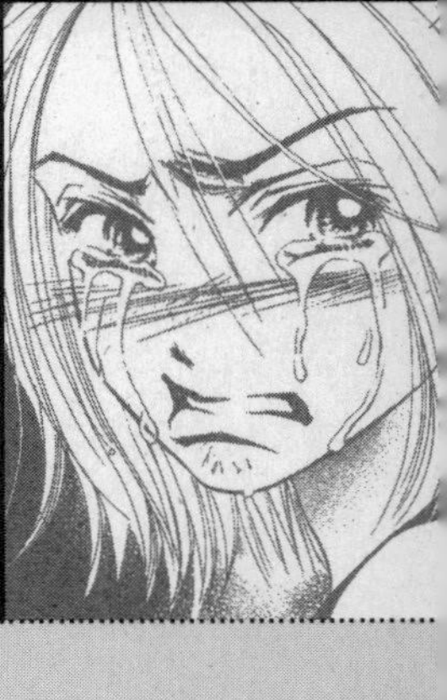

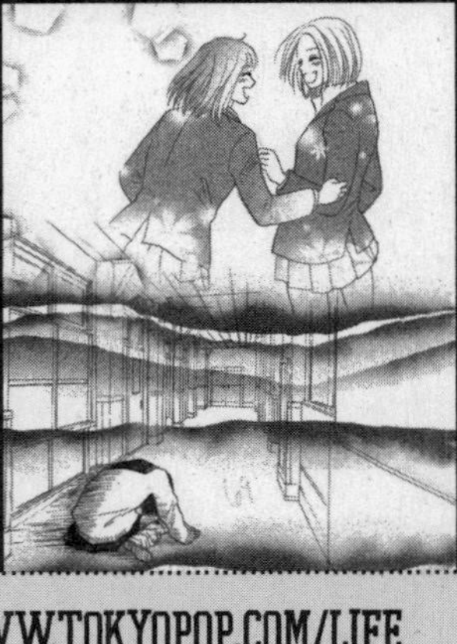

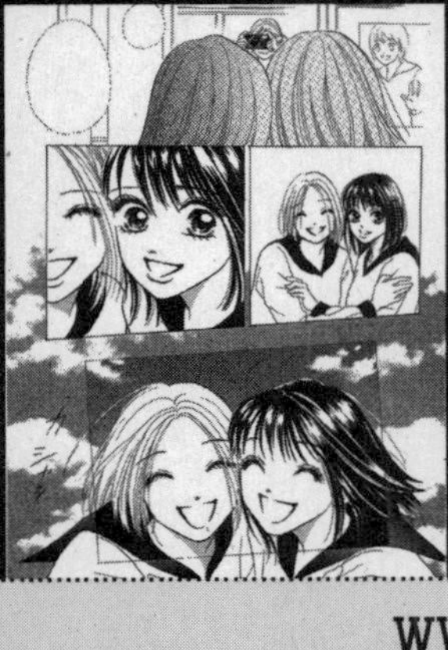

WWW.TOKYOPOP.COM/LIFE

LIFE
BY KEIKO SUENOBU

Ordinary high school teenagers...
Except that they're not.

OT
OLDER TEEN
AGE 16+

READ THE ENTIRE FIRST CHAPTER ONLINE FOR FREE:

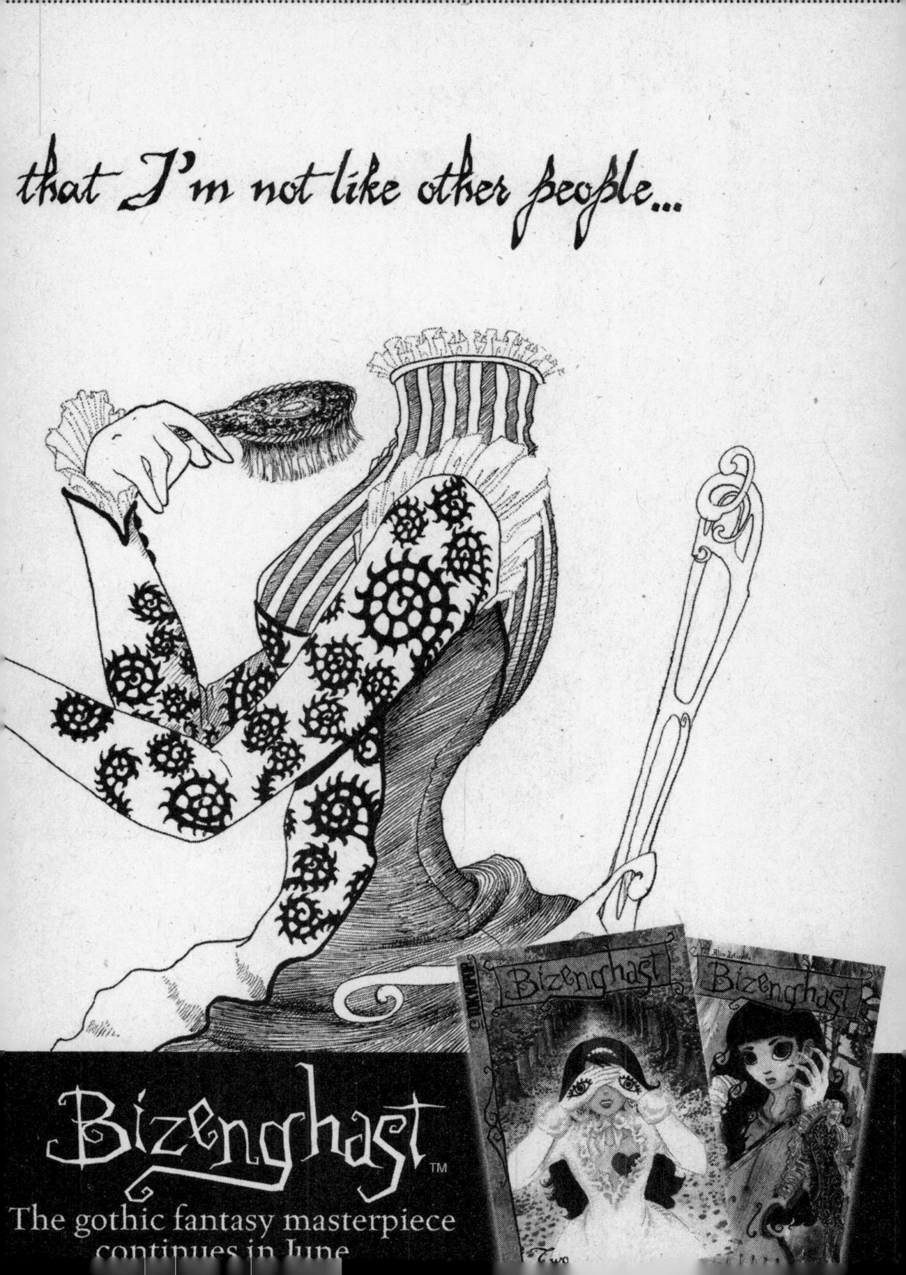
that I'm not like other people...
Bizenghast
Bizenghast
Bizenghast™
The gothic fantasy masterpiece
continues in June

Dear Diary,
I'm starting to feel

When a young girl moves to the forgotten town of Bizenghast, she uncovers a terrifying collection of lost souls that leads her to the brink of insanity. One thing becomes painfully clear: The residents of Bizenghast are just dying to come home. ART SUBJECT TO CHANGE © Mary Alice LeGrow and TOKYOPOP Inc.

THIS FALL, TOKYOPOP CREATES A FRESH, NEW CHAPTER IN TEEN NOVELS...

For Adventurers...

Witches' Forest: The Adventures of Duan Surk

By Mishio Fukazawa

Duan Surk is a 16-year-old Level 2 fighter who embarks on the quest of a lifetime—battling mythical creatures and outwitting evil sorceresses, all in an impossible rescue mission in the spooky Witches' Forest!

BASED ON THE FAMOUS *FORTUNE QUEST* WORLD

For Dreamers...

Magic Moon

By Wolfgang and Heike Hohlbein

Kim enters the enigmatic realm of Magic Moon, where he battles unthinkable monsters and fantastical creatures—in order to unravel the secret that keeps his sister locked in a coma.

THE WORLDWIDE BESTSELLING FANTASY *THRILLOGY* ARRIVES IN THE U.S.!

TOKYOPOP SHOP

WWW.TOKYOPOP.COM/SHOP

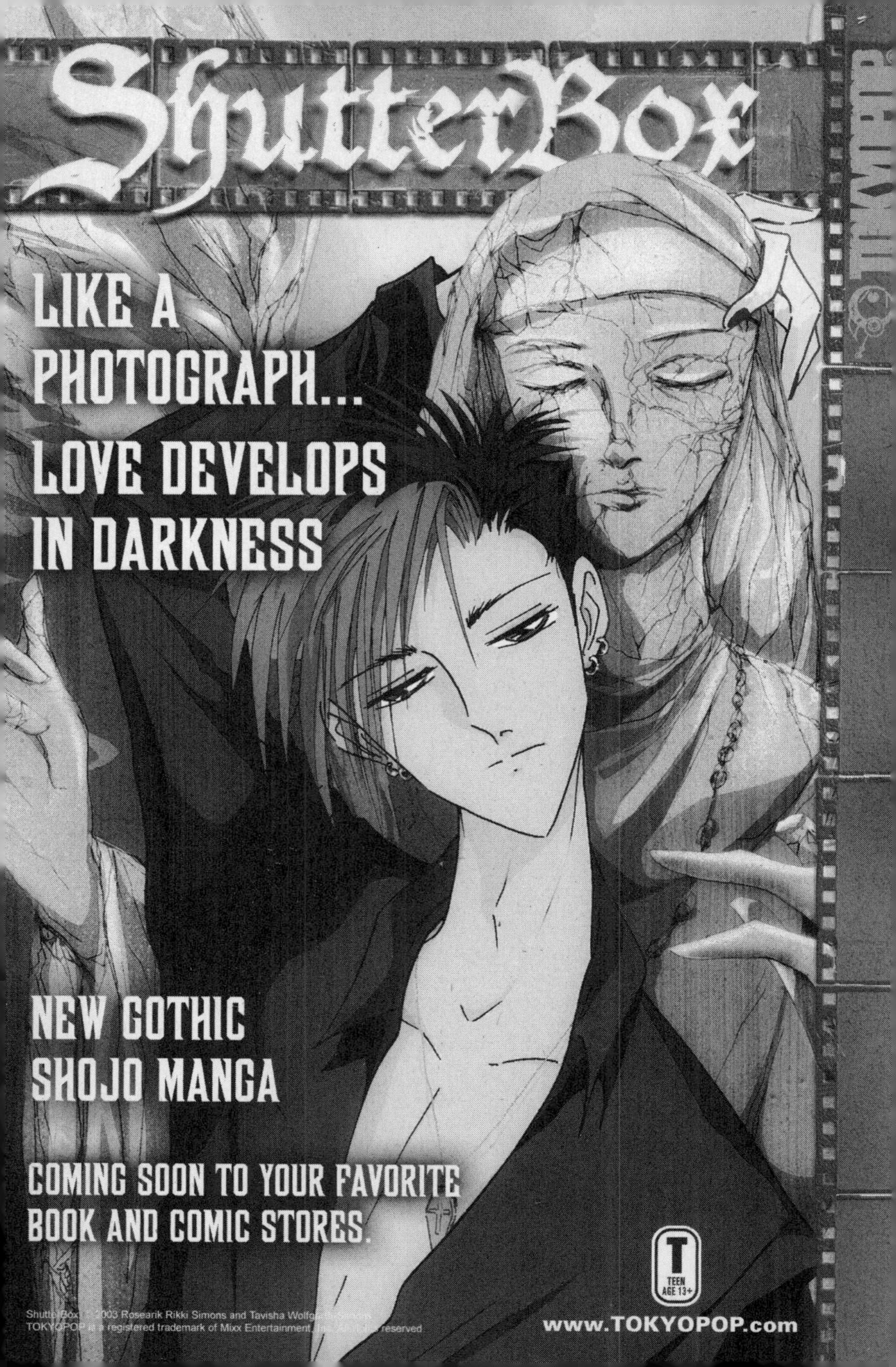
ShutterBox
LIKE A PHOTOGRAPH...
LOVE DEVELOPS IN DARKNESS
NEW GOTHIC SHOJO MANGA
COMING SOON TO YOUR FAVORITE BOOK AND COMIC STORES.
T TEEN AGE 13+
ShutterBox 2003 Rosearik Rikki Simons and Tavisha
TOKYOPOP registered trademark of Mixx Entertainment reserved
www.TOKYOPOP.com

Fruits Basket

Life in the Sohma household can be a real zoo!

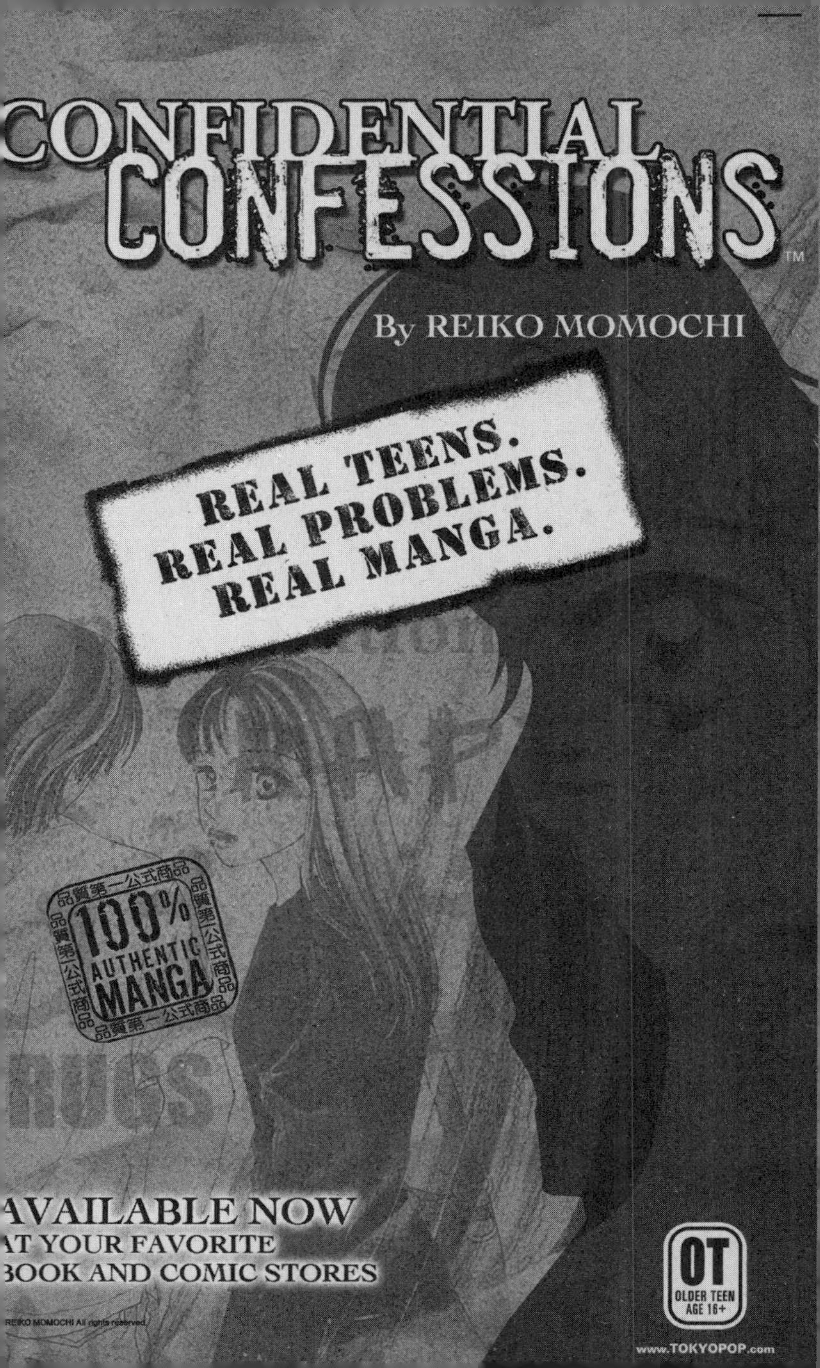
CONFIDENTIAL CONFESSIONS™
By REIKO MOMOCHI
REAL TEENS.
REAL PROBLEMS.
REAL MANGA.
100% AUTHENTIC MANGA
AVAILABLE NOW
AT YOUR FAVORITE
BOOK AND COMIC STORES
OT OLDER TEEN AGE 16+
REIKO MOMOCHI All rights reserved.
www.TOKYOPOP.com

STOP!

This is the back of the book.
You wouldn't want to spoil a great ending!

This book is printed "manga-style," in the authentic Japanese right-to-left format. Since none of the artwork has been flipped or altered, readers get to experience the story just as the creator intended. You've been asking for it, so TOKYOPOP® delivered: authentic, hot-off-the-press, and far more fun!

DIRECTIONS

If this is your first time reading manga-style, here's a quick guide to help you understand how it works.

It's easy… just start in the top right panel and follow the numbers. Have fun, and look for more 100% authentic manga from TOKYOPOP®!